THE PHOENIX OF
FLORENCE

By Philip Kazan

The Black Earth
The Phoenix of Florence

THE PHOENIX OF FLORENCE

Philip Kazan

Allison & Busby Limited
11 Wardour Mews
London W1F 8AN
allisonandbusby.com

First published in Great Britain by Allison & Busby in 2019.
This paperback edition published by Allison & Busby in 2020.

A CIP catalogue record for this book is available from
the British Library.

10 9 8 7 6 5 4 3 2 1

ISBN 978-0-7490-2223-5

For T, F & P

BOOK I

CHAPTER ONE

When Sergeant Andrea Gherardi started banging on my door that night in August, I was asleep. It might be more precise to say that I was negotiating one of the hazy and feverish realms between true sleep and wakefulness, because the stifling air of a Florentine summer night had not let anyone in the city sleep properly for days, and my rank as one of the Grand Duke's police officers did not exempt me from the common suffering. I rolled and kicked at the damp sheets, sometimes dimly aware, sometimes trapped inside shallow dreams like a fly caught in the filmy surface of a puddle. The dreams were the usual ones: palimpsests of memory, scraped off and redrawn, rubbed away and drawn again, line by line into the same dull scene, made up of things I recognised but knew had never happened. A country road, a common track of chalk and dust, climbing steadily up a smooth, brown hillside. On the other side, a town with a market, and my father waiting for me. But the track never reached the skyline. The crown of the hill receded imperceptibly. I stopped to drink at a fountain, and when I looked up, the track was running through fields, or a vineyard. The sun slipped from zenith to dusk. My father was waiting.

I turned and, finding a miraculous little patch of cool linen, groaned with pleasure. The landscape changed. A copse of holm oaks hiding a spring, water dripping over emerald moss. I was leading a horse, who dipped its head to drink. Flies hummed like a plucked lute string. Above the dream, in the thick night, a thread of breeze trailed in through the window and brushed across my damp skin. I stretched and let myself surrender to the flickering shadows of the leaves.

At first I thought it was my own heart that had woken me, thumping so hard that I could hear it. I rolled onto my back, unpleasantly alert. The inner workings of my body were something that, for as long as I could remember, I had regarded with unease. Every soldier knows that the body of a man is nothing but meat, and that whatever animates it is not only invisible but fickle. I had seen men die from scratches no worse than a shaving cut. On the other hand, people I knew had survived the loss of arms, legs, even, once, a sizeable chunk of skull. I'd seen men clutch their chests and fall off their horses, stone dead, killed by their own hearts. So I felt a brief surge of relief when I realised that the knocking was coming from the outer door of the house and not from under my ribs. Relief which faded when I heard a familiar voice.

'Comandante! Are you there? Comandante?'

'For God's sake . . .' I pressed my thumbs against my eyelids and sat up, muttering. The knocking continued. 'Be quiet, Andrea!' I rasped. The calling and knocking did not relent. I staggered upright. 'Sergente Gherardi!' I called, louder, wincing as my voice cracked. 'Shut up! You'll wake the whole street!'

Even though the heat was almost unbearable, I had slept in a linen shirt. Cursing, I tightened the laces and tied them with a savage tug. My undergarments and stockings were folded on a nearby chair. I pulled them on. Toes groped for slippers. Despite the closeness, I swung my cape, the long black broadcloth one I used for night work, around my body. Gherardi was still hammering away as I stamped downstairs, crossed the courtyard and unlatched the street door.

'What is it that couldn't have kept until morning, Andrea?' I croaked, as the large man stepped into the courtyard. Andrea Gherardi of the *sbirri* of Florence grinned and planted two meaty fists on his hips. He was sweating in thick beads and his dark clothes were soaked through at the chest and under the arms.

'Guess who's got himself killed, Comandante?' he asked, when we were both inside. His chest was heaving, I noticed, as if he'd run here.

'Tell me you didn't wake me up to play games.'

Andrea laughed. 'There's been fun and games, all right.'

'Oh, just fucking tell me, Andrea,' I snapped.

The big man pouted in mock disappointment. Then he brightened. 'You'd have guessed it in three goes or less, Comandante. Pietro Vennini!'

'Vennini?' I frowned. Part of my mind was still watching the light dance on that cool, green spring water. Then it cleared. 'Ah. Yes, I would have guessed that, you're right. He didn't just die, I suppose? Someone killed him?'

'*Cazzo*, Comandante! Someone? The bastard was cut to sausage meat by a whole gang. Right on Ponte Santa Trìnita.'

I sighed and dragged my fingers through my damp hair. 'When?'

'About half an hour ago. Haven't seen anything like it for a while. The bridge looks like a slaughterhouse. There're two other stiffs apart from Vennini.'

'You can stop smiling, Andrea. Three people dead?'

'Oh, come on, Comandante. We all know that Pietro had it coming to him. The whole of Florence knew it.'

I sighed. 'Let me get dressed. Who's there at the bridge?'

'Tedesco and Gualdi.'

'Just two men?'

'I sent word to the Bargello before I came here.' The sergeant paused and scratched his nose, glancing slyly at me. 'I was going to get the *capo*, but . . .'

I sighed. 'You did the right thing. Scarfa wouldn't have appreciated it in the slightest. Not that I do, mind.'

'That's what I thought. He'd be like a bear in winter. Make our lives a misery for the next month.' The sergeant folded his arms.

'Can I get dressed, please, Andrea?' I said pointedly.

'Go ahead.' The sergeant looked at the nearest chair, obviously planning to make himself comfortable.

'Jesus . . .' I growled in frustration. 'There's a jug of beer in the pantry. It should still be cool. Please, go and help yourself.'

The sergeant grinned and rolled off in the direction of my outstretched finger. When he was out of the room, I went up to my bedroom and locked the door. I was buttoning my black doublet when I heard Gherardi stamping up the stairs. I unlocked the door as quietly as I could and met him on the landing.

'Was the beer cool?' I asked, taking down the lantern I used for night business from its hook near the door.

'Nah. Warm as piss.' Gherardi blinked as he remembered who he was talking to. 'But most welcome, Comandante. Most welcome indeed. Here . . .' He took the candle from his own lantern and lit mine with it. 'Yes, most welcome. It's going to be a long night.'

We didn't have far to walk. My house was in Borgo Ognissanti, just past the hospital of Santa Maria dell'Umiltà, the orphanage which everyone knew as the Pietà. As soon as we crossed in front of the Palazzo Ricassoli and turned onto Lungarno Corsini, I saw the glow of torchlight just ahead. There was an excited buzz of voices as well.

'Quite a crowd,' I said to Gherardi. 'Tedesco and Gualdi should have sent them off to their beds.'

'Everyone's a bit worked up,' he answered. 'The heat and everything. And Vennini was popular.'

The two policemen had managed to keep the crowd, which was a good fifty or sixty strong, off the bridge itself. Gherardi walked straight into the throng, big elbows hammering left and right, and I followed him. In the torchlight, the faces around me drifted in and out of shadow and focus. Working men, mostly: weavers and dyers, my neighbours from Borgo Ognissanti and the streets round about, their features stained and prematurely aged by poverty and hard labour. Closer to the bridge, Gherardi shoved past some better-dressed men and they rounded on him angrily, only to step back, muttering, when they saw he was wearing the livery of the police. I looked them up and down, running my eyes over faces, clothes and hands, but there was no blood and they were sweating from the heat, not recent exertion. Tedesco, a recent recruit to the *sbirri*, was gripping the shaft of a halberd and his expression told me he was enjoying himself.

'The first one's here,' Gherardi said, pointing. A long, dark shape was laid out at an angle across the pavement where the bridge started to rise over the first arch. I bent down and shone the beam of my lantern into the corpse's face. A youngish man with dark, curly hair and extravagant mustachios; his light brown eyes were still shining, and his lips were curved in a half-smile as if he'd just lowered himself into a warm bath. Blood had run from his nose and the corner of his mouth. I turned him over onto his back: his dark red doublet was stained even redder and was torn in at least three places. Dark liquid welled up through the rips as the cloth settled against his torso.

'Recognise him?' Gherardi shook his head. 'Me neither. That's a soldier's moustache, though.' I stood up, and a ripple of excitement ran through the crowd behind me. 'Tell those idiots to go home,' I said. 'Tell them I'll fetch the Lanzi if they give me any trouble.'

The threat of the Grand Duke's German guards had the desired effect. With a lot more muttering, the crowd began to thin and then evaporate. I watched them drift away up Via de' Tornabuoni or along the riverbanks. The workers would go home, the gentlemen would be heading for the brothels and gambling dens near the Mercato Vecchio. I sighed and walked over the curve of the bridge to where Gherardi was standing, holding his lantern over a man who was sitting against the parapet of the bridge, legs splayed out in front, chin bowed to his chest. He could have been a sleeping drunkard, but when I came forward and held my own light close, I saw that one limp arm was attached to the body by not much more than a laced doublet sleeve, and that the top of the man's head was crushed like the top of a boiled egg. Blood and brains plastered his hair to his face. I drew my dagger and lifted the sticky curtain aside.

'Don't know him,' said Gherardi.

'I do,' I said. In spite of the deep slash that had almost taken off his nose, I recognised the pinched cheeks and long, narrow jaw. 'He's from Siena. I don't remember his name, but he knew some friends of mine. He was a *sergente* in Scipio Piccolomini's company in Flanders.' I straightened up. 'He's in quite a state. Did Vennini kill both these fellows, or did he have friends with him?'

'From what I can gather, it was just Vennini against six or seven attackers,' said Gherardi. 'Want to see him? Over here. He's in a worse state than this poor sod. A lot worse.'

The third corpse was a dark heap in the shadows at the far end of the bridge. He had almost made it home. Pietro Vennini's house was in Borgo San Jacopo, just around the next corner. The other policeman, Gualdi, was holding back another crowd, thirty or so faces, their grimaces licked by torchlight. Gherardi trotted over to them and began to shout the same threat he'd made just now, and again, the faces began to draw back and fade into the darkness. When they had mostly gone, I squatted down next to the dead man.

Vennini had been handsome. One of the most handsome men in Florence, depending on whom you asked. The face in the flickering light from my lantern was barely a face at all, though. He had been stabbed through one eye, and the left side, from ear to mouth, had been sliced clean away, exposing clenched teeth. There was another wound in his forehead that had punched clean through the skull, and his neck had been hacked down to the bone. Vennini had been wearing a doublet of defence, a jacket of quilted and ruched leather studded all over with ornamental strips of gilded steel, but even that had been cut to pieces. One arm, hand still grasping the hilt of a sword, lay a little to one side. I looked back across the bridge. A trail of blood – drops and footprints, some distinct, others dragged and smeared – ran from the direction of Via de' Tornabuoni.

'He put up a proper fight,' I said.

Gherardi had come back and was standing over me. 'That he did,' he said. 'Two dead, and judging by the amount of gravy, a few more seriously damaged.'

I stood up, imagining what had happened. He'd have been wounded further over the bridge but had kept his attackers at bay as he retreated. The temptation to turn tail and run for the safety of his house must have been overwhelming, but he'd resisted it. Or perhaps he couldn't run. I stooped to have another look, wrinkling my nose at the smell of blood already starting to turn foetid in the heat. Yes, there was a deep gash in his left thigh. He would have been gushing blood. He'd stopped here, then, and made his last stand. The wounds to his face and neck had been made while he was still upright, but the others . . . I narrowed my eyes, seeing blades rising and falling, hacking at the fallen man.

'This wasn't just a brawl,' I said. 'Those two were soldiers. Who wanted him dead?'

'Comandante!' Gherardi chuckled. 'Only half the husbands in Florence.'

Vennini's stock-in-trade had been the seduction of women of noble or gentle birth, young women harnessed to older men for the furthering of bloodlines and fortunes. Usually the cuckolded husbands kept quiet, fearing shame and laughter, but a few years ago one of them had challenged Vennini to a duel and got himself killed, for which crime Vennini had been exiled. He had been back for almost a year, having done some favour for the Grand Duke in Rome. Pietro Vennini had a few important friends, being from one of those Florentine families that had been here for ever, but the Venninis hadn't been anywhere near power in the city since before Old Cosimo's time. This death wouldn't ruffle many feathers: far more people would rejoice than would mourn. But something wasn't right. Supposing the two dead attackers were part of a bigger gang of soldiers for hire, and Vennini hadn't simply crossed them in some tavern or brothel, someone had paid to have him cut to pieces very publicly.

'Who was he screwing?' I asked Gherardi.

'Who wasn't he screwing?' The sergeant made a face and pumped his fist back and forth.

'For God's sake . . .' I rubbed at the scar on my neck. My throat was starting to feel tight. Soon my voice would fail altogether. 'Find out. I want to know first thing in the morning. And names: those two over there, and whoever else might have been here. I want witnesses.'

'Yes, Comandante,' said Gherardi, his buoyant mood evidently punctured.

'Get on with it. I'm going back to bed,' I told him, and started off towards the north bank. The smell coming up from the river, which was very low and running sluggishly between festering, muddy strands, was catching in my throat. As I passed, I looked down at the man from Siena. His name was on the tip of my tongue, but I couldn't catch it. I remembered him more clearly now, though. He'd been one of those men who make a nuisance of themselves when there is no fighting to be had, gambling and whoring around the taverns of Brussels. He'd fought one of my men – yes, that was right. I had been in charge of my company's security back then, and I'd had to complain to his *condottiere*, Piccolomini, a Sienese patrician who had settled matters reluctantly and with a lot of well-bred flouncing. It wasn't particularly surprising that he'd washed up here in Florence. There were plenty of ex-mercenaries floating around Italy these days, now that the endless wars had actually come to an end. I yawned. This would be over in a couple of days. Vennini had slept with the wrong wife. As Gherardi said, it was bound to have happened sooner or later. It was a demonstration of power, and the man who had ordered it would not keep his involvement secret. He was probably already on his way to Milan or Rome, to save himself the bother of a trial, bribes and exile.

There was something else to all this, though, and I knew I wouldn't get back to sleep tonight. Vennini had no doubt been killed over some affair that had been discovered. But there are at least three parties to any affair: the wife, the lover and the cuckold. A cuckolded husband who had taken the trouble to murder his rival so very extravagantly had another person to deal with. As I walked past the hospital and the Casa della Pietà next door, where a hundred and fifty orphaned girls lived and worked, I knew that somewhere in Florence, a woman was waiting for her killers, or was already dead, and there was nothing I could do about it. A couple of cloaked figures slipped into an alley to avoid the beam of my lantern. I was the *sbirri*, the Grand Duke's police: the very sight of me made people afraid. Those two: coming or going from some gambling den. Or perhaps they were a pair of sodomites. Both those likelihoods put them under my jurisdiction. But I wasn't in the mood for any more excitement tonight. There would be enough of that in the morning, and morning wasn't very far away.

My bed was as damp and unwelcoming as when I had left it, and though I slipped into the shallowest of sleep, all it brought me was the familiar phantoms. Soldiers' dreams, as thin and clinging as a bloody bandage. Here they came: the barber-surgeon's trembling hands forcing a needle and thread through my flesh; the clack of boot-soles on stone stairs; a horse, kicking with a broken leg, its great, soft brown eye begging for understanding. When I woke at dawn it was, as usual, a relief.

CHAPTER TWO

The bell towers of Florence began, one by one, and then in a galloping, tuneless chorus, to welcome the sixth hour of the day. Santa Maria dell'Umiltà's old, off-pitch bells were clanging too loudly for the stinking air of this last day of August, filling up Borgo Ognissanti, and my head, to bursting. There had been a lovely few minutes before sunrise when a cool breeze had slipped in through the open window of my bedchamber and I had got up and stood naked, looking over the rooftops to where the mountains were just forming out of the darkness, letting the cold air play across my skin. I had gone down to the courtyard, drawn a bucket of water from the well and, still in my nightshirt, poured it over my head. Then I had dressed and slipped out into the daylight, which was as hot and jaundiced as old melted butter.

The curfew was still in effect and the parish of Ognissanti was silent, though the stench of urine from the dyers' workshops on each side of the street was so strong that it almost had its own sound: a thin whine, as insistent as a trapped wasp. Piazza della Signoria was empty of anyone and anything, except a flock of pigeons. By the time I got to the Bargello, it was as if I hadn't slept at all. My boss, Captain Benedetto Scarfa, had already arrived, which was a rarity; I was almost always the first in to the office, and I guessed that Scarfa's presence didn't bode well. I was right.

'You're late, Celavini,' the captain said. By the sound of his voice, he had slept as well as I had.

'Late for what?' I replied, looking around pointedly at the empty room.

'For last night's murder.'

'Late? By a few minutes. The blood was still steaming when I got there, I can assure you, Capo.'

'Keep up, Celavini. There's been another one.'

My stomach lurched, even though I had been expecting this. 'Of course there has.'

'Another one, Celavini.'

'I heard you. Pietro Vennini's lover, no doubt.'

'You're a hard man to surprise. But yes, you've got it.' Scarfa crossed himself with a world-weary flourish. 'She was called Zanobia Linucci, God rest her soul. You'll find her in Chiasso Cornino.'

'Linucci?' I frowned. I had expected a name I recognised, the wife of a patrician or a rich merchant. 'I've never heard of her. Are we sure that she's part of this?'

'The servants say that Vennini was a regular visitor. And the whole city knows Vennini.'

'Who is she, though?'

'That, my dear fellow, is your exciting challenge for today. And a write-up on last night's little cavort, if you please.'

I rubbed my stinging eyes and shook my head, wishing it would clear, wishing I didn't feel as if I had the worst hangover in the world, though I hadn't touched a drop the night before.

'They didn't waste any time,' I muttered at last, settling into my chair. The stack of papers on my desk seemed to have grown in the night, as though the wood had been infected by some particularly aggressive fungus. At least it was quiet right now. The office of the *sbirri* is next door to the torture chamber of our employers, the *Otto di Guardia*, the Eight of Public Safety, and the magistrates don't mind how early they begin to interrogate their suspects.

'Unlike you,' said Scarfa. 'Off you go, Celavini. I want a report on all this mess for the magistrates. I want it before luncheon. Well before.'

I smelt the blood before I had even reached the bottom of the stairs. The narrow house on Chiasso Cornino looked ancient on the outside but the interior was done up in the newest style. I noted a very fine tapestry in the entrance hall, and my shoes sank luxuriantly into the long pile of a Turkish carpet as I walked towards the stairs. The stairwell was lined with crisply carved panelling, and the plastered walls were brightly frescoed with cherubs and greenery in the ancient Roman style. There was a rich scent of polish, of laundry and fine beeswax candles in the air. But over it all was the thick, rank sweetness of blood spilt into August heat. A small crowd of people blocked the top of the stairs: servants, from the scullery maid to the steward, all whispering busily to each other. None of them looked particularly upset. Quite the reverse. I recognised the muted holiday mood that often attended these miserable affairs. I sighed wearily and cleared my throat, and the two footmen who were blocking my way started guiltily and stepped aside.

'Let the *comandante* of the Bargello through!' It was the voice of a man who had slept even less than I had, and sure enough, when I peered through the crowd, a square-shouldered man in Medici livery was standing in front of a painted door.

'Good morning, Andrea,' I called, and saw one of the servants, a lady's maid by the quality of her dress, frown at the harsh, cracked sound of my voice. It was worse than usual this morning; the heat and the lack of sleep had dried out my throat, and I knew I must sound horrible. No more horrible, though, than what was behind that door. 'Something of a fairground up here. It's worse down in the street.'

'No one ever gets bored of blood,' said Gherardi.

'Really? I'm getting a little tired of it, for one. Seems like we've been wading through it lately. When did you get here?'

'I stayed on duty last night, Comandante.' *He looks as rough as I feel*, I thought.

'And someone came and reported the crime?'

'Someone . . .' He scanned the gaggle of servants. 'That one there,' he went on, pointing at the youngest footman.

'Time?'

'Around four of the clock.'

'And you've been here ever since?'

Gherardi rubbed his stubbled chin. Twenty or more years older than I, like most of the police, the sergeant drank too much and was ageing by the minute, so it seemed, under the strain of trying to marry off his three daughters. 'Well . . .' He looked down knowingly at me. 'There wasn't any need to hurry, was there?'

'No?'

He shrugged. 'Dead is dead, Comandante. Am I right?'

'And she *was* dead?'

'Oh yes.' Gherardi chuckled grimly. 'There wasn't any rush. Well, you'll see, sir.'

He shifted to one side and opened the door. I paused. 'Anyone else been inside?'

'The priest just left.'

'All right. Thanks, Andrea.' I ducked under the sergeant's arm and stepped into the bedchamber.

The heavy curtains were still drawn across the windows, and the room was dark, except for one candle burning in a candlestick that stood on the floor, carefully placed in the centre of one of the geometric medallions of the rug, a few inches from the naked foot of the young woman who was half lying, half sitting against the side of the four-poster bed. Her nightdress was rucked up around her splayed thighs, its white linen dark red now and plastered to her body. Her head lolled back against the coverlet at a right angle. There was almost nothing to hold it in place: the wound that divided the waxy skin of the woman's neck was so deep that I could see the yellowish bone of her spine. Her eyes, already filmed with dust, gazed blindly at the coffered ceiling, and her lips were drawn back in a rictus, exposing white teeth and blackened tongue.

'Donna Zanobia,' I murmured. I knew her name; it

seemed impolite not to use it. I walked carefully across the room, noting the bloody footprints that dotted the bright colours of the rug, guessing that the priest had knelt on one of the clean patches. He hadn't wanted to get too close. If he was the parish priest, then I knew him: a fastidious little man who would be upset by stains on his cassock. *You should have closed her eyes*, I thought, bending over the woman. I reached down and touched her cold eyelids with my fingertips, pulling them gently down over the glassy pupils, but when I took my fingers away one lid opened again, slowly. Nothing but a reflex of dead tissue, yet there was something almost complicit in the way the eye continued to stare. *We both know what we see*, the dead woman seemed to be telling me.

'I know, I know,' I said to the empty room. I shook myself, trying to shift the stifling mood that had been weighing on me ever since I had walked into the house, went over to the windows and pulled open the curtains. 'No one is surprised, are they? Not even you.' I turned back to the bed and saw that the low sunlight pouring in through the windows had made the body more grotesque, less human. It was a relief.

I squatted down on the carpet and pinched out the candle. The dead woman's bare feet, stained crimson where she had slipped in the cascade of her own blood, had perfectly manicured nails.

'Come in here, please, Andrea,' I called. The sergeant came round the door and stood, looking bored, at the edge of the bloodstain that had swallowed half the rug. 'Any witnesses?'

'Plenty.' Andrea scratched his nose idly; the dead woman was keeping him from his breakfast.

'How so?'

The sergeant shrugged. 'The steward was woken by a banging on the door – as I said, around four of the clock. Two men with their faces masked—'

'Masked? What sort of masks?'

'Hoods with eyeholes cut in them. Black. And they wore black robes. Like the Misericordia, is what the witnesses all said.'

I grimaced. The city confraternities who tended the dying and collected the dead hid their identities, for modesty's sake, behind black hoods and robes. And they would be along, shortly, to collect Zanobia Linucci. 'The Misericordia, or the Battuti Neri.' The masked men who also accompanied those condemned to die on their last journey to the gallows pulled on their legs to make sure they died quickly.

'They had a sense of humour, at least.' Andrea scuffed idly at the rug with the toe of his shoe. The dead woman was nothing more to him, now, than an impediment to breakfast.

'Is that what you'd call this?'

'I mean, after what happened to Pietro Vennini, she might as well have been waiting on the gallows.'

'That seems to be what everyone thinks.'

'Everyone.' Andrea nodded in placid agreement. 'You still need me, Comandante?'

'Yes. Who was she?' I asked.

Andrea cast a weary glance ceiling-wards, giving me a view of the bloodshot whites of his eyes. Then he shook his head. 'Good question. As far as I can gather, she's a widow from down south . . .'

'South? Naples? Rome?'

26

'South in Tuscany. No one's very clear about where.'

'Siena?'

Andrea shrugged. 'Can't get a clear answer.'

'But she's a widow?'

'That's what they say.' Andrea looked around the room. 'Married young and married very well, by the looks of this place. Rich husband with the decency to turn up his toes before she lost her looks.'

'She was carrying on with Vennini, but she's a widow. Why kill her?' I looked down at the carpet. It had a decidedly masculine air about it. Would a young-ish woman have chosen it for her bedroom? 'So she was someone's mistress. Kept. Who owns the house?'

'Give me a chance, Comandante!'

'Get the witnesses together so I can question them. Then you can go. I want the deeds to this house on my desk before lunch.'

'Very good, sir.'

Andrea went out and closed the door behind him. I looked around the room again: fine old furniture, a well-painted portrait of a man in armour with a bullish face, another painting of a classical nymph. Above the table, which was scattered with pots of face creams and paints, a Venetian mirror was hanging, from which I was staring back at myself: a small and slight man, a head shorter than my sergeant, with close-cropped, straight brown hair under my neat cap. Clean-shaven, with an old scar running up from the high collar of my doublet, scribbled like a crack in porcelain across my pale skin, a red line from the hollow of my throat to just under my left ear. A fresher scar, hardly healed, smeared across my right temple. Small and rather fine nose, broken at some point, skilfully reset. Brown eyes, almost unnaturally large in the setting of a delicate face.

I turned my back on him and knelt again on the rug. It was new, I saw: golden-yellow medallions like knotted stars laid out across reds and purples and blues, everything geometric, repeating obsessively. A muffled hubbub came to me through the door, but the loudest sound inside the room was my own measured breathing. I traced one of the golden patterns with a finger, smoothing the soft nap of the wool. Complicated, but once my finger had travelled through every angle, it arrived back at the point where it had begun. The stars were mazes with no way out. In that way they reflected the life and now the death of their owner. I stood up, drew in a deep breath and took hold of the corpse under its arms. The dead woman was heavy and beginning to stiffen, but I lowered her as gently as I could to the floor, straightened her legs and crossed her arms over her chest. I pulled a sheet from the bed and covered her with it, watching as the fine white cloth ballooned gently before settling on her limbs and face. Then I knelt beside her and began to pray.

The steward shifted uncomfortably against the carved panelling of the main room. He looked like a disgruntled bullock trying to scratch an itch. A large, dark-haired man with bramble eyebrows and steel-blue bristles on his cheeks, he wasn't happy that I had caught him trying to slip away through the kitchen.

'Who killed your mistress?' I asked, for the second time. My voice gave the words a jagged edge. The man shrugged. 'You can tell me now, or I'll put you in front of the *Otto*. You can tell the magistrates. You're a big fellow: not ideally suited to the *strappado*, I wouldn't think.'

The man swallowed. 'Why would they torture me? I'm just a servant.'

'Because you're acting a bit suspiciously, aren't you, Simone? First you open the door to a couple of masked men who swan upstairs and butcher your mistress, and then you try and sneak out when the *comandante* of the *sbirri* arrives.' I cocked my head. 'If I was the *Otto*, I'd torture you, to be honest. Give you a couple of drops, whether you needed them or not.'

'All right! All right. But I don't know who killed Donna Zanobia. They were wearing masks, like I said. That's the truth.'

'Who sent them? Actually, no, let's not waste time here. Who kept Donna Zanobia? Whose mistress was she? Who owns this house?'

'Donna Zanobia owned it.'

'Do I look like a simpleton? Who bought it for her?'

Simone pursed his lips until they were white, then let out a deflated sigh. 'God in heaven. I warned her, you know. I told her what would happen. But she knew what she wanted, and, well . . .'

'The house, Simone.'

'But she really did own it! I worked for her; we all did. Donna Zanobia came up from the south two years ago. Her husband had died: he was a gentleman from Pitigliano. A wine merchant or something like that. Brother of a bishop, I think. I was hired after the house was bought, to arrange for her arrival. But you're right, Signor Celavini. I don't think any of this was paid for by Donna Zanobia. It was very clear that she had been installed here in the city as a man's mistress. I wasn't happy about that. My career has been respectable . . .'

'No doubt.' I let myself soften a little. 'So, this man.'

'Will I be safe? If I tell you, I mean?'

'You're going to tell me or the *Otto*, Simone.'

'But all these deaths!' The big man wasn't being shifty, I saw; he was terrified.

'You'll be a witness in a murder case. The magistrates have every reason to keep you safe.'

He gritted his teeth and let out a sort of moan. 'I . . . I know he didn't kill Donna Zanobia, because I'd have recognised him, mask or not.'

'Oh yes? Why?'

'Because he has a crooked back.' Simone arched his spine back and to the side. 'Like this.'

'So he's a hunchback?'

'No. Not crooked like that. He isn't exactly a cripple, just twisted. As if he'd had an accident: fallen off his horse, or been wounded, but a long time ago. He doesn't accept it, if you know what I mean. If he'd been born that way, he wouldn't be so . . . angry about it.'

'About his back?'

The steward groaned. 'I don't know what I mean. All I can tell you is that he's tall and his back's twisted. His name is Don Bartolomeo. It isn't his real name, though, I swear.'

'Bartolomeo? Just Bartolomeo?'

'No, no. That could be real enough. It's his family name. I just never believed it.' He relaxed slightly. 'I'm a Florentine, signore, and my people have lived here since Caesar's time. I

30

have a little education, and the history of our city is my passion.'
He crossed his arms over his chest, warming to his subject. 'I
daresay I know the name of every family, great and small, that
has lived inside these walls since before the Duomo was built.
The Black Guelphs, the White Guelphs—'

'I believe you. But I don't want a history lesson. I want a name.'

'That's just it. Don Bartolomeo's family name hasn't been
used in Florence for centuries.'

'Bloody hell . . .'

'No, signore! Listen to me. It used to be a really important
family, one of the most important. But they died out in the
time of Dante's exile.'

'Fascinating, Simone.' I pulled at a strand of my hair,
something I only did when I was at the limits of my patience.
Next, my hands would be around his neck. 'And what is this
extinct name?'

'Ormani, signore. The man who kept Donna Zanobia calls
himself Don Bartolomeo Ormani.'

CHAPTER THREE

'Ormani?'

'Yes, signore. Ormani. They were one of the prominent families in the Quartiere Santa Maria. Some of them changed their name to Foraboschi, the rest were exiled or died out. But that was two and a half centuries ago, at least.'

I swallowed. My throat was closing up. 'And that's why you think it's a false name?'

'Yes, sir.' He drew himself up proudly. 'And I'll gladly tell that to the *Otto*.'

'That's good. That's . . . good.' I scratched the scar on my neck. It was beginning to throb. 'Where does he live, this Bartolomeo Ormani?'

'That I don't know,' said Simone eagerly. We were friends now, apparently. 'But not in Florence. He comes into town once every six weeks or so, stays for a few days and leaves again.'

'Is he here now?'

The steward shook his head.

'When did you last see him?'

'Two weeks ago.'

'You have an address for him?'

He shook his head again.

'Then how did you keep in touch?'

'Through his bank. There's an agent there . . .'

'And when did you tell him that Donna Zanobia was sleeping with Pietro Vennini?'

'My God, sir!'

'Oh, come off it. Do you think I don't know how these arrangements work? The lady was a possession; her servants were her keepers. Keepers, and spies.'

'It wasn't me! I was fond of Donna Zanobia. She was kind. And she wasn't vulgar. Not like one of those courtesans.'

'Who, then?' I snapped my fingers in front of his face.

'I . . . Probably Riccio the cook or Lisabetta the lady's maid,' he said hurriedly.

It had been Riccio. He wasn't in the slightest bit shy about admitting it, either. 'That's what Don Bartolomeo pays me for,' he said.

'A jealous fellow, is he?' I asked.

The cook was a nondescript man on the borders of old age, with a heavy Prato accent and few teeth. 'Prudent, that's all. You know what women are like.' He sucked air wetly across an expanse of mottled gums.

'So you tipped him off, knowing full well what would happen to your mistress,' I went on. I had arranged myself casually against the kitchen table, but my hands were gripping the edge hard enough for my nails to dig into the scrubbed wood.

'Straight away! A man's honour was at stake!' The cook raised a dandruff-flecked eyebrow at me in puzzlement.

'How much did he pay you?'

'Four lire a month. There'll be a bonus for me now, though.' He smacked his lips happily.

I left him to his cooking: a pot of ribollita was *plip-plipp*ing over a low fire and there was a basket of carp ready for the knife. There would be a lot of excited mouths to feed today. I was looking for the lady's maid when a twittering broke out on the floor above me, and four black-robed men in tall, pointed hoods came around the bend in the staircase, carrying a stretcher between them. They manoeuvred their burden expertly down the last of the stairs. I looked at the body on the stretcher; it looked smaller than the dead woman I had seen upstairs, wrapped in the sheet I had draped over her, which had now been tied at the head and feet.

'Comandante.' One of the hooded men nodded at me. I recognised the voice: a lawyer from the parish of Santa Croce. I knew most of the brothers of the Misericordia, but you didn't get familiar with them while they were at work.

'Good morning, brother,' I said. 'Where are you taking her?'

'She has no relations here in Florence,' said the man. 'We're taking her to the Bigallo. If no one comes forward to pay for a funeral, we will have to bury her in the common grave outside Porta San Francesco tonight.' I held the door open for the men and watched as a fifth hooded figure greeted them with a grave bow and led them off down the street, ringing a large hand-bell that tolled out a loud but flat note. There was quite a crowd outside, and they all crossed themselves busily and craned their necks to get a good eyeful of the corpse. One of the *sbirri*, an old soldier called Colino, was on guard by the front step.

'Make sure no one leaves this place with anything that doesn't belong to them,' I said. 'Which means anything at all. I'll send you some help. When they get here, clear the place and seal it in the name of the *Otto*.' I went back inside and found the steward, who was helping himself to his mistress's good wine.

'Where is the strongbox?' I asked. He got to his feet rather unsteadily and led me back upstairs. There was a small room furnished as a chapel next to the bedroom, and against the wall stood an iron-bound chest.

'Key,' I said, waggling my fingers at him.

The steward produced a large key from inside his doublet and rattled it into the lock. There wasn't much inside the chest: some silver candlesticks and trenchers in a velvet bag, and several pouches of coin. I lifted one up: gold.

'There should be more here. Where's your mistress's jewellery?' I demanded.

'The murderers took it all,' he said.

'So it was a robbery?'

'No, no. They said they were reclaiming their master's goods,' the steward said. 'Though . . .' He frowned into the chest, reached in and released a catch. A hidden lid sprung open, revealing a coil of pearls and some fine golden earrings. 'These are her own things,' he said, 'but there should be more. A pendant that she treasured. A ring – no, the ring was given to her by Don Bartolomeo, but she loved it so much that she kept it here. Perhaps she was wearing them when they came for her.'

His face fell, and he looked away towards the door. 'I tried to stop them,' he said quietly. 'But they were the kind of men . . .' He looked at me and lifted his hands weakly. To my surprise, I found myself believing him. 'You know what kind of men they were, Comandante.'

'I do.'

'I don't think Don Bartolomeo trusted me,' he went on. 'Because I worked for Donna Zanobia, not for him, and I . . . I . . .' Without warning he buried his face in his hands and began to sob. 'She didn't deserve it,' he said, his voice wet and muffled. 'I would never have stolen from her. I wanted to get away in case Don Bartolomeo thought I'd been part of it. Her affair with Don Pietro. As if I'd been her pimp! Oh, Jesus . . .'

'Don't worry, Simone,' I said. I upended the bag, counted the coins and handed two of them to the steward. 'There's two *scudi* here. Buy your mistress a proper funeral.'

'Two *scudi*?' The steward's tear-streaked face brightened. 'That will pay for candles! A feast! We'll bury her here, in San Biagio!'

'Donna Zanobia will be at the Bigallo,' I said. 'Give the money to the brothers.' I held up a finger. 'They'll give me a full accounting, master steward.' I dropped the bag into the chest and locked it. 'This goes to the magistrates.'

'Of course, of course!' He actually grinned. 'You are a good man, Comandante.'

'You sound surprised,' I said, turning to leave.

'If I find out anything about Don Bartolomeo, I'll come straight to you,' he called after me. I lifted my hand in acknowledgement.

* * *

36

I didn't go straight back to the Bargello. Instead I walked through the crowds around the fish market, across the Piazza della Signoria and into the Palazzo Vecchio. The office where the state tax records were kept was a long, dingy room at the back of the palace that smelt of mildew. The river had got inside during the flood of 1557, and the place had never been properly redecorated. It was all due to be moved into Messer Vasari's new office building around the corner, but the packing had only just begun. I looked around for the head clerk and found him kneeling in front of an ancient-looking document chest.

'Comandante Celavini,' he said unenthusiastically. The *sbirri* tended to put a lot of enquiries in the way of the tax office, but niggling, time-consuming ones that the clerks seemed to find even more onerous than the paralysingly dull work of their day-to-day. 'How can I help our oh-so-diligent police today?'

'Two names,' I said. 'I don't need you to calculate anything; I just want information.'

'Two names.' The clerk, whose name was Boschi, raised his eyebrows sceptically.

'Zanobia Linucci and Bartolomeo Ormani.'

'And what information do you want?'

'Anything.'

'Can you give me a little more to go on?'

'One's dead.' I paused. 'And the other . . .'

'Ormani, you say? That's an old, old name.' Boschi hunched his shoulders and frowned. 'No Ormani has paid tax in Florence for a very long time. It's a name from before this palace was built. In fact, the tower used to be theirs: the palace was built around it. They were called the Foraboschi then, of course.'

He stalked over to a huge stack of shelves holding vast ledgers, their damp-puckered leather spines secured by rusting chains. 'I expect there are Ormanis somewhere else in Italy, maybe even in Tuscany. I can have a look if you really need me to.'

'Thank you. The only thing I know about Zanobia Linucci is that she was possibly from Pitigliano, and she was a widow, so Linucci may be her husband's name.'

'Pitigliano is outside the State of Tuscany,' said Boschi peevishly. 'It's a fief of the Orsinis.'

'Yes, I know. I said *possibly from*, Signor Boschi. But she was from south of here.'

'Was?'

'She was murdered this morning.'

'Ah. She was that Vennini fellow's lover.'

'Dear God.' I shook my head in amazement. Even this half-fossilised tax official had caught the latest gossip. 'Yes, that's her. Do what you can, please. You have a friend in the chancery, don't you? Ask him too. Your reward will be that if Donna Zanobia has died intestate, the state now owns a very nice house in Chiasso Cornino.'

'That's nice,' said Boschi, folding his arms.

'Our usual arrangement will apply,' I assured him.

'Good. I will send word when – if – I find anything of interest,' he said, and turned his back on me.

I had the sudden need to be outside again and made my way back to the piazza. I looked up at the clock in the tower that had once belonged to an extinct family called Ormani. There were still three hours to go until noon. I walked to the Mercato Vecchio and threaded my way through the stalls, through crowds of merchants and shoppers, clouds of flies and wasps, flocks of sparrows, strutting gangs of pigeons and pickpockets, until I came to a stall stacked with an extraordinary arrangement of cheese. Ash-rubbed rinds, hay-wrapped wheels, some new and golden, some aged underground until they were almost black. Bottle-shaped *caciotta* cheeses hung from the cross-bar. A wiry little man in a greasy apron was arguing loudly and blasphemously with a cook who, I knew, worked in one of the nearby inns that doubled as brothels. I waited until the cook had reluctantly parted with a handful of coins for two cheeses from Pienza, then strolled up to the stall.

'Good morning, Umberto,' I said.

'Comandante! Are you buying today?'

'I need your very best,' I said.

'You'll like this,' he said, and, picking up a knife with a handle made from a goat's horn, he cut a thin wedge from a cheese with a rind the colour of tarnished brass and held it out to me. I wasn't hungry; in fact, my stomach had been jumping with nerves ever since I had left the house of the murdered woman. But to be polite I nibbled an edge, and it was, indeed, excellent: creamy, a little sour, a hint of the sheep who had given the milk.

'It's a *Marzolino* from Monte Amiata,' he said. I closed my eyes and, despite my mood, took another bite and found myself imagining the rustle of chestnut leaves and the artless clank of sheep bells.

'Delicious. Yes, I'll buy one of those,' I said.

'Anything else?'

'A *caciotta* with peppercorns. And I want to know if any

wounded men were treated in the city last night or this morning. Sword wounds.'

'Hmm.' Umberto stuck his fingers in his mouth and whistled twice. As he was unhooking one of the hanging cheeses, three young men appeared behind him. They were dressed in clothes that, a few owners ago, had belonged to rich and stylish gentlemen but were now shabby, though still rakish. Umberto and his sons had been my most useful informers for several years. I turned a blind eye to a few of their schemes, mostly procuring and gambling, and in return for this, and a judicious distribution of lire, they supplied me with detailed information on the Mercato Vecchio's comings and goings, dirty dealing, fraud, the activities of their rivals (several of whom were also in my pocket) and the sort of gossip that didn't make it to the ears of tax clerks in the Palazzo Vecchio. The sons grinned toothily at me, nodded their heads at their father's instructions and drifted off into the crowd.

'The lads will tell me if anyone so much as stubbed their toe,' Umberto told me as I counted out three times the value of the cheeses I had bought into his hand.

'Have these sent around to my house,' I said. 'And, Umberto, do you know anything about a woman called Zanobia Linucci?'

'Aha! So it's about that rumpus, is it? Thought so,' Umberto said, rocking back on his heels. 'As it happens, I know her cook. Riccio from Empoli. He's an arsehole.'

'So he is,' I agreed. 'He was the one who betrayed the poor woman. Do you know anything about her? Or about her patron?'

'As a matter of fact . . .' Umberto turned and called to a chubby teenager with bad impetigo who was sitting on a barrel behind the stall, throwing gravel at the pigeons. He was delegated to mind the business, and then Umberto led me across the square and into one of the alleys that led off the west side.

We were behind the church of Santa Maria in Campidoglio, one of the seediest parts of the city. 'Just step in here,' he said, unlocking a door in a damp, mossy wall. The houses around here were so old that some of them looked like candles melting into the ground. Beyond the door was a dim but cluttered space. I trusted Umberto within the confines of our business arrangement, but I kept my hand near the pommel of my dagger as I walked past him into a small warehouse that smelt strongly of sheep. Cheeses were stacked on rough pinewood shelves, and huge wicker-bound glass flasks of wine and oil stood between them. Plaster was coming away from the walls in sheets. A large ginger and white cat with only one ear glared at us from his perch on the sill of a high, barred window.

The cheese-seller shut the door behind us, bolted it, and brushed past me. 'Your pardon,' he muttered. 'Now then . . .'

He extracted a key from inside his hose, opened a rather fine old cabinet that was leaning against one wall, kept off the damp floor with bricks, and began to rummage inside. 'Here it is.' He locked the cabinet again, tucked the key back between his legs, and held something out to me.

It was a pendant on a gold chain. I took it over to where a beam of sunlight shone past the cat onto a patch of drying olive oil on the tiled floor and held it up. 'Jesus,' I muttered.

The heart of the pendant was a cameo of a woman in profile, in brown and cream agate, which was obviously Roman, framed by curlicues of gold enamelled in red and green. Four baroque pearls, embellished with gold to resemble tritons, were fixed to the frame. At the top, two little gold mermaids flanked an enamelled shield, into which the pendant's ring was fixed. The shield, though tiny, was so detailed that I could make out the coat of arms on it. A white field was divided by a gold stripe. Below, angled red stripes, and above, a tiny red rose.

'Where did you get this?' I asked Umberto.

'That arsehole cook,' he replied. 'You know I have a bit of a sideline as a fence, Comandante. Just a dabbler, that's me. A dabbler, and no rubbish either. Anyway, that Riccio came looking for me, which I take as a compliment to my reputation . . .'

'Don't push your luck,' I reminded him.

'No, no and indeed, no.' Umberto held up his hands in mock surrender. 'As I said, Riccio sought me out, asking if I'd be interested in some choice pieces. I said I might. You know, Comandante, can't be too careful. A couple of days later he brings me this. And, Mary's tits! What a beauty, eh?'

'When was this?'

'A few days ago.'

'And he just stole it from under her nose?'

'Extraordinary, isn't it? A little shit like that, pulls off something a master thief would count as the pinnacle of his career.'

'Did he say how?'

'Just that the lady was distracted. Distracted! I ask you. Meanwhile, he said there would be more. The next day, he said.'

'And was there?'

'Well . . .'

'Umberto,' I said reprovingly.

'You're too sharp, Comandante,' he muttered, fishing behind his codpiece again for the key. This time he opened his hand like a bored conjuror and presented me with a ring. I plucked it from his palm, holding the pendant out of his reach when he tried to take it.

'I'm taking these,' I said, putting them both in the pouch that hung from my belt.

'Comandante!'

'I'm saving you a lot of bother, Umberto. A lot. The men who killed Zanobia Linucci took the rest of her jewels. They belonged to the fellow who kept her as his mistress. And no, I don't mean Pietro Vennini. Someone who paid to have Vennini cut to pieces and his own mistress almost beheaded. I don't think you want him or his bravos after you.'

'If you put it like that, Comandante.' Umberto bit his lip, then gave a mirthless smile. He gave no sign of being angry, but I knew the man, and his cheery varnish hid a dangerous soul. But he was no fool either. The mirth returned. 'I heard all about Vennini. No, I've no wish to end up as *bistecca*.'

'I'll put something your way,' I said. 'Don't worry.'

'As if I would, Comandante. Now, shall we? I don't like leaving Cadere in charge of the stall for too long. His face doesn't encourage the buying of fine cheese.'

I left Umberto to lock up his warehouse after he'd promised to send one of his sons to me as soon as he had any information, and walked slowly back to the Bargello, so deep in thought that I was almost trampled by a pack horse on Via Calimala.

Captain Scarfa was waiting for me. 'My report, Don Onorio?' he said, as soon as I walked into the office.

43

'That's going to take a while,' I said.

'Hmph. A while, you say.'

'It's turning into a difficult one,' I said, carefully. 'You know how we hadn't heard of Zanobia Linucci? Well, the man whose mistress she was is from outside Florence, and he seems to have used a false name.'

'For fuck's sake.' Scarfa made two fists and banged them together, hard enough for the bony knocking to carry around the office. 'That bastard Vennini. I knew he'd leave us with a bloody mess to clean up, sooner or later. So what can you tell me?'

'Two hooded men were let into Donna Zanobia's house this morning around four of the clock. The steward let them in – he's a sound fellow and a good witness – he says neither of them were her lover, who apparently has a crooked back. The cook, a Riccio of Empoli, was the one who informed on her. I need a warrant for him; he's a nasty piece of work. The lover calls himself Bartolomeo Ormani, but there's every reason to believe it's an assumed name. He ordered the killers to take back all the jewellery and silver he'd given her.'

'Ormani? No one's—'

'Yes, I know. No one's carried that name in Florence for centuries,' I snapped. 'I've got the tax office and the chancery working on him. Donna Zanobia as well – she's a mystery too. But you should see this.' I took out the pendant and dropped it into Scarfa's open palm. 'The steward thought his mistress came from Pitigliano. And look here.' I pointed to the tiny shield above the cameo. 'That's the arms of the Pitigliano Orsinis.'

'Orsini, eh?' Scarfa squinted at the pendant, then took the pair of eyeglasses he kept on a cord around his neck and fitted them to his nose. 'This thing is worth a fortune. I thought you said the killers took everything.'

'Riccio the cook stole this and took it to my friend Umberto to fence. Umberto naturally brought it straight to me,' I said.

'Naturally.' Scarfa licked his lips. 'The magistrates won't like this. They're giving me all sorts of aggravation about the business on the bridge. The Grand Duke is upset about it, and I don't blame His Highness one bit.'

'The men who killed Vennini were mercenaries,' I told him. 'I recognised one of the bodies: he was in Flanders when I was there. No doubt Donna Zanobia's killers were mercenaries as well. I've got people checking the hospitals and the shady barber-surgeons. Vennini hurt at least one of them very badly.'

'Good swordsman, Vennini,' Scarfa said thoughtfully. 'I suppose you'd have an opinion on that, Don Onorio?'

'He was a braggart, but yes, he was an excellent swordsman. He challenged me once, as you know.'

'And backed out when you accepted. You might have saved everyone a lot of bother if you'd killed him then, Comandante.'

'Less paperwork, anyway.' We shared humourless soldiers' grins. He wasn't a bad fellow, Captain Scarfa. He drove people hard, but he was a Florentine, and as such, a realist at heart. We had probably crossed paths at some point in our former lives, because we had both been mercenaries ourselves not so long ago. Because of that I always knew where I was with him, and him, I suppose, with me.

'I'd better go and talk to the magistrates, or they'll be hanging on my balls like bell-ringers on Easter Sunday,' he said. 'Bring me somebody by sundown, Celavini.'

'I'll do my best. Does it matter who?'

'No. It really doesn't.'

He made a face and headed off in the direction of the magistrates' offices. I sat down at my desk, wrote out a warrant for the arrest of Riccio the cook and a request to have all the assets of Donna Zanobia Linucci seized, had Gerardo the office boy take them to the magistrates for approval, then went out into the furnace of midday.

CHAPTER FOUR

I spent the next few hours criss-crossing the city, talking to my informers, calling in favours and handing out bribes. The heat had either drugged people or put them on edge, and I was constantly cajoling and pacifying. Umberto shook his head when I walked past his stall: no news yet. Andrea had rounded up some witnesses to the fight on the bridge, who would be talking to the magistrates later, but now we knew that it had been six men against one. Pietro Vennini really had been an expert and very brave swordsman. What I'd said to Scarfa had been true: I had nearly fought him myself. Shortly after his return from exile, someone had accused Vennini of trying to cheat them over the sale of some property. I had been sent to investigate. Vennini saw this as an affront – typically for a man who spent his life dishonouring others, he guarded his own honour jealously – and had challenged me to a duel. I had joined the *sbirri* while he had been in exile, so he hadn't known anything about me. His friends soon told him that the man he had challenged was the victor of the notorious Duel by the Sea, and very soon after that he had, with no little charm, apologised to me and called things off. I understood why: he had wanted to kill a man who had insulted him, not be part of the circus that inevitably surrounds a duel between two famous swordsmen. And there had been no hurt feelings, especially as he had been cleared by the Eight of any wrongdoing. I wondered, now, how it would have been to fight him. It would have come down, as it always does, to which one of us had the most to lose.

Vennini must have been going home after sleeping with Donna Zanobia. He would have known that Ormani was a dangerous man to cross – his lover would have told him, and also, I guessed, Simone the steward had tried to save his mistress by warning Vennini away. But it hadn't made a difference. He'd been careless, and that is what kills us in the end.

I was rolling these thoughts around as I walked across the Ponte Santa Trìnita. The blood had been washed away, more or less, but at the far end there were still gobs of Vennini's hair and brains between the cobblestones. *What did he have to lose?* I thought. *Nothing much.* It was always going to end like this for him. This was the disaster he had been courting his whole life. But Zanobia Linucci: she had also been made to pay horribly for her lover's carelessness. And Vennini probably wouldn't have cared, if he'd lived to hear the news. He had been the sort who makes love to women but is really making love to himself. Donna Zanobia's life was not the first he had ruined.

It wasn't far from the bridge to Chiasso Cornino. The house was under guard, and I had a few words with the soldier at the front door. But I didn't go in. Instead I carried on up the street to the little church of San Biagio. The priest, Father Iacopo, was in the vestry. He greeted me with polite distaste. Father Iacopo was a fastidious man, neat and correct in appearance, habit and manner, and he knew my presence meant untidiness in his life. Because his parish bordered on the seedy edges of the Mercato Vecchio district I had dealt with him a few times in the past and had found him censorious and judgemental when it came to the less fortunate members of his flock.

'Comandante,' he said, putting down the chalice he was polishing. 'No doubt you've come to ask me about the unfortunate Linucci woman.'

'Unfortunate might be understating it, Father,' I said. 'You saw what they did to her.'

'A most unsettling experience,' the priest said, and pursed his lips. *You didn't even bother to close her eyes*, I thought.

'What can you tell me about her?' I asked.

'Very little, I'm afraid. I was not her confessor.'

'But she worshipped here?'

'Yes. She was diligent.' The man's narrowed eyes told me that he would have preferred it if she had worshipped somewhere else.

'Who did she come with?'

'I only ever saw her with her maid and the steward, Simone.'

'Never with Bartolomeo Ormani?'

The priest frowned. 'Who?'

'The man who kept her in that house. You knew she was someone's mistress, didn't you?'

'I keep my opinions to myself, Comandante.'

You bloody don't, I thought. 'You've never heard that name mentioned in the parish? Ormani? It's unusual. And he was a hunchback or crippled in some way. A crooked back.'

'Oh. Indeed, I have seen a man fitting that description. He comes and goes, you know.'

'I don't know. I want you to tell me, Father.'

He winced, as if using his memory on my behalf was too much of an imposition. 'I would say that he appears fairly regularly. Once a month, perhaps? No, every six weeks. Always with a small retinue of rough-looking fellows.'

'Rough?'

'Soldiers. Or ex-soldiers.'

'I expect you've heard about Pietro Vennini.'

'I do not waste my time with gossip.'

'Ah! Then you're the only man in Florence who hasn't heard that he was cut to bits on Ponte Santa Trìnita last night, and that he was Signora Linucci's lover, which is why . . .' I chopped the edge of one hand into the palm of the other. The priest sighed.

'A woman like that will inevitably collect the wages of sin sooner or later,' he said.

'A woman like that?' I repeated, aghast.

'A courtesan. A whore, Comandante.' Father Iacopo picked up the chalice again with a contented little smirk.

'She seems to have been a lady of noble birth,' I said. 'And by the way, she will be laid to rest in this church after a fine and proper funeral. I'm sure I'll see you here, conducting the proceedings with the respect and piety you accord to the worthiest members of your flock.'

I could feel the priest's stare consigning me to hell as I left the church, but I didn't care. I couldn't stand priests like Father Iacopo, squatting like toads in their parishes, growing fat on the gifts of their rich patrons and ignoring the poor. It was getting on for five hours past noon, and I walked north, back to the Mercato Vecchio, where Umberto was packing away his stall, loading cheeses onto a handcart to which the pustular Cadere was harnessed.

'Comandante!' he said. 'I've had the *pecorino* and the *caciotta* sent around to your place. And . . .' He lowered his voice and led me towards the Column of Dovizia, where ragged children were playing jumping games over the chains that surrounded the pillar. 'My lads combed the city. Combed it, mind, as finely as a monkey mother checking her kids for nits.'

'Good. And?'

'And they found a surgeon who'd treated a man for a sword wound in the arse. The arse!'

'That's excellent, Umberto. Is he still treating him?'

'No.' Umberto rolled his eyes apologetically. 'He left around noon.'

'Fuck. Who, and where?'

'The surgeon's name is Spinelli, and he lives on Via dei Macci, just across from the Poor Clares.'

'Thanks, Umberto. I'll see that your boys find their efforts have been worthwhile.'

'You always do, Comandante. Incidentally, about that pendant and ring . . .'

'You can't have them back. They're evidence.'

'Ach.'

'I'm sure there's plenty more in that cabinet. Which, at the moment, I'm disinclined to remember ever having seen,' I said. 'Let alone where you keep the key.'

It was a long walk in the heat to Via dei Macci, and when I got there, Spinelli was not at home, or in any case he didn't answer when I banged, with growing irritation, on his shabby door. Fine. I would come back tomorrow with a warrant.

It was getting dark by the time I got back to the Bargello. Scarfa had gone over to the palace for a meeting. Andrea Gherardi told me that Riccio the cook was in custody, and I told him to arrest Spinelli as soon as he showed himself.

'You look wrung out, Comandante,' he said, after I had leant back in my chair and closed my eyes. 'I'm going home. Scarfa won't be back tonight. You should go home too. Get something gentle to eat. Something easy on the stomach. There's a veal torte waiting for me.'

It wasn't my stomach that was bothering me, but I didn't tell Andrea that. My head was throbbing, from walking miles in the heat, and from something else. Yes, I would go home.

I did, but not before stopping at the chapel attached to Santa Maria dell'Umiltà. It was a small, shabby room which smelt of boiled kale and laundry, the cross on the altar looked as if it had been picked off a dust heap, and the framed Virgin and Child that hung above it hadn't been painted by a maestro, but it was where I always came to pray. The only people I ever found in there were girls and women from the Pietà: orphans, rejected girls, abandoned girls, who spun raw silk into thread and wove cloth from dawn until dusk. The prioress, Sister Brigida, was a tough, solid woman who had spent her whole life in the orphanage. I had helped her a few times when her girls, as she always called them, many of whom worked outside the Pietà, got into trouble with their employers, or were accused of stealing or selling themselves. They were never guilty, those girls, and invariably I would find myself threatening some lustful weaving master or shopkeeper who believed all poor women had been sent by God to satisfy the itch between their legs. I knelt down to pray, and time drifted by. I prayed to the Virgin, and to my patron saint, Santa Celava, who finds things that are lost. When at last I rose, rather stiffly, and reached into my purse for something to put in the offering box, my fingers found, among the coins, a metal hoop. Zanobia Linucci's ring. I took it out and held it up to the nearest candle.

It was a thick, gold circle formed out of the long bodies of two hounds, their tails entwined, their heads encircling a cushion-shaped bezel inlaid with a rough-cut diamond the size of a grain of wheat. I felt a shock go up my arm, or perhaps I imagined it, but the next thing I was aware of was the sensation of cold tile against my cheek. I looked up: there was the altar, the candles, one of them bleeding a neat line of black smoke from an untrimmed wick. The pinkish light of the faint was receding from my eyes. I hadn't eaten anything all day, I told myself. The heat, the miles walked . . . I rolled over and got up onto my haunches. There was something in my hand. I opened it, and there was the ring.

It wasn't far to my house. I unlocked the outer door and stepped into the courtyard. When I locked it behind me, I was alone, quite alone, for the first time that day. The courtyard, no more than six paces from end to end, had a brick well with a worn marble cap at its centre. One side was the street wall. Adjoining houses made up two other sides, but their windows and doors had been bricked up a long time ago. On the third side was another, slightly newer door, two small windows on either side and one larger one above, all pointed in the ancient style. My house was at least three centuries old and it seemed a kind of miracle that it had survived that long, as the mortar was crumbling between its stones. In the courtyard the air smelt of old stone and cats, and the things that grow in places where the sun can't be bothered to shine, but the throat-catching fumes of the dyeing vats of Borgo Ognissanti had barely seeped in. Orange and grey lichens mottled the walls with streaks and bullseyes. There wasn't really enough light for the orange trees and the date palm I had planted in big pots and they were looking sickly. Sparrows were making a racket in the leaves and in the vine growing up the side of the house. I told myself I should consult a gardener about the trees, and then wondered how I had managed to have such an ordinary thought.

My housekeeper had left hours ago. I closed the shutters on the windows that gave out onto the street and stood for a while in the dusty near-dark. Then I went upstairs. Though the house was empty, I locked the door of my bedroom. Old habits are hard to break. I shuttered the window and pulled the curtains against the last gleam of dusk that was coming in through the cracks. I let the darkness swaddle me, then I groped for the tinder box on the dresser and lit some candles. The room was sparsely furnished: the dresser, a high-backed chair next to the fireplace, an ornate bed in dark, richly carved wood that had come with the place. The walls were bare, except for an oblong frame draped in heavy black velvet.

The housekeeper had left me a clay jug of wine and a glass on a pewter tray. The clay, beaded with moisture, had kept it cool. I poured a glass and took a deep drink. Then I began to unbutton my jerkin. Even though it was my lightest, it was still too heavy for August: dark grey, almost black leather, pinked in lines and studded with silvered steel, designed to stop a knife thrust or the attentions of an unskilled swordsman. I shrugged it off and let it drop noisily to the floor, rolling my shoulders until the muscles understood they had been released. I unbuckled my belt and stepped out of my breeches. Then I unlaced the collar of my shirt and pulled it off. The binding around my breasts had somehow worked itself tighter through the day, and I tugged at the knot impatiently, loosening the fine linen bandage and unwinding it until I was free. I stretched gratefully, feeling the blood return. Kicking off my breeches, I went to the chamber pot in the corner and squatted. Then I stood for a moment in front of the black-draped frame before pulling at the velvet and letting it drop to the floor. There I was, reflected.

Thin, white as milk, still almost young; breasts streaked with red where they had been crushed against my ribcage. I took a deep breath, and then another, letting my flesh settle and become itself again for a little while. I stretched again, staring at the woman in the silvery glass. There are always a strange few moments, a sort of slack tide in my head, before I remember that I am Onoria, not Onorio. Then it passes, because I know who I am again.

My mirror. It is where I find peace, in so far as I ever really am at peace. I take off my armour, my false skin, my actor's clothes, and let Onoria be at ease. Alone and behind a locked door, I am still hiding, though not from myself. You might say that a locked door makes a prison. Ah, yes, but I have the keys. The thing of metal that fits the lock is one, but Onoria can't just turn it, open the door and be free. The real key is the bandage for her breasts, the commander's costume, the proud codpiece laced over a very different sex. When Onorio goes out, Onoria must stay behind to guard our ghosts. In a way, the locked door is really for them.

I talk to myself. That is another of my secrets. We talk in the same voice, Onoria and I: the same broken voice. We tell each other the things we have never been able to say out loud, the things that come to us every night when we sleep, but which we can't allow out into the daylight. Our ghosts. We . . . I sometimes have to remind myself that we are the same person. I can live with these ghosts locked up inside me. If they haunt my dreams, I suppose that's the bargain I have made with them: they may live while I am dead to the world, but when I am awake and trying to live, they have to return to their graves. It is a reasonable exchange for the living to make with the dead, and it has served all parties well – until now.

I looked in the mirror and I imagined myself in Donna Zanobia's place, lying on a stone slab in the Bigallo, stripped and exposed, my secrets flying out into the world. Just another dead woman. Although the room was hot I was shivering painfully, as though I had a quartan fever. Picking up the pall of velvet, I covered the mirror and stumbled over to the window, pressed my hands against the shutters through the curtain. My ghosts, I knew, were no longer contained by this locked door. They had been released and had sniffed the air of the living. I had felt them around me all day, though I'd tried to ignore them, walking back and forth across the city as if I might have lost them, shaken them off, made them slink back here to wait for my return. But they had stayed close by. From the moment I'd heard my name, and my brother's name, coming from the mouth of a stranger, my ghosts became a part of this story. So if I am not to sound mad or deceitful, I will need to let them speak.

BOOK II

CHAPTER FIVE

You can see the whole world from her bedroom window: the puckered golden floor of the valley, far below, soft hills that seemed, here and there, to have been gnawed by giant teeth to reveal the grey rock beneath the grass. To the south, the mount of Radicofani jutting up, its flat top a little bit tilted; if she screws up her eyes, she can see the tower of the castle. Further on, a line of low mountains that changes colour hour by hour, day by day: black, purple, green, hazy pink. Sometimes, in the summer, they aren't there at all. Beyond the mountains, the sun rises and the world's edge curves like the trembling arc of a soap bubble. Sometimes a raven swoops down from the woods behind the village that climb up to the summit of Monte Amiata; the girl will hear the hiss of wind across its great wings, then it will be in front of her, and for a moment she will be looking along its broad, glossy back, glinting oily blue and green. Then she will be riding out across the great gulf of air, breathless with the joy of it, until the bird grows smaller and vanishes into the hazy light and she imagines herself suspended above the earth, hovering on wings of her own. The Ormani crest is three black ravens on a white ground, standing in a row above a field of red. Her father sometimes tells her what his grandfather told him: that the first Ormani was a raven who flew down from Amiata and landed on a bare crag, where an old woman happened to be sitting. The old woman had been a saint, and she had turned the raven into a man. And the red? That was blood, her father will say, then laugh and change the subject.

The girl likes to tell Bartolomeo, her brother, that Radicofani is the stump of the greatest tree that had ever lived, with a crown so high that the sun had been one of its fruits, that it had been cut down by giants, the same ones that had used the crag on which the village perched as a chair. He will roll his eyes and tell her that Radicofani, like everything else in Creation, has been made by God. The girl doesn't see why God couldn't have made an enormous tree, or giants, but Bartolomeo says He hasn't, and that is that.

The girl lives in the castle with her brother, and her mother and father. Once, a very long time ago, the whole village had been the castle. Some knight had climbed up here looking for solitude or safety and built a strong wall around the crag that jutted out from the skirts of Monte Amiata. As years turned into centuries, people realised that no one would be foolish enough to attack such a place and began to build their own houses inside the castle walls. They called it Pietrodoro, after the cliff that drops away from the end of the crag which, when seen from a distance, looks like a great seam of gold. The castle church became the village church. The Rocca, where Onoria lives, is just the keep of the original knight's castle. There is an even grander house in Pietrodoro, a palazzo that stands across the little village square.

Onoria doesn't like to go inside that house, but her friends live there: her best friend, Federigo, his older sister, Smeralda, and their two little brothers. They are the only children she is allowed to play with, because they are of the same rank. It isn't an easy thing to understand, especially when the children of the farmers and artisans who also live in Pietrodoro seem to know how to enjoy themselves. But there it is: Onoria's family, the Ormanis, and Federigo's people, who are called the Ellebori, have lived in Pietrodoro for ever. *The Ormanis have been here as long as the mountain itself* – so the villagers say. *But not as long as the Ellebori*, might be the reply, depending on who you were talking to.

Onoria has to go there today. It is time for the fencing lesson that her father gives her and Federigo almost every day when he is at home and the weather is kind, and she has to fetch her friend, who is usually on time but hasn't appeared yet. She wanders across the piazza, ignoring the looks she is getting from Father Giovanni, the village priest, and from the two older women drawing water from the deep well in front of the church. As usual, she is wearing a set of her older brother's fourth-best clothes: Bartolomeo has never cared about his appearance, and the doublet and hose are drab and frayed. Still, she likes the way the hose feel against her legs, and the freedom they give her. You can climb over a wall in them, do things you could never do in a dress. Which, as she has always supposed, is the whole point of being a boy. It isn't the state of her clothes that makes people stare at her – she understands that well enough. 'I don't want to be a boy,' she's explained countless times to her mother, to Federigo, to anyone who questions her. 'I just want to be *like* a boy.' It is because she chooses, whenever she can, to dress like a boy. Smeralda, in

61

particular, disapproves, but that is because she is jealous, Onoria supposes. Her skirts don't allow her to keep up when they chase pine martens through the olive groves or run races along the track which joins Pietrodoro to the mountain, a straight, flat, paved way running along a narrow spine of land between two rows of ancient cypress trees. Smeralda's mother gets angry if she catches her shooting at targets in the old archers' butts at the edge of the cliff below the church. But Smeralda, who is pretty – black hair, a little turned-up nose and rather small eyes that just make her freckles more adorable – is also a decent shot with a bow, and her skirts don't get in the way of archery. Onoria has told Smeralda, more than once, that when she grows up she is going to be a *condottiere* in charge of her own company of mercenaries, and Smeralda has laughed rather sadly and said, 'That's just something you've made up. Girls don't become *condottieri*.'

'Go on, Ralda! You could be one too, if you wanted to be! We could ride together: Federigo, you and me,' Onoria will say, although she knows it isn't true. She only gets away with acting like a boy because her father indulges her. One day her mother will put her foot down and Onoria will be in a dress, listening to her parents arrange a marriage for her.

She shivers as she goes through the big arched doorway of the Palazzo Ellebori, because the house always greets her with a waft of chilly, damp air, no matter how hot it might be outside. She pads through the entrance chamber, not bothering to look at the glowering Ellebori portraits, the enemy standard from some ancient battle, the antlers, the scrofulous wolf pelt. Somewhere below her, so her friends say, there is a little church carved out of the living rock, filled with the monuments and bones of countless dead Ellebori. The thought of that makes her shiver again: the living grown-up Ellebori are bad enough, let alone dead ones. Lodovigo Ellebori is about the same age as her own father, but has a creased, sun-polished face that looks to Onoria like a Roman mask in one of her mother's books. He is thin and wiry, and always seems to be moving as if he is wearing armour. Lodovigo was a soldier like her father, but that isn't something the two men ever talk about. His wife should be beautiful, but her delicate features, a more developed version of Smeralda's, always seem to be hiding from themselves. Benedetta Ellebori walks two steps behind her husband, and Onoria has never heard her say anything to a grown-up that isn't a reply to someone else's question, though her tongue can be like a razor when she turns it on her children.

But the person Onoria likes least is the oldest brother, Augusto. He is at least ten years older than Smeralda, the child of a previous marriage, of a woman who has left no trace whatsoever of her existence in Pietrodoro apart from her son, though Onoria supposes that her bones are somewhere below her, mouldering in the family crypt. And Augusto is the first person Onoria sees that day, coming down the stairs in his usual costume of baggy, heavily slashed hose and stockings in a dirty shade of crimson striped with white, a padded doublet of the same colour with puffed-out sleeves, untied to the waist to expose an expensive but grimy linen shirt. His dark brown hair is long and greasy, and his face resembles his father's, but where Lodovigo Ellebori's features are mask-like, Augusto's are mobile, always twisting into one expression or another, but all of them, to Onoria's eyes, mocking and unkind. He wears a beard, but it is thin, combed out to a straggly point, and his moustaches bristle on either side of his thin lips like the whiskers of some dangerous, night-dwelling beast. He is tightening the laces of his codpiece, and Onoria knows he is doing it because she is there when he gives them a particularly hard tug so that the hard leather bulge rears up between his legs. He leers straight at her.

'Signorina Ormani,' he says. His voice sometimes reminds Onoria of a burning fuse, smoking and sizzling with contempt. 'I think I'll join you today. I saw your father last night and he seemed to believe that I could assist him in his lessons. Hurry up, Federigo!' he shouts up the stairs.

Onoria's friend wanders into sight across the landing. Federigo is Onoria's age and looks like a male version of his sister: freckled, fine-featured, but with blonde curls instead of straight black tresses. This morning, like most days, he is dressed like Onoria in cast-offs. When he sees her, he waves sheepishly.

'It's so hot, Onoria! I thought perhaps Maestro Amerigo might spare us today.'

'He was going to, but I insisted!' Onoria grins. 'Come on, lazy bones! There's a bit of shade in our courtyard.'

'Yes, hurry up, Federigo,' says Augusto. 'When you're a soldier, there'll be no turning up late when there's action.'

'But I don't want to be a soldier,' says Federigo. 'Onoria's going to be the *condottiere*, not me.'

'Ha ha,' Augusto says, an unpleasant smile twitching his beast's whiskers. 'A boy who acts like a girl, and a girl – you are still a girl, are you not, Signorina Ormani? – who believes she is a boy. How amusing Pietrodoro has become. Like a Roman whorehouse.' He brushes past her and goes out into the square. Onoria rolls her eyes at her friend and they follow him. The only good thing about

64

Augusto is that he doesn't spend much time in the village. He has been in Rome, Federigo told her yesterday, and before that with a mercenary company. Onoria is sometimes able to admit to herself that one of the reasons she dislikes Augusto Ellebori so much is that he is living a life that she will never be able to lead herself. Augusto is always 'in Rome' or 'in Naples' or 'with the Count of Pitigliano'. When she reaches his age, she'll be locked up in someone else's house, pregnant with her fourth child.

As they cross the piazza, Onoria sees Smeralda going into the church of Santa Clara. She is becoming more pious lately, Onoria has noticed. Then again, she is almost fifteen, and her parents are already looking for a husband. *Perhaps she'll become a nun*, Onoria thinks. *Better than being married.* Gianozzo, her father's steward, is talking with Francino the groom in the gateway of the Rocca. They bow respectfully to Augusto, and Gianozzo gives Onoria a wink after Augusto has strutted into the courtyard beyond the gate.

'It's hot today, Signorina Onoria. I'll have Carlo send up some cold lemon water.'

'Thank you, Gianozzo!' The Rocca's servants are almost equally divided in their approval or otherwise of Onoria's strange habits. The steward is one of her allies, which is important. In fact, her father's servants indulge her, and her mother's do not. Onoria has long ago decided that the maids and the housekeeper just envy her. Who, after all, would choose to wear skirts and a bodice when there are doublets and hose in the world? It is absurd.

CHAPTER SIX

'Here.' Her father jabs at the open page, his finger coming to rest on one of the pairs of figures stacked across the paper: little men in shirts and tight hose, each one stretched wide into dancers' poses, each one armed with a longsword and a dagger. 'And here!' His finger traces a circle around one pair of men. She leans over to see better, almost bumping heads with Federigo. In the drawing, both men are lunging, legs impossibly far apart, but one man's sword has gone right through the other's head and his dagger has lodged in his adversary's chest, while the other man's blades hover uselessly in the air. The poor man's mouth is making a shocked O and little drops of inky blood are dropping from where the sword has gone into his face.

'Oh dear,' she whispers.

'Yes, well, that's . . .' Her father, Maestro Amerigo Ormani, blinks apologetically.

'The whole point. I know, Papà,' she says, and smiles to show that she doesn't mind, even though she does, a little bit.

'You'll never see such things, of course, *cara*,' says. 'You, on the other hand, Federigo . . .' He reaches out and ruffles the boy's hair affectionately.

'Mmm.' Federigo grimaces and shoots her a quick glance. She grins by way of reply. Her friend's blonde curls have been tied back away from his face with a strip of rag, and she has done the same to her own straighter hair, pulling the knot as tight as she can so that her hair is as flat and as smooth against her head as sealskin.

'See. You hold the dagger thus.' Augusto is standing next to the maestro. He reaches behind him and pulls his own blade from its sheath, flourishes it in front of the two children. The steel flashes in the sunlight, and Onoria's eyes are filled for a moment with strange blue and purple shapes. She blinks.

Augusto is missing the middle finger on his left hand, which, wrapped around the hilt, looks like a fat, pale spider. When he first returned from the wars, Federigo – to whom his brother was more or less a stranger – asked him how he had come to lose his finger. Onoria, as usual, was with her friend, and Augusto leant down and breathed into their faces. 'Well, since you ask, little brother, I put it up the hole of a Tyrrhenian witch. And she bit it off!' He barked out the last words and leant back, roaring with laughter at the children's gaping mouths. 'A woman's hole bit off your finger, Augusto?' Federigo breathed, looking green, and the man grinned evilly, but just then the Ellebori family confessor shuffled in the room, and Augusto grinned and shook his head. 'No, no. It was an arquebus ball at Scannagallo,' he said, so that the priest could hear.

'I know he's your brother, but that thing he said was disgusting,' Onoria said to Federigo, later, when they were hunting lizards in the olive groves outside the wall.

'Could it, though? You know . . .' Federigo glanced towards Onoria's lap with a look of near terror.

'No! Don't be so ridiculous!' she snapped, and Federigo went pink with relief.

A shutter creaks, and Onoria looks up to see her mother leaning out. The sunlight, slanting into the courtyard at a late afternoon angle, gleams on the pearls at her neck and in the lobes of her ears. A dark corkscrew curl comes free from the elaborate arrangement of plaits that crowns her head, and springs against her cheek. Onoria feels a warm surge of love. 'Amerigo,' Maria Ormani calls. 'The bookkeeper needs you.'

Her father sighs. 'In a moment,' he calls back. He turns to Augusto. 'I'll let you carry on with the lesson.' Onoria, who knows her father better, she reckons, than anyone else in Creation, marks a slight frown that passes across his face after he says this, but then he is gone. Amerigo likes Augusto Ellebori as little as she does, but treats him with more respect than he deserves. It is because Augusto is a soldier, as her father once was, though her father led a famous *condottiere* company in Lombardy, and Augusto . . . no one exactly knows what Augusto did in the wars besides lose a finger, though he has a deadness around the eyes, and uses a blade with a skill that Onoria – as expert in such matters as the daughter of a fencing master can be – has to admit is more than reasonable. But Onoria knows that the real reason why her father puts up with Augusto is pity. The war that Augusto returned from was the fight between Florence and Siena; Duke Cosimo against Sienese and Florentine rebels fighting for the French king. Augusto had been fighting on the Sienese side, and they had lost.

The children dutifully pick up their wooden daggers and allow Augusto to shape their hands around the quillons. He is more gentle with Federigo; when it is her turn, he stands too close and makes sure that the hard orb of his codpiece is rubbing against her hip. His breath smells of garlic and cheese, and she doesn't like the way the stump of his missing finger, smooth and polished like another little codpiece among the other fingers, kneads her skin.

While Augusto leans against the trunk of the walnut tree that grows in the corner of the courtyard, the two children thrust and feint at one another. The dagger feels unnatural in Onoria's left hand, but when at last they are allowed to pick up their swords – carved, like the daggers, from ash wood – she finds that she likes the way her hands balance each other out. Augusto makes them study the book again, prodding first one picture, then another. When Onoria tries to question one posture and puts her own finger on the paper, Augusto bats her hand away.

They go at it again, circling one another in the centre of the courtyard, Augusto shouting directions and commands, sometimes demonstrating with his own sword, which sizzles through the air like a hornet. For a brute – for Augusto is exactly that – he moves with quick, sinewy dexterity, the grace of a predatory creature. Dancing, Onoria thinks, is taking pleasure in both your own grace and another's. Augusto's grace is entirely for his own pleasure, for his own use.

The children shuffle, spin and strike, repeating the same exercise until their arms burn, then another. *What is keeping Papà?* Onoria begins to ask herself. Augusto takes their daggers and shows them, with his sword, what to do next. He smells of sweat and stale orris root, and his shirt is stained yellow under the arms, so Onoria is glad when he goes back to his place under the tree. 'Ready?' she asks Federigo, who rolls his eyes in exasperation and nods.

Onoria likes the way her feet move as if she is dancing and not pretending to fight. When Augusto at last decides to see if they have learnt anything, and tells them to square off and fight each other, Onoria finds that she can easily twist out of the way of Federigo's weapon and slash him – lightly, because she doesn't want to hurt her friend – across the legs and shoulders. When she has lured him towards her and slipped her sword along his arm so that it presses into the hollow below his collarbone, Augusto barks, 'Stop!' He pulls his brother, who is rubbing his shoulder, over to the shade of the tree, and shows him something in the book. Onoria is panting slightly: the sword, though made of wood, is still quite heavy. But she doesn't want Augusto Ellebori to think she is tired, so she goes through the postures, twirling the sword above her head and lunging, side-stepping, lunging. She is trying to imagine what it might feel like to face someone with an actual sword, to have its point flashing across her vision, the terror of knowing you could be cut, or run through, in the blink of an eye. Or to do it yourself. She shakes off the thought and assumes the guard of the unicorn, left hand behind her back, sword at the level of her forehead, pointing forward. She shuffles, steps, twists her wrist and cuts the legs from under her invisible enemy.

Augusto sends Federigo back towards her with a shove. The boy has a thin-lipped look that signifies annoyance. *I want to stop too*, she's going to say, but just then Augusto orders them to begin. Federigo raises his sword, and Onoria crouches. She lets him come on, then taps him across the wrist. Federigo steps back, takes a lower guard; Onoria feints and lunges. The wooden blade slips across Federigo's chest and under his arm, but instead of stopping, he grabs both her wrists. She has time to see him squeeze his eyes shut before his foot comes up and he kicks her, hard, between the legs.

Pain comes down over her like a black hood. She dimly feels herself fall to her knees. *I'm going to be sick*, she thinks. A hand touches her arm and she flails it away. Hot tears force her eyes open. She sees Federigo's shoes. 'You . . .' she croaks. He squats down and takes her shoulders. His face is white, and his mouth is twisted. Behind him, she sees Augusto, legs apart, fists on his hips, mouth wide. The ringing in her ears changes to his ugly laughter.

'I'm so, so sorry, Onoria!' Federigo hisses. 'I'm sorry! He made me! That . . .' He drops his voice even lower. 'My brother said I wasn't to be bested by a girl. He said he'd tell our father. And he showed me what to do in the book. I wasn't going to do it, but I thought . . . I didn't mean to kick you that hard, and I thought, seeing as you're a girl . . .'

'Oh, Madonna.' Onoria wipes her face with a dusty hand. 'Because I'm a girl, eh?' she says through clenched teeth. 'One day I'll kick *you* there and then we'll see!' She pushes him away and stands up shakily. Federigo stands up too.

'That's enough for today, Augusto,' the boy says, a surprising edge in his voice. He picks up his sword and slashes it angrily through the air. 'I hate all this,' he mumbles. 'I'll never be a soldier! I'll tell Father when he comes home, you'll see.'

'If you can pull a filthy trick like that just because someone . . .' Onoria bites down on the words that want to come out. Augusto is a brute – worse – but he is her best friend's brother, and she has learnt respect from her father. '. . . I thought you were my friend,' she mutters. But this time she lets him take her arm and help her up. 'Go away,' she says, trying to grin to show that she doesn't really hate him. But perhaps she does. When the nausea ebbs, she goes over to Augusto and is about to hand over her sword when she sees an unpleasant little movement in the wrinkles around his eyes. Amusement, disdain, and something else that hangs in the air between them, as feral as the stink of his sweat.

'Thank you,' she says, and makes a pretty curtsey. Then she hesitates, deliberately. 'My father says you are a good swordsman. I was wondering, Don Augusto . . . There's an attack that I don't quite understand. Could you show me?'

'Attack, eh?' Augusto's lips pull back, showing a black tooth. 'What do girls know about attack?'

'It's this one.' She goes to the book and flips forward until she finds the page. 'See, here. Can you explain the footwork?'

Augusto snorts. 'So easy.'

'Oh! Perhaps you could show me!'

She can see him considering, a little string of tics across his face: dubious, proud, then cruel. 'All right, then,' he says. 'But don't cry to your father if I'm not gentle.'

'I promise,' she says. She backs away from him, into the open yard. 'The defence is like this, I think.' She puts her weight on her back foot and holds the wooden sword upright in front of her, making it look clumsy, like a tired altar boy trying to hold one of those long candles straight. *Porta di ferro*, but badly done. Augusto has picked up his brother's sword. He advances on her with a bandy-legged swagger.

'Right,' he says, taking position. He bounces a little on his knees, like an ape that Onoria once saw at the Viterbo fair. 'It's like this.'

It isn't hard to guess what he's going to do: he's going to hurt her, enough, probably, that she'll never want to play at swords again and humiliate his little brother. He sniffs, rolls his shoulders. His left fist goes behind his back, his sword comes up. 'Watch my feet,' he barks, and obediently she drops her eyes, but only for an instant. As his wrist rolls and his sword hisses towards her forehead, she crouches and twists her body to the right, turns her sword across her chest, *rovescio tondo*. There is a clack of wood, and her sword is almost jerked from her, but she expected that. Her grip is good. Rising, she turns his sword, and all the force he has put into his blow – everything he intended to hit her with – carries him almost off balance. As his point drops towards the flagstones she catches her own blade with the flat of her left hand, pushes it forward, throws all her scant weight onto her front foot and lunges. The tip of her sword catches Augusto square on the breastbone. These wooden swords have soft, inch-wide rounded ends, but even so, the man paws at his chest with his left hand as he staggers backwards, wheezing in alarm. His heel catches the edge of a loose stone, and he trips and lands heavily on his backside.

'Thank you for my lesson, Don Augusto,' says Onoria. She bows to him, noting that his face has gone an apoplectic shade of red. 'I found it very useful.' Without waiting for a reply, she walks as steadily as she can from the courtyard.

The Rocca is old, one of the oldest houses in Pietrodoro. The two noble families, whether they sprang from the mountain rock or not, have been facing each other across the village square for as long as anyone has been telling stories. Ormani and Ellebori, forever on opposite sides: Guelph and Ghibelline, Pope and Emperor, Florence and Siena. An Ormani died at Montaperti, centuries ago, when Siena massacred the Florentine Guelphs, and an Ellebori was killed at Benevento, when Florence and her allies got their revenge.

But Pietrodoro, tiny, clinging to its crag like a swallow's nest, is a long way from Florence or Siena. Inside its old walls, most people measure time by watching the mountain's shadow move across the wide, golden valley below. Guelphs stopped fighting Ghibellines long ago, and young men went off to war for money, not honour. There used to be Ormanis in Florence, but no one in Pietrodoro has heard from them in generations. The Ellebori, who are cousins to the Siena Salimbenis, feel things more strongly, maybe, and since Florence conquered Siena, things have been tense again in the village. Augusto went off to fight for Siena, but he did it for money, not for love. Onoria's father stayed out of the whole affair. 'I'm retired,' he said, and made a point of inviting Augusto's father, Lodovigo, to the Rocca for a grand dinner. And Lodovigo accepted, because, since Grand Duke Cosimo became ruler of Tuscany, everyone has put aside the old rivalries and hatreds, and become Tuscans, pure and simple.

This is the world as Onoria knows it. The old stories, to her ears, are all too complicated and stupid. Her father sometimes tells her how his grandfather and Federigo's great-grandfather fought a little war across the square, with crossbow bolts thudding into the shutters and men shouting rude words to one another from the towers. And also, how men from each family would run out and fight in the square. What her father hasn't told her, but which Bartolomeo, who always has his nose in some book or other, has found out from the family records, was that during this miniature war, her father's great-uncle killed Federigo's great-great uncle and hung his body upside down from the top of the palazzo tower for the whole town, including the poor man's wife and mother, to stare at for days, until the families made peace and the great-great uncle was taken down and buried. She asked her father about it, and he went very serious and even bit his lip, which he only does when something has really upset him. So perhaps, she decided, it didn't happen after all, and Bartolomeo made it up to frighten her.

The castle of Rocca di Pietrodoro is old, a tall, narrow keep sticking up out of the top of the village like a broken flagpole. The place was built, so her father says, in the time of the Lombards, though some of the people who live in the village are of the opinion that it grew up out of the mountain itself to protect them from Saracen raiders. She climbs painfully up the rock-cut steps that lead to the front door, a great, ancient archway carved with flowers and strange beasts, all now melted into stranger forms by centuries of wind and rain. The castle rises above her in two tiers: a more or less square block topped by fishtail crenellations, with slightly bulging walls which are a patchwork of old brick and older marble blocks, Roman columns and capitals, from which the keep of tallow-coloured stone juts up, stained with rust from the windows that pock it at odd intervals. Some recent Ormani lord topped it with a modern battlement which sits on the pinnacle like a fashionable hat on a crumbling statue. Other buildings cluster inside the curtain wall: the armoury, the bakery, storerooms.

Onoria stops in the cool of the downstairs hall and puts her head against one of the tapestries that hang there: Hercules wrestling the Nemean lion. She loves Hercules, but she loves the lion more. She usually finds him comforting, but today the silence and stillness seem to make the pain worse, somehow, and she has to squat down and lean against the wall, eyes screwed shut. She thinks of Augusto's crotch pressing against her and his slug-like finger stump, and then a picture appears in her head: Augusto, hanging head down from the tower. At that, the pain recedes.

'Onoria?' She looks up to see her father standing above her. 'Are you all right?'

'I . . .' The words are on the tip of her tongue: *Augusto made Federigo kick me between my legs, then he laughed at me.* She won't tell him that. 'Nothing. An accident. Federigo got me in the stomach with his sword.' She looks up and smiles crookedly, deciding not to tell him about her sparring with Augusto. 'He's getting better, I think.'

'Oh! My poor darling.' Amerigo helps her up gently. 'Your mother is right. I shouldn't make you do all those things. She'll have my ears for a necklace when she sees you.'

'Don't tell her, then!'

'Dressed as a boy, spending time with animals . . . with men like Augusto Ellebori. Dear God, I am a neglectful father.'

'No! You aren't. Please don't tell Mamma. I would die, really die, if I had to be a proper girl!'

'Holy Mother!' Amerigo crosses himself. 'What on earth are you, if not a proper girl?'

'Of *course* I am. But . . . Bartolomeo wants to be a priest, doesn't he? Priests are proper men.' She cocks her head at him, daring him to deny it.

'Let us not get into theology, *cara*,' her father says hastily. 'I mean, yes, plainly they are.'

'But they aren't manly, like soldiers.'

'Honestly, Onoria . . .' But she knows her father. He's uncomfortable because he doesn't exactly disagree.

'So Barto can be a priest, but I can't be a *condottiere*. Boys can be unmanly priests, but girls can't be ungirly soldiers.' She folds her arms. 'Well, I'm a girl and if I can't be a *condottiere* like you, at least I want to learn how to fence, Papà. And when I'm as good as you . . .' She tilts her head up and looks at him slyly. They both grin at the same time. 'When I'm a bit older I'll do what Mamma wants. But not just yet. Please, Papà.'

'Ach.' Her father sighs and shakes his head. 'Perhaps . . . Well, Onoria, it can't go on. You understand, don't you? People are beginning to whisper. They're mostly idiots, I do know that, but still. And that damned Father Giovanni gave me a lecture yesterday. In my own house.' His voice is beginning to growl. Onoria knows that her father doesn't like her mother's confessor very much. Her father isn't pious like her mother. It is an argument they often have: her mother trying to get her husband to go to church more regularly, her father growling that he is a soldier with a soldier's honest faith, that he's talked to God often enough on the battlefield to know that he is in good standing. Her parents argue quite a lot, but it is never very serious. Mostly, her father scolds her mother about Bartolomeo, who has never shown any sign of wanting to be a soldier like him, and her mother scolds her father about Onoria. So in a way, a convenient sort of balance is maintained.

Onoria lies awake for a long time that night, wondering if she should tell her father about Augusto, how he turned Federigo against her, and how she beat him at swordplay, although she also humiliated him, she knows, and that is a bad thing. But the next day, her father leaves for Montalcino, where he is thinking of starting a school of swordsmanship, and it is raining. The day after that, Federigo comes around as if nothing has happened. But something has happened, a good thing: his brother has left Pietrodoro as well, to join a *condottiere*'s company. The two go back to their life of chasing lizards in the walls of the Rocca, hunting rabbits in the olive groves and climbing the old oak trees that line the road down to the valley, but in the mornings Onoria has lessons with her mother and Bartolomeo, where she must wear a dress or be punished. Endless hours of Virgil from the big book in her parents' bedroom. Aeneas and his Trojans. So horribly, horribly boring.

There is a half-collapsed stone hut in the terraced groves below the Rocca, still with part of its roof, some sticks that had once been peasants' furniture and a small bread oven set into one wall, which is where Onoria keeps another set of boy's clothes – hose, tunic, serge doublet and a pair of worn but tough shoes, all once belonging to Bartolomeo – rolled into a bundle along with her rabbit-hunting bow and arrows. Every time she pulls them on she thinks how funny it is that her brother's old cast-offs allow her to do all the things he disapproves of.

He isn't really a bad person, her brother. In a sense – this is something Onoria is just beginning to understand – he is caught just as painfully in the trap of expectations as she is herself. It's the fault of her mother's uncle, Archbishop Capacci, who went to Rome to be made a cardinal but caught the plague and died instead. Bartolomeo is going to complete that journey for her mother's family.

It isn't the journey that her father wants, though. Onoria barely remembers her oldest brother Tommaso, who was the little swordsman, the little *condottiere*, the joy of Amerigo and the future of the Ormanis. Tommaso, who fell off his pony and broke his leg, only for the bone to fester and kill him before his twelfth birthday. Onoria is older, now, than Tommaso will ever be. Bartolomeo, at ten, was promised to the Church, and her mother won't let her father change that.

And Onoria herself? Well, daughter of an Ormani and a Capacci, she is destined to be married. No more or less than that. Her husband will be a nobleman from one of the old Tuscan families that align themselves with the Medici Grand Duke. Her father wants to restore the Ormani fortune. He has his eye on some of the rich land around Montalcino and a place under the new Medici sun. With a son in Rome and a daughter married to a Pucci or a Ruccelai, or even an Orsini cousin . . . The Ormani name will be gone, but Onoria will carry the Ormani blood into a bright future.

Meanwhile, Bartolomeo, who will never be Tommaso but will be a cardinal, and even, one day, pope – why not? – will be leaving soon. At the end of the summer he will be ordained, and then he's off to Bologna to study law. A distant cousin of her mother's, who happens to be a Monaldeschi, has secured him an important benefice in Orvieto. He'll be a bishop before he's twenty. For now, he is teaching her Latin grammar, not because anyone thinks that girls should know such things, but mainly to keep her from climbing trees and coming home covered in dirt. She'd much rather be taught by him than by Father Giovanni, who smells and leans too close to her. Even her mother, usually the kindest of women, gets peevish when she teaches Onoria. But her brother, in so many ways a storyteller's idea of a scholar – pale, on the thin side, careless of his appearance, but also surprisingly handsome – loves books the way she loves swordplay. She understands that.

'I want Papà to come home, so he can go on teaching me to fight,' she says to him one morning, just to annoy him.

'I know you do,' he answers, surprisingly patiently.

'Wouldn't you rather be outside too, Barto? It's such a lovely day! I could show you a sparrowhawk's nest . . .'

'You always want to get away, don't you, Onoria?' he says. To her continued surprise, he shuts his primer and steeples his fingers on top of it, one of his strangely mature habits.

'Yes!' she says defiantly.

'And you can, for now. Papà lets you get away with all sorts of nonsense.'

'You're just jealous!' There is sunshine being wasted, and all of a sudden, she is furiously resentful.

'A little,' Bartolomeo says calmly. 'I can't pretend to be Tommaso. I'm just not made that way. So I'm glad you

80

can make Papà happy by letting him teach you his art. He deserves happiness.' Onoria's mouth falls open. She's never heard her brother talk like this. 'But soon Papà will have his fencing school,' he continues. 'He's buying a grand house outside Montalcino.'

'I know *that.*'

'I'll be gone by then. No, it's you I'm worried about, sister. You'll be married in three years. No husband is going to let you roam around the countryside, let alone mess around with swords. You'll be shut away. In *his* house. What are you going to do then?'

'I'll escape!' she says petulantly.

'Really? You won't be here in Pietrodoro, you know. You'll be wherever your husband lives.'

She clenches her teeth so hard that she feels the sinews in her neck standing out like lute strings. 'Why are you doing this?'

'Because, Onoria, I'm giving you a way to escape.' She makes an uncomprehending face at him, but he persists. 'Books, sister. You read as well as I do. Your Latin isn't bad at all. Books are the window you can jump through. This' – he thumps the book in front of him – 'Ovid's *Metamorphoses.* Have you paid attention to *any* of it?'

'No,' she snaps. It's true: she hasn't.

'Then I advise you to begin.' Bartolomeo stares at her owlishly, like the priest he has almost become, then he grins and ruffles her hair, as though she really were a younger brother. 'But let's have another lesson. Why don't you fetch one of Papà's books on swordsmanship? You can show me how well you read, and teach me a little, too.'

'Priests don't need to know how to fight,' Onoria points out.

'Oh, no? What about Pope Julius? He rode at the head of a papal army. Like a *condottiere*.'

'Really?'

'Really. Would I lie about a pope? It was a long time ago, though – before Papà was born.'

'So is that what you're going to do?' Onoria suddenly forgets that she's annoyed with him. 'Be a soldier priest?'

Bartolomeo folds his arms behind his head and laughs. 'Not if I can help it! But get that book and show me some things. Just in case.'

CHAPTER SEVEN

It is mid-August, and the little village bakes in the sunshine. Exposed on its crag, Pietrodoro sometimes feels like a metal spur glowing in a blacksmith's forge. It is far too hot to play in the terraces, where the grass has been cooked to golden hay, and the praying mantises and lizards are the only things moving. The only good thing about high summer is the village feast, which happens on the eleventh day of August, Santa Clara's day. That morning, as Onoria and Bartolomeo watch the villagers set out the long trestle tables in the piazza, Bartolomeo explains – it is a ritual the two of them have had for as long as Onoria can remember – that Pietrodoro's Santa Clara is not the Clara who was Saint Francis's companion. Their church, a puzzle of Roman columns and bricks, Lombard dragons and Norman arches, all shrunk together like a fig left out in the sun, is much too old to be dedicated to her. No, the saint of Pietrodoro was a woman who, perhaps in Roman times, perhaps later, climbed up to this lonely place to live as a hermit. It was her little shelter – perhaps a cave – that became the church, and she is the tiny black Virgin enshrined on the altar. Over the centuries her name was forgotten and she became Santa Celava, the Hidden One, and that, in turn, became Clara. After Clara of Assisi's death, the two names, and even the feast days, became confused, and the ancient saint merged into the new one. No one really cares now, as Bartolomeo says, not even Father Giovanni. 'Why do you care, then?' Onoria always asks him, and he always shrugs and says, 'Because the truth is important.'

Onoria cares too. What she especially likes is that Bartolomeo has entrusted this knowledge to her. It feels like she holds the secret of the village. And wasn't it Celava who turned a raven into the first Ormani? Santa Celava is part of her. As the tables clatter and scrape into place on the flagstones, as olive branches and festoons of vines, boughs of pomegranate and almond heavy with fruit begin to decorate the church, she mutters the saint's name under her breath like a spell. *Celava. Celava.* The word is as mysterious as the hermit herself. *What was she hiding from?* Onoria wonders. Then her nose catches a whiff of roasting lamb meat and her stomach growls in answer. She forgets all about Santa Celava.

Her mother scrubs Onoria's face – Onoria is getting much too old for this, but she lets her mother do it anyway, because it is a special day – and brushes her hair. When she struggles into her best set of clothes, she submits to her mother's fingers as they pinch and pull, tuck and tighten. When she is enough of a girl to satisfy her parents, she follows them out into the piazza to the shrieking of bagpipes and the thudding of goatskin drums, fourth in line in the little procession of the Ormani household, from her father to Belardino the stable boy. Her father is magnificent in his black Venetian doublet and hose, her mother in Florentine silk. Even Bartolomeo looks almost fashionable in a plain but expensive doublet. Hanging from his belt is a long parrying knife that was once Tommaso's. Onoria wonders how much badgering from her father it took to make him wear it.

Another procession, a mirror of their own, is leaving the palace of the Ellebori. She sees Federigo and waves, but he frowns slightly and doesn't wave back. Then again, the grown-ups all look serious. This part of the day is serious business. Lodovigo is limping: an old wound that has been getting worse this year. Benedetta is gripping his arm tightly. There is no Augusto, she notes with relief, but his younger brothers, Antonio and Girolamo, are there, with Smeralda.

In Pietrodoro, which the two families have struggled to dominate since, perhaps, the time of Santa Celava, neither the Ormanis or the Ellebori are allowed the place of honour. Instead, a boy and a girl are chosen by popular vote, dressed up as nobility and installed, with a lot of play-acting and bagpipe howls, at the top table. Then come the familiar rituals: dancers, some of them masked, acting out a legend of the old hermit and a shepherd; a horse race, both absurd and dangerous, with four riders careening around the square. More than once this has ended in disaster: horses crashing into tables, riders being dashed against walls. But today all is good. Onoria shouts until her throat is raw and screams as her horse comes in first. Then the food, endless toasts and singing until the sky fades to rose, to orange, to blue and then black.

It is boring after a while, and she cannot quite talk to Federigo over the noise and the width of the table. She eats ravenously and rehearses fencing moves in her head. Just after the sun sets, she notices that Lodovigo Ellebori has stood up and is toasting her father. He smiles broadly and does the same. Lodovigo reaches over and grasps her father's arm. One of the brothers – Girolamo, the younger – reaches over and raises his goblet in front of Bartolomeo, who, surprised and no doubt embarrassed, stands awkwardly and knocks his own goblet against Girolamo's. Onoria tries to catch Federigo's eye, and raises her own cup of watered-down wine, but he is ignoring her. His mind has plainly been somewhere else all day. The older men, though, are laughing and joking in a way she can't ever remember seeing before. Servants are running back and forth, filling wine jugs from the barrels set up by the fires where lambs, kids and pigs are turning on spits, where cauldrons of tripe, cabbage soup and beef stew are steaming. The whole village seems to be singing. All at once, she is happier than she has ever been in her life.

It is late when her mother finally makes the ritual excuses and leads Onoria back to the house. Onoria stands, swaying a little from the wine. Her drink had been watered almost to nothing, but it had been hot in the piazza and she feels as if she has drunk a barrel's worth of something. Her stomach is full to bursting and she keeps giggling as her mother fumbles with the ties of her bodice.

'Ow!' she squeaks as her mother catches her bare skin with a fingernail. 'Are you drunk, Mamma? I think everyone in Pietrodoro is drunk tonight!'

'What do you take me for, Onoria?' her mother says, and then she kisses her daughter to show she isn't serious. But she is: as an Ormani woman, just like an Ellebori woman, or any woman, her duty at the feast is to sit, polite and ornamental, next to her husband.

'I've never seen everyone so happy!' Onoria says, spinning free of the confines of her skirt. 'Papà and Don Lodovigo – like proper friends!'

'That is a good thing,' her mother says.

'Is it because Augusto is gone? I hate Augusto,' says Onoria, and claps her hand across her mouth, because she never talks like this in front of her mother. But her mother just raises her eyebrows.

'Grand Duke Cosimo has brought peace to Tuscany,' she says. 'Maybe he has even managed to bring it to Pietrodoro.'

'Cosimo de' Medici . . .' Onoria is wriggling into her nightgown. 'A real soldier. Papà told me that Duke Cosimo led the army himself at Montemurlo.'

Her mother clicks her tongue. 'Why are you *so* interested in such things, girl? What do you know about Montemurlo?'

'Papà was there! The Grand Duke beat the Florentine rebels . . .'

'Yes. Well, girl, my uncle was killed there. He was a nobleman, and he had his throat cut by some peasant arquebusier. Please don't talk to your father about fighting. "Wars, horrid wars," that's what Virgil says, and it is true. Now, to bed with you.'

'Are you going to bed too, Mamma?'

'I'm going to pray for a little while in the chapel.'

'Goodnight, Mamma.'

'Goodnight, little one.' She turns towards the door, then pauses and sits down on the edge of the bed into which Onoria has just climbed. 'But you aren't so little now, are you?' She brushes a stray lock of hair away from Onoria's forehead. 'Let me plait it for you. I was watching you today, you know. You're not a girl any more, Onoria.'

'What do you mean, Mamma? I don't . . . I mean, I don't have anything here yet,' Onoria says, folding her arms across her chest. But it is hard to be annoyed as her mother gently plaits her hair, fingers working deftly, the most comforting sensation in the whole world.

Her mother laughs softly. 'That will come by and by. That's not what I meant, though, *cara*. The way you hold yourself. So confident. You'll never be a great beauty, but that's a good thing.'

'I don't care about that,' Onoria says, trying not to sound defiant.

'I didn't mean to be cruel. You have the kind of face that someone might want to paint. A face that will get you a good man for a husband.'

'You're beautiful,' Onoria says, puzzled. 'And Papà is a good man.'

'I was lucky. Anyway . . .' Her mother takes a ribbon from where Onoria has an untidy collection of objects and ties off the plait. 'There you are. You have lovely hair.' Then she sighs. 'I saw the Ellebori boys looking at you.'

'Mamma! What – Antonio and Girolamo? That's horrible! But . . . at least it wasn't Augusto.'

Her mother sighs again. 'God forbid. Anyway, we'll be leaving Pietrodoro soon. Your father has just bought a fine house near Montalcino. Maybe, in the autumn, I'll take you to Florence. Would you like that?'

'Florence?' Onoria has only ever been to Viterbo and Orvieto. 'Why?' she asks suspiciously.

'You're thirteen, my darling. It's time we started looking.'

'I don't want a husband. You know that. I never want to get married.'

'I said exactly the same thing when I was your age. I expect every single girl that's ever been born has said it.'

'If I have to get married, then I'll marry a *condottiere* who'll take me off to war with him.'

Her mother shakes her head and kisses Onoria on the cheek. 'Then we'll have to find you a *condottiere*, won't we?' She stands up.

'No, you won't.'

'Oh, no? My parents found one for me.' Her mother turns from the door and touches her fingers to her lips. 'Sleep well, Onoria.'

'Goodnight. I love you, Mamma.' But her mother has already gone, and the latch clicks softly behind her.

Though Onoria's room is on the top floor of the palazzo, the only room in the stump of what was once a high tower, and faces away from the square, it is still noisy enough that she doesn't fall asleep for a long time. Voices and instruments rise and fall, sometimes a whisper, mostly a roar. It is hot, of course, and though she kicks off the sheets, her nightshirt still binds to her damp skin. Finally, she rolls out of bed, takes her rosary from its drawer and kneels on the floorboards, which are more or less cool, and prays for a long time. She usually prays to Santa Celava, who has some power to find things that are lost, and so she does tonight, asking the saint to intercede with the Holy Virgin and help her to stay unwed. Her thoughts drift: she is stepping back, then forward, lunging, parrying. Then the saint's face appears, tiny, age-black and rimmed with tarry gold, and she goes back to her entreaties. At last she feels the energy in her body begin to ebb, and she crawls gratefully back into her bed. She is asleep almost at once.

She is dreaming about a battle: there are men running all around her, and though she has a sword in her hand, she is standing like a statue in a great field of brown grass which is on fire, a line of flames burning towards her, birds flying up through the smoke like they do when the farmers down in the valley sweal their fields in autumn. A man stops beside her, an arquebusier dressed in half-armour that shines like mercury. He raises his gun and fires, *bang!*, again and again, *bang! bang!*, without pausing to reload, into the fire.

'What do we do?' Onoria shouts at him in her sleep.

'They're killing us,' says the man, and his grin, in the shadow cast by his helmet, spreads like a bloodstained summer crescent moon. He raises his gun again.

Bang!

The door latch scrapes and suddenly the room is full of something, a man, a roaring, stinking man and his unwashed smell: bad teeth, dirty armpits, spit and wine. There is a dirty red light coming from somewhere and it ripples across the sheen of his black doublet. In her terror, she doesn't recognise him straight away, this black horror leaping towards her with a dagger on his hip and a short sword hanging behind, though he knows her name, screaming it, screaming at her with his mouth working madly, all teeth and tongue and foam-freckled lips.

Bang!

I'm still asleep, she thinks, and the thought is clear, like a thought in a dream, but she seems to be sitting up in bed, her legs caught in the sheets, and then he grabs her.

She is falling, the bed coming up to meet her at terrible speed as she understands that she is wide awake. Then her nose and mouth are smothered in the embrace of hot, damp cloth. She knows.

Augusto Ellebori's hand, twisting the heavy rope of her plaited hair, is pushing her face deeper into the bolster. She tries to cry out, because she knows, now – 'Oh, God help me! Holy Mother have mercy on me!' – but the hand pushes harder, and then there are iron fingers at her neck, something hard running across her throat, and then a twisting, a tightening, pressure, the sudden agony. A knee is thrust into the curve of her back. She feels muscles tearing in her neck as her spine arches backwards. Her hands thrash against the sheets, finding nothing to grasp. She is drowning in a sea of white linen. Her lips, forced into a rigid O by the ligature around her neck, search desperately, hopelessly for air. There is nothing, though, except pain. Not even fear. Her mouth is full of blood.

Suddenly, the pressure lessens. She gasps reflexively, breathing in her own salty blood, hands scrabbling at the leather strap cutting into her neck. She hears Augusto panting with exertion. One of his hands twists the ligature again, and the other rustles for a moment with the linen of her shift before the fingers, hard as iron, rake up the inside of her thighs. One of his knees forces her legs apart. Through the blood singing in her ears she can hear the rasp of his breath. She tries to lift her head, but he pushes it hard into the bedding. Augusto's fingers find what they are groping for and he laughs. Suddenly, the pressure at her throat lessens. For an instant she is weightless, and then she is staring up at Augusto's face, lips drawn back, tongue out like a hanged man, eyes wide and black, full of the polluted cruelty she saw that day in the courtyard. She drags a thread of air into her throat, which is surely splitting apart, flesh parting against its will, above and below as his hand shoves into her again, her body turning into one great wound. Fingers fumble, thrust, and leave again. As the room turns red, she sees his free hand fumbling with the ties of his codpiece.

His voice, slick with greed and triumph, cuts through the soft red darkness that is sucking her down, mercifully, away from her terror and humiliation. 'Filthy little boy-girl! So you like to fight, eh? Fight me, then!' He slaps her face, but she barely feels it. 'Now, which hole will I choose?' She wants to drown, but something is keeping her afloat. A heat inside her, stronger than the pain. Anger. *What a stupid thing to feel now*, she thinks, because her thoughts are beginning to do what they want despite her: they are softening, beginning to drift out of terror towards a stillness, a radiant peace that is coming closer She is so close. There, not far now, is the end to all this.

Santa Celava, help me to my death now. Help me find God's hidden mercy.

It is death that her hands are scrabbling for, clawing at the air, far beyond her control. Her nightgown rips. She is reaching through dirty red darkness for the kind black face of Santa Celava when her right hand finds something else. Smooth, cold, something the memories that live in her fingertips recognise, even if her mind does not. Maybe she is dreaming after all, because the slowness, the care with which she clasps the hilt of Augusto's left-hand dagger has the underwater feel of deep sleep. Augusto is trying to split her in half with something blunt and hot. She closes her eyes, though they are blind now anyway, and sees the hermit saint, a knife in her tarry black hand.

There is a howl, which must be her, though how can she

be howling, now that her throat is almost cut through by the leather thong? Then she feels a hot gush across her right hand. The thong comes loose. She takes in a vast lungful of pain, but there is air as well, and she opens her eyes as Augusto bucks on top of her, his body arching backwards as he screams again. He rolls away from her, scrabbling behind him, his thing bobbing vilely between his legs, and she shoves herself in the opposite direction, toppling over the edge of the bed without warning. She somehow gets on all fours and vomits, almost choking again as she breathes in. She can't even sob; her breath comes out of her in growls and whistles. Augusto . . . He screams again. 'Little cunt! I'll fucking . . . Jesus, I hurt!'

Onoria drags herself over to the window and pulls herself upright against the sill. The air outside is red. She drags in another lungful and tastes smoke as well as blood. Forcing herself to turn around, she sees Augusto kicking at the pillars of the bed, letting out little shrieks as he tries to reach the knife, which is sticking out of his doublet below his right shoulder blade. She is staggering towards the door when she trips over something: Augusto's sword. Without thinking she squats, gasping at the pain between her legs, and picks it up. A short, wide-bladed *storta*, a murder-sword. That's what her father calls them: murder-swords. Some distant part of her mind sees blood and hair clotting on the steel. She stands, turns. Augusto has got hold of the dagger and is trying to pull it free. The stump of his missing finger twitches like a blind grub. Rolling on his back, his breeches half down, hairy white skin stark against black cloth, he sees her. 'I'll fuck you!' he bellows. Onoria takes two steps across the floorboards, grips the sword with both hands, raises it high above her head with every spark of strength she has left, and brings it down across his body. He makes a noise like the bray of a donkey and, eyes tight shut, she strikes him again. Then she is on the landing. Whimpering in terror, she begins to stagger, as fast as she can, down the stairs.

Bartolomeo's room is directly below hers. As Onoria steps out of the stairwell she is looking straight through its open door. In the dim glow of a rush light, all that she sees at first is a great spray of dark, shiny wetness across the white of the bedsheets. And then, on the floor, head towards the door, her brother, sprawled on his stomach. He is half dressed, his shirt slashed and soaked with blood. His head is twisted all wrong. She drops to her knees in front of him and shakes his shoulder.

'Barto!' Onoria pleads, but his head lolls away from her. His chin knocks against the floorboards with a clack of bone and teeth. She pushes herself away from him like a crab and can't stop herself from being sick next to his half-open clothes chest. Bartolomeo is neat, but someone has been rifling through his clothing. The sleeve of a black doublet trails down to the floor. Onoria is shivering so hard that the muscles in her stomach have cramped. She is almost naked, she realises. Her nightgown is hanging from one shoulder, plastered against her skin with her blood – or Augusto's blood . . . She sits, rocking, for a moment. Then she drops the sword and tears what's left of her gown away, then pulls out the doublet and manages to get her trembling arms into the sleeves. It is too big for her, of course, but not very much so. Her fingers are numb, and she only gets three buttons done up, but her breasts are covered. In a frenzy, she digs down through the clothes until she finds a pair of breeches: trunk hose, with a modest codpiece sewn into the crotch. Standing to put them on, she sees the deep scratches on the insides of her thighs, the streaks of blood. She has to lean against the wall to stop herself from falling. The rough cloth chafes horribly against her wounds and the breeches are too wide for her, but in amongst the heaped clothes she sees a belt. Faded and cracked, it was once bright red, with gold tooling. As she buckles it, she pictures it around Bartolomeo's waist. Her father had brought it back from Rome for him and she had been so jealous . . .

Down on all fours again, she crawls over to her brother and tries to heave him onto his back, but he is too heavy, and when his head lolls towards her, she meets the stare of his white, unblinking eyes. 'Oh, God, help him,' she prays, yet nothing comes from her throat but a thin wheezing. Feverishly, she tries to turn him again, and as he comes over onto his side, something clatters onto the floor: Tommaso's dagger. She grabs it. Something she knows well; it fits into her hand and the reassurance of it calms her enough so that she can lean down and kiss her brother's head, eyes closed so she doesn't have to see his.

There are loud men's voices coming up from below, and smoke. What was before a taint in the air is now a thick haze. Onoria peers round the door, then she sees the bloody footprints leading from Bartolomeo's body towards her bedroom.

'Augusto! What the fuck are you doing up there?' someone shouts from downstairs.

'Fucking!' someone else barks. There is laughter. 'Come down, you dick! The place is on fire!'

'Keep your voices down, fools!' Onoria recognises this voice. It is Lodovigo Ellebori. And now Onoria knows what has come to her home. 'I want every one of them dead. Do you understand? The priest, Antonio – is he taken care of?'

'Yes, Father.'

'Go and fetch Augusto. You, idiots. Go with him.'

War has come back to Pietrodoro. Their own little war, which Onoria was so certain was just a story. 'I fly to Your protection, O Holy Mother of God,' she whispers. 'Do not despise my petitions in my time of need . . .' She crawls into the hallway, pushes herself upright against the wall and runs down the short corridor that leads to her parents' room. With the awful predictability of a nightmare, the door is open. Her father is in bed, on his back as if asleep, except that his throat has been cut so violently that his head is almost off. Her mother is on the floor, half under the bed. All that Onoria can see is her bare white legs, and the blood. Her mother's body is an island in a lake of her own blood. Booted feet are clumping up the stairs behind her. Onoria turns, the dagger out in front of her in *porta ferro*. *Let us all die*, she thinks. *But I'll kill some of you, you beasts. You'll see how he trained me. You'll see . . .*

At that moment there is a crash from outside, and a flurry of sparks swirl up past the open window. She turns to look, sees the window, her mother's writing desk next to it, a book – the fat old Virgil – open where she had left it. And beyond . . . Onoria knows what's beyond the window. She has been staring at it for years while her mother has tried, so patiently, to educate her.

The Rocca forms part of the walls of Pietrodoro. In some places those walls merge with the living rock of the mountain and plunge a hundred feet or more towards the olive groves. Below the palazzo, though, is the old road which used to lead to the Rocca, disused now, except by shepherds. At some point in the past an arbutus sapling got its roots into some hidden vein of soil and has grown until its topmost branches come halfway up the palazzo's walls. One of the thicker ones is just outside the window. Her father was meaning to have someone cut it off, because it is scraping the mortar, but it is such a beautiful thing, with its shiny toothed leaves and tasty fruit, that he never quite got around to doing it.

Another gout of sparks. The outbuildings must be blazing. Boots are coming closer. She looks at the dagger in her hand. *If I had a sword . . .* But her legs are almost giving way and the pain between them is savage. She knows, because she has been taught to understand her body like a duellist, that they will fail her. A man will come through the door, take her blade, push her down . . .

'I am sorry, Papà,' she says, though only she can hear the words that are trapped in her swollen throat. 'I can't stay with you. Goodbye, Mamma. Until we're reunited.'

Tucking the knife into the belt in the small of her back, she climbs onto the writing table, her knees sliding across pages of Virgil, takes hold of the window frame and steps out, as she has done countless times in her imagination, into the air. Just for a moment she is falling, and then she is clutching the rough bark of the branch, surrounded by pointed, shiny leaves that are reflecting the flames licking out of the lower windows. She pulls herself along until she is inside the crown of the tree.

Branches surround her like a cage, and she knows she is hidden from the sight of anyone looking out of the palazzo. Men are shouting above her, in her bedroom.

'Is he dead?' She recognises Antonio Ellebori's voice.

'It was the boy! Must have been!' A rougher voice, in an accent that isn't from Pietrodoro.

'Augusto! Is he dead, for God's sake?'

'Bartolomeo must have done this! The little fucking priest! But he's in his chambers . . .' Girolamo Ellebori, his young voice laced with rage and confusion.

'He must have crawled down there to die. Christ, Augusto's really bleeding, Father . . .'

'Where's the girl?' Lodovigo Ellebori sounds out of breath.

'He's breathing! Augusto!'

'Augusto, where's the girl?'

'Grab his legs. We need to get out of here, lads. The whole place will be ablaze in a minute!'

'What about the girl?'

'The little bitch must be hiding. Don't worry, she'll burn, like the monster she is. Get a move on, now!'

Onoria works her way through the branches until she has the whole crown of the tree between her and the palazzo. Gingerly, her limbs barely under her control, she lowers herself until she is hanging by her arms and drops the last foot or so to the ground. It is no height at all, but even so she lies there winded. When she is able to stand, she sees fire, great hungry tongues of flame, shooting up from behind the courtyard wall. As she watches, the ground floor windows are lit from inside by a red glow, and an instant later, flames are groping out into the night. The Rocca is old, and its timbers are bone dry. It seems to take no time at all before it is a stone shell bursting with fire. It jets from the tower, from behind the battlements, with a vast, strangled roar. Onoria is transfixed. Her parents, Bartolomeo – Holy Mother, what about the servants? – are gone. A moment ago, she was looking at their corpses, and now they must be ash. The flames pouring from the nearest window seem to beckon. She could just climb back inside and let herself be consumed. Why not? She gathers her courage. But as she stands there, contemplating – there will be heat, horrifying pain, but it will be over so quickly – she realises that she feels alive. Not in the way she does when she spars with her father, or shoots hares in the olive groves, or races across the piazza with Federigo; she feels alive simply because she is not dead. She is in pain. The sheer horror of what Augusto did to her is only just beginning to cut through the numbness in her mind. Her family is dead. But she is still here, barefoot in the dry leaves. She can feel the sparks that are pouring down onto her, stinging like jewelled wasps. She can feel that she wants to be sick again. She closes her eyes and sees Santa Celava, her face burnt black with age but filled with kindness, with holiness. Our Lady of Hidden Things. 'Why do you care what she's called?' she'd asked her brother. This morning. It had been this morning. And he'd replied, in his kind, serious way – a cardinal, one day, everyone said so – he'd told her, 'Because the truth is important.'

'Santa Celava, what should I do?' she shouts, but the pain of the words almost chokes her. 'I repent all my sins!' Her voice is a hiss of air through a wound. 'If I have ever done anything to offend thee, I . . .' She can't remember any prayers at all. Her mother would know what to ask for. She looks up at the burning window. 'Please help me, dearest Santa Celava! Help me, Mamma!'

Something in the heart of the Rocca gives way, and a huge gust of flame and sparks is thrown into the sky. The blaze jets from every crack, every loophole, and from her parents' window a fist of smoke and fire punches out, unravelling in a cloud of light. And, whirling inside it, what Onoria thinks at first is a bird with beating wings of fire that hangs in the air, caught in a vortex of heat, and then begins to fall, its feathers unravelling: a book. The great Virgil, tumbling and dissolving into floating cinders.

Oh, Onoria, don't fidget. Look, here, what Virgil says: 'Endure, and preserve yourself for happier days.' Well, he says 'yourselves', but honestly, cara. You're as miserable as Aeneas's followers. Could you at least try? Sometimes – some things, Onoria – we just have to endure.

Dogs are barking. Suddenly the church bells start to clang. She can hear shouts from beyond the fire, distorted by the heat like her own voice. The last of the numbness in her head clears. She turns and slips over the edge of the terrace, clambers down a low stone wall and begins to run.

Inside, the ruined hut is almost pitch-dark. The dirty red glow of the fire in Pietrodoro hasn't made its way in here. Onoria finds her way to the old bread oven by touch, hands patting along stone and crumbling wood until they find the oven's mouth, pull away the rock she has blocked it with, and grab the roll of clothes, and the bow and quiver of arrows inside.

She has to strip again to put on the hose and shirt. Wondering hazily about scorpions, she pulls the worn hose up over her legs, finding the smallest grain of comfort in the familiarity of the things she has always worn for play. She can barely manage to tie the points of the hose to the old serge doublet. The newer, larger one fits over the other like a short jacket. When she slips her feet into the shoes she realises she has cut through the skin of her soles.

She can hear voices above her in the village: no words, just sounds that could be men and women, or the howling of beasts. The church bell is still ringing.

What about the girl?

The little bitch must be hiding . . . It was Lodovigo Ellebori's voice, hoarse with smoke. Now she remembers his words. *Don't worry, she'll burn, like the monster she is.*

Onoria pulls her plaited hair from inside the jacket. As she feels its smooth weight she remembers her mother's fingers working through her hair, and the feeling of contentment it always brought. Then she sees, horribly clearly, her mother's bare legs splayed in the great pool of blood, and the pain as Augusto almost tore the braid from her scalp. Without thinking – or so it seems to her – she picks up Tommaso's knife and begins to saw at the plait at the nape of her neck. The knife is sharp, and in three strokes she is holding her braided hair like a limp, dead thing in her hand. She stares at it in confusion. Something seems finally to have broken. Not her body, but something deeper. It must be her soul. That thought is the last thing she remembers as she runs, as fast as her wounded feet allow, into the night.

CHAPTER EIGHT

Morning – is it the morning after, or some other morning? Onoria has no idea finds her lying on an uncomfortable nest of twigs and leaves. She is in a cave . . . No, under a pile of branches. She crawls out from under them. She is in a steeply sloping wood and has been sleeping under a fallen tree. She stares wildly around her, rubbing her stinging eyes. Chestnut trees and holm oaks. She fumbles with the points of her hose, squats and makes water. It hurts. Everything hurts. Her neck feels as if she is wearing a collar of briars. She can barely swallow. Then she remembers how he choked her as he did that thing . . . Retching, her empty stomach knotting and unknotting in waves of nausea, she stumbles down the slope until she comes to a gap in the trees. Not far away, across a deep valley, a pillar of black smoke is rising straight up into the clear blue sky from a golden village that sits like a carefully placed coronet on the skull of an almost bare hill.

She knows where she is now. The chestnut forests of Monte Amiata spread their skirts wide, and this is a fold of them where she has often played with Federigo. She retches again and whimpers at the pain. Federigo, her best friend. He'd sat across from her at the feast, next to his brothers. Next to Lodovigo, who'd stood up and toasted her father, again and again. The brothers, drinking with Bartolomeo until his face was red and his eyes out of focus. But Federigo . . . He'd kept his face away from her. She'd tried to joke with him, but he hadn't been able to look at her. He'd known. He'd *known*.

A breath of wind cools the back of her head. Onoria lifts a hand to the unfamiliar sensation and finds that her hair is almost all gone. Stubble at the nape, where the skin beneath is almost too raw to touch, longer above her ears and forehead. She thinks she must have done this herself, but she can't quite remember. She shakes her head and it's as if she can feel her brain sloshing around inside her skull. Suddenly she's very thirsty. There is a spring further down this slope that often runs in the summer – she thinks that's right, though all these thoughts might belong to someone else. She's been here before, but this is the farthest she has ever come from home.

Home.

She retrieves her bow and quiver from under the dead tree and makes her way downhill, walking like an old crone. Sure enough, the spring, a crude fountain cut out of the rock a long time ago, is running, a thread of water trickling noisily into a shallow stone basin. She leans over to drink, and sees a creature staring back at her. There is a monster drinking out of her hand.

'Holy Mother, what has happened to me?' Onoria gasps. But she has no voice, just a hollow whisper like wind hissing through bare branches. Half of her face is purple-red and swollen. Her eyes are bloodshot, and one is ringed with a bruise like the yolk of an overboiled egg. Blood has crusted between nose and top lip. An uneven fringe of short brownish hair covers her head like some kind of crude felted cap. But worse, much worse, is the gash that runs across her throat below her chin, across the crook of her jaw and up towards her left ear. It is a deep crease filled with dried blood and crusted yellowish matter, swollen and crinkled at its edges, surrounded by black bruising.

She dabs at her neck with a wet hand, and though the pain is appalling, she dips and pats, dips and pats until it is more or less clean. Then she scrubs at her face. The water in the fountain is pinkish now, threaded with blood. She forces herself to look again.

Filthy little boy girl.

She stands up, and she can see the whole of herself, the perspective stretching her away towards the sky. Skinny legs in dirty hose. Hips, crotch, waist hiding under a sagging pair of breeches, with a padded codpiece bulging from the centre. Revolting thing. She gropes for her knife, thinking to cut it off, but something makes her pause. Her upper body is wrapped in her old doublet, and Bartolomeo's bigger doublet sits squarely across her shoulders, widening them. The handle of a long, naked dagger, smeared with mud and leaf mould, juts from the belt cinched too snugly around her waist. Above, there is the disaster of her face and the hideous remains of her hair. It isn't a girl reflected in the water, what she sees there is a stranger. A stranger in every possible way.

Every way, though? Not quite. As she stares at the distorted contours of her face she begins to see other faces appear and

104

vanish. Her brother Bartolomeo, when he was younger, softer in the chin and cheeks; when he was plump and unbearably superior, and she called him Cardinal Piglet, because it made him cross. Someone from longer ago, too: the dimly remembered eyes and nose of the first one to die. Tommaso. Her dead brothers rise below the surface of her own skin like the faces of drowned boys drifting under milky water, reaching for the light and sinking down again into the forgetful dark.

Bartolomeo had never come here. Or perhaps he had, but not with Onoria. Yet now she remembers something he once told her: *This is Santa Celava's spring.* The legends of Pietrodoro had got it wrong: the ancient hermit had lived in these woods, not on the crag, and she'd drunk from this spring. Grandfather had told him about it: how, when he'd been a boy, unimaginably long ago, old village women remembered when the village had made a yearly procession here, and how their mothers had come to the spring to ask for Celava's help in finding things they had lost – mostly lovers, Bartolomeo added, with a judgemental sniff.

'But *I'm* lost!' Onoria blurts, in the hiss that seems to be her new voice. She squeezes her eyes shut, so tightly that red and purple lights flash across the blackness. The praying space, where Our Lady comes to listen sometimes, and God too, and always little Celava. Now there is no answer, except for a squirrel or a jay rustling far above her in the chestnut trees. 'Celava, dear one, it's me who's lost!' She opens her eyes and sees the filthy little boy-girl still looking up at her. Hardly a girl at all. A ragged, damaged, filthy boy. She understands. Santa Celava always finds hidden things. The saint's message is so hard, so painful, that she has to fight not to be sick again. But when she stands and limps away into the wood, she understands.

Onoria wanders through the woods all day, angling across the steep slopes, steering away from Pietrodoro, whose smoke is still rising like the gnomon of a sundial behind her. She isn't hungry – at least, her head doesn't want food, but her body is starting to grow impatient. Close to sunset she sees a family of rabbits in a glade and shoots one of them with her bow. When she picks up the limp creature, though, and feels the warmth of its life leaking out through her fingers, she feels like a murderer. Worse, she has no idea what to do with it. She doesn't have any means to make a fire and doesn't know any of the tricks with sticks and leaves that boys are always boasting about but never seem to actually do. So she tucks the little corpse under some roots and stumbles on. It is getting dark, and Monte Amiata's wolves will be waking up. When it is too dark to find her way, she scrambles up into the crown of a fallen chestnut and props herself against its lattice of dead branches.

Wolves. When they begin to howl, they're much closer than Onoria has ever heard them. The forest is alive with alien sounds. Something large grunts and snuffles for a long time beneath her tree. She is too frightened to sleep, but when the short night is over she is glad, because she knows she has at least been spared the dreams she might have had. She climbs down, feeling as stiff and crooked as she imagines the old ladies of Pietrodoro must be, and carries on her slow, limping way. In the east, the sky is clear. Her home must be cold ashes now.

She soon forgets how long she has been walking and sleeping, walking and sleeping. She drinks from springs and eats the only thing she recognises: unripe chestnuts, which fur up her mouth with bitter juice after their spiky shells have pricked her fingers. At some point, around noon (but on what day?) she wanders into a long-abandoned garden: four walls surrounding a thicket of trees heavy with fruit. Figs, apricots, apples, pomegranates, even some misshapen citron. Behind it, a small ruined hut. A snake, one of the fat, striped vipers that live on the mountain, is guarding the door in the wall, but as Onoria stoops to pick up a stone she sees that it is only the sloughed-off skin of the creature, still fresh and colourful. She steps past into the small enclosed space, which is alive with wasps gorging on the spoiling fruit. She ignores them, lurching from tree to tree, swatting the insects away and feasting blindly like a bear. There is a small roofed space in the ruin, and she huddles on a stone table, curls up around her full belly and goes to sleep. When she wakes again it is almost dark and she discovers that she has been asleep on an altar. The building is an abandoned hermitage. That makes her feel safe, and she goes to sleep again. In the thin light before dawn she opens her eyes to the scrabbling of a gecko in the rafters above her head. The pallid creature is stuffing a huge white moth into its wide mouth with its strangely human thumbs. She laughs, because the sight is so ridiculous, and finds that her throat is not quite so sore. This would be a good place to live, this little ruin. Plenty of fruit, a wall to keep out the wolves. Could she stay here? But when she considers, she decides she doesn't want to. As she has wandered, she has only felt two things properly: fear and anger. Onoria doesn't know where she is, but she does know that she can't be far enough away from Pietrodoro and the Ellebori to be safe. She has only been out of sight of Pietrodoro twice (she doesn't count Pienza or San Casciano, because you can sort of see the village from there). Her mother has relations in Orvieto, but she doesn't remember who they are and she thinks they might be dead; Viterbo was grey and depressing. As she lies there, watching the gecko eating the moth as if it were a tiny unplucked chicken, she decides she has to go somewhere. The only places she can think of are Florence and Rome, so she makes up her mind: Florence, because her family came from there, a long time ago. Maybe she'll find some Ormanis there. Maybe they'll look after her.

Because – and the idea shocks her, sending a strange heat through her veins – she wants to stay alive. She wants to become strong and fierce. She wants to . . . Onoria rolls over and feels the knife against her hip. She looks down at her body, the gangly limbs, the dirty male clothes. Santa Celava showed her, back by the spring. She has lost herself, yes; left Onoria Ormani behind in her bedroom in Pietrodoro, but that was just her old skin, sloughed off like that snake outside. There must be a new creature underneath, because – she sees it clearly now – that was what the saint was trying to tell her. A new Onoria, as strong and supple as a viper. And as dangerous.

She takes off her jacket, knots it into a sack and fills it with fruit. Sunrise finds her at the edge of the forest. In front of her, a short slope falls towards open country, golden, rolling, stitched with tree-lined paths and stippled with vineyards and olive groves.

CHAPTER NINE

The first thing she steals is fire. Making her way as carefully as she can along a narrow, overgrown valley that snakes outwards from the skirts of the mountain, she eventually comes across a little hamlet of houses clustered so close together that they are more or less one building. A little off to the side is a hut from which puffs of dark smoke are rising, and the clang of metal striking metal. A smithy. She runs over to a patch of reeds and pushes her way into it. After a long time has gone by, the hammering stops, and a large man in a sweat-soaked tunic stumps out and, swearing loud enough for her to hear, goes over to a ditch that runs between the smithy and the hamlet. He turns his back and begins to fish inside his breeches. Without hesitation, she slips out of the reeds, sprints over to the smithy and darts inside, her heart banging in her ears like fireworks. Her eyes flick desperately around the small, cramped space: the furnace, against one wall; a huge pair of tattered bellows folded like a giant sleeping bat; the stump of an oak tree in the middle of the floor with an iron anvil set into the top; hammer; tongs of all sizes. She knows what she wants. She knows . . . For a horrible moment she forgets. And then she remembers. There, by the furnace: a wooden box filled with shards of flint. She runs over, scoops out three sharp flakes. The other thing she needs is everywhere. Flakes and lumps of raw metal. Bars and ingots. Nails . . . She grabs a big iron nail, drops it and the flints into the quiver, where they rattle down through the arrows. There is a gourd with a string tied around its neck on the ground near the furnace. She picks it up. Then she sees something else: half a loaf of greyish bread and a hunk of cheese. Her stomach leaps with yearning and she is reaching for it when she hears a paroxysm of coughing just outside. She turns and runs. A figure, no more than a shadow, yells in profane surprise. Her arm brushes against damp cloth and firmer flesh. Horror floods through her. When she stops running, she is in an olive grove, and the hamlet is no more than a blur in the distance. Her chest is heaving, and the inside of her throat feels as if it has been raked with a carding comb. She climbs up through the grove's gentle terraces, and at the top she finds a family of rabbits grazing a patch of thyme. She shoots the biggest cleanly through the chest and carries it down to where, on the other side of the ridge, a fold of rock has gathered a small stand of cypress trees into itself, forming a perfect shelter. She makes a pile of dry twigs and curls of cypress bark, and fishes her stolen prizes from the bottom of the quiver. She has never had her own tinderbox, but she has watched people use them many times. Even so, she is delighted when she knocks the flint against the nail and produces a shower of sparks. She does it again, and again, and then threads of smoke begin to rise from red points of light in the bark. With a sudden *whoosh!* the pile of twigs is alight.

110

She laughs aloud. It is the first time she has felt pleasure since . . . No. She won't allow it, and lets the wet, revolting business that needs to be done with her knife and the dead rabbit drive the feelings out. But as she works, she can't help remembering. Hunting with Federigo . . . She won't allow that either. But she can see Giacomo in the kitchen, paunching the rabbits and hares she brought him. His mocking laugh the first time he ribbed a hare out of its skin 'like *this*!' – mocking, but kind. He'd given her a sip of wine to settle her stomach, then shown her how to stuff the empty body with herbs and salt, spices and pepper, thread it onto a spit. The herbs she gathers – rosemary, thyme and some pungent mint – just fall out again, but she sharpens a straight stick anyway, pushes it through the limp, pink thing and props it on some stones over the fire. The smell of searing meat is unbearably good.

Onoria will wonder, later, whether the stolen fire and the roasting meat had forced her mind back to the burning palazzo. But that evening under the cypress trees, it doesn't. Or perhaps she is just too hungry to think of anything at all. When the rabbit is blistered brown-black all over she rips it to pieces, burning her fingers in the process, and tears every scrap of meat from the bones with her teeth. Her throat is still so raw that she has to chew the meat to pulp before she can swallow it, and her jaws are aching by the time she has finished. The gourd, which she had almost forgotten about, is empty and smells of stale spit, so in the failing light she makes her way down the hill to where a line of reeds tells her water must be running. She is right: there is a tiny stream filled with watercress where she washes and fills the gourd before climbing back to her shelter, where she stretches out beside the warm ashes of her fire and

111

watches the Milky Way begin to drift like smoke across the sky.

That was the first day away from the mountain. By the third day, she is lost. At least this is what she tells herself, as if this is something new, as though she once knew where she was going. Florence. She is heading for Florence, where the Ormanis had once been a rich and splendid family, and which is somewhere to the north, between the rising and the setting sun. Florence is a great city. If she just keeps going north, she's bound to just bump into it eventually. But by now she's had to leave the last of the hills that spill out from the edges of Monte Amiata like bristly piglets keeping close to their mother. The country she finds herself in is a gently undulating patchwork of fields burnt almost white by the sun. She can see the few settlements there are from a long way off and takes a long detour around each one. There are some hills a long way in front of her. There are rabbits and partridge and long-legged bustards to hunt. When she shoots and cooks a bustard, there is enough meat left over for her to wrap in fig leaves and take for tomorrow's lunch. She walks, hunts, eats, sleeps – though her nights are feverish and hateful dreams wake her again and again. She can feel Augusto Ellebori's crushing weight on her, his scrabbling fingernails, the awful sensation of choking. Every morning feels like a deliverance from evil. She walks, telling herself she is well, that she is free, walks until she has to eat, until her body gives her no choice but to revisit the hell of sleep.

She keeps to the flatlands. A wide valley seems to be leading her northwards, and that, she thinks, must be a good omen. More than once she has to wade across the shallow river that meanders across the valley floor. She creeps past a couple of small villages at dusk, nondescript places that are nothing like

Pietrodoro. Halfway through one of these days it starts to rain, a light, warm drizzle at first, then a deluge. There is nowhere to shelter, so she makes sure her bowstring is tucked safely inside her breeches where it will be more or less dry, and trudges on.

The rain doesn't stop. The rabbits are all in their burrows. She loses an arrow shooting at a pigeon, and by nightfall she is hungry, cold and soaked. She crawls under an abandoned cart that is sinking into the earth in a corner of an overgrown vineyard, finding a little respite beneath the rotting wood and rusting iron, but the next morning the rain is still coming down in thick pleats. She wakes up cold and trembling, and the chill only deepens as she begins to walk. She isn't in a valley any more: around her stretches a rolling plain of fields under sodden corn or freshly ploughed, a vineyard here and there, and lines of poplars and willows to mark a river or ditch. Everything is grey and dead brown. She finds a half-sunken track that seems to be going in the right direction, puts her head down and begins to walk.

It might be midday; it might be almost dusk. She's been limping along for hours, her shoes completely sodden, wet leather raising blisters on her skin. The air is muggy, and she is sweating inside her clothes, though she still feels cold. Her stomach is rumbling. 'Plenty to drink,' she says aloud to herself, because it sounds like the kind of thing people could say at times like this. But she doesn't really know if that's true. She is so far outside her own experience that she feels completely raw, like a skinned rabbit. She is so hungry. 'I'm starving' was something she said all the time when her mother was there to listen, when Giacomo had been ready to cook something for her. But now the words feel different. They describe something real, something frightening. After she has stumbled and landed on her knees in a puddle for the fourth or fifth time, she notices that her legs and hands are shaking. She must find something to eat, but what? Even if she shoots a bird or a rabbit, she won't be able to cook it. Then she'll have to steal, she tells herself. But when she scrambles out of the track, which has become more of a culvert, there are no houses to be seen through the heavy mist that is lying across the plain. The valley seems to have narrowed. There are soft, cypress-spiked hills on either side of her, nothing but faint, velvety grey silhouettes. Closer to hand, chalky outcrops rise to her left, and on her right, a spinney of holm oaks. At least there she'll be dry, she thinks. She might be able to start a fire. She starts towards it, but the mist and the thin, wet light has deceived her. The spinney is on rising ground, further away than she thought. The freshly ploughed field she is crossing sucks at her feet. By the time she gets to the far side, her shoes are encased in two globes of clay, as heavy as lead. It takes what seems like hours to knock them free against a stone. When she looks up, though, she sees, crossing the next field, a small group of bustards. They stalk and stop, bend and peck, their feathers silver with water. Her numb fingers fumble for the bowstring, which is miraculously still not wet, and strings her bow. There is a low hedge along one side of the field, and she crouches and makes her way over to it. Hidden by its screen of bushes, she creeps along, planning to outflank the birds. They are quicker than they look, though. Peeping through a laurel bush, arrow nocked to her bowstring, she finds that they are already beyond the ploughed land and climbing the slope of the nearest hill. She moans with annoyance, but there is something else there in her chest: fear, as if her heart were being patted by a cat with only half-sheathed claws. She closes her eyes and says a prayer to Santa Celava, then starts to wade through the wet grass and bracken towards the birds. They bob here and there, stopping and starting. She's almost close enough . . . The biggest bustard pecks, looks about him. Onoria begins to draw back the arrow. Then he nods his head and stalks away. Suddenly he's gone. There is a fold, a wrinkle in the land before it rises smoothly again towards the blurred horizon. A curse, a proper oath, the kind her father used when he thought she wasn't around to hear, rises in her throat. She runs along the hedge, which stops abruptly at the lip of a shallow gully. Thick scrub hides the northern end. The stand of holm oaks is less than a quarter of a mile away. The bustards are browsing contentedly amongst some thorny shrubs. She slithers down the slope on her bottom and hunkers down behind a mastic bush. Down here, she finds she is underneath the mist, which hangs above her like a hazy ceiling. Hoping her bowstring hasn't got too wet, she aims at the nearest bird, draws, murmurs Santa Celava's name and lets her arrow go. There is an almost human cry and a whirl of feathers. The bustards take off all at once, but one of them is still on the ground, long legs twitching, Onoria's arrow skewering it through the middle. She runs over. The bustard claps its beak once, twice, then its eyes go dull. She pulls out the arrow; bending down, she wipes it clean of blood on the grass, and drops it into the quiver. The only thing she can think about is the taste of roasted meat. The shelter of the holm oaks is just ahead. The trees are thick so the ground will surely be dry. She picks the bustard up by its curled, sharp-clawed feet.

'That was a good shot.'

She drops the bird and wheels round. There is a man standing in front of the mastic bush where she has just been hiding. He is neither tall nor short, and he has a sword and a dagger hanging from his belt. His hands, though, are empty. In fact, he has his arms folded across his chest, and is watching her with a sort of bored amusement.

Time slows. She feels the bow in her left hand, plots the path of her other hand around to the quiver, is able to imagine tugging out an arrow, nocking it, aiming . . . She drops the bow. She has been carrying Tommaso's knife shoved through her belt, and that is what her right hand finds, almost of its own accord. The pommel fits against her wrist, the twisted wire of the grip feels alive against her fingers. Suddenly, in a way she doesn't understand, she feels almost whole again. This is Onoria Ormani, daughter of Amerigo. She draws the blade, and as she does, time speeds up again. Now it is running faster than it should. She feels weightless, surrounded by light, although the day has only grown more gloomy.

As her sword comes up – *It's a knife, just a knife*, she corrects herself – she sees the man as if for the first time. He isn't that small after all: much bigger than her, anyway, broader, solid as a statue. He is wearing dirty riding boots and a much-worn leather doublet of defence, quilted and pinked and stitched in stern decoration. His crimson sleeves and breeches are baggy and slashed into wide ribbons, revealing black cloth striped with yellow beneath. On his left arm he wears a chain mail sleeve. His cap is broad-brimmed, slashed like the rest of his clothing, and slouched to one side, with a spray of pheasant feathers drooping wetly from a silver clasp. His face is lined, skin loosening over taut muscle, and his short beard is halfway between black and silver. His eyes are narrow like slits notched into his face with a broad-bladed chisel, each with a fan of crow's feet. And the eyes

116

themselves are sharp as flints and the colour of steel.

She has taken the tense, uncertain guard she assumed for Augusto that day in the courtyard, the *porta di ferro*, because she reckons he's a soldier, and because he's a soldier he's also an arrogant pig who'll act like the animal he is. The brute is looking at her, but all he sees is a girl, she tells herself, defenceless and soft. *He'll come to take what he wants, what he thinks he sees, and I'll stick him in the gut. He won't be expecting that, the pig.*

But then she looks into his eyes. He is still standing with his arms crossed, big hands in light riding gloves tucked calmly against the gaudy tangle of his sleeves. A man alone with a tired, hungry girl in the middle of God knows where. He's going to kill her, no matter what else happens. 'If this is my death, then so be it,' she whispers, 'but you'll do it in the way I choose, and I'll hurt you before you do.' She raises her arm so that her knife is higher than her head, turns her wrist and points it straight at the man's face. Left fist tucked into the curve of her waist. Knees flexed. *Becca cesa.* She hears her father's voice, feels his hand on hers. *Keep it steady. Like the scorpion's tail.*

When he sees Onoria do that, the man shakes himself, like an animal, a bear, and suddenly his sword is in one hand and his dagger in the other, and he too has taken a guard, left foot forward, blades held low. *He is a proper swordsman*, Onoria thinks approvingly. And this is good. Now she will die with honour.

'Come on then, sir!' she calls, although her voice is nothing but a hiss. So she stamps her foot and lets her spine arch backwards. Alive. She feels alive.

Then the man does something with his hands, and suddenly he is holding both dagger and sword by their blades in his left hand. With another flourish, he buries them both in the shiny green leaves of the mastic bush.

'I'm not going to fight you for that big chicken,' he says. 'Put your spur down, little gamecock.' The man's voice is surprisingly friendly. He speaks Tuscan with a seasoning of other places. 'What's your name?'

She stares at him. Her hand is starting to sweat around the grip of the knife. She could rush at him, get him through the neck before he can pull his sword out of that plant. But his arms are folded again. She can't see his hands. Her blade stays up, but she scuffs her feet a little, letting her toes in their wet leather sheaths find a better purchase on the ground. He can have her name, and then . . .

'Onoria,' she says, and because her voice still won't work properly, she says it again, carefully, pushing the sounds out from her wounded throat. 'Onoria!'

'Well met, Onorio!' The man touches a finger to his cap with a little twirl. It isn't mockery, though. Not exactly. 'Onorio. It suits you, young sir. And do you have a second name, boy?'

And then she . . .

And then I told the first great lie of my life.

'Onorio Celavini,' I said. 'I am Onorio Celavini.' I had been praying to the saint in my heart and perhaps it wasn't me who decided that her name would be mine from now on. The finder of lost and hidden things, she is, but also, perhaps, the protector of those things that wish to remain hidden. But is it wrong to use a saint to cover what I did that afternoon? Because I threw away truth as if it had been a rabbit bone I had picked clean.

I abandoned my family. I abandoned my sex. And my life? That had been the one thing I'd planned to throw away, and now I found myself clinging to it again, desperately, as I had done when I found Augusto's knife as he was killing me, and afterwards when I had left the bodies of my mother and father, of my brother and jumped from the window. And when I had, the next day, turned my back on the smoke rising from my gutted world and began to stumble through the forest. I didn't know, at that moment, exactly what I had done, or precisely why I had done it. It's easy, now, to say that I just hoped this terrifying stranger would be content with this exchange, would touch his cap again and flash his steely eyes, and leave me to steal away to the woods and cook my prize.

It wouldn't be the truth, though. What is true is that I was a young girl, alone, lost, starving, soaked to the skin, who already knew what men would do to me simply because . . . I didn't really understand that part. But this stranger in his slashed hose and feathered cap was dangerous because he was a man and I was not. Except that now, suddenly, miraculously, that had changed. Onoria, by some swift, strange alchemy, had been transformed into her opposite. She had become he. Onoria, Onorio. It was terribly, terribly easy. So easy that I didn't believe it myself until the man spoke again.

'Listen, boy,' he said. 'I'm going to put my blades back in their scabbards, yes? Perhaps you'll do the same?'

Boy. He'd said it again. *Boy*. I kept a tight grip on the knife as he turned and, with slow and deliberate movements, pulled his sword and dagger from the bush, wiped the steel on his hose, slid them into their sheaths and held his hands towards me, palms out. Only then did I lower my own blade and, feeling slightly foolish, slipped it between my belt and my doublet.

'Celavini. I've not heard of that family. Where are you from?'

My blood rushed to my head. 'I . . .' Thoughts were spinning around, and I couldn't catch on to any of them. 'There was a fire,' I blurted. 'I'm the only one who . . . who . . .'

'You escaped from a fire?' The man dropped his chin towards his collar and observed me, frowning. *He knows*, I thought. *He's been sent by the Ellebori. He's been hunting me.* But when he started speaking again, he didn't sound like a hunter. 'And you've been wandering for . . . how long?'

'I don't know,' I said truthfully. 'A long time, I think.'

'What happened to your voice?'

'A man tried to   .' I blurted and shoved a knuckle into my mouth to stop myself.

To my horror, the man closed the distance between us with two long strides. His hand was on my chin, fingers clad in damp leather cupped gently around my face, tilting back my head. I tried to grab my knife, but he dropped another heavy hand onto its hilt, and I froze.

'Quite a pretty boy, and all alone. He hurt you badly. What did you do?'

'I killed him,' I said, opening my eyes and staring up into his.

'I believe you,' said the man, letting go of me. 'He has done you some damage, the animal. It sounds as if your voice box is crushed.' He shook one of his gloves free and put a cold hand against my forehead. 'You're feverish. When was the last time you ate?'

'Days,' I said. Now that he'd said it, I could feel the fever

120

threading its way through my blood. My teeth began to chatter.

'Hmm. Where did you say you were from?' I pointed vaguely south. 'And you're all alone? Quite alone?'

'Everybody died,' I whispered.

'Relations?'

'I don't know of any.'

'Where the hell were you going, boy?' The man sounded genuinely concerned.

'Florence,' I said.

'Dear God.' The man bent to pick up his glove. The back of his neck appeared, pale and grubby, between his hair and his collar. I could have pulled out my knife and stabbed him there, between the bumps of his spine. I could have killed him in a moment. A child could have killed him. A girl . . . But I didn't. And then he straightened, and the moment was gone.

'You're a fighter. Who taught you to fight?'

'My father. He is a famous . . .' I stopped myself, but my voice had begun to whistle again, and the man hadn't heard me properly.

'Your father? Was he a soldier?'

'In his youth. He was a fencing master.'

'So they have fencing masters here, eh? I don't know this part of the country. Anything south of Siena is a mystery to me. Well, well. Tell me, what was the guard I took when you so gallantly drew on me?'

'*Cinghiale porta di ferro*,' I whispered.

'Oho! Yes, very good, very good.' He pulled his glove back on, wiggling his fingers. Seeing me watching, he winked. 'So what is your plan, Onorio? Do you know how far it is to Florence?'

'No,' I said, and bit my lip, because I sounded young and foolish.

'It's a long, long way. Why are you going there?'

'My mother's family is from there. Was. I don't know.' I was going to cry, and that was the worst thing that had yet happened.

'Pick up your bird, then,' said the man. 'Let's go.'

'Where? Who are you?' I demanded.

'Me? I'm Orazio del Forese. Don Orazio del Forese of Lucca. My men are waiting for me up there a little way. We'll cook that bustard for you and someone will look at your throat.'

'But I'm going there!' I turned and pointed, absurdly, at the dark mass of the holm oak wood, which was starting to gather wisps of mist.

'It is a damn fine wood, boy, but if you don't get looked at by a surgeon, you'll be there for good.' He shrugged. 'Someone might find your bones, after the foxes and the badgers are done with them, but is that where you want to leave everything your father taught you? *Cinghiale porta di ferro?* What a waste that would be. Don't you agree?'

I shrugged. 'You're a soldier, aren't you?'

'Well done,' he answered patiently.

'Were you at Montemurlo?'

'Montemurlo? Why on earth . . . Yes, I was, though that's a bizarre question for you to be asking. It was only a little battle, you know. More of a skirmish.'

'What side?'

'What do you mean, boy?' Don Orazio del Forese's eyebrows lifted ominously.

'What side did you fight for at Montemurlo?'

'Why, the Grand Duke's, of course! Don't tell me you're one of those damned Sienese . . .'

'My father fought for the Grand Duke there,' I interrupted. 'My mother's uncle was killed.' I picked up my bow and put it over one shoulder, took hold of the bustard's scaly legs. 'If you're soldiers . . . If you are men who fight for Grand Duke Cosimo, I'll go with you.'

Don Orazio laughed out loud. 'We're honoured, I'm sure,' he said. 'Though you'll more likely be dead by nightfall, by the look of you. Come on, boy.'

He led me up the northern lip of the hollow. There was a horse grazing there, reins dragging on the ground. The land here was more creased than I'd thought, and I wouldn't have seen it as I'd stalked the flock of birds. It wore an expensive-looking saddle with a high pommel and cantle, much like my father's, the one that had always stayed on the wall. Without warning, Don Orazio took me under the arms and lifted me up, dropping me astride the horse's neck in front of the pommel. I felt him climb smoothly into the saddle, and then he was draping the reins around me. 'Hold on,' he said, but I was already almost lying against the horse's mane, feeling the beast's warmth seep into me. Don Orazio clicked his tongue, and we moved off at a fast trot, the horse obviously trained to follow the most subtle of commands.

There wasn't far to go. If it hadn't been for the heavy mist, perhaps I would have heard the noise of about a hundred and fifty men, thirty or so women and at least two hundred horses, a short line of carts and wagons: a company bigger than every man, woman and child in Pietrodoro put together. If I had heard that low, steady rumble of voices, rattle and chink of harnesses, that whinnying of horses – impossible to believe that I hadn't, I told myself, as we rode towards it – I would never . . . But I had not heard it. The *colonnello* of Don Orazio del Forese was another hidden thing waiting to be found that day, muffled in the cape of Santa Celava. It was waiting for Onorio Celavini, the boy who had not existed even one hour earlier. The boy who was helped down from Don Orazio's horse by a couple of frowning, slightly amused soldiers, who had to untangle his cold, cramped fingers from a nest of stiffening bird claws, who was half led, half carried to one of the carts, where a pock-marked, large-bosomed woman sat me down on an upturned cask, wrapped a blanket around me and gave me a flask to sip from, filled with some bitter liquid that burnt so horribly going down that I screamed, though no sound came out. The boy who the company surgeon examined, though only my neck and throat, because I pulled the blanket around me as closely as I could and heard Don Orazio whisper loudly in the surgeon's ear, 'Someone tried to bugger the child. I shouldn't prod him and poke him too much if I were you.' The boy who climbed into the back of the wagon fell dizzily asleep and woke up to the rocking and creaking of movement under a darkening sky, unable to remember where he was. Or his own name. Or that he was, from now on, a boy.

CHAPTER TEN

That evening I sat in front of a fire, shivering with fever and wrapped in a heavy blanket that smelt of horse. The large woman, who was the surgeon's helper, or mistress, or most likely both, had been instructed to mash up my portion of the meat together with almonds and milk, but the very fact that it had been seasoned with salt and long pepper and a sprinkle of cinnamon seemed like a miracle to me. It was almost painless to eat, and I realised how much I had been suffering as I'd tried to keep myself alive. The other men in the circle – there were many fires, many circles on the level pasture where the *colonnello* had set up camp for the night – watched me with expressions that ran from curiosity to indifference, but no one was out-and-out unfriendly. Perhaps Don Orazio had told them to show me kindness, or perhaps they were used to picking up strays; I didn't know, and I didn't honestly care. I ate my fill, drank some more of the repulsive liquor that, I had to admit, did soothe my throat.

I was ill for three days, shivering in the surgeon's wagon as the company moved south into the valley of the Orcia river. It was my great good fortune that the surgeon and his mistress were kindly, reasonably talented but basically incurious creatures, and apart from the odd dose of liquor and some undeniably good food, they left me completely alone. I would leave the wagon to piss, and if people had noticed that I only squatted, I would have told them that my guts were in disarray. But no one did. There were no further examinations, no attempts to undress me. I was not much more than a piece of baggage.

What a relief it was to find that I'd been asleep as we passed within sight of the crag of Pietrodoro. That evening we made camp a little south of Radicofani, near enough to the Via Francigena that we could hear the pilgrims on their way to Rome chattering early in the morning, because pilgrims, apparently, rise even earlier than soldiers.

The next day I felt better. I could turn my head without my neck feeling as if it was splitting apart like a rotten fig. I could also speak for more than a couple of words without my voice turning into the hiss of an angry goose, although it was now high and rasping, and would crack if I talked for too long, or spoke too loudly, and so it has remained. Feeling almost restored, I climbed down from the wagon and looked around me. We were in a kind of sparse forest of low, spindly pine trees. Radicofani was there in the distance, leaping up out of nowhere, dark and crooked like the sole surviving tooth in an old man's mouth. Men were packing up their bedding and tending to their horses. No one was paying any attention to me. The chatter of voices from the pilgrim road was quite loud, and I could pick out four or five foreign languages. Now, I thought, would be the perfect time to slip away. I could easily vanish into the trees. I doubted I would be missed, and when the company had moved off, I would join the pilgrims on the Francigena and make my way to Rome, where surely . . .

'Master Onorio! To me, please!'

I spun around guiltily. Don Orazio was beckoning me over to where he stood in a small group of men. They were all dressed like him: doublets of defence, slashed hose and sleeves in many bright colours, riding boots. I waved to show that I had seen him, but I was horrified. Thinking fast, I gestured that I needed to piss, and trotted away to where the trees were a little thicker on the far side of the wagon. Once I was more or less out of sight I checked my appearance in a panic. Bartolomeo's old clothes were looking even older now and fitted even more badly, because I had lost a lot of weight on my journey. I hitched up my hose so that the codpiece was snug between the fork of my legs and tightened my belt to its last hole. Then I trotted over to the men, trying not to look like an obedient puppy or a terrified girl.

'This is the boy,' Don Orazio said, patting me on the shoulder.

'He's a runt,' said one of the others, a tall, thin man with one eyelid sewn shut, from under which a constant thread of tears ran that had burnt a permanent red line down his cheek. He didn't sound unkind, though, just matter-of-fact.

'And he would have fought you? You're joking. He's hardly a boy. Looks more like a girl.' The man who spoke next was rather plump, with heavy, black-stubbled cheeks. His curly hair sprung out from under a beret of pinked and ruched crimson felt. He didn't sound kind at all. My mouth went dry.

'Why don't you ask him, Gianbattista?' Don Orazio folded his arms in what seemed to be one of his favourite poses.

'You. Runt. You dared to draw a blade against Colonnello della Biassa?' The man stepped towards me. His belly, caught behind the swell of a red doublet studded with gilded metal, almost bumped me in the chest. He was wearing a sword with a looping, German-style guard, and a large hand was resting on it, fingers slightly hairy and covered with gold rings set with stones of all different colours. I noticed all this as I breathed in his smell: sweat, horse, good civet perfume, unwashed arse. Repulsion caught me by the stomach and turned almost immediately to anger. I skipped backwards and stuck my chin out defiantly.

'I'll draw my blade on any man who sneaks up on me while my back is turned,' I hissed.

'You little . . . I'll thrash you!' The man began to draw his sword, but Don Orazio grabbed him by the wrist.

'What did I tell you, Gianbattista?' he said, chuckling. But Gianbattista was not amused.

'The little faggot. I won't be spoken to like that by a stray dog!'

'Why don't you fight him, then?'

'Fight it? Don't joke with me, Colonnello. I'm not in the mood.'

'You're full of piss this morning, Gianbattista. Stone playing up again?' the tall, one-eyed man asked innocently.

'Fuck off, Daniele. I'm going to punish this runty little turd properly. And then, if it's a girl like it looks to be, my lances can have it for a bit of fun.'

I gritted my teeth. My knife was back in the wagon, or I would have drawn it. Then I saw that Don Orazio was watching me. It was a strange look. He should have been annoyed with me, or angry. I was nothing to him, just baggage, and now I'd riled one of his officers. But his eyes weren't angry. Instead there was something else. He was watching me with an intense curiosity and with something that might possibly have been affection.

'Would you fight Don Gianbattista, Onorio?'

'If I had my knife,' I spat. I wasn't sure I actually meant it, but I certainly wasn't backing down now, not in front of these stinking men. And after that thing the man had said, I couldn't, for my life. *Looks more like a girl. My lances can have it for a bit of fun.* Damn them. Damn them all. If I was to be a boy now, I'd damn well be a boy.

'He's small, but he's a gamecock, Gianbattista. Son of a fencing master. I shouldn't chance it if I were you.'

'Like fuck!' the heavy man exploded, shaking off Don Orazio's hand and swinging at me with his open palm. I dodged further back. Don Orazio took hold of him again, this time less gently.

'You see, he's called Onorio. Honour. He can shoot a bird through the heart at fifty paces and knows his fencing guards. He almost fought me. I'm curious to see what he knows. Seeing that you want to teach him a lesson, why don't you two have a little fencing match? Sebastiano, find Onorio a sword. A proper one. Asdrubale will have something suitable. Onorio, go with him.'

Sebastiano, the youngest man there, gave me a slit-eyed look and strode away towards the middle of the camp. I had no choice but to follow. Asdrubale turned out to be the company armourer. He glanced at me with the air of a man who has seen everything in the world more than once, bent his finger, and led me to another wagon piled with iron-bound chests of various sizes and lengths. Opening one to reveal more swords than I had ever seen in my life, he pulled out a bundle of them, held like a bouquet of strange metal flowers in both his large hands. He clicked his tongue a few times, laid the swords back in their box and took out two of them, which he held out to me hilt-first. I drew the first one. It was quite plain, with straight quillons and simple enarmes around the ricasso. It was short, made for a small man or a boy. There were German words on the blade but Italian on the enarmes. The other sword was the same length but a little more ornate: the quillons curved like a letter S, and the pommel was fluted like a Turk's turban. I weighed them both, swapped them from hand to hand. The fancier sword felt lively and looked nicer, and I almost chose it, but at the last moment I slid it back into its sheath and took a guard with the other blade.

'This one,' I said. It was purposeful. It was balanced. It felt like something with which you could kill a man. Asdrubale nodded approvingly 'Well done, sonny. Lucky choice – that sword was made by Melchior Diefstetter in Munich. I want it straight back,' he added to Sebastiano.

'I want a left-hand dagger too,' I said, surprising everyone, even myself. Asdrubale shook his head, opened another box, took out a short dagger with curved quillons in a battered black sheath. 'There. Take it or leave it,' he snapped.

'I'd be praying now if I were you,' Sebastiano said as we walked back. 'You'll be dead in a few minutes.'

'I pray all the time,' I said to him. 'Don't you?' Which was true, as far as that went. Santa Celava was never far from my mind. I felt her protection around me like my mother's cloak. I supposed that counted as prayer.

Gianbattista had taken off his doublet to reveal a fine linen shirt stained ivory-yellow with old sweat. He was heavy, I noted, but not as fat as I'd thought. His arms were thick with muscle, though his belly bulged over the waist of his trunk hose. I hadn't noticed his codpiece before: sculpted in red velvet and as big as a blackbird, it curved upwards between his legs. A boy with dirty hair and a fading black eye beneath a scabbed eyebrow was holding out an armoured glove, which Gianbattista pulled on over the ringed fingers of his left hand.

'When I kill him – *her* – I don't want any nonsense from you, Orazio,' Gianbattista said loudly, obviously for my benefit. 'You'll mark it down that I executed it – we shall call the creature "it" when we record its demise – for insubordination. Agreed?'

'Certainly,' Don Orazio said. 'Are you ready, Onorio?'

I drew, and handed the scabbards to Sebastiano, who didn't look at all pleased to suddenly be acting as my second. 'Ready!' I said, as cheerfully as if I had been about to fight Federigo with a wooden sword. I suppose I should have been scared out of my wits, but the truth is that I have never really been scared with a sword in my hand. My father had never taught me to fear; perhaps it was a lesson, a sensible one, that he had been saving. Instead he had taught me to attack, to make myself nerveless, to use my body as if it were a marionette controlled by the greatest swordsman I could imagine – who, of course, had been my father himself. I had a good sword, and when I closed my eyes I could see my father's great book with its pictures. In any case, I didn't think this Don Gianbattista actually intended to kill me. I was to be humiliated, punished and . . . It was what would happen afterwards that terrified me.

So, with a surprisingly clear mind, I decided that, if I couldn't win, I would certainly not lose. If I showed this swaggering ape of a man what I was made of, perhaps Don Orazio would intervene on my behalf. No matter that I had no real idea who or what Don Orazio was, whether he could be trusted. He seemed to have just thrown me to the lions. But then I remembered that look he had given me. It was too late now, anyway. A crowd was gathering around us. The other officers had backed away and seemed to be placing bets on what was going to happen next. Don Gianbattista had only a sword, and so I handed my dagger to Sebastiano, knowing my father would have approved. My opponent grinned and flexed his knees, looking more ape-like than ever, making his codpiece dance suggestively. I saw Augusto standing before me in the courtyard of the Rocca and shuddered. Saying a prayer to Santa Celava, I raised my sword in salute. Don Gianbattista didn't even bother to return the courtesy.

He dropped into the low guard of *coda lunga e stretta* and I raised my sword high over my head, *guardia alta*, to show that I wasn't afraid of him. Almost instantly he came at me, fast, springing on his bandy, muscled legs. He made a thrust, which I parried easily, and another, whirling his sword through the air as if he were practising in a garden surrounded by admiring ladies. He postured, and flashed his teeth at me, and I retreated, letting him prance, letting him puff himself up. He was teaching me a lesson, all right. I guessed he was planning to drive me backwards until I tripped, then beat me with the flat of his sword, or simply get inside my guard and knock me down, but he wasn't really paying attention to me at all. I guessed that he liked to hurt children, if that boy's eye was anything to go by. I probably wasn't much more to him than a dog, as he had already said. But it was not hard to deflect the flurry of blows he was aiming at me, all from quite far away. If any of them had reached me, they would only have grazed my skin. It was all a show. I ducked under another pretty sideswipe and turned his blade so that he staggered a little, then darted back out of reach, just to let our audience know I was still fighting.

And then it happened. Don Gianbattista caught his balance with a neat little hop and a skip. He took the *coda lunga* guard again and I dropped the point of my sword below my knee, *larga*. He feinted, I parried, and suddenly he lunged with the full force of his body behind his sword. I saw it coming with a split second to spare and managed to twist out of the way. He hit me with the inside of his arm and I fell, rolling out from under his feet and scrambling up just in time to see him take the guard of the unicorn and advance. If that lunge had hit, his sword would have impaled me through the chest right to the hilt. It had been a killing blow. Don Gianbattista had decided to make his lesson a final one. I thought all this, panting, blinking dust from my eyes, watching the man sidle towards me, sword poised like a viper's fang. He wasn't expecting to fence any more. He was just coming to finish me off.

Energy flooded through me, sickeningly strong. I could hear the shuffling of feet behind me, and voices, laughter, though my blood was ringing in my ears. The sword felt huge in my hand, the grips slippery with my sweat. The man in front of me clenched his left hand in its ugly steel glove. Sunlight glinted off the gilding on the hilt of his sword. The red codpiece bobbed and reared between his legs. Through the singing of my blood I heard the chink of coins changing hands and, louder, the rasping of my own breath. I blinked, and there was my father's finger, tapping a page. *You're not with me any more, Papà*, I thought. *I'm alone.*

And so I was. It was I alone who straightened my backbone and felt that it was supple and hard like steel. It was I alone who deflected the great thrust the man aimed at my breast and, following through, flicked the point of my sword across his forehead, so that a flap of skin, pouring blood, was suddenly hanging over one of his eyes. I alone faced his bellow of rage, ducked as he swung at me, felt his blade hiss through the tips of my hair. And alone I rammed the pommel of my sword into the man's neck, felt his Adam's apple break, and as he lurched backwards, tripped him with a twist of my leg so that he fell like a rotten tree onto the ground. Whether it was Onoria Ormani or Onorio Celavini who stabbed him under the breastbone, I don't know. Which of us pushed until the steel was grinding into the earth beneath his body, and watched as bright red blood frothed out of his mouth and his legs kicked and went still? Time has rubbed away those things, and I no longer have the answer. But when I pulled out the German blade and stood up in that ring of men and women, who had now gone quite silent, I knew I had made my final transformation.

'Does anybody else wish to call Master Onorio a girl? Or perhaps a runt? Or a dog? No? Then I say this affair of honour is settled.' Don Orazio was looking down at the body of the man who, a minute or two ago, had been one of his captains. No one said a word. I could hear nothing but the chirr of cicadas and, faintly, someone on the pilgrim road singing in a lilting tongue I couldn't understand. The *colonnello* was holding out a handkerchief to me. 'Clean your sword, Onorio.'

'I need to give it back to Messer Asdrubale,' I said stupidly. My throat was beginning to close, and I felt dizzy.

'I don't think there's any need for that, do you?' Don Orazio clicked his fingers and pointed to Sebastiano. 'Caposquadra Morelli, bring the scabbard, please.' He let his hand drop onto my shoulder, not gently, but as though he had forgotten I was not a full-grown man. 'To the company I say this. I, Orazio della Biassa, take Onorio Celavini into my lance, to serve under me from this day on. The lance that was Gianbattista Tascha's is now under the command of Caposquadra Roderigo di Bondi.' At last there was a faint cheer. Some sort of enchantment seemed to have been broken. The circle began to dissolve as voices rose, some in laughter, some babbling with the release of tension, others angry. Don Orazio heard those. 'Come with me,' he said, and, hand still on my shoulder, began to lead me on. As we walked away, the crowd surged around the body. People sounded angry, I noticed, but nobody sounded particularly upset.

A large tent was pitched at the far end of the camp. Don Orazio held back the flap for me to enter and came in after me. It was sparsely furnished: a simple cot with rumpled sheets; a folding table with gilded legs holding a pewter jug, a cup and the remains of a loaf of bread; a leather-backed scissors chair, into which Don Orazio lowered himself. I stood in front of him, holding the sword like a choirboy holding a candlestick.

'Half of my men – oh, more than half – are out there at this very moment, saying how fortune deserted Gianbattista Tascha, how a boy was amazingly lucky and managed to kill this man who was far superior to him as a swordsman, a gentleman, all the rest of it.' He picked up a half-moon of bread crust from the table and pulled off the end with his teeth. 'But it wasn't luck at all, was it? You fought very, very well. Beautifully, one might say. Pure

Scuolo Bolognese. Your progressions: Manciolino or Marozzo?'

'*L'Arte della Spada,*' I said, seeing the beautiful title page of my father's book in my mind's eye. 'But mainly Maestro Altoni from Florence. His book is called *Monomachia.*'

'Aha. Of course! The Florentine style. And your father taught you? Taught you well. Very well indeed. Was there a single point where you were not in control?'

'I didn't think he wanted to kill me,' I said. Hearing my voice break, Don Orazio poured something from the jug into the cup and handed it to me. I gulped at it eagerly. It was strong wine, and I almost choked.

'Careful,' Don Orazio said, amused. 'To tell you the truth, I thought the opposite. It says all you need know of the man's character that he would have killed a child in front of the whole company . . .'

'And you would have let him, sir!' I burst out.

'Yes? Would he have killed you?'

'He tried!'

'To try is one thing. To succeed, quite another. I never thought you were in any danger, boy. I would not have allowed the thing to happen if I had.'

I was about to answer that he had not merely allowed it, he had instigated it. Instead, another, far more disturbing thought struck me.

'So . . .' I took another sip of the wine. It burnt, but my voice came easier for it. 'I thought you set Don Gianbattista on me. But really . . .'

I was standing in front of a man, a powerful man who I barely knew and hardly trusted. I had just killed one of his officers. My life, at that moment, was worth less than nothing. For all I knew they were digging a grave for me between the spindly pines, next to the man I'd run through the lungs. I really had nothing left to lose, so I might as well find out whether I was right about what had just happened. I swallowed, painfully, and handed the cup back to Don Orazio.

'But really, sir,' I rasped, 'I might almost think that you were setting me on him.'

Don Orazio looked genuinely surprised. Then he grinned. It made him look much younger.

'Might you, indeed? Are you a gambler, Onorio?'

'Of course not!' I said, shocked. Which I suppose was funny, considering what I'd just done.

'No, no. You're too young. How young *are* you, incidentally?'

'Fourteen,' I lied, though it didn't seem like a very big lie compared to the others I'd told.

'You're small for your age. Anyway, I gamble a little. About as much as I need to. But I'm very, very good at it. I gambled on you beating Gianbattista Tascha. Oh yes, on you killing him. I'd have wagered my entire fortune on it without the slightest fear of losing.'

'I . . . Why, sir?'

'I'm a good judge of men. I'm also a student of the art of the sword. Don't mistake me, Onorio. When you first took a guard against me, I knew you were destined to be a great swordsman. But you should also know that Tascha was rather a poor one.'

'I meant, why did I have to kill him?'

'Because he needed to die,' he said bluntly.

'Why?' I repeated.

'You expect me to tell you?'

'You expected me to kill Messer Tascha.'

'True.' He stood up, paced over to the cot, straightened the sheets. 'You've been feverish or asleep since I brought you in. Have you any idea who we are?'

'You're mercenaries,' I said.

'Ho ho. Yes, I suppose we couldn't be anything else. This is my company. I've led it, in one version or another, for twenty – let me see – twenty-three years. I'm also the Marchese of Castelnuovo Valdarno, just outside Florence. When our new pope came to the throne last year, he saw fit to strip me of my title.' Don Orazio folded his arms. 'You'd have to know that for years my family have been allies of Spain, and Pope Paul hates Spain worse than he hates the Protestants. I expect your father will have told you about Pope Paul.'

'Ah . . .' I was about to deny any such thing, but Don Orazio wasn't listening to me.

'The Pope, whose arse is the worst to nestle itself on the cushions of St Peter's throne for two hundred years, has made an alliance with the King of France, and invited him into Italy. Because this is treachery of the basest kind, I have offered my services to the Duke of Alba, who has ordered me to join the Spanish armies at Naples. Gianbattista Tascha, who thought himself the cleverest of men, was plotting to take us over to the French. And to usurp me as head of the company, obviously.' He laughed aloud. 'He didn't know that I had discovered his faithlessness – couldn't conceive of such a thing, because he fancied himself a genius at plotting, as he fancied himself to be a genius at everything. I had made up my mind to get rid of him last week, but a mercenary company is a delicate thing – politically, that is – and I did not want to call him out as a traitor, because that would force any factions to show their hand. I wanted to deal with one traitor, not split my company. Anyway, I'd thought of poison, you know . . . Then he insulted you.'

'You hadn't planned this?'

'No. But there was an opportunity and I seized it. Don't look so upset, boy. That is what one does in war.'

'I'm . . . I'm not upset, sir,' I managed to say, although 'upset' barely scratched the surface of all the emotions I was suffering at that moment. 'So, is there a war?' I said shakily. It had seemed so peaceful here in the woods until a few minutes ago.

'The war is over,' said Don Orazio. 'Thanks to you. That little war, anyway. The bigger one hasn't even begun yet.' He leant back in his chair. 'Onorio. You've lived up to your name and served me well. And you'll make a fine soldier. You must be proud.'

'I don't know!' I blurted. 'I want to go home!' But those last words came out as a fit of coughing, and then I was spitting blood onto the trampled grass floor of the tent as Don Orazio tried to put the cup of wine back in my hands.

'You're not healed yet,' he said gently. 'But I meant what I said. You'll be joining my lance. I've never met a boy so plainly destined to be a fighting man. Fearless. Quite fearless. How many men can say that of themselves with any truth?'

Later, as I lay curled up in the surgeon's wagon as it lurched south along the Via Francigena, I thought about what Don Orazio had said. Fearless? When he had come upon me that afternoon I had been terrified. I had stood against him out of fear of what he would do to me. I had known almost nothing of the world outside Pietrodoro, and then it had come flooding in. The world, to me, meant only pain and terror, shame and death.

I don't remember, now, if I had ever believed I was going to live longer than a few days. I was going to Florence, but had that been anything more than a story I'd been telling myself, to keep my failing body moving? The truth was that I'd been waiting for death, and I had thought Orazio della Biassa was my end. The creature he'd seen as a brave boy was, in reality, a little girl whose contrary nature and loving father had turned her into . . . what? An 'abomination', the Ellebori had called me. 'Capricious', my mother would say, when I'd come home covered in mud, or burrs, or blood. Perverse creature. A girl who liked to pretend that she was a boy. A skilful, innocent little actor. That is what Don Orazio had stumbled across. An actor.

My father, may God have mercy on him, was the finest swordsman of his time. I have heard that from many people, over the years, none of whom would ever guess my relationship to him. Like most men, he had expected to have a son into whom he could pour all that he valued about himself: his skills, his qualities, his honour. But for my poor father, that had not come to pass. His warrior son had died, and his bookish son had lived. And then there had been me. I had never wanted to be a girl – not for any strong reason, but simply because I envied the things I saw boys do. They were free. I wanted to run, to climb trees, to knock down old walls, to swear and cackle and fight. I hated the feel of heavy skirts. I didn't flinch, as Bartolomeo always did, when my father fired his arquebus. So my father had let me pretend to be dead Tommaso, and of course I had played the role with every atom of my being. He'd taught me his art, and I would never have a finer teacher. Perhaps he'd never had a more eager pupil. But everything I learnt – and I learnt everything – I did so that I could play my role. It seems to me that a real boy would have gone along with this education for the love of the fight itself, of the sword, of blood. It seems strange to say, then, that I learnt to fight because it would teach me about being a boy. The rest of it happened – I have always, as I told you, been a perverse creature – almost by accident. What I am trying to say is that when I had drawn my dead brother's knife and faced Don Orazio, I had been acting. For the last time, as I had thought. I was going to die in the way I thought men died, although I was beside myself with fear. What the *colonnello* had seen first had been my skill, my *guardia becca cesa*, the one part of me that wasn't play-acting. The rest . . . He had been taken in. I had fooled him.

Had I been acting with Gianbattista Tascha, though? He'd called me a girl – dear God, he'd seen, or guessed, what I really was. He'd threatened me with all the foulness I had escaped from at the hands of Augusto Ellebori. I'd had no choice but to stand up to him. It is an unpleasant thing to admit, perhaps, but I never felt a moment's guilt for killing him. When I'd fought him, it had been with everything I'd learnt from my father. I hadn't been a girl pretending to be a boy, I had been my father's pupil; and no, I hadn't been afraid. Because that was what my father had taught me.

'Turn fear into judgement,' he'd said, whenever I'd flinched away from his wooden sword. 'These guards you're learning, these parries: they come from fear, from our instinct to protect ourselves, but we turn that fear into judgement. We don't step out of the way of a blow because we fear it, but so that we can judge our opponent.'

'Aren't you ever frightened, then?' I'd asked him.

'Of course! In a fight, a real fight, there is always fear. Fear comes from nature. It can't be destroyed. That is why you practise, so that when you're close with your enemy and his blade is right there in your face so that all you see is the glitter of the edge, how sharp it is, how deadly, you aren't afraid. Instead of fearing your enemy, you judge your response. Conquer fear and you are left with prudence, discrimination. Have I told you this before?'

'You have, Papà.'

'Then let's practise.'

There in the wagon, I could hear his voice, patient but firm. All the time I had been acting the part of his son, my father had been teaching his daughter how to live. Fear becomes judgement. It was a strange thought. I was tangled up in things I didn't understand at all, though I had done my fair share of the tangling. As I was remembering my father's voice, I heard my mother's as well, saying what she usually did, with a heavy sigh, when I came in for my lessons scratched by briars or with a black eye: 'Mercy, Onoria! Why do you make yourself so ugly? One day the cock will crow, and you'll be stuck that way for ever.'

CHAPTER ELEVEN

Well, the cock had crowed. Over the next few days I slowly learnt exactly what this was going to mean to me. Because I was still hiding, but now I was hiding in plain sight. It would have been simple if I could just have forgotten Onoria and reinvented myself as someone else. But I was not just changing names, I was abandoning one sex and taking up another, which was – as people, most particularly my brother Bartolomeo, had never ceased to tell me – a sin against both God and nature, and probably (although details were never supplied) against the actual laws of Tuscany as well. I had always been amused by this, but now that I was, in the crudest sense, trapped in the guise of a boy, I discovered that my situation was anything but funny.

Nature was, however, on my side, at least partly. I was fourteen, but my monthly cycle had not yet started. My mother had begun to nag me about it. She blamed my boyish habits, particularly riding astride, and just that year had begun to issue vague threats about doctors and – worse – priests. Though when

I had asked her about her own entry into womanhood, she had admitted, grudgingly, that she had not begun to bleed until her sixteenth year. Nor had my breasts really begun to grow. In this, I guessed I also took after my mother, who was not voluptuous. 'Flat-chested,' she would sometimes complain to my father, I think so that he would reply, as he always did, 'Not as flat-chested as Grand Duchess Eleanora, but far more beautiful,' which always made my mother blush, as the Grand Duchess was widely thought to be the loveliest woman in Tuscany. Now, the shirt and doublet which were my only clothes fitted badly enough to hide my natural shape, and if I hitched up my hose and kept my belt tight, the codpiece hid what was missing between my legs.

But there, of course, lay my most vexing challenge. I might have changed my name, but I still had to piss. In a company of two hundred men, where privacy meant almost nothing, I was in danger whenever my bladder was full. At first, I pretended I had the flux, which wasn't so far from the truth. I would stagger away from the wagon, find the nearest bush and squat down. But in the camp, and especially when we were on the move, it was the habit of most men, when the urge took them, to simply pull down their hose, pull out their things and let fly. You will perhaps laugh when I tell you how shocking I found this at first. I, who had thought to master every point of acting like a man. But at home, my father had never done that; Bartolomeo certainly hadn't. Federigo was a modest sort and usually went behind a tree. The village peasants knew not to piss in full view of Donna Onoria. And now here I was, assailed virtually all the time by the sudden appearance of hairy, spotty bums and streaming male organs. It seems almost unbelievable, but so innocent was I that the only word I knew for the organ of generation was 'thing', although by the end of my first week with the company of Don Orazio della Biassa I knew dozens, as it seemed impossible for soldiers to utter the simplest sentence without inserting some reference to sexual parts, the generative act, or defecation. Of course, as part of my disguise, and because their inventiveness was, I had to admit, quite extraordinary, I learnt all these words.

But while I learnt how to swear, I still didn't know how I was ever going to piss in public. Fortunately – the good fortune appears in retrospect, but it certainly didn't seem fortunate at the time – my dilemma was solved by one of the riders in Sebastiano Morelli's lance. He was an almost handsome man, around thirty years old, who I first noticed because his taste in clothing was particularly gaudy in the way of soldiers' fashion, which in those days meant doublets and hose artfully and expensively slashed to resemble rags: pinked and ribbed leather, dangling laces, metal eyelets and studs. It was the style of the Swiss landsknechts, though I didn't know that yet, and indeed I had heard men call him Il Svizzero, but I didn't pay him much mind until I began to notice that, whenever we were close to one another, he kept his eyes fixed on me. At first, he just stared, but soon he got bolder, contorting his face into all manner of leers and grimaces, which at first I took for the symptoms of a rotting tooth. Then he took to grabbing his codpiece and rubbing it whenever he saw me, and I knew exactly what he wanted.

By that time I had left the wagon. The surgeon's mistress had more or less thrown me out. I think she was bored with cooking for me. So I had taken up my place in Don Orazio's lance, which, I discovered, was a squad of twenty-five mounted men. There were seven lances in the company, each with its *caposquadra*. I had no rank at all. Don Orazio found me a horse, an old gelding whose back was starting to go but could still carry the weight of someone small, and I rode along behind the lance, keeping my head down. The majority of the company ignored me: most because I was insignificant, a few because they had liked Gianbattista Tascha. Most, that is, except for Il Svizzero.

We were on the border between Tuscany and the territories of the Pope, in the high country just north of Lake Bolsena. The company had halted for the midday meal on a plateau dotted with clumps of pines and oaks. I badly needed to piss, so I hobbled my poor old horse, picked out a line of scrubby oak trees and made my way over to them, in some discomfort as my bladder was so full. My sword was hanging from my saddle, but I was wearing Tommaso's knife, for which Messer Asdrubale had found a sheath. He was more interested in me now, after the fight, and after he'd heard that I was the son of a master swordsman. I was trotting across the patch of open ground between the company and the trees when I happened to glance behind me. A group of seven or eight men had gathered and another man was striding, quite quickly, towards me. The others were talking in loud, harsh voices, and they seemed to be egging him on. I could see from his clothes that it was Il Svizzero. He saw me notice him and began to pump his fist in front of his crotch.

That all men want to put their thing inside women was a fact I'd learnt, in the most roundabout and delicate terms, from my mother. That some men also want to do that thing to other men, and even boys, was something I had discovered only since joining the company. 'Oh, and Onorio,' Don Orazio had said to me, the morning he had formally introduced me to the lance. He'd spoken quietly, out of the hearing of the other soldiers. 'There is every kind of man in an armed company. Good, bad, mostly both, as and when it suits them. We haven't had a young fellow like you with us for a while. A few of them will want to fuck you. They'll think . . .' He'd pointed to the puckered, healing scar across my face and neck.

'What will they think?' I stammered, blushing and horrified.

'They'll think that someone's done it before.' He shrugged.

'But they didn't! They didn't!' I was Onoria in that moment, but once again my ruined voice saved me. The indignant squeak that came out meant that only Don Orazio heard me. Which, of course, was for the best.

'You can look after yourself. I give you leave to defend yourself in whatever way you please. I'm sure you'll be fine. But be careful.'

Il Svizzero was gaining on me. I was almost at the trees. I couldn't turn back, because then he would catch me in the open, and do the dreadful thing to me while the whole company watched. And then they would all, of course, discover my secret. They would kill me, no doubt. No doubt I would want them to. But here was the edge of the small copse of trees. There was no time to think. The man was right behind me. I could hear the flapping of his ridiculous doublet. I darted between two pine trees and into sudden shade.

I almost tripped on a branch and took a panicked glance around me. Woodsmen, perhaps charcoal burners, had been at work recently: most of the oak trees had been roughly coppiced, and I was in a small clearing where the ground was thick with twigs and small branches. The bigger trees were quite widely spaced, and bushy cypresses were growing up into the sunlight, looking like a conference of big green bears. Somehow, I remembered my father's advice: turn fear into judgement. Il Svizzero was already crashing through the outermost trees. I picked up a sturdy sawn-off branch and pushed myself into the frondy embrace of one of the cypresses.

Just in time: an instant later, Il Svizzero shoved his way into the clearing. I swear he was panting. His eyes were as big as saucers; if he had been a dog, his tongue would have been halfway to his shoes. 'Where are you?' he called, in a rough voice full of sharp foreign corners. 'I want my fun!'

If Il Svizzero had ever read the *Metamorphoses* of Ovid with the same diligence that my mother had forced me to spend on it – though I'm sure Il Svizzero couldn't read a single letter; he didn't appear to be the scholarly type – if he'd spent hours, as I had, on the story of Apollo and Daphne, he would have beheld a sort of Daphne in reverse. He stood there panting, dancing on the balls of his feet with the energy of his lust, and turned his head eagerly as he heard the rustle of branches, in time to see me step out of the heart of the cypress tree, my wooden club gripped in both hands. Something changed in his face, though whether it was triumph or fear I never found out, because I brought the branch down onto his ridiculous slashed cap with all my strength. He dropped straight down, as though his legs had vanished into thin air, and pitched backwards into a snarl of twigs. I hadn't intended to kill him . . . Or had I? I'd chosen the club and not my knife. But in any case, I saw with a certain amount of relief that he was still breathing, although blood was running freely from a long gash in his scalp. It was then that my body reminded me why I'd come here in the first place. I pulled down my hose and prepared to squat, then had another thought. Stepping out of my hose entirely, I planted my feet wide apart and conducted my first experiment in pissing while standing up. It wasn't altogether successful, and extremely messy, and Il Svizzero got quite a splattering, but I saw how, with a little practice, it could be managed.

After I'd restored my clothing I relieved the would-be rapist of his dagger. He was beginning to stir, moaning feebly. I thought for a moment, then bent down and sliced through the lacing of his codpiece, pulled it off and shoved the dagger through it as if it were a thrush for roasting. Then I sawed through his belt, cut off the buttons of his hose and the points attaching it to his doublet. He was blinking now and trying to make words. I gave him a kick and, carrying the spitted codpiece before me like the trophy it was, left the wood and walked back to the company. Il Svizzero's comrades were waiting where he'd left them. When they saw me come out alone they began to hoot and bray, thinking, I suppose, that their friend was still savouring his conquest. They were nudging each other, and as I got closer they began to shout, to ask me who I wanted next. Then one of them pointed to something behind me. I had reached them by that time and they had seen that I held a dagger in my hand. Glancing over my shoulder I saw Il Svizzero stagger out from among the trees, his hose halfway down his thighs and his face covered in blood. The man nearest me was a bearded, older fellow from Sebastiano

Morelli's lance, one of the men who had been making it a habit to leer at me. I walked up to him and held out the dagger, so that the point was a foot or so away from his chest, but loosely, so that the codpiece dangled limply, laces flopping like the legs of a dead creature. Or like a jester's sceptre. He gawped. I didn't say anything, and neither did he. There was nothing, really, to be said. I went back to my horse while Il Svizzero's friends rushed over to see what had befallen him.

From that day on I wasn't troubled again by any randy soldiers. I had triumphed: over a grotesque oaf, over lust, over the entire species of men. I thought so, at least. Looking back through the clear and honest lens of time and experience, it is plain to me that I was incredibly, undeservedly lucky and nothing more. For one thing, the landsknecht was not, despite his audience that day, a very popular man. Even his nickname would have told me that if I'd understood those things at the time, because he was a German landsknecht and so the sworn enemy of all things Swiss. As I learnt after more time with the company, men who openly preferred other men or boys were not tolerated by the others. It was acceptable to use a boy if the natural urges that overcame a sturdy, healthy man could not find a female receptacle. It was also accepted that, from time to time, if a young fellow with little power got ideas above his station, he might find himself singled out by the more powerful men, who would use him as the leader of a pack of dogs uses his subordinates, until he learnt his place. Men who used other men in this way always claimed that they did it out of necessity. Il Svizzero was one of those who, so gossip in the company went, enjoyed these things rather more than a proper, natural man should. His friends had plainly egged him on to violate me because I had upset the natural order of things, to do a suitable, even necessary thing. But when I had humiliated him in his turn, that had also redressed an imbalance of nature. He had come after me as a righteous man set to punishing the strange boy who had burst into their world and killed one of their leaders. But it was just as satisfying to the general sense of justice that, when he had failed, and failed so dismally, he should become the all-too-willing sodomite punished for his unnatural lusts. It was my good fortune that Il Svizzero was as much on the edge of our world as I was.

Equally as lucky – and this I did understand, even then – was that the man had been so blinded by his urges that he had blundered into the most pathetic of ambushes. For all his affectation, the landsknecht had a reputation as a ferocious warrior. He had fought in the recent wars and was undoubtedly a better swordsman than Gianbattista Tascha had ever been. I only bested him because he allowed his thing to lead him blindly – for a man's thing is as blind as a mole, no matter that it drags him wherever it wishes – into a child's ambush. I hadn't deserved to escape with my life.

Il Svizzero recovered from the knock I'd given him, though the surgeon had to stitch his scalp back together. But he lost his swagger, and his warlike tatters never seemed to look as dashing. He became nervous, a man who was always looking over his shoulder, and his friends, such as they had been, abandoned him. He disappeared one day, somewhere in the Liri valley, no doubt to try his luck with the papal armies and sample the fleshly delights of Rome. So the shamed sodomite lost, and I, the imitation boy, triumphed. It hardly seems fair now, though it certainly did to my younger self. But then I spent that strange and desperate part of my life in a constant negotiation with justice, with fortune, honour and with truth itself. I was becoming something I was not; I could not be what I really was. The harm that had been done to me, I sometimes passed on to others so that I could keep myself safe. How much justice was there in that? Not much for those who suffered. For me, though, justice was being served. Every day that I remained alive was revenge against the world that had wronged me. The wrong was great. And my need for revenge, though I hardly knew it, was growing every day. I hid it within myself, like a tainted lake hidden in porous rock, and there it remained, though I told myself it was a pure spring and called it justice, and honour, and truth. Like all things, concealment becomes a habit. You forget who you are hiding from. You forget who is hiding.

CHAPTER TWELVE

After that day, my life became easy. Easy, that is, to the eyes of any observer who did not know my true nature, and that, of course, was everyone. My triumph over Il Svizzero had won me respect and demonstrated that I was someone of virtue and good morals. To my relief I slipped into the life of Don Orazio's company and vanished into its rhythms and complexities, as so many others had done before me. It is in the nature of a mercenary company to pick up strays as it journeys from place to place. I was not the first oddity to be taken in, and I wouldn't be the last. Once the novelty of my presence had worn off, I was just Young Onorio of the Colonnello's Lance.

The company rode down to Naples. We joined the army of the Duke of Alba and rode back again to Rome, where the Pope surrendered to us before we had even begun to lay siege to the city. The French marched down from the north to relieve the Pope. The Duke of Alba, who was a great soldier but also a prudent and exceedingly careful strategist, decided to let his enemy, the Duke of Guise, exhaust himself and his troops by chasing us around Italy. We won the war by keeping just out of range. When we finally met Guise near Ascoli, we all but destroyed his army. I watched from a nearby hillside. Don Orazio thought me too young to fight, and in any case, out of the men of a lance, only two would go into battle on any given day. I couldn't see much: thickets of pikes disappearing into cannon smoke, the rattle of arquebus fire. It was almost dull.

The Duke of Alba went back to Spain. Don Orazio took us north and then down into the Kingdom of Croatia, where he signed a contract with the parliament there to fight the Turk. Croatia looked to me much like Italy, though the people spoke a strange language. On a day in late autumn, as we rode through the country south of Skradin, we came across a Turkish battalion with numbers a little larger than our own. Don Orazio and his squadron leaders decided to give battle. We were drawn up into ranks using the manoeuvres we had practised countless times.

To my joy – even by then I was still young, only fifteen – Don Orazio ordered me into the front rank. By that time, we had adopted the tactic called the caracole, that is, where you ride at the enemy in ranks, each rank firing his pistol as soon as he is within range before wheeling away to let the next rank fire. I was a good horseman by then, and fast, because I was still small and did not weigh much. I had acquired, by various means, a suit of armour pieced together from different sources that more or less fitted me, and I had a good pistol that was absurdly heavy in the hand but with which I could burst a turnip quite reliably from twenty paces.

I sat on my horse, looking across a flat, scrubby meadow

dotted with sunburnt broom and tamarisk bushes. Not very far away was the enemy, a line of bright colours and strangely shaped headgear, and banners of all different shapes and sizes waving overhead. It was hot. My armour was making me sweat, steady rivulets running down my body and soaking into my underclothes and into the linen band I had wrapped tightly across my breasts. I fiddled with the strap of my helmet, one of those tall-combed morions with an open face. Our company was silent, except for the snorting of excited horses and the occasional yell of a *caposquadra*, but a steady, deep thrum of drums drifted across from the Turk. Don Orazio gave the order to charge and we set off, trotting at first through the scrub and then cantering.

I had time to notice that the failing year was letting some green back into the grass before we began our gallop. I straightened my arm. The pistol felt like a block of lead and all I could think about was that I was going to drop it. Suddenly there were faces, not much more than blurs: moustaches, eyebrows, dark shapes that were mouths opened to scream things I couldn't hear. Turbans, feathers, steel reflecting the early afternoon sun. The arrows flying past looked like a flock of little birds.

The man next to me discharged his pistol and the shock of it made me pull my own trigger. There was a sound like a sheet ripping down the middle, and then we were turning, wheeling away, doing what our bodies had learnt to do in defiance of good sense and reason. We were galloping across their front, that sound of tearing still in my ears, then back across the meadow, past the Croatian arquebusiers who were advancing in a ragged line. That was my first battle. The Turks retreated, and the Croatians chased them until they came face-to-face with a much larger force and ran away, by which time we were inside the local castle, celebrating our victory with Venetian wine. Caposquadra Sebastiano Morelli – who had, since the day I had fought Gianbattista Tascha, sometimes acted as a species of unwilling guardian, though no one had asked him to do it – came and sat with me in the corner where I was cleaning my pistol. I'd only fired it once, and I hadn't even drawn my sword.

'Congratulations, Onorio,' he said. 'You did well. I thought you would.'

'Thank you, Caposquadra,' I said.

'It was a tight thing,' Sebastiano went on. 'Their musketry was good, for Turks, and their cavalry gave us a fright. It would have been good if someone had noticed them hiding behind that ruin.'

'Cavalry?' I hadn't noticed any cavalry. I hadn't noticed any musket fire, but that, no doubt, had been the tearing sound. I'd shut my eyes reflexively as my pistol had gone off, and when I'd opened them again, all I had seen was smoke.

'What did you think of them, eh? All that screaming? Wild desert men from Syria, most likely. The second rank had a hot time.'

'I thought we would attack again,' I said, though I hadn't at the time. I'd just followed the lances back to the rear, where I'd joined in the shouting and backslapping, even though I'd still been almost deaf.

'What, and exceed the terms of our contract?' Sebastiano laughed. 'Don't worry. We're going to attack them again tomorrow. The *colonnello* is renegotiating with the Croats as we

156

speak. Another caracole, and a melee, if they give us the chance. Swords, Onorio. You'll be in your element.'

He was right, as it turned out. It wasn't a large battle, though bigger than the first. The main Ottoman army was elsewhere, and this was a force sent out to probe the Croats' flank. But there was a company of janissaries, and the cavalry were spahis, Turkish gentlemen who spent their lives training for war. This time we charged, fired our pistols, flung them away and drew our swords before crashing into the enemy line. And I was not frightened. Yesterday I had fretted as we waited for the order; today I was nerveless. I'd been thinking about my father, perhaps that was one reason. War, at its heart, is only about death, and who better than a ghost to guide me into it? So as I waited in the second rank, rubbing the sole of one boot against a stirrup, working out how best to carry my cocked pistol so that it didn't accidentally discharge and kill me, my horse or the man next to me, I remembered one of the stories he'd told Federigo and me as we'd sat at his feet under the fig tree in our courtyard. About a battle, a charge, how he'd lose himself in the great turmoil of the fray. I don't remember the details now. Strange: now I can only remember the robin who hopped around us, waiting for a crumb from the cake my father was eating. Then, I had clung to every detail, every horror, storing it away to use in my act, all the refinements on what it meant to be a man, as imagined by a small girl.

But when we attacked, I understood. My body understood. It was my years of training, of course, but it was more: I – Onorio, Onoria, whoever I was – dissolved. I fired, threw my heavy pistol into the white teeth of the man in front of me, drew my sword, twisted and turned as my horse plunged through the wall of men, stabbing and hacking, my mouth wide in a silent yell, because I had no voice that day. And I knew exactly what to do. It was so simple. Guns went off next to me – an arrow *tink*ed against my helmet – these were voices telling me, *You are alive! You are alive!* I was with my comrades, those men, those other men. I rode, and slashed, and saw how force – the weight of our horses, our armour, our fury – met resistance, human flesh, rage and fear, and what happened. Simple, predictable, like throwing stones into a stream and making the water go this way or that. The enemy was water, and we were the stones. A tall man with a taller white headdress waving a red and gold flag appeared in front of me. I ran him through the throat and took the flag as it fell. The water parted for me. When the cavalry came at us with their lances, I felt nothing but joy as we met them, because I saw that they couldn't stop us. We turned them and chased them through the olive groves to where the arquebusiers were waiting. There was blood then – I remember the horses screaming as the guns killed them, and not the men. Those I saw die in battle, those I killed or helped to kill, come to me when I sleep, or when I pray. But in battle, they were water, nothing but water, and I was the rock for which they parted.

I was given my own lance after that, the youngest *caposquadra* ever known in Don Orazio's company. The *colonnello* had been given his patrimony back by then – Pope Paul had died, and the new pope was a friend to the Emperor and to Tuscany. Some in the company had feared that the *colonnello* would retire to his lands now that he was a marchese again, but when I had asked him, he'd just scoffed. 'I'm a soldier, not a farmer,' he'd said. Don Orazio, who had more or less ignored me after getting me to kill

Tascha for him, had taken me under his wing since I had captured the janissary standard. I see now that he had been watching me from a distance, seeing if I would live or die in those first days and then, when I survived, steering me gently to where I would flourish. Now that I had my own lance, he had begun to take me into his confidence, in so far as he ever let any man get close to him. I came to know him well, but I think I owed that to the circumstances of our meeting – I had surprised him, and he was a man not easily surprised – and to the fact that he had revealed to me how he had schemed to get rid of Tascha, though he had probably been honest with me because he thought I'd soon be dead. He had also discovered that I was educated, which made me a rarity among mercenaries, and for the first time in my life I was glad that Bartolomeo had drilled the principles of mathematics into me across so many tedious hours. From Don Orazio I learnt the hidden, humdrum things that keep a mercenary company on its feet: accounting, supply, the law of contracts. How to manage fundamentally unmanageable men.

How to avoid them, too. I had no one who could be called a friend, but this was my choice. The one great friend of my life had betrayed me. Whenever I felt lonely, which was often, I would recall the eyes of Federigo Ellebori watching me across the table at the feast of Santa Celava. He had known. Perhaps he hadn't been happy, but he'd known. So apart from Don Orazio, who was much too grand for me to ever call a friend, I kept even the people I needed at arm's length: my pages, who came and went; and my second-in-command, a Roman called Paolo. About ten years older than me, who wore his bushy beard in the combed-out German fashion, he'd been one of the men who had egged on Il Svizzero, but since then he had become strangely devoted to me. I scared him, I think. Paolo was one of those men with a mind that is lively but lacks capacity. He needed to understand things, but didn't quite have the quickness to manage it. I was something he didn't understand at all. I think – no, I am sure – that I scared him, but I fascinated him too. It was my strangeness, of course. He was the type who paid money at fairs to see the mermaid or the talking monkey. To him, as to the other men, I was either a freak or a madman, but to soldiers, both of those things can be lucky. Paolo kept close to me because I was a curiosity, but also out of superstition. I didn't really care, as he was a good cavalryman and the lance did as he ordered.

We left the Kingdom of Croatia when the parliament there ran out of money to pay us. A year later we were in France, lured by the war that had broken out between the true Church and the Protestants. Don Orazio made a contract with the Duke of Guise, who had only recently been our enemy, and we fought at the Battle of Dreux, charging with Maréchal Saint-André to rout the Huguenot infantry. Dreux was a bloodbath: our company alone lost thirty men. Sebastiano Morelli was wounded and froze to death in the night before we could find him. The living was good in France for us: we were on the side of the king and we were winning. It was a fat country and we barely needed to lift a finger to keep ourselves fed. I looked after my men. It was in France that I began to earn a reputation as one who worked as hard off the field of battle as on it, a man who made sure that his men's purses were as full as their bellies and who dealt out justice with an even hand. We joined in the siege of Orléans, but then our employer was assassinated by a Huguenot, after which a treaty was drawn up, and we were jobless. That was a strange time: no wars were being fought in France, in the lands of Italy or Germany. Spain was at peace. So were the Low Countries. We had no choice but to go east again and hope someone would pay us to fight the Turk.

As we travelled and fought and travelled again, I grew into a man. I grew, anyway. I would never be tall, but I reached a respectable height: tall for a short man, you might say about me. I was and still am of slight build, a little wider in the hips than most men, a little narrower in the shoulders. My voice would never recover from Augusto's belt. As Don Orazio had guessed, my voice box had been crushed, but this meant that no one was surprised when my voice never deepened. These were the rudiments of my disguise, but fortune continued to help in other ways. My breasts never grew to any great size, perhaps because I began to bind them before they had even begun to develop. My lunar cycle, too, came late and never brings much blood, though it has always pained me horribly. I quickly learnt to use rags, and to wash them in secret.

More dangerous for me was my hairless face. I was surrounded by men with bristling beards, and those who went clean-shaven were shaving stubble from their faces every day. I watched them carefully, and when I thought the time must be right, around my fifteenth birthday, I bought a razor and learnt how to shave myself, soaping and scraping my smooth skin, and making sure that everyone saw me do it. If anybody asked why my beard was so sparse, I would tell them what a doctor had told me in Mantua: that the injury to my neck and face had no doubt caused a shock to my skin. Sometimes, after such a thing, a man's hair may fall out entirely, I'd been lucky, I would say. I could have been left as bald as an egg. Regarding my bodily functions, fashion came to my aid. It was at that time that the fashion for martingale breeches was spreading, those things that come with a flap in the front – the martingale, to which the codpiece is attached – that one may loosen with just the untying of a couple of laces in order to piss or shit without the unseemly bother of pulling down one's hose and underwear. I didn't have to expose my backside, which I supposed must look like a woman's, though I had no clear notion of what that might mean. The greatest effort I put into my deception was to commission, from an alchemist in Venice, a set of copper tubes, about the length of my forefinger, one end flared to a design I had carefully drawn for him. I always keep one in a little pouch sewn into the lining of my martingales. With a little sleight of hand, one of these allows me to let fly with as manly a stream of piss as any fellow in the world.

I have often wondered how easy it would have been to maintain my deception in ordinary society, where women and men live side by side in equal numbers. Men, I have come to understand, are fundamentally unobservant. If they have no reason to look for something – the motivation of spite, perhaps, or greed, or jealousy – they won't. Is that true of women? I don't know, because I have spent so little time in their company, but I have always thought that women are far keener, far more astute at seeing the subtleties of life. I think I am. But is that just my own temperament, or something common to my sex? Again, I don't know, because I have abandoned womankind. True, there were a few women in the company: some of the men had wives or mistresses who followed them; there were professional cooks; and a small, ever-changing band of whores who were not officially part of our number but who pursued the company as closely as egrets follow a herd of water buffalo. I kept all of them at arm's length, and so the men called me a shy boy. That, at first, suited me. But like all men I was building a reputation, and I knew my reticence with women would not be a useful addition to mine. So I hid behind honour, as men often do. I let it be known that I held women to be my ideal, that my guide was that book my father had given me, the romances of King Arthur written by Rustichello of Pisa. The men in my lance were forbidden to treat a woman – any woman – with anything less than courtliness. The rule of our company was that rape was punished with death, but it was never enforced. When one of my men raped a farmer's wife outside Orléans, though, I had him strung up. The company thought I was mad, but as I have said, madmen are lucky in battle, so with the perverse logic of soldiers I gained more respect, not less.

Did I still want to be like a man, as I had when I was a girl? As I slipped into my twenties, that question didn't trouble me very often. I had to be Onorio. He was the hiding place that Fortune had given to me, a gift of great worth and great complication. Onorio was the castle I had occupied to keep me safe, the palazzo which the Ellebori had not burnt. I had come to know him better than I had ever known Onoria Ormani, that little girl who had played at being someone, anyone, other than herself. And everything that Onorio did made him more real. He was in other people's stories now. My lie had its – his – own life. He was more real, far more real, than Onoria. But Onoria was there too. She followed me everywhere, like the women following the camp. She was there between my legs, under the bindings around my chest, in my beardless skin. If only my comrades knew that I slept with a woman every night, that I shared her dreams. Someone once told me that breathing is a habit, not a natural reflex like the beating of our hearts. We learn it, and we can forget it too. Keeping Onoria secret was a habit as close to the very essence of my life as breathing itself. But I could never forget her, not for a moment.

Then something happened, and it all changed, for both of us.

We were in Croatia again, with a contract from the Habsburg commander to keep Ottoman raiding parties out of the flatlands along the coast. It was dull work: the Turks made it their business to keep us moving but not fighting, the worst thing for a company of soldiers. It was the spring of 1564. We had been resting, tired and frustrated, near a little Dalmatian town that sat among wheat fields and salt pans on one of the many peninsulas that jut out into the Adriatic Sea. There wasn't much to do. I spent most of my time preventing the men from stepping across the line between foraging and pillaging the local population. There wasn't much to pillage: a few farmhouses, a couple of hamlets, the usual windmills. On one of my solitary patrols I found a whitewashed church on a low hill overlooking the town. The people in those parts being Catholic, I decided to go in and pray to the Virgin and Santa Celava. I was kneeling in front of the altar when a nun appeared, looking disturbed to find a soldier in dusty boots and mail in her church. I let her know that she had nothing to worry about, and she brightened when she heard me speak Italian, because, as it turned out, she herself was from Venice and had come here, many years ago, to join the small convent which, to my surprise, I discovered was just behind the church. We talked for a while, about the news from Italy and the politics of the new pope, which interested her a great deal – another surprise – but she was Venetian, and those people have an insatiable thirst for news. I gave her some money so that she and her sisters in the convent, which was called Izvor, would pray for the souls of my family, and she promised she would do so.

It was a few days later when, without warning, a strong force of Turkish cavalry appeared at the top of the peninsula. They had come to sack the town and weren't expecting to find us there. As soon as the patrol galloped back with the news, the camp erupted. It was like the end of Lent: finally, there would be some action. There wasn't time to get into our armour. I was already wearing a steel-studded doublet of defence, as I usually did, so I grabbed my helmet and my armoured gauntlets, shouted at my page – he winced, as he always did, at the cracks in my thin voice – to load my pistol, and buckled on my sword. My lance were mounting up, all of them jabbering excitedly. I rode to the front, and Paolo took his place next to me. The page – Martino, I think that one was called – handed up my pistol. Don Orazio came striding over.

'You and Gentile are leading, Onorio,' he said. 'I want your lance on the right. Gentile will take the left. Give me something I can boast about to our employers. They're beginning to question our value for money.'

It was the kind of skirmish we had fought many times against the Turk. Today, our enemy were mounted raiders of the kind the Ottomans called *akinji*, lightly armoured with long dresses of chain mail and commanded by an Ottoman *effendi*. When we found them, he was riding at their head, a magnificent sight in his fluted armour, horsehair standard, and flag of red and green carried behind him by a bodyguard of armoured men with turbans tied around their helmets. We came upon them two miles up the road, at the point where our peninsula began to be pinched off from the mainland, where the land rose on one side in a long, low ridge. Not very far away, behind us, was the convent of Izvor, where I had met the Venetian nun. I pointed it out to Gentile Rondoni. He was a good, steady man from Florence who'd fought for Duke Cosimo at Manciano.

'There are nuns there,' I told him. 'We can't let the dogs reach it.' Gentile crossed himself and squinted into the sun.

'They haven't seen us,' he said. 'And we're above them.'

Ahead was a place where the ridge dropped unobstructed by walls or trees. 'There?' I asked Gentile.

'It'll do very well,' he agreed, and we formed the lances up in ranks at the top of the slope among some grazing sheep. We had about a third of the company all told, eighty men against perhaps one hundred and twenty. It wasn't long before they saw us, and there was a sudden blaring of horns and rattling of drums. Their ranks, such as they were, began to dash around, getting into the crescent formation in which the Turks liked to fight. I nodded at Gentile, and he nodded back.

'Order the charge,' I said to Paolo, because my voice wasn't good that day. 'Draw swords, no pistols.' Paolo stood up in his saddle and yelled the order. We began to canter, the slope giving us more weight and speed, ignoring the arrows which were flying un-aimed towards us, and were into the Turks before they could set their spears. Their line buckled like thin tin struck with a hammer, and then it was all hand-to-hand. Gentile went down almost at once, hit on the helmet with a battle-axe, but he staggered to his feet and began looking around, dazed, for his mount. The *effendi*, the sun glinting off the gilding on his armour, his pointed helmet plumed with peacock feathers, was levelling his spear at him, and I spurred my horse at the Turks, tugging the reins to make her rear and plunge. Her hooves knocked the spear out of the *effendi*'s hands and caught the Turkish horse on the head. It must have been blinded, because it turned and bolted wildly through the press of fighting men, the *effendi* shouting at it and pulling uselessly at its reins. I tore after them, slashing at a figure in a huge feathered hat who was raising his bow at me, kicking away another's horse with my spurred heel. I managed to draw my pistol and fired it at the *effendi*'s back, but I hit his horse instead, sending up a fountain of blood from the back of its skull. It dropped dead in full stride, and the Turk flew over its neck and crashed into a pile of stones left by a long-ago ploughman. I reined in over him, sword ready, but it was obvious he was as dead as his horse. I dismounted quickly, thinking that this was a sad end for a brave man. But he would have a purse, and there was a dagger in his sash with a handle and scabbard of gold studded with gems. I found his purse and took the dagger too, thinking to give them out later as a prize.

But I had to get back into the fight. I had chased the man right through the press of men and beyond it. Some of the Turks had seen that their commander had fallen and were beginning to run away. I vaulted up onto my horse and pulled her head around. As she reared and wheeled, I saw three horsemen break away from the fight and gallop towards me, one of my men right on their tails. My horse jumped towards them, and I stood up in the stirrups to aim a blow at the leading man. As I swung at his head – I was aiming backhanded at the long moustaches flowing back across his cheeks, as his head was swaddled in an enormous red turban – I realised, too late, that the next man in the group had dropped the point of his spear and was coming at me full tilt. My sword was already hissing through the air. It met the Turk's face, and the impact jerked me up and back. Blood sprayed, and through it I just had time to see the second man's teeth bared in a furious grin, before the point of his spear caught me between the legs.

I screamed, though I felt nothing except a great numbness, and found myself pitching out of my saddle onto the shaft of the spear that had impaled me. It almost took my weight before it sagged and snapped. The last thing I saw before the ground flew up into my face was Paolo's sword going through the Turk's neck.

I must have passed out, because I opened my eyes, maybe only moments later, with a sensation that I remembered from childhood: that I had had a dream of pissing and woken to find that I had pissed in my bed. I was lying in a warm wetness that was spreading out from between my legs, though one of them, my left, I couldn't feel at all. Hooves slammed into the earth a few inches from my head, and I instinctively curled into a ball, though that leg refused to move. There was a rushing in my ears and a bright purple light, and when I could see again I was looking up at Paolo, who was kneeling over me. I could feel his hands tugging at something below my waist and long moments passed before I remembered that he shouldn't be doing that. No matter what the reason, he must not do that.

'No,' I said feebly, and tried to bat his hands away, but my arms felt as if they were boneless.

'You're bleeding to death, Capo,' Paolo said. His fingers continued to tug and pry. I knew what he was doing: untying the stays of my martingale.

'Stop!' I hissed, but it was too late. I felt the laces give, and the flap of cloth and its bulging codpiece being pulled roughly aside. I tried to push my hands down, to hide . . .

'Oh, Jesus!' Paolo's voice was full of the deepest horror. He was staring between my legs as if into the mouth of hell itself. I managed to lift my chin to see as well. There was my martingale and codpiece, drenched in blood, lolling against my leg like a freshly skinned rabbit. And in the fork of my legs . . . nothing. Nothing but a welling pool of dark blood. With that sight came the pain, worse than anything I'd ever felt.

'Don't tell, Paolo! You mustn't tell!' I pawed at his arms, because this was the end, the end of my great lie. 'Go away,' I begged. But it wasn't me. It was Onoria speaking in her woman's voice, the voice she would have had if I'd ever let her grow into a woman. 'Go! Leave me to die here, for God's sake!'

'I'm not leaving you, Capo! Look, it's . . . it's not so bad, perhaps . . .' I felt his hand on the inside of my thigh. That was worse, almost, than the pain. His fingers fluttered, brushed across hair, folds, absences . . . 'Oh, Holy Mother, Capo. I'm so sorry. I'm going to bind it . . . I don't know what to bind!'

Despite the pain, or perhaps because of it, my head was beginning to clear. And as it did, I found something. A spark, an idea. A fragment of my shattered lie. Whatever it was, I let it fill my mind. I tried to move my arms again, and found I had command of them. I looked down again. What looked like a bowl filled with blood was, I realised, the blood-soaked front of my shirt, knotted up against my groin. With as much strength as I could find I grabbed Paolo's wrist and pulled it away. I hoped I had done it soon enough.

'What's . . . what's *left*?' I managed to say. I could still act. It somehow made the pain less bad. 'It's still there . . . Paolo, tell me it's still there!'

'The spear's gone right through your thigh. But I think your . . . I don't want to say it, Capo.'

'For fuck's sake . . . Cock? Balls? Oh, fuck – both? If it's both, in Christ's name just strike off my head now, Paolo!'

Paolo bit his lip. The poor fellow looked as if he was in more pain than me. I still held on to his wrist. I could feel my nails digging into his flesh. But I saw. It was plain on his face: he didn't know. His fingers had told him one thing, but his head hadn't believed them. It had told him another story, and he couldn't even bring himself to believe that. Because there was no worse thing that one soldier could tell another: that his manhood was gone. He didn't want to tell me that. I could see it in his eyes. Meanwhile, the idea in my own head was still unfurling.

'I can *feel* them,' I said, my voice choosing that moment to drop into one of its odd growls, which seemed to convince Paolo, because he crossed himself with bloody hands and tried to smile. One of the Turks was lying beside me; Paolo drew his dagger and began to cut strips of silk from the corpse's robe, which he bound tightly around the wound in my thigh, while I pressed my wadded shirt up against my groin. 'What's happening?' I asked, to distract him from thinking too hard about what he was doing. 'I saw Rondoni go down. Is he all right?'

'Far as I know,' he said. 'Look, we're chasing them, the fucking dogs.' He gasped as I tried to raise myself. 'No, don't sit up, Capo!'

'Listen, Paolo.' I took hold of his collar and pulled his face down towards mine. 'There's a convent, a Catholic convent, about half a mile from here. I want to be taken there. One of the nuns has some skill in medicine. I'd rather have a nun examine me down . . . down there, than Brunetti the fucking surgeon. Can I trust you?' Paolo nodded eagerly. 'I knew I could. Because I want no one to hear about this. Do you understand? Brunetti would tell the whole camp. The fucking Sultan would hear about . . . about this. Take me to the nuns. And don't tell a fucking soul, Paolo. Swear it.'

'I swear, Capo.'

'Swear you'll go to hell if you don't keep this secret.'

'I swear! I'd never—'

'I know. Now get me onto my horse.'

'Jesus, Capo! What are you talking about?' He glanced in horror to where my hand was clamped between my legs. 'You can't ride!'

'I'll ride side-saddle. And that's another thing you'll never breathe a fucking word about.' I even managed a grim little chuckle.

It wasn't even half a mile to the convent of Izvor, but every step my horse took brought a fresh refinement of agony. Paolo had lifted me bodily into the saddle, and I let myself fall against her neck, my right hip taking all my weight, the pommel digging into my ribs. I told Paolo to ball up the cloth of one of the dead Turks' turbans and put it between my knees, to keep my legs apart. Then we set off, Paolo leading my horse by the reins. Now that I was off the ground, I could see for myself how the lances had chased the Turks back the way they had come and were now hunting stragglers across the flatland between where we were riding and the sea. The pain didn't let me think of anything except keeping my body in the saddle. I watched as the church appeared out of the heat haze, white shimmering, coming together into roof, bell tower, door. The nuns must have come out to watch the battle, because we were still some distance away when two black shapes detached themselves from the white dazzle of the church and hurried towards us. It seemed like another day of agony, but I suppose it was only a few minutes more before hands were reaching up to me.

'What will I tell the company?' Paolo asked, as he carried me like a child into the church.

'Tell them that the sisters are tending to me. Tell them I am wounded in the leg. And that is the truth, Paolo. You don't even have to lie.'

There were three other women kneeling in front of the altar. An older nun stood up and, tutting with disapproval, led us to a door in the side of the church, and out into a tiny cloister. Two more nuns emerged, fluttering their hands in shock. There was an infirmary, a whitewashed cell no bigger than a horse stall, with a low cot and a slit window. The Venetian told Paolo to lay me down.

'Get back to the company,' I told him. 'And remember . . .'

'God keep you, Don Onorio,' he said, crossing himself, and let the nuns shoo him out. As soon as he had left, the older nun turned to me.

'We saw the Turkish raiders coming,' she said. She spoke the heavily accented Venetian dialect of those parts, though it wasn't the language of her birth. 'I decided we would spend our last minutes in prayer, but then we heard the sounds of battle. And see, God sent you and your men to us.' She clasped her hands and breathed deeply. 'Having said that, you are a man and our rule forbids men inside our house.'

'Heavens, Mother!' The Venetian knelt down beside me and took my hand. 'The man is wounded! He is bleeding!' Her eyes ran down my body, and her face suddenly went pale. 'Fetch me hot water!' she called to the other nuns, who were gathered in the doorway.

'Sister Vittoria, you know very well—'

'Mother Superior,' I croaked, 'I need to confess something.'

She looked at me, frowning. 'Young man, are you a Catholic?' she asked sternly.

'Of course he is!' Sister Vittoria began, but the older nun ignored her.

'I am,' I said.

'Because a Catholic would know that a nun cannot hear confession. Only a priest—'

'Yes, yes, I know that.' The numbness was creeping back into the lower regions of my body, and I knew I had to hurry. 'I need to tell you something. Not my last words. You can send for the priest if it comes to that.' I glanced at the women in the doorway, a bouquet of sunburnt faces framed by black, white-edged veils.

'Please, sisters. Just to you. In private.' I let my head fall back onto the hard pillow. Was I still acting? If I was, I was overplaying it, I thought, but no, I was suddenly fighting the urge to vomit. It occurred to me that I might really be dying. The Mother Superior must have thought so, because she turned and shooed the others away and shut the door.

'Go on,' she said.

'Good sisters, please look on me with mercy. I told a lie to my comrade. I told him that one of you had some skill with wounds. I don't know if that is true or not, but I had him bring me here, because this is the only place I could come. You must understand. I'm wounded, and I may die from it. But that isn't . . .' My voice trailed off into a dry rasp. It was about to fail me, I knew, so I did the only thing I could. One of my hands was still clamped between my legs. Almost crying out from the pain, I pulled away the sticky mass of linen and drying blood. 'Look,' I whispered. 'Look. I am not . . .' The purple light was coming again. Sister Vittoria's hand tightened in mine, and I squeezed it as hard as I could. 'No one else knows. God help me. I am a woman,' I said, and fell into the light.

CHAPTER THIRTEEN

When I woke up, I was still in the little cell, still on the bed, though I was covered with a rough wool sheet and a blanket. There was a steady, horrible pulse of pain in my thigh, and my body felt both hollow and burning. My first thought was that I had died, and the nuns had embalmed me, taken out my organs and washed the cavity of my chest and belly with vinegar. Then I heard a noise and found Sister Vittoria standing with her back to me, washing strips of linen in a steaming earthenware basin that stood on the only other piece of furniture in the room, a rough olive-wood table. She must have heard the change in my breathing because she turned around and gave me an uncertain smile.

'You're awake,' she said, and paused, mouth open to say something else. Instead she twisted the linen band she was holding until water began to fall into the basin. We both watched the drops fall in silence. Then she shook out the linen and draped it over her arm. There was a jug and a cup on the table, and she poured some clear liquid into the cup and knelt down beside the bed. She put her hand under my head and helped me lift it, holding the cup steady until my lips could reach it.

'There's a spring nearby,' she said. 'Izvor: the name of this place. The water is sweet. Drink.'

I sipped, and let the cool liquid trickle down my throat, easing the dryness. It stung, but I drank some more, and this time it went down more easily.

'Can you speak?' asked Sister Vittoria.

I nodded. 'Thank you,' I whispered.

She seemed to be making up her mind about something. 'What is your name?' she asked, after another silence.

'My name.' I hesitated. My senses were returning, and I could feel that I was naked beneath the sheet. There would be no secrets here.

'I'm Onoria.' I caught my breath. My voice felt like a dull blade. 'Onoria Ormani.'

To my surprise she took my hand and held it gently. Her skin was hard and cool. 'You were lucky, Onoria Ormani. The lie you told was not a lie after all. I do have a little skill with healing. My father was a doctor of medicine. When I was with the order in Venice I worked in the infirmary there. Sometimes when our fleet had fought with the Turk, when the ships returned, the wounded sailors from our parish might be brought to us. Twice lucky, really, because your wound . . . It was a spear?' I nodded. 'The spear went cleanly through the meat of your thigh. An inch higher . . .' She winced. 'A finger's width to the left or right, and the great artery of your leg would have been cut. You'd have been dead in two minutes. As it is, you've lost a lot of blood. Had you been a big man, perhaps you could have afforded that. But that isn't the case, is it?'

'Oh,' I said. I lay back and closed my eyes. 'Sister, I wanted you to save me. But now that I find myself alive, like this . . . It would have been better if I'd let myself die there on the field.'

'Why?' Sister Vittoria let go of my hand. She pulled back the sheet, and my heart jumped in alarm to see my nakedness: my unbound breasts, pale and still streaked red where the bindings had pressed into them; the little swell of my stomach, and below it, the tuft of hair. My left thigh was bandaged up to my groin. I looked so small. 'Why do this? Why deform your body and hide it inside those warlike things? Why would a woman disguise herself as a . . . as a brute?'

'Was I a brute when I came into your church last week?' I asked. I could feel tears start gathering in the corners of my eyes. A woman's habit I had erased: soldiers do not cry. But now the tears were running down my face.

'No, my daughter. No, you were not.'

My chest heaved. No one had called me 'daughter' since that last evening in Pietrodoro. And that had been a long time ago.

'I should leave you to rest,' the nun said. She pulled the covers up over me and, leaning down, wiped away my tears with the sleeve of her habit.

'Please don't!' I hissed. 'I want to tell you. Will you listen, sister? Please listen.'

'You'll tire yourself,' she muttered, but nevertheless she settled herself on the very edge of the narrow bed and took my hand again.

177

I told Sister Vittoria. My story: all of it, from the moment Augusto Ellebori had burst into my bedroom, to when I had turned to find Don Orazio watching me hunt for bustards. She listened, her face betraying nothing, only stopping me when my voice began to break to help me drink. The words poured out of me: my words, my story. My ugly voice. Perhaps it would be my last confession after all, because I could feel myself weakening by the moment, but I had to finish.

'This Marchese del Forese, he mistook you for a boy straight away?' Sister Vittoria asked when I had reached the end.

'He did. But Don Orazio made an honest mistake. It was me who told the lie.'

'You did it to protect yourself. You were a frightened little girl. I don't think God wished you to die.'

'I was not so little, sister. I knew very well that it was wrong. I knew that God asks us to tell the truth. But it was because I was praying. I'd been praying the whole time.'

'To Santa Clara?'

'The Church calls her Clara, but she's Celava, sister. The saint of our village. She looks after things that are lost. And I felt – I knew – that Celava had given me this chance. A chance to live. Is that wrong?'

'God works through his saints, my daughter. I can see that your devotion is honest, and I don't believe anything else matters.'

She smiled for the first time since I had begun my story. It made her face look younger. I studied it now, through a haze of tears. She was in her late forties, and though her features had been shaped by her austere life, by the stillness of contemplation and the sun in the garden where she worked, tumbled like a

178

pebble in a stream until it was all hard, smooth curves, there was a kindness that shone through it, and a hint that perhaps she had never quite left her own youth behind.

'And you've lived all this time. With all those men.' She pursed her lips, but her eyes were laughing.

She gave me something else to drink, and I think it had poppy juice in it, because I slipped almost instantly into a deep, velvety sleep. Pain woke me, and there was Sister Vittoria, changing my bandages. I was shaking, and the sheets were heavy with sweat. The cup appeared at my lips, and I drank and slipped back into the velvet darkness. I had no idea how much time was passing in that way: sleep, waking, pain, the comfort of hands, a voice I couldn't quite hear, then sleep again. When I finally opened my eyes, I found that my head was clear, that my sheets were dry.

'Your fever has broken.' The Mother Superior was watching me through the open door. I wondered how long she had been standing there. 'And your wound is closing well. Good morning . . . my daughter,' she added after a significant pause.

'Good morning, Mother Superior. Thank you. I would have died without your care.'

'That you would. No, don't move!' I was trying to sit up, but she had raised her hands in horror. 'You'll open it up!'

'Sorry.' I lay down again. 'I am not used to being so still.'

'No. Of course you aren't. You have been living as a soldier.'

'You find that a terrible thing. Which is probably true.'

'I do not understand how you could do such a thing. Practise such deception with your whole being. But Sister Vittoria told me how you came to be . . .' She fluttered her fingers at me. 'This.'

'I am a woman now,' I said, smoothing the sheets across the contours of my unfettered body.

'And will you stay a woman?' The Mother Superior shut the door and sat down on a three-legged stool that sat on the floor near the head of the bed. It hadn't been there before. People had been sitting with me while I slept. The thought of it made me want to cry again.

'I . . . I could stay here,' I said, putting words around something that had just come into my head.

The Mother Superior harrumphed. I couldn't tell if she was amused or disgusted. 'Could you, indeed?' she said. Then she smiled. She had the same smooth, weathered features as Sister Vittoria. *They might be sisters*, I thought, and that made me smile too. 'Could you join our order and serve God as a nun? Let me see. You have lived a life of great discipline. You have turned your back on the world that nature intended for you. You have abjured the flesh: you are still a virgin—' I opened my mouth in shock, but she silenced me with a flourish of her hand. 'We had to examine you, girl. Who knows where that spear might have gone? All is well, by the way.'

'Good,' I muttered, uncertain what the news meant to me.

'All of that, on the face of it, might make you seem an ideal candidate for the sisterhood. But you aren't. I have contemplated your story. And I've prayed to God for guidance. Hmm.' She steepled her fingers and propped her chin on their tips. 'You could become a monk.'

'Mother Superior!' I burst out laughing.

'Ah. You find that ridiculous. Why? You've passed yourself off as a man for how long? Ten years? In the very heart of their world. A monastery would be no challenge at all.' She chuckled, then stopped herself abruptly. 'But there's the thing, Donna Onoria. Or Don Onorio. You have a gift: you can make yourself who and what you please. A boy, a man. *Capo* of a lance of cavalry. And another gift: you can hide who you really are. But to serve God as a nun . . .' She took a deep, slow breath. 'To serve God, you cannot hide. You must find who you truly are, the very heartwood of your being, strip yourself of everything else, and as that pure thing, that heartwood, you stand before God. He sees everything, you know.'

'Yes, I know.' I struggled upright in bed, despite the Mother Superior's upraised hands. 'So I couldn't do that? You don't believe I could be pure?'

'Oh, for heaven's sake, be careful with your dressings, girl! I think you have a purity all of your own. It isn't mine, of course, nor Sister Vittoria's. I don't profess to understand it. But I see it.' She stood up and touched the crucifix above my bed. 'What you have is a purity of intent. Ours is a purity of devotion. Do you see the difference, my daughter?'

I did. I saw it very clearly.

'Perhaps I should go back to my company,' I said.

'Your *condottiere* has sent his prayers for your speedy recovery. You seem to be a valued . . . man to them.'

'Has anybody come to see me?' I asked. The thought hadn't occurred to me before, and now I wondered why it hadn't.

'I told that soldier, the one who brought you, that men are utterly forbidden here, and that I made an exception for you only because you were so near death.' She touched her lips with her fingers and raised her eyebrows at me. 'Could it be

181

that you miss your life? Your disguise? Perhaps deception feels more real than the truth?'

'Mother Superior, I have no choice!'

'You don't? You could not live as a woman? The world is a very big place, my daughter.'

I actually laughed. Her suggestion was absurd to me. 'I spend my life with men, Mother Superior! They count women as little above farm animals! And of a good less account than their swords or their horses. I might have lived my whole life as nothing more than a man's goods! I think of my mother, who might have been a teacher at a university if God had made her differently. I shut my eyes and see her butchered by men who, I daresay, barely gave their butchery a second thought. She died as my father's wife, not as . . . not as someone who read Virgil and Ovid and Aristotle. She was a clever woman. She wanted me to be clever too, to be more than just a wife, to have more than she had, even if I had to keep it all in my head. And if I had not been wayward and spoilt . . . No, I did learn. I learnt from her death, that power will always triumph over gentleness. That there is no safety for us.'

The nun had listened to my outburst with a tiny smile lifting the corner of her mouth. 'There is safety in the shelter of God,' she said calmly.

'It was the men of my company that gave you shelter from the Turk,' I reminded her. 'Forgive me,' I added hastily, as a wave of guilt washed over me. But the nun merely chuckled.

'Oh, you are right, you are right. And we are thankful. But you have not answered my question. Could you not live as a woman again? Perhaps I should be clearer. Not *should* you, but *could* you?'

'I come from a noble family. Women of my station marry a man, or they marry God. Without a dowry – and I would not marry, not even if my life were at stake – what would I become? What life waits for a woman alone, with no family, no name? One thing alone suggests itself: to turn to whoring, but my looks' – I turned my scarred face into the light – 'such as they ever might have been, are ruined.' I grinned joylessly. 'But there are men who will pay for a spoilt face. And a woman who looks like a man. So, there is my new life: a whore for men of what one might call slanted tastes.'

If I had hoped to shock the nun, I failed. 'You think so little of yourself?' she asked.

'I think little of Onoria Ormani. I wouldn't give *this*' – I snapped my fingers – 'for her prospects. But Onorio Celavini? Caposquadra Onorio? He has a man's prospects. He can stride through the world and it will stand aside for him as he passes.' I had to ease myself back against the pillow: the nun's questions had stirred up emotions and thoughts I had spent years trying to avoid. 'I wish it weren't so, Mother Superior. But I was robbed of the life that by rights I should have lived. It wasn't me who upset the balance of nature. You said something about intent. You're right – what else do I have? My life is poised on the edge of disaster. I'm like an artilleryman who must fire his mortar by lighting both the fuse on his bomb and in his gun. The touchhole must be lit, then he must grit his teeth and lean into the mortar's jaws with his match, knowing that if he has cut his fuse too short, he will be blasted to rags in an instant. I take that risk with every breath God gives me, but I intend to stay alive, even if I am an offence to the proper order of things. I would like it to be otherwise, believe me.'

'I do, my daughter. It must be hard to have saved your life at the cost of your nature.'

'I want to live because they tried to take my life from me! Theirs is the offence!' I croaked. The conversation was taking a toll on me. My heart was pounding, and my eyes were stinging. 'Those men killed my mother, my father, my brother, our people, and yet mine is the offence, because I wear breeches and a sword and live a life of . . . of honour?'

The nun sighed. 'Tell me one thing, Onoria. What is it that drives you, truly? Is it anger? Is it the desire for revenge? Because, my daughter, I am not a scholar like your mother, but I have studied as much as my poor intellect has allowed. The Book of Deuteronomy tells me that God forbids a man to dress as a woman, and a woman to dress like a man. But if you hadn't practised that deception, you would have condemned yourself to death, and that is the greater sin. Perhaps this is sophistry. I am not wise enough to know. But I do know this: God reserves vengeance for himself, and himself alone. Do not use a lesser sin to mask a greater one.' She patted my hand. 'I've tired you. I had not fully understood your dilemma, Onoria. Plainly, I still don't. You confuse me. I'm a dull old woman living an exceedingly dull life. I am not used to confusion.'

'I would like to stay here,' I whispered. 'I cannot tell you how much I wish that I could.'

'I know, my daughter. But you belong to the world.' She smiled. 'Or is it the other way around? Now, sleep. It will give you back your strength. You of all people need to be strong.'

* * *

The nuns had washed and repaired my clothes. I found them waiting for me one morning when I came back to my cell after hobbling around the lovely little garden behind the convent. I had been on my feet for two days, though at first I could do nothing but walk out into the cloister and back to my bed. There didn't seem to be any serious damage to my thigh. It had been a small miracle, Sister Vittoria said, the spear had missed both my stockings and my breeches, which must have ridden up as I stood in the saddle, and there were no pieces of dirty cloth in the wound. So, while the hole in my thigh was still leaking yellowish fluid into the bandages, it was giving me an honest pain, like a freshly cut finger, and not the dizzy heat of infection. One of the sisters had brought me an old crutch, and another had sewn me a rough shift out of old bedlinen, not much more than a long white sack with wide arms and a hole for my head which, when I pulled it on, looked a little like a shroud. That was how we buried men in the company: wrapped in white cloth. I had been wondering how many men had been buried after the skirmish and, looking down at myself, naked beneath the crude drapery, I felt another pang of the guilt that had been growing in me since my fever had broken. That day I limped around the cloister until my leg ached, then rested on the single stone bench, breathing in the scent of the rose bush that grew in the centre of the gravel square, then limped again. The nuns – there were five of them, apart from the Mother Superior and Sister Vittoria – came and went on their daily errands or followed the fixed ritual of the holy hours. At first, they had found me interesting, but that place moved to its own inexorable rhythm, and had little time for novelty. The convent

185

was not one of those places where daughters of good family are deposited out of convenience, or where girls from questionable families are locked away to protect them from the appetites of men. It was a place, so Sister Vittoria told me one day as she was changing my bandages, where nuns from several other convents down the coast had come after their own houses had been overrun by the Turkish advance. There was no one here without a true vocation. I liked the fact that I could be so easily ignored, even though every sister knew my story by now. I felt invisible yet cared for, like the ghost of someone whose family misses them, and is glad when they hear footsteps in an upstairs room, or the sudden, soft brush of an unseen robe. It was how I wished I could spend my whole life. But I could not.

I closed the door of my cell and stared at the clothes on the bed, laid out in order, as though they had clothed a corpse that had rotted completely away. My sword looked obscene lying on the nuns' scrubbed linen. I hesitated, then picked up my armoured doublet. It seemed so heavy: a brutish thing that didn't belong in that tiny, pure space. My shirt had been washed and stitched, though the lower quarter was stained a rusty orange. Even the codpiece on my breeches had been cleaned. I felt a pang of guilty revulsion when I imaged the gentle sisters setting diligently to work on it. There, inside, was my copper pissing-tube in its little sleeve. How ridiculous it looked, how foolish my concerns appeared now that I could walk out into the garden and feel the warmth of spring on my unbound skin.

These clothes were Onorio's skin, which he'd sloughed off like a snake. But a snake can leave those papery husks behind and go off into the world all new-made. Onorio would not be given such a blessing. He would have to put his old skin on again and let it shape him into the creature he had, perhaps, thought to escape. Had I really believed that I could?

'I'm so sorry, my daughter.' I jumped, startled, and my hand, of its own accord, reached for the hilt of my sword. Sister Vittoria was standing in the half-open doorway. I pulled my hand away, my face burning with embarrassment.

I yelped. 'You startled me, sister!'

Sister Vittoria pretended not to notice. 'We had word from your colonel this morning. He is taking the company north. I'm afraid, Onoria, that you shall have to leave us.'

'Oh, Holy Virgin,' I breathed, and sat down heavily on the little stool. 'I'm not ready.'

'I understand. You have found peace here.'

'Yes, I have,' I said, and began to cry, properly, unashamed.

'But you have only put your life to one side, my dear.' She nodded towards the sword on the bed. 'The habits of the flesh are deeply engrained in every one of us. And you, you've made your life, actually crafted it, like a goldsmith who makes a fine statue. Mother Superior told me you thought you might stay here. I should like that very much, if it was possible. People are remade in places like this. They are redeemed. God takes the gold, melts it in His crucible and recasts it into something new. But you, my daughter, you are both statue and sculptor. You are your own creator. You will have to find redemption yourself.'

'Will I, sister?' I wiped my face on the rough linen of my shroud tunic. 'Do you think I can?'

'If it is in your power to make a fragile young woman into a man of war, I imagine you can do anything. But . . .'

She paused and ran her fingers down the beads of the rosary around her neck.

'What is it?' I asked.

'Don't mistake yourself for God. You – your Onorio – is a work of art. But even the greatest artist is herself created. Never forget that.'

When she had gone, I knelt and prayed for guidance to God, the Holy Virgin and Santa Celava. But in that place where they should, by rights, have been close by, I felt completely alone. So, very slowly and painfully, I dressed myself. Standing naked on the cold tiled floor, I pulled on the man's underwear that I had tailored myself so that they fit tight across my hips, with the wide slit I had cut and hemmed from front to back. Then the stockings. If I had had a mirror, if I could have seen myself, I'd have still seen a woman. I lifted my arms and stretched, feeling my breasts lift, feeling the life there, a life that was and was not mine. Then I bound them, and tied myself into the heavy, bulging skin of Onorio Celavini.

CHAPTER FOURTEEN

We were on our way to Sicily, where a great Christian army was being assembled. While I had lain in the convent, an Ottoman fleet, a vast armada of two hundred or more ships, had invaded the island of Malta and laid siege to the fortresses of the Knights Hospitaller. A messenger had brought Don Orazio a letter from an old friend of his, the *condottiere* Ascanio della Corgna, inviting him to join the army that Don García de Toledo, the viceroy of Sicily, was gathering for the relief of the island. The whole of Christendom was in a panic, so I learnt, because if Malta fell, the Sultan would have the Mediterranean Sea at his disposal, and was already planning to invade Italy and beyond. I was most interested because Ascanio della Corgna was someone I had heard of for most of my life, being at that time the most famous swordsman in Italy. My father had told me stories of a great duel the man had fought in Bologna many years before I was born, and now perhaps I would meet him.

These were the thoughts of Onorio Celavini as I rode down through Italy, past Ravenna, across the mountains to Rome and into Campagna. I had healed. My skin was my own again. Perhaps because the freedom I had found in the convent had been so blissful, so tempting, I wrapped myself even more tightly in manhood, and after only a little while I began to tell myself that my experience among the good sisters had been terrible, a violation, that they had flayed poor Onorio and I had been forced to grow a fresh skin, as if Ovid had written the story of wretched Marsyas in reverse. That had been one of my most hated passages in the *Metamorphoses*, though Bartolomeo had told me I should like it, because boys liked gruesome things. I had never been able to convince him that I did not want to be a boy, that I wasn't trying to go through my own metamorphosis, but simply to be as free as he was, though he squandered his freedom in books and candlelight. And now I was growing more like one of Ovid's subjects with every year that passed.

The company had welcomed me back with wine and roasted flesh, and I had allowed myself to celebrate, or at least to pretend, because drunkenness was as terrifying to me as a poisoned well. How could I indulge in something that, as I saw almost daily, stripped people of their defences, their natural reserve, and released what men like to think of as their true selves to brawl and rut like beasts? My men were forever trying to get me drunk. It was a good-natured game, good-natured as all things are until men cross their particular line. I had long ago demonstrated that I wouldn't allow their sport to go past a certain point, by beating one drunken idiot around the camp with the flat of my sword. I suspect the men, though they feared me, wanted to see what would happen if they succeeded, like those fellows who insist on smoking their pipes next to barrels of gunpowder.

We had lost three men in the skirmish with the Ottomans: two from my lance, one from Gentile's; Gentile himself had broken his arm. He was sure I had saved him from the *effendi* and greeted me with actual tears. No one else had been seriously hurt. Paolo had clearly embroidered the story of my exploits in the battle, because I returned to find my reputation higher than it had been before I had been wounded. But something was different. I took Paolo aside and made him swear many ferocious oaths that he had said nothing about my injury. The poor fellow denied it again and again until I saw that he believed what he said. But Paolo was a man who liked his wine and, though he was always happy in his cups, was the kind of man whose tongue begins to flutter like a pennant in the breeze after he had drunk too much. I wondered what he had said, and to whom. I caught men staring at me, who hastily turned away when I met their eyes. There was a certain kind of laughter that was quickly stifled in my presence. But they also seemed to be somewhat in awe of me, as though I had become even more of an exotic creature.

I decided that Paolo must have talked about my wound. But he plainly hadn't believed the truth that I feared his hand must have told him, because if he had . . . I didn't like to think what would have happened then. There had been a woman from Cremona who had impersonated a man and been a respected *condottiere* a hundred years ago, but she might have been a legend. The Maid of France had not met a good end. Women do command troops from time to time, but only as women, and always queens or nobility. It would be my deception that would put me in danger now, not my sex. But that was not, it seemed, in question. I guessed there was a lot of speculation about my privy regions, and how much, if any, had survived the Turk's spear. If it amused them, so be it. I was amused to know that, though they thought I might be missing something important, none of them had the balls to challenge me about it.

Don Orazio promoted me to man at arms. I still had command of my lance, but now I had responsibility for the company's security. I settled disputes between men that were too petty to drag in front of Don Orazio himself. If we stopped in a village or town, I made sure the men did not cause too much offence, and if one of the locals did anything against us, I was responsible for sorting those problems out as well. I was remaking myself, just as Sister Vittoria had said.

I tried not to think about Sister Vittoria, or the Mother Superior, or the little convent that had smelt of clean stone and damask roses. I made myself forget how I had felt there. What I had been. I made myself forget Onoria, with her slender body that did not need to be hidden, that told its owner things about herself that she had never before tried to understand. I never let my mind linger on the moment I had seen my soldier's clothes on the bed and had thought that perhaps I would tell the sisters to give them to the poor and ask them to sew me a black novice's robe.

'The men respect you a great deal,' Don Orazio had said when he gave me the job. 'They also fear you, which is good. But none of them understand you, and that is excellent. I don't understand you myself, Onorio, but I don't have to. I know I can trust you, and I don't care about anything else.'

You are right: you don't understand me, I thought. *And you never will. But you can trust me, because I can wear your trust like a mail shirt. I can wear it like the striped skin of the snake, that makes it invisible as it lies among the rocks.*

We arrived in Sicily at the beginning of August. I had never been on a ship before and left a trail of my vomit across the Strait of Messina, but so did the rest of the company. The army of Don García was gathered at the western end of the island in an encampment of ten thousand soldiers, carpenters, sailors, farriers, armourers, cooks and camp followers – a sprawling landscape of tents as big as a middle-sized Italian town. There I finally met Don Ascanio della Corgna. He was a hawk-faced man with sunken cheeks and one eyelid sewn shut over an empty socket. Don Orazio must have told him about me because he sought me out one day and we talked for a long time about swordsmanship.

It was only a couple of days later that a man bumped shoulders with me as I walked through the camp with Paolo, discussing two of the men from my lance who were on the verge of blows over a whore. It was a hard bump, and I turned angrily. I recognised the man who had done it. I'd seen him the night before as I made my rounds. He'd been drinking with some men from Gentile Rondoni's lance, boasting loudly and belligerently in a Neapolitan accent.

'No balls,' he said loudly, when I stopped in my tracks. 'No cock either. And you pretend to be a soldier?'

'Do I know you, sir?' I asked. Paolo's hand had gone to his sword, but I stepped in front of him.

'Alexandro de Ricca.' He smirked. He was dressed to the

hilt: apricot silk quilting on his doublet, sleeves slashed into thin ribbons, silver sequins on his cap. 'My lady,' he added.

I burst out laughing. Perhaps it was relief, because this was my worst fear realised, and now it was already past.

'Tell him to show you his cock,' said his companion, who I'd not noticed: a thin, nervous-looking fellow with the unmistakeable silky sheen of a nobleman.

I looked around me. We were on the border between Don Orazio's company and the next, which was the much larger contingent led by Ascanio della Corgna. And indeed, della Corgna's tent was only fifty or so paces away from us. The man himself was sitting with a group of other men, one of whom was Don Orazio. I could tell him by his hat. De Ricca looked shamelessly in their direction.

'If it please you to show me your organ of engenderment, you may go on your way,' he said to me, loudly. We were surrounded by other soldiers, and they had caught on to what was happening. Men were already gathering, others running in all directions to fetch their friends. I had no idea if this de Ricca had any reputation, but I did, and I guessed, by the sudden uproar, that plenty were putting good odds on his chances against me.

'Do you proposition many men like this? Though by the prettiness of your clothes, it wouldn't surprise me,' I said. My mouth was a little dry, but I felt calm. Almost blissfully calm.

'I thought you Tuscans were proud of your balls?' he said, with a little swagger.

There was tittering from our audience. *Palle* was the word for the balls on the Medici coat of arms, and the cry of their supporters. '*Palle! Palle!*' some wag began to chant.

'But why wouldn't you be?' de Ricca went on. 'Tuscans are the greatest sodomites in Christendom! Though a eunuch need not be a somite,' he added. 'Simply a man-woman.'

'You say I am a eunuch, sir?' I asked, politely.

'I do, sir!' He grinned.

'Prove it,' I said.

'It can be proved if you will remove your breeches, sir!'

'Oh, I think it is up to you to prove it. I will not do your work for you. I will not. So, do you still persist in your accusation?'

'I do, indeed!' he crowed.

If I had not spent the last few years abroad, I would perhaps have known that Alexandro de Ricca was, at that time, probably the most famous swordsman in Naples, if not the whole of Campania. I suppose it might have made me pause for another few moments before answering. But only for that long.

'Then you lie, sir,' I said, and gave him back his grin.

'You call me a liar?'

'Your actions are the proof. I am merely the witness. But yes, you are an infamous liar.'

'You'll satisfy my honour with your sword, Signor Eunuch. Or is there nothing of any length, any hardness that you can show me, as I said?'

'You may see my sword whenever you like. Name the time and the place, sir.'

'I think here and now would suit me.' De Ricca glanced towards della Corgna's tent again. Now I understood. He wanted to fight me in front of Italy's most famous duellist. What better way to put more gilding on his reputation?

I blew out my cheeks and shrugged. 'Very well,' I said.

'I'll be your second, Capo,' Paolo said at once.

'Thanks,' I said. I wondered if he knew how the rumours had spread, after all. Still, he was a decent, strong swordsman. 'While we get ready, please fetch Don Orazio. I should make this right with him before it happens.'

'Immediately, Capo,' he said, and pushed away through the growing crowd.

'Do you need to send for anything?' I asked de Ricca. 'A buckler? A dagger?' He ignored me and turned to whisper something to his friend. I felt as if I were standing on a stage with no lines to deliver, so I sighed and leant down to brush some dirt from my knee. I heard a gasp from the crowd, like a wave drawing back from a pebble beach, and looked up to see that de Ricca had drawn his sword and was coming at me.

As chance would have it, I was wearing the German sword with which I had fought Gianbattista Tascha all those years before. Though it was quite short I still carried it sometimes, for sentimental reasons, perhaps, and because a short sword is useful in a crowd, and my job as head of security sometimes put me in those positions. If I'd chosen a longer sword that morning, maybe I wouldn't have been able to draw it in time, or would have got it caught in the scabbard, but as it was it took little more than a flick of my arm and it was out. De Ricca had been too hasty, and that, too, saved me because I twisted away, his thrust went through the cloth of my left sleeve, and our bodies crashed together. I smelt the perfume of expensive civet and last night's wine before ducking under his arm and skipping backwards. That was when I saw that his friend had also drawn, and the two of them were coming at me again, their swords in high guard. My eyes told me in a flash that the friend was the inferior swordsman: something in the tightness of his sinews, the way he held his sword, and I didn't hesitate. Stepping sideways, I feinted, and when he lunged, I parried and let my blade hiss along his, and into his chest. He staggered back, a look of bewilderment on his handsome face, and I cut his throat.

It has become quite famous, the duel I fought in Sicily. I won't dwell on it. For me, once I had killed de Ricca's companion, whose name had been Buenaventura de Consillariis – ironic, as he clearly wasn't prone to good luck – I was able to fight de Ricca himself as though it was nothing more than a sparring match with my father in Pietrodoro. It was the release, I suppose: the worst thing that could have happened to my living self – almost the worst – had happened, and I had survived. But whatever the reason, my feet, my body, my arms all moved with magical ease, like the illustrations in my father's book come to life. People who care about such things still remark on how my footwork was a perfect example of the Florentine style as taught by Francesco Altoni. De Ricca was a classical swordsman of the Bolognese school, and so the *cognoscenti* regard ours as a duel between two schools as much as between two people. The real fight, of course, was an invisible one between a man and a woman, though I wonder, if that had been known, whether the whole matter would have been mysteriously forgotten.

Whatever the truth of it, we fought for almost fifteen minutes, which is a terrible length of time in the heat of an August day in Sicily. In the end, it might have been exactly those things which de Ricca had accused me of having lost which were his undoing, because as we duelled, neither of us with any great advantage over the other, his man's pride began to rise, and with it his anger. It is a trait of men, that prideful rage. I have learnt to imitate it very well, but I don't believe I have ever really felt it. But I can see it in others well enough, and I saw it in his overeager movements, the impatience in his steps. As he strutted, I stalked him. Della Corgna was in the crowd, in the front row, standing with Don Orazio, and I knew, I could almost feel, that de Ricca was performing for him, a young gamecock displaying his ferocity to an older one.

He was an excellent swordsman, though, and I felt something like regret when he let his guard slip for the blink of a dry eye and I slashed the point of my sword across the upper part of his left arm. He cursed, staggered back, and circled me, carefully, knowing he was bleeding – not a terrible wound, but in that heat it would drain him quickly. He took the guard of the unicorn. I decided I needed to tire him, stepped in for a thrust, but instead of parrying he countered and the tip of his blade flashed past my eyes. I felt a sting on the side of my head and a warm wetness on my neck. He grinned. His sword came up again, inviting an attack, which I made, watching his eyes, knowing they were seeing my blood. I could feel his sudden eagerness, and showed him what he wanted to see, my chest left exposed by a mistimed thrust. He lunged across my blade, I turned my wrist, sent his arm wide, and with a perfect, stiff-legged stance, knees straight like one of Altoni's own drawings, I lunged and thrust my sword into his ribcage up to the guard. I felt a great shiver go through him: it travelled into my hand through the steel. He was dead long before I stepped back and let him fall to the ground.

When we finally took ship for Malta three weeks later, I was still something of a celebrity. As it turned out, de Consillariis had been a man with a dark reputation: a minor aristocrat from the countryside behind Palermo, he had killed several men and, so it was rumoured, his first wife, whom he suspected of having an affair with a servant. Both de Consillariis and de Ricca had been famous in their way, and that fame passed to me, as though it had been a contagion of the blood. No one whispered any more as I walked past or glanced down between my legs to see what my codpiece might be hiding. 'Eunuchs don't fight like that,' I overheard someone say. 'He certainly has something left down there.' But such things were never said to my face. Even Ascanio della Corgna seemed impressed, which I counted as a great compliment. Just before we had set sail for Malta, he and Don Orazio had staged a mock duel with wooden swords to keep the men amused, and I had seen just how well he deserved his reputation. Not that my commander was far behind the master in skill, and after it was over, he told me that he had been della Corgna's second in a famous duel near Perugia.

'Ascanio told me he'd like to fight you,' he said, and when I blinked, had laughed. 'In friendship, Onorio. I would take that as a compliment. He'd kill you, of course, in a real fight.'

'I suppose he would,' I said. 'But I'm younger. And I have both eyes.'

'The arrogance of youth!' Don Orazio said.

'God keep me from being arrogant. I don't want to make a life of this,' I told him. 'Let me do my fighting at the head of my lance.' But that wasn't true. In my heart I remembered the Mother Superior's words to me and swallowed the guilt that rose like bile in my throat.

'I think you'd probably kill me, though,' Don Orazio muttered, but I pretended I hadn't heard.

What we did on Malta has been written about many times, and I will not dwell on it. Besides, after all the waiting, it was over very quickly. We landed, Don Ascanio led us in a charge against the Ottoman army, who were already tired of the siege and beginning to retreat. It was a great victory and a dreadful massacre. When the survivors sailed away, they left thousands of bodies. After that, we were stuck on a ruined island peopled, it seemed, mainly by the dead. I couldn't wait to leave, and we soon did. Don Orazio made an agreement to fight for the Habsburgs again, this time in Hungary. We arrived too late for the Siege of Szigetvár, though we saw some fighting with Turkish border raiders. I hoped our journeying would take us past the little convent on the coast, but we never went near there again. The next year we took ship to Spain and then to the Low Countries, where we fought with the Duke of Alba against the Protestants there, who were in open revolt against the Spanish crown. We stayed in that damp, grey country for three years. There were battles, but the men we lost – and we lost many – fell mostly to disease. Agues, winter fevers, consumption. Paolo coughed up his life in a Brussels hospital.

I came to dread the winters, with their snow and frozen rivers. Though we were losing men, we were gaining more, and before the Battle of Jemmingen the company was twice as big as it had been in Malta. Don Orazio promoted me again. I had been a captain, in charge of my own *famiglia* of cavalry, two hundred men under my command; now I was constable, second in command of the company. This suited me: I could hide behind my rank and, anyway, I enjoyed the humdrum stuff of keeping a little army fed, housed and paid. I was imposing order on things. I was maintaining balance.

Then, in 1570, the Holy League came together to fight the Turks, who had captured Cyprus. We turned our backs on the flat, dreary north and marched down through France into warmth. My joy when I saw the first olive tree is something I will never forget. A few months later we were back on Sicily. Ascanio della Corgna was there, and when we sailed out against the Ottoman fleet that was massing off the coast of Greece, our galleys were next to his in the first line.

Lepanto. I will never escape it. A battle fought at sea, on lurching ships. We won. I lived. It was not the biggest battle I ever fought in, or the bloodiest, but there was a special horror to it. Men died in every way that a man may die: from water, steel, fire. Men died of fever as we rowed towards the enemy, and of exhaustion as they strained at the oars. Our ranks were filled with amateurs, high-born men who had joined for glory, but knew nothing at all of war: men in armour that it would have taken me a lifetime of fighting to pay for. And the Turks were not the raiders we had fought in Croatia and Hungary. They were the cream of the Sultan's troops. Men on our ships heard the drumming and skirling of their musicians and puked in terror. But after all that, we won. We sailed back to Sicily. In Messina, while we were waiting to cross over to the mainland, Don Orazio announced that he was retiring to his lands. We would go to Rome and he would pay off the men and dissolve the company. The *colonnello* recommended me to a friend of his, a *condottiere* from Mantua, and I joined him as constable. We went back to Flanders, and laid siege to Alkmaar and Leiden. It was at Leiden that I received a letter from Don Orazio, who was in Rome. There was talk of the new pope resurrecting the Holy League, and the *colonnello* had gone to petition for leadership. He wanted me at his side. I was heartily sick of Flanders, and I resigned my post and rode south.

I found him in the palazzo of his brother the cardinal. Don Orazio had caught a cold riding south from Florence through a rainy November. 'I just need to rest,' he told me when I arrived. 'This is a good opportunity for you. You'd make a good *colonnello*, Onorio. We've known each other for . . . how long is it now?'

'Twenty years,' I said, and the number seemed extraordinary to me.

'A lifetime. And you are still as much of a locked book as you were when I first met you. Do you remember that day?'

'Of course.'

'When I've shaken off this bloody cold, I'll help you gather your own company. Men will follow you, Onorio. A good leader has secrets. I'll tell you a few of mine when I'm better. I owe you that, at least. So, goodnight, Onorio. I'll see you tomorrow.'

Two days later, Don Orazio died in his sleep.

CHAPTER FIFTEEN

Rain was drifting in thick, grey cobwebs out of the mountains beyond Fiesole, and I was soaked to the bone as I rode through the Porta al Prato and into Florence in the early afternoon of a January day. I had no real idea what time it was, but as I rode across the muddy open space inside the walls and into the Via della Scala, it became unpleasantly obvious that I had missed lunch. People were trudging about: the better off wrapped in cloaks, the poorer ones in bits of oilcloth or blankets. Everything was dull – even the painted Virgins in their wall niches seemed to have swapped their aquamarine cloaks for slate grey. The air smelt strongly of mildewed straw. I had never been to Florence before in my life, though I had heard about it countless times from my mother and father. Florence was the heart of everything good in the world, everything noble and rich and clever. The Ormanis had come from here; they, too, had been noble and rich. The city wasn't making a good impression so far, though.

A bedraggled woman near the steps of San Lorenzo was holding a tray heaped with rushes, through which threads of steam rose enticingly. 'Carp tortes,' she croaked as I passed, so I dropped a coin into her hand, and waited as she rummaged beneath the rushes and handed up two almost hot pies. I ate quickly as I rode down busier streets towards the Duomo, licking my fingers and cursing as I saw that buttery flakes of pastry were melting into my cloak. I wanted to make at least a reasonably good impression, after all, and I had almost arrived at my destination.

Being back in Tuscany was still strange to me. We had ridden up the Via Francigena alongside the covered wagon carrying Don Orazio's body, through Viterbo, past Lake Bolsena and across the high country beyond Acquapendente. My companions were my second in command Lorenzo Guarini, Gentile Rondoni, two other *capos* and six men, most of them from Don Orazio's own lance. One day we had ridden over a wooded ridge and I was suddenly looking down into the country where I had been born. We dropped down into the long, wide valley towards the fang of Radicofani. We stayed there for a night, after we'd ridden past the place where I had fought and killed Gianbattista Tascha. The next morning, I woke feeling ill. Perhaps it was the vile food of the inn where we were staying, but I mounted my horse with a heavy sense of dread as well as a heaving stomach. We hadn't had good weather for our journey, but that day the sky was blue, and the air was like crystal. The dark bulk of Monte Amiata, which I had been staring at for two days now, passed slowly on our left. The road rose and fell across the brown hills and limestone gullies of the Val d'Orcia. This was the golden country I had looked down on, that I had dreamt of soaring above, when I was a girl. It wasn't golden now, but dun-coloured and muddy, yet still I knew that I was tracing paths that I had once traced with the tip of my finger, eyes screwed up against the sun. The laden wagon trundled on, pulled by two long-suffering oxen. We stopped for lunch, even though I told my companions I would rather push on to Bagno Vignoni. I refused the evil-smelling salami from the inn, and sipped on watered wine as I waited for the others to finish. Soon enough, they did. We crested another ridge and, as one of the long arms of the mountain drifted behind us, I saw it.

High up. That was how I remembered Pietrodoro. High up, on a crag of honey-coloured stone that, below the church at the tip of the village, dropped sheer into terraced slopes of olives. Had I really thought I could keep my eyes from it? The sun was bright and starting to sink towards the top of the mountain. I rode along with my eyes on the track, but how can we resist our dreams? So I looked up. Of course, I looked up, into the sun, and saw it. A golden smear, a brush stroke, a fleck of loose gilding – nothing more.

Perhaps I thought that it hadn't been real after all. Perhaps I thought I really had dreamt it. I looked away, and back again, and it was still there. *Just a village*, I told myself. *I never lived there*. It was true: I understood, with a lurch of the bad food in my guts, that Onorio Celavini had never lived in Pietrodoro. I had to lean forward and rest my head on my horse's neck.

'What's wrong, Condottiere?' Lorenzo asked me.

'Nothing. I was . . . I was thinking about the *colonnello*. He made me who I am, you know. We would ride through country like this – poor, bad soil; mean little villages – and he'd say to me: *This is the kind of place where soldiers come from, Onorio. They don't come back to them, though.*'

'Sounds like the *colonnello*, all right,' Lorenzo agreed. 'We rode right past my parents' farm once—'

'I remember that.'

'And he made some comment or other. He was right, though. I'll go back, stay for a year. Find some girl, knock her up, and *woof!* I'll be off, looking for another company to join.'

'The *colonnello*'s going home,' I pointed out.

'The *colonnello* is dead, Condottiere.'

We rode on, and I didn't look back. That night we stopped at the pilgrim hostelry in Bagno Vignoni. The landlord insisted on welcoming the body of a hero of Lepanto by killing a pig and sending a boy to the church to have the bells rung. Later, as we were eating – a far better meal than the night before, but my gut was still unsettled – the landlord, who spoke in a thick dialect which, with a shock, I recognised, because it was almost the same as that of Pietrodoro, asked us if we'd had any trouble on the road. I said we had not, that I thought Duke Cosimo kept the peace in these parts.

'Ah, the Grand Duke, God keep him,' the landlord said. I detected a less than enthusiastic tone in his voice and told him so in a friendly way. Over the years I had lost my own accent and spoke like what I was: an officer in command of men from all corners of Italy and beyond. I would have passed for a gentleman in Milan or Palermo. A foreigner, anyway, to this fellow. He sighed and poured us all some more of his best wine – 'The pilgrims don't get this,' he'd assured us, though it wasn't much good – before leaning back in his chair and scratching his round belly.

'Duke Cosimo. Yes, we're all his subjects now. All Tuscans together. And that's lovely. I'm a Tuscan man to the marrow in my bones. But Duke Cosimo is in Florence, and all these nice laws of his, they flutter down here like tired swallows and expect everyone to magically follow them, just because they smell like Florence and have the Medici balls on the seal.'

'No great love for Florence, then?'

'Were you at Scannagallo?' the landlord asked, his eyes suddenly narrowed.

'Scannagallo? In 1554? I was twelve,' I said.

'Of course, you would have been.' We all laughed. 'Well, before Scannagallo we were part of the Sienese Republic down here. A lot of us remember that.'

'And that still causes trouble?'

'It wasn't so long ago.'

'I suppose not.' I could have told him that my father had fought in that battle on the side of Florence, and so had the man whose body was currently resting in the landlord's barn. Instead I said, 'I thought the last of the Sienese surrendered to the Duchy a long time ago. 1559, wasn't it, at Montepulciano?'

'Ah, but there are some who haven't.'

'Haven't surrendered?'

'I won't say that. Who haven't lost hope in the Sienese cause, more like.'

'You one of them?' asked Lorenzo bluntly, waving a well-picked pork rib at him.

'Me, sir? Holy Virgin, no! I'm as good a subject as Duke Cosimo could wish for. You don't sound like a man from these parts,' he said to me. 'I'm a good judge of voices – I hear them from all over Christendom here. I'd say you're from . . . don't tell me! Padua!'

'I'm from Mantua,' said Lorenzo disgustedly. 'He doesn't sound anything like a Paduan. Where are you from anyway, Condottiere? I thought you were from Orvieto.'

'Close enough,' I said.

'Oh, well. You don't sound like an Orvietan either.' The landlord sniffed. 'As I was saying, if you *were* from these parts you'd know of the great families – the Aldobrandeschi, the Piccolomini, the Capacci . . .'

'You don't have to be from Tuscany to have heard of the Aldobrandeschi,' I pointed out.

'No, indeed. But as I was saying, there are some from those families, younger sons mostly, I should say, who won't bow their neck to the Medici yoke. Their words, not mine,' he added hastily, holding up a finger. 'Wild types. They take to banditry from time to time. There's a band of them who live up on the other side of the mountain, and they come down here sometimes if a rich mule train is coming through.'

'And the duke does nothing?' I said. There was an uncomfortable feeling building inside me. Those names: Capacci. My mother had been a Capacci.

'He sent a company of gendarmes a couple of years ago. They chased the boys around for a bit, then gave up.'

'Good country for bandits,' said Lorenzo. 'They'd be fools to come near us, though.'

'They won't do that.' The landlord chuckled. 'This time of year they stay in their fortress over on the Maremma side, those that don't go back to their own homes.'

'Sensible of them.' Lorenzo took out a silver toothpick he had taken from the body of a Turkish lord on Malta and began to rid himself of pork fibres.

'They'd have been looking down at you passing by, though,' said the landlord.

I bet you tell the pilgrims all sorts of stories, I thought. *Probably hire out guards too, for a hefty price.*

'Oh, yes?' I said aloud.

'You rode almost beneath one of their strongholds. I'm sure you noticed it. Little village on its own spur of Amiata. Like the prow of a ship. Pietrodoro it's called, because of the big streak of golden stone which you can see from miles away.'

My stomach almost turned itself inside out. I swallowed hard. 'Really,' I said.

'Oho, yes! They're a bad lot up there. Not all of them. But the family that owns the village, the Ellebori? Old Lodovigo—'

'I'm off to the privy,' I interrupted, standing up so hastily that I knocked the last of my meat off its trencher.

'Gut's been bothering him,' I heard Lorenzo explain as I left.

I could feel the mountain behind me as I rushed outside. The night was clear and cold, the stars as bright and unblinking as sequins on a funeral pall. The air settled me almost at once. I was expert in mastering my emotions, after all. But although anyone coming upon me would have found me completely calm, I was roiling inside. I went to the barn. Candles were burning on long sticks at the head and the foot of the wagon-hearse. One of the men was keeping vigil.

'I'll take over,' I said. 'Go and get some food. The wine's bad, but the landlord has a heavy hand tonight.'

'Thanks, Condottiere!' he said, and trotted off without a backward glance.

I sat down on the stool the soldier had left. It was frigid, but I thought my nose was catching a faint smell of decay. I hoped the cardinal's plumber had done a good job sealing the coffin as we had at least another week on the road. It wasn't Don Orazio in there, I knew. Our mortal bodies are but vessels for the soul – nothing more. I tried to find some comfort in that. But what was a soul, anyway? Something like air, that lived inside the body? In the heart, some said, or in the head. Perhaps. I'd seen inside men's bodies and skulls. A pig's heart does not look so different from a man's, though the Church tells us that animals have no souls. For myself, I wondered if it might be something different, but then again, I was made differently from other people. Because in a way, Onorio was my soul when I was out in the world, and Onoria took up the role when I was safe and alone. Both a part of me, and yet different. Onorio was better: an ideal. The Church would have something to say about that, all right: pure blasphemy.

Whatever the truth, and it was a truth that I don't think even the greatest philosopher could deduce, the mention of Lodovigo Ellebori's name had turned the soul within me colder than the air outside. Lodovigo – still alive. It didn't seem possible. But then I forced myself to think. He hadn't been much older than my father when . . . when it had happened. My father had been, what? Forty years old? Dear God. That meant that Lodovigo might not even be sixty. An old man, certainly, but not a dotard. I thought about what the landlord had said – *the family that owns the village* – and a picture formed in my mind: Lodovigo

Ellebori, whose face I could not bring myself to remember, even now, squatting in the centre of Pietrodoro and looking down at those rolling, golden lands I had so loved, directing his malevolence here and there, wherever his will took it, until it was all grimed and foul with his evil. The next day, I knew, we would be moving into a wider landscape, the flat country I had stumbled through with my bow and arrow. I'd been dying then, perhaps. The man in the coffin had saved a little girl, and he'd created someone else, without ever knowing. Now we were back here again, and one of us was a corpse. I couldn't help wondering if it was fair that it should be this way round.

I sat and prayed for the soul of Don Orazio for hours. But I couldn't help thinking about Lodovigo, even though I tried not to. It was only when I began to pray to Santa Celava that my pain began to recede. The hermit, the hidden one: she'd looked down on this country too. Had she sent the *colonnello* to find me, old finder of lost things? 'Dear one, keep me hidden now,' I whispered, because, despite everything, I was a little girl again, starving, wounded, alone. Then Lorenzo, drunk but still dutiful, came to find me, and I was Onorio. Not hiding, but hidden.

I was glad when we inched our way out of those lands.

We came to Florence by a roundabout way, because Don Orazio had asked that his body lie for a day and a night in the chapel of his ancestral home. Castelnuovo Valdarno was a gnarled old castle with a few half-hearted modern embellishments in the farmland between Empoli and Florence. The whole of the countryside seemed to have turned out to pay their respects. It was a loud and lavish homecoming, and I knew that my old captain had looked forward to a day like this for many years. What a trick Fortuna had played on him, I thought, as I watched his coffin welcomed by his own people, while the man himself was far, far away, beyond the reach of all worldly emotions.

And here I was, in Florence at last, riding through a grey, dismal city with crumbs on my cloak. Our little procession turned into Via de' Tornabuoni. The tower of the Palazzo Vecchio was there, rising over the rooftops, not very far away. I recognised it from a painting that had once hung in my parents' house. Somehow, I'd thought everything would be bigger, the city itself and its buildings. It had all the people I had imagined, though, and more. Even in the rain, the street was thronged: black-robed lawyers, priests, merchants, all milling about, all on their way to somewhere else, somewhere dry, but negotiating chance encounters with friends or colleagues, debtors or adversaries.

The church of Santa Trinita, where the del Forese family had buried their dead for centuries, was in a piazza at the end of the street. Beyond, a bridge spanned the river. We were met by a priest, who sent to fetch some pallbearers. We waited for half an hour in the rain until they arrived. The coffin was borne with much wheezing and muttering into the church, and set down in the del Forese chapel. After all the pageantry of our journey through Tuscany, our grand entry into Florence had been so muted that we might as well have been invisible. We made arrangements to stay at the spartan hostel connected to the church, which we found ourselves sharing with a small party of Vallumbrosan monks.

The funeral was that night. I had been frantically coordinating it by letter with Don Orazio's quartermaster, who had come to Florence ahead of us. Lorenzo and I had brought our best armour, and we helped each other with buckles and laces as the monks watched disapprovingly from a distance. Then I went and supervised the moving of the coffin into position before the altar, where a grand *baldacchino* of gilded wood draped in black cloth, obviously brought out for the best funerals, had been erected. The side chapels had all been hidden by black cloths, and boys were hurrying around, setting up great banks of candles. The quartermaster, a Florentine of noble birth, was checking lists, and jogging up and down the aisle. Night was falling outside. The candles were lit, and the mourners began to arrive. Almost all men, many holding themselves like soldiers, all wearing that curious loose garment like a Roman toga that the quality of Florence had adopted because they believe it lends them the dignity of the ancient republic, though it makes them look like furtive nightwatchmen. I knew there were lofty and important people here; I'd looked at the quartermaster's list: Strozzi, Petruzzi, Ricci, Capponi, Pucci, Frescobaldi. I recognised no one, of course. Don Orazio was being buried by strangers.

We stood, Don Orazio's men, as an honour guard while the priest gave the service, hands on the hilts of our swords. It was over too fast. I was still remembering the first time I had met him as the coffin was being heaved into its niche in the del Forese chapel wall and the masons were mortaring the carved slab into place.

'What will you do now?' I turned around. A man, one of the noble mourners, swathed in his odd toga, was examining me with friendly curiosity. 'You were his second in command, were you not?'

'I left Don Orazio's service nearly five years ago,' I said. 'Though we fought together on Malta and at Lepanto. I owed him a great deal. He was going to sponsor me with my own company. I had gone to Rome to discuss it with him when he died. It seemed fitting that I should accompany him on his final campaign.'

'That's admirably loyal of you, Condottiere Celavini.' The man was quite serious. He had a long, pale face and small, piercing eyes. 'And will you lead his company now?'

'If I knew with whom I have the pleasure of speaking?' I bowed politely.

'Antonio Serguidi,' he said. 'I am secretary to His Highness the Grand Duke.'

'I am honoured, Signor Secretary No, Don Orazio's company has been dissolved. My last contract expired two months ago. I am a *condottiere* without men. I am . . . free.'

'What will be next for you?' Serguidi narrowed his eyes.

I shrugged again. 'To be honest, signore, I don't really know. There is fighting in France, and I am a soldier. But for the moment, I'm enjoying my freedom. I may pass a day or two in your famous city before I leave.'

'And you are welcome. A day or two, eh? Such a brief visit? Unless—' Serguidi folded his arms. 'How long have you been soldiering, Celavini?'

'Since I was fourteen and smooth-faced, sir.'

'Still smooth-faced.' Serguidi gave me a sharp look down the length of his narrow, straight nose.

'I've hardly needed to shave since I got this,' I said, touching a finger to my scar. 'All my hair fell out. The surgeon said it was with the shock of it. My scalp recovered; my beard did not.'

'Honestly come by.' Serguidi nodded. 'Where did you get the wound?'

'In Croatia,' I said. It was such an old lie that I barely thought about it.

'Not tired of fighting?'

'Perhaps a little, sir. I'm not the youngest man any more, and I've had my share of knocks.'

'You're no more than twenty-five, surely!'

'Almost thirty-four.'

'A good age for a man to settle down. Are you married?'

'I've barely stayed long enough in one place to take off my boots, let alone marry, Messer Serguidi.'

'No matter. Now then, I have a proposition for you.'

'A proposition?' I blinked in surprise.

'What do you know of Florence, Condottiere Celavini?'

I frowned. 'In terms of . . .'

'You know nothing. That gives you a distinct advantage.' He chuckled.

'Signore?'

'How would you like to join our *Otto di Guardia e Balia*? Our Eight of Security? Other cities have police, of course, but none as good as the *Otto* of Florence.'

'Police?' I laughed politely. 'I'm a cavalryman, Messer Serguidi.'

'So much the better. The *Otto* are based in the duke's palace, and in the Bargello. They themselves are magistrates, but they have at their disposal a force of policemen, the *sbirri*. There is a *capo*, and two *comandantes*, one of whom has just died of . . . Well, he's dead. His position could be yours.'

'Signore, I don't know what to say.'

'But you are interested?'

I opened my mouth to deny it, but something stopped me. I was a mercenary. I existed from contract to contract, and a *condottiere* who did not have a sheaf of job offers tucked away in case of misfortune was, in my experience, a man who did not have to work for a living. 'Perhaps,' I said. 'I'd need to know a great deal more.'

'Plainly! Only a fool would take a job before he knows what it entails. Go to the Bargello tomorrow. Say, at the ninth hour. Ask for Capo Scarfa. He'll explain everything.'

'Very well. Thank you, Signor Secretary, for considering me. I'm very flattered. But you seemed to know that I would be interested.'

'At this stage in my life I can just about admit that I'm a decent judge of men, Condottiere. Besides, if you'd turned me down, I would simply have asked that fellow over there.' He pointed casually at Lorenzo. 'Goodnight, Messer Celavini.'

CHAPTER SIXTEEN

The next morning, I rose early and left my companions snoring away the wine they had drunk at Don Orazio's funeral feast, from which I had slipped away after the first round of toasts. The city was already wide awake, and the sky was a piercing blue, washed clear by weeks of rain. I walked across the bridge close to our hostel, listening to the roar of the brown, swollen Arno as it rushed over the weir just downstream. There were mountains in the distance.

I strolled through the poor neighbourhood on the other side of the river, navigating by the tower of the duke's palace, and back over a bridge lined with shops. There was a fish market just beyond, and then I was walking across the piazza in front of the Signoria itself, between the statues that stood dotted around like pieces of an abandoned game of chess. I decided to ask one of the landsknechts guarding the Signoria where I might find the Bargello. He looked down on me disdainfully but gave me directions in German-laced Italian. After a number of wrong turns, I reached a small piazza. A massive, defiantly grim building jutted into the far corner.

That was the first time I saw the Bargello. It is, to all intents and purposes, a small castle marooned in the middle of the city. The walls are topped with crenellations, and the windows are small and look out threateningly like the many eyes of a spider. All of Italy knows it by reputation: the central prison of Florence and of the whole Duchy of Tuscany. I had spent most of a lifetime in the company of men who had been inside it for one reason or another – none of them good. And I had known at least one man who had never come out again.

I walked past the guards in red and white Medici livery on either side of the main door, glancing up at the crossed keys and shields carved above it. A couple of furtive-looking men were hanging around beneath the cloisters that ran across one side of the courtyard beyond. Another liveried man was coming down the open staircase in front of me.

'I'm looking for Capo Scarfa,' I said.

'Wait with the rest of them,' he said curtly, pointing to the men lurking in the cloister.

'I think he might be expecting me.'

'They all say that. Unless you've come to inform on the fucking Emperor, you can wait there.'

'I'm not an informer,' I said indignantly. 'I was told to come here by Messer Serguidi, the Grand Duke's secretary.'

The man's expression changed. 'Oh, is it court business? Your pardon, signore. We get all sorts of rubbish drifting in and out of here,' he went on brightly, leading me across the

218

courtyard to a heavily studded door. 'Not that . . . Anyway, the *capo* is in here, sir.'

He twisted the ring handle, which clacked ominously, and pushed open the door. 'Capo Scarfa!' he called, to someone I couldn't see. 'Someone to see you. Sent by Messer Serguidi, he says.'

'Send him in, Renzi,' a voice came back. A soldier's voice, roughened from yelling commands. I stepped across the threshold into a large, lugubrious space. The high cross-vaulted ceiling was decorated with dark and faded designs from before the time of the Medicis. Heavy tables of age-blackened oak covered the floor, each one piled with stacks of paper and vellum. The air smelt instantly familiar: men in heavy clothes, their breath, sweat, food, farts. Barracks air. I half expected to recognise the man who was making his way over to me from a table raised up on a small dais at the far end of the room. But Captain Scarfa was a stranger. Of middling height, with a thick waist and thicker arms, his shiny black beard was trimmed close to a face that was beginning to be mottled by the effects of wine. Square jaw, large broken nose, surprisingly pale eyes under heavy brows. A purposeful face, made for use, like an engineer's tool, or like a weapon.

'Are you the man Secretary Serguidi met last night?' Scarfa demanded. His expression of studied boredom was really as sharp as a needle. 'The mercenary?'

'Apparently,' I said.

'Apparently.' He snorted. 'Serguidi thinks you might be a replacement for the late Comandante Milanesi. According to the worthy secretary's memorandum, you were Orazio del

Forese's second in command.' He eyed me sceptically.

'A few years ago, yes,' I said. 'More recently I served Don Pietro della Tamerice in the same capacity.'

'Is that so?' Scarfa looked more interested. 'So you were at Lepanto?'

'I was. And Malta.'

'Hmm. Sit down, sir.' He led me over to his raised desk and waved to one of the chairs in front of it. I sat down, and he took the other. 'Your name is Celavini. What is your family?'

'We are Tuscan. My father's family were local nobility from the hills around Montalcino.' My false past rolled off my tongue as glibly as it always did.

'You, presumably, are a younger son.'

'An only son.'

'Oh, really? But you will not inherit?'

'No, Capo. There is nothing for me to inherit. We lost our lands. And my family lost their lives.'

'Lost?'

'After Scannagallo there were some local upheavals between those loyal to Siena and those who supported Duke Cosimo. My family always stood with Florence. These things run almost as deep as the mountains, Capo. I won't bore you, but I was the only one who escaped. I was very young.'

'Hmm.' Scarfa grunted, evidently satisfied by this. 'So you became a soldier.'

'It was my father's trade. He led his own company; in fact, he fought for Duke Cosimo at Scannagallo, under Il Medeghino. It was my fortune to be taken up by Don Orazio, who found me when I was a fugitive. My father was a master swordsman,

220

and I was my father's favourite pupil, which has always helped me.' I allowed myself to tap the pommel of my sword, almost playfully, but I saw Scarfa's eyes glance down and then up again. 'Yes, I became a soldier, Capo. I believe that's the usual career for a dispossessed gentleman. Though I confess I never considered the Church. Is it too late, do you think?'

To my surprise, Scarfa raised an eyebrow and gave the briefest of grins. 'It's never too late, Condottiere.' He lifted his chin until the point of his beard was aimed at my face. He wrinkled his brow and puffed out his chest. Then he appeared to come to some internal decision. 'Lepanto,' he said. His head came down and he offered his hand. I took it, the captain's rough palm and bulging knuckles almost swallowing mine. He squeezed, and I dutifully squeezed back.

'Lepanto.' Scarfa was growling again. 'Lepanto. Hmm. Can you read and write?'

I blinked. 'Of course.'

'Of course?' Scarfa sounded incredulous. 'Do a lot of soldiers of your acquaintance read, Condottiere?'

'I was taught by my mother. She . . . really did want me to go into the Church.'

'But instead you became a mercenary? That's an interesting change of plan.'

'I had no choice.'

'No.' Scarfa sighed, and there was a moment's silence in the gloomy office. 'No, one rarely does.' He rubbed his nose thoughtfully. 'Wait a minute. Celavini . . . Are you the man who fought that duel in Sicily? What was the man's name . . . Ricci? Riccardini?'

'De Ricca. Yes, that was me.'

'I've read an account of it. Almost as famous a duel as the one Ascanio della Corgna fought outside Bologna.'

'I don't really think that's true.' I smiled politely and looked around at the office of the Guardia. Three of the desks were unoccupied, and at the other two, men in red, white and blue Medici livery were working, one studying a dirty roll of parchment, the other scratching something in a ledger with a quill that had seen happier times.

'Don Onorio.' His attitude had completely changed. 'Listen. You will be used to a different sort of life. This work isn't for an adventurer. A good policeman has few friends and he should want fewer. He must harbour no desire to be loved. There is little enough reward. Look at poor Ginori Milanesi. He lived alone, you see. No one knew he was dead until the holiday was over. I wouldn't wish this life on a man who has seen the grand sweep of things. Lepanto! You'd go mad with boredom, Condottiere.'

'You were a soldier once too, unless I'm mistaken, Capo Scarfa.'

'I suppose it's obvious. Yes, I was. But I haven't seen any action for a long time. Unless you count the time we went chasing after Vico Aldobrandeschi a couple of years ago, in the Maremma.' He sighed at the memory.

I'd only been half listening as I looked around again at the men at their desks, none of whom were remotely interested in me. Everything seemed blurred with boredom. But now Scarfa had my attention. 'You have authority in the south?' I asked. 'To deal with the bandits there?'

'Well, yes. But we didn't have the men or the funds . . .'

'Tell me, Capo. How much does this job pay?'

Captain Scarfa chuckled. 'Twenty lire a month.'

'That's . . . what? Thirty-five *scudi* a year?' I was almost lost for words.

'Dreadful, isn't it? A bank clerk here in Florence makes three times that amount. Of course that isn't really what you would earn. Every fugitive from justice trails a reward, and in the city, only one of the Guardia may collect that reward. There are a lot of fugitives, and it's a small city.'

'So you work not for pay but for plunder?'

'That's more or less it, exactly.' Scarfa grunted. 'But this is Florence. Everyone comes here sooner or later. Bees or flies; shit or honey. Take your pick. But even the worst outlaws can't keep away.'

'Is that really true?'

'It is. This is the centre of Tuscany. The heart. Every man of ambition, every fool with a scheme, every bandit or outlaw noble: there will be something they need or desire here. They come, we catch them, we get paid.'

In the blink of an eye, everything came into sharp focus. I rubbed my scar, trying not to seem too eager. 'Any other inducements?'

'There are two *comandantes*. They split the work between them. Two months on, two months off, which gives a man time for . . .' He shrugged. 'Other pursuits. A house comes with the job – Ginori's house. It's in a dismal neighbourhood. I wouldn't exactly call it an inducement.'

'You've been very honest with me, Capo Scarfa. Soldier to soldier, may I repay the compliment?' I said. Perhaps my mind was already made up, but if I was going to jump into the dark,

I did at least want to make sure I wasn't wearing a blindfold. 'I am tempted, I must admit,' I said. 'But here's the thing, sir: what I know of your *Otto* is that they are the instrument of your Grand Duke's tyranny; that they have spies everywhere in the Duchy and indeed in all of Christendom; that they use deceit, and torture, and assassination, all at the whim of Duke Francesco, who is nothing more than a modern-day Nero. They oppress the many and enforce silence. That the duke rules with fear, and the *Otto* are his instrument. And, of course, they are monstrously corrupt and venal. This is what I know. Will you tell me I am wide of the mark?'

We stood staring at each other for a very long moment. Then Scarfa broke into a wide and genuine grin.

'Well done, sir! I know, I know: you aren't looking for a job, but honestly, you have all the qualifications. You are unreadable, you can fight. You are, if you'll forgive me, unremarkable and yet oddly striking. And you're right, of course, the whole world regards our *Otto* with equal measures of loathing and fear. Men talk about us up and down the length of Italy. In France – even in London. Some of what they say . . . I wouldn't like to play you at cards, sir, your face is like a wax mask. Yes, I'll be frank with you. The *Otto* are reviled by His Excellency's enemies, and he has many enemies.' Scarfa lowered his head and stared at me from under his brows. 'Yes? You know all this. You served with Ascanio della Corgna, who had more than one Florentine exile in his ranks. You fought alongside Don Paolo Giordano: the Romans who are his followers are full of opinions about His Highness. So yes, what you said is true, and then again it is not. It's true that we – the state – use spies. What state doesn't?

It's true we use torture. Again, name me a judiciary anywhere in the world that does not. But compared to Venice, say, we are the gentlest of states. As for Duke Francesco, well, he is a ruler. But I have known this city all my life and I can assure you that Medici rule owes far more to Augustus than to Nero. They bring peace and stability. The *Otto* are their instruments.' He looked up. 'Oh, God's teeth. Excuse me, Don Onorio.'

A man in courtier's clothes was picking his way reluctantly through the maze of tables and desks. 'Capo Scarfa,' he called.

'Messer Antinori,' Scarfa said with studied politeness. 'I expect you've come about your friend Rinaldi.'

'Hardly my friend, Capo. Can we . . .' Antinori glanced at me.

'We can speak in front of Don Onorio. Yes – Rinaldi. It was obviously him. There was no need for torture – just came right out with it like a true gentleman.'

'You wouldn't have tortured him, surely!'

Scarfa laughed humourlessly. 'Of course not. Meanwhile, I've talked to the chief magistrate, and he said he will be fine with Rinaldi just staying away from Florence for a couple of years. He'll have to pay a small forfeit, of course. Do you want to speak to the magistrate?'

'No need. I'll write a report for His Highness and I think he'll agree. It won't be such a dreadful thing to keep Rinaldi locked up for a few more days.'

'Really? I'm having to keep him in fine wine and choice delicacies.'

Antinori chuckled. 'I'll bid you good morning, Capo.'

'Two years' exile,' I remarked when Antinori had gone. 'He can't have done anything too bad.'

'Actually, he killed his niece.'

'He's a murderer?'

'Well, the niece was betrothed, but she started an affair with someone else. As the head of the family . . .' Scarfa made a gesture that spoke of inevitability.

'So murder is not much of a crime here in Florence?'

'Not if you own half the Mugello and go hunting with the Grand Duke's son. If it had been anyone else, they'd certainly have got a longer exile. And a much bigger fine.'

'A fine.'

'A large one. Just because honour demands something, it doesn't mean that there are no consequences.' Scarfa, finally seeing my frown, raised his hands. 'Rinaldi is an absolute shit, to be blunt – I'd ask you not to tell anyone I said that. And the whole city knew his niece, who was beautiful and . . . intelligent.' He rubbed his chin sadly. 'Witty. I expect the boy was to blame. It's a dreadful thing. But if Rinaldi hadn't killed her, someone else would have. That's the way of the world.'

'What about the boy?'

'Vanished. He's either halfway to Milan or they'll find him in a fish trap downstream.'

With that, my mind was finally made up. I stood up and put out my hand. 'I won't keep you any longer, Capo Scarfa. I'd be delighted to take up the position of *comandante* if you're still offering it.'

Scarfa laughed delightedly and pumped my hand. 'Excellent!' he said. 'Welcome! I'll need to . . . No. Come back tomorrow. Your counterpart, Comandante Mondavio, has two more weeks of his shift to complete, which should give you time to put things in order.'

'My things are perfectly in order, Capo,' I said. 'Now, you said something about a house.'

'Ach.' Scarfa looked around the office. 'Poverini!' he shouted. A young man with an ambitious moustache decorating his pleasant face came over. 'Celavini, this is Lugotenente Damiano Poverini. He'll be directly under you. Poverini, this is our new *comandante*, Don Onorio Celavini.'

Poverini grinned. 'Welcome, sir!' he said.

'Do you have time to show him around poor Milanesi's house?'

'Of course! I'm not on patrol until eleven.'

'Until tomorrow, Capo.' I bowed, and Scarfa slapped me on the shoulder.

'Delighted,' he said.

'Likewise.'

I followed Poverini out onto the street. Perhaps I should have been wondering what I had just done, but oddly, I had never been so certain of a decision in my life.

CHAPTER SEVENTEEN

'What happened to Comandante Milanesi?' I asked Poverini.

We were heading east, and he had been pointing out things of interest as we went along: *The Piazza della Signoria is just down there. Over there is the Church of Orsanmichele. This? It's the Mercato Nuovo . . .*

'The gossip is that poor Comandante Milanesi died of neglect. Actually . . .' The lieutenant lowered his voice and looked around himself conspiratorially. 'What nobody is saying is that he killed himself. Dreadful scandal if it got out. But it was the loneliness. A woman turned him down, I understand, and after that he festered there in Borgo Ognissanti for years, until . . .' He rolled his eyes superstitiously. 'It isn't the most cheerful place to live, signore, I warn you.'

'Let me decide that. Is it far?'

'It isn't all that near,' Poverini said. 'But it's a beautiful day, signore, and the sun will even be shining in Borgo Ognissanti.'

'What's wrong with the place?'

'It's a rough neighbourhood. A slum, basically. Mostly dyers. The farther towards the walls you go, signore, the more dyers there are.'

'Why is that?'

He shrugged. 'You know what dyers are like – or perhaps you don't. They're like savages from the Indies, all patterned with dye, only speaking to their own kind. Their vats stink. But to be honest, they don't cause as much trouble as other people.'

We passed the church of Santa Trìnita, where men were dismantling last night's funeral, and carried on eastwards. 'Palazzo Corsini,' my guide intoned. 'That's the Ponte alla Carraia.' The river was very close, and the sound of the weir was a constant roar. The street we were in now was narrow, and the houses were interspersed with patches of waste ground. But the street itself was full of life. Men were pushing barrows and pulling handcarts piled with cloth, rags, leather, firewood. The doors of most houses were open, and from inside came the sounds of hammering, of clacking shuttles. We went past a large, shabby building, part chapel, part house. 'This is the Casa della Pietà,' said Poverini. 'One of the homes for abandoned girls. You'll become well acquainted with this place. And here we are, sir. We've arrived.'

Poverini was standing in front of an unprepossessing door. The house was on the corner of Borgo Ognissanti and a narrow alley, a few steps from the church of Ognissanti. From the far end of the alley came a welter of noises: the clanging of a hammer on tin fought it out with a screeching baby, a barking dog and several men having a conversation at the tops of their lungs. I examined the door. It was old, made of plain oak, bleached by the weather, its nails and hinges losing a long war against rust. Poverini's nose was twitching with comic revulsion, and it was true: the air was heavy with a complex stink which seemed to be made up of the briny tang of iron and the eye-watering vapours of old, concentrated piss. It was far from pleasant, but I had smelt far worse. This was nothing to the below-decks of a fighting galley, or the aftermath of a town sacking. It was merely people dyeing cloth. That thought seemed quite comforting.

'Open it, then,' I said.

Beyond the door was a small square courtyard, no more than eight paces from end to end. In the centre was a brick well with a worn marble cap. One side of the courtyard was the street wall. Adjoining houses made up two other sides, but I saw that their windows and doors had been bricked up a long time ago. On the third side was another, slightly newer door, two small windows on either side and one larger one above, all pointed in the ancient style. The building was at least three centuries old and it seemed a kind of miracle that it had survived that long, as the mortar was crumbling between its stones and looking up, I could see plants, even a small tree, growing from the gutters. In the courtyard the air smelt of old stone and cats, and the things that grow in places where the sun can't be bothered to shine, but the throat-catching fumes of the dyeing vats had barely seeped in. Orange and grey lichens mottled the walls with streaks and bullseyes. A pile of olive twigs, stacked for firewood, was slowly rotting in a corner. It was as private a place as you would ever find in a city like Florence.

Poverini picked his way over the mossy flagstones, carefully pushing a dry cat turd out of the way with the toe of his shoe.

'Lovely, eh?' he said cheerfully. The key, which was large and archaic, barely clicked in the lock, much to Poverini's surprise, and the door swung open on hinges that had been recently oiled. We stepped into a room that was as neat as the courtyard outside was unkempt.

'A fastidious man, was he, this Milanesi?' I asked. I knew next to nothing of policemen, but it seemed appropriate that tidiness might be important to them. To keep order, one should be orderly. Was that anything like me? I had never lived in a house for more than a few weeks since I'd fled from Pietrodoro. My travelling chests were tidy, my accounting ledgers meticulous. That had to be a good start, I decided.

'It's no palazzo,' Poverini said. 'This was Milanesi's study—' He pointed through a door, and I looked into a small room with plastered walls that had once been crudely frescoed with geometric patterns and, very optimistically, faded heraldic devices. There was an old table and a plain, high-backed chair with a fraying upholstered seat. A pair of newer bookshelves was empty. The chair was positioned so that its back was towards the window, which let out into the street. Shutters hung half off their hinges.

'He'd nailed them shut,' Poverini explained. 'All of the windows. I was one of the ones who found him. He was upstairs in his bed – they had to burn the mattress and all the linen.' He shuddered, and his face suddenly lost all of its good cheer. 'Across there is the kitchen. He had a woman who came and cooked for him, but he'd sent her away.'

'I'm going upstairs, Poverini. You don't have to come.'

The staircase was as old as the rest of the house, but the

treads did not creak as I climbed. I imagined Milanesi at work with nails and oil. I was beginning to like him. There were two rooms at the top of the stairs. One was completely bare: no furniture, no hangings on the wood-panelled walls, no rugs, only a dead tortoiseshell butterfly on the windowsill. In the other room, a surprisingly ornate bed of dark brown wood took up most of the floor, its four posts carved with elaborately twining vines and topped with satyrs leering through pointed beards. The headboard was decorated with geometric garlands and masks in the grotesque fashion. Where the mattress should be, the ropes sagged forlornly.

'They should have burnt the hangings too,' Poverini said behind me. 'But they had to sell them to pay Milanesi's debts. Owed a small fortune to his tailor, though I never thought he looked that remarkable. He bought the bed for his bride-to-be, and . . .' Poverini went over the window and opened it. Dead flies and maggot husks crunched under his shoes. 'Venetian silk hangings. Bloody hell. It still reeks in here. Can't you smell it?'

I could, but this was old death, no more than a spoilt sweetness and an acrid musk. At Orléans, I had been trapped in a strongpoint with a man whose wounded leg had turned gangrenous. It had been a week, in an airless redoubt, in the summer. After that, the world had always smelt more or less bearable to me.

'They scrub down the rowers' benches in galleys with vinegar. I'm sure that will work just as well here,' I said. 'What happened?'

'He was lying in that bed. Gone for a few days, in high summer. Around here, bad smells don't attract much attention, obviously. When he'd missed too many days of work, Scarfa sent us round.'

'No, I mean with this.' I touched one of the bedposts. It was smooth and solid. 'The bride.'

'I don't know very much. Do you mind?' Poverini slipped past me with evident relief and started down the stairs. I followed. 'Milanesi was from a good family – not the best, but good. Like me.' Poverini grinned over his shoulder. I was starting to like him too. 'His people were silk merchants, I think. He was a second son, or a third. Oldest brother inherited the business . . .' Poverini clicked his fingers. 'The usual stuff. Milanesi became a soldier, went to work for one of the big families in Rome, made enough to come back here and set himself up in his own right. He wanted to get into the silk trade, but his brothers didn't want him competing with them. He had some connection or other in the Signoria who got him a good position with the Guardia.' By this time, we were out in the courtyard. Poverini locked the door. 'Meanwhile, when he'd gone to Rome he'd left his childhood sweetheart behind. When he came back he had the money and the prospects to marry her. And she'd waited for him, apparently. They were betrothed. He bought that bed, poor bastard.'

'So what went wrong?'

Poverini went over to the well, opened the moss-encrusted lid and peered in. 'The girl was from a slightly better family. Her father was a minor banker who'd got involved in financing one of the old duke's grand schemes. I think it was the new walls of Fivizzano. In any case, he was discovered with his fingers in the money chest. A bit of embezzlement. Very minor – he was able to bribe his way out of it – but his wife decided that he must have been falsely accused. And then she decided that the

Otto had been to blame, and that people in the Bargello had conspired to ruin him.'

'So she forbade her daughter to marry Milanesi.'

'Yes.' Poverini let go of the lid. It fell back with a damp thud. 'It ruined him. His whole life had been leading to that one thing. He fell prey to the blackest of humours. Melancholy is a terrible affliction, so I hear. A policeman must armour himself against the dark, or it will swallow him: that's what Capo Scarfa always says.' He jumped down from the well's plinth and went over to the door. 'Well, it swallowed poor Milanesi. After you.'

We walked out into the *borgo*. *Did he kill himself?* I wondered. I must have spoken aloud, though I hadn't meant to, because Poverini answered.

'I don't really want to think about it. Do you? The most mortal of sins. Because he was in such a state when they found him I don't think they know one way or the other. A fever could have done it. He could have had an apoplexy. A stroke. He wasn't a healthy fellow towards the end. Maybe he had an accident. There are many ways for a man to die alone.'

'It sounds like you've thought about it quite a lot.'

'I'm not a person who can bear loneliness, signore. I dread it.' He laughed cheerfully, to show he was being frivolous, but I caught an undercurrent of something else.

'And the father of his betrothed. The embezzler. Is he still alive?'

'Still alive and thriving. The girl married someone else.'

'Of course.'

'Yes, of course.' Poverini sighed deeply. 'Well, perhaps now I should introduce you to some people who can find you a proper place to live.'

'But you don't need to, Lugotenente. The house is perfect. I just need to buy a mattress, and some furniture.'

'You're joking!'

'I'm not.'

'But you'll be all alone out here! In that place . . . You'll never get rid of Milanesi, you know.' Poverini wrapped his arms around himself. 'You can feel him.'

'You and I are opposites, Poverini. I don't fear loneliness. I like it.' I patted him on the shoulder. 'And if you've been a soldier for as long as I have, the dead don't bother you. Milanesi is the one who won't be lonely. I'm bringing so many ghosts with me that he'll never lack for company.'

Poverini just shook his head in bemusement. 'What is there to like in loneliness? You might as well say you like rainbows at night,' he said.

He left me on the steps of Santa Trìnita. His mood had risen as soon as we had left Borgo Ognissanti, and by the time we reached the church he was his cheerful self again. He gave me the name of a merchant who could help me with a mattress, and promised that a small army of Bargello servants, armed with vinegar, would have Milanesi's house as clean as a nunnery by tomorrow night. He kindly offered to put me up at his own house, but I turned him down as politely as I could, though in the end he was so insistent that I had to make up a story about an old friend I had promised to visit. When he had finally gone, I went into the church and lit a candle in the del Forese chapel. There were still crumbs of mortar on the tiles in front of his tomb.

Later I went in search of the Florentine branch of the bank whose services I had used for years and drew some money against my letters of credit. I'd never had a chance to spend the money I had earned over the years and I guessed that, by most men's reckoning, I was rich. That had never meant anything to me, until now. Now, I had a house, and a door that locked.

Then I found a soldiers' tavern on the far bank of the Arno that I'd heard about. It was half empty, and the landlord was happy to give me a room to myself, the only one with a door that locked from the inside. I wrote a short letter to Captain Scarfa, formally accepting the position as commander of the Bargello. When I gave it to the innkeeper's servant to deliver, together with a large coin, his face went through a complicated procession of emotions when he heard the address: surprise, distrust, curiosity and fear. Then it closed completely, like a mask. I nodded to myself. I'd made the right decision after all. I had the landlord send my supper up to my room and went to bed to await my ghosts.

CHAPTER EIGHTEEN

My first week as a policeman was a *bravura* lesson in boredom. In other words, it was exactly as I had expected it to be. How different, after all, could a police force be from a mercenary company? Most of the *sbirri* were ex-soldiers. We operated a military hierarchy. Policing the streets of Florence would be no different, in many ways, from keeping order in a big military encampment. The Bargello opened its doors to me, and I slipped inside my new life, leaving barely a ripple.

I arrived at the Bargello at dawn on the first day, this time earning a proper, if still grudging, salute from the guards on duty at the baleful entrance. By doing this I had thought I might gain myself an hour or two in which to quietly establish myself in the quarters of the *sbirri*, but no sooner had I stepped inside the big chamber, which was lit only by the wavering light from a candle and had the expectant feel of empty space, when a rasping voice hailed me from the far side of the chamber, which had seemed to be empty.

'Good morning to you, Comandante!' A shadow loomed up behind the candle, and Captain Scarfa made his way towards me between the desks. 'I've been waiting for you.'

'I'm sorry, Capo,' I said hurriedly. 'We never formally discussed . . .'

'Formally? Christ and the Virgin, man!' The captain was moving stiffly, as though he had been sitting behind his desk all night, which, I reflected, might in fact be true. 'But of course, I'm forgetting that you are still fresh from soldiering. We are not very formal here, Celavini. Except when we are. Who decides, you are wondering. Well, I do.'

'I wouldn't have dared assume otherwise, Capo,' I said, resisting the urge to salute. Did they – *we* – salute in the *sbirri*? I had no idea.

'But then, I am merely an extension of the Grand Duke's will. Which has decided to keep me here all bloody night, looking at informers' reports.' Scarfa stopped in front of me, put his arms behind his head and stretched. The bones of his spine popped like chestnuts in hot coal. He smelt of unwashed clothes, old spittle and ink. He must have known it, too, because he dragged his fingers down his unshaven cheeks and winced. 'Anyway, welcome, sir.' He stuck out his hand, and I took it. 'You've done me a good turn, taking this job. A damn good turn.' He grinned. 'And in recognition of that, I'm handing you those bloody reports. Those towers of papers on my desk. You remember where your own desk is? Excellent. I'm going to get some breakfast.'

Scarfa limped off without another word, leaving me alone. After he had gone, I looked around again. I was here at last, and yet it wasn't as I had expected it to be. There were stacks of ledgers everywhere, heaps of documents, shelves full of rolls trailing seals and ribbons. Where was I going to begin? *Why be impatient?* I told myself. *Begin here. You have your orders. Do your duty.*

Feeling oddly self-conscious in the empty chamber, I dutifully transferred the piles of documents to the desk that had been Milanesi's. Only when I had sat down in front of them did I realise that Scarfa hadn't told me anything about them. They must be reports of crime or criminals – that much was obvious. But what was I supposed to do with them? Put them into alphabetical order? Sort them by severity of crime? As I knew almost nothing, that morning, about the Grand Duchy's criminal code, they were as open to me as a book written in the holy language of India. Nevertheless, I began to sort through them, because I had nothing better to do, and because I couldn't help wondering whether Scarfa had not gone to get breakfast at all but was watching me through some crack or spy-hole.

The documents were letters – some several pages long, some no more than pieces of paper or parchment – written in hands that varied wildly from the neat script of well-educated men to the wild scrawls of the barely literate. I flipped through the larger pile first, hoping that Scarfa had done most of the work already, but there was no order that I could discern. The smaller pile – much smaller – seemed to concern people and events in Florence, so I went back to the larger pile and found that, while almost every letter had an origin within the borders of Tuscany, they came from places as far afield as Empoli, Pistoia, Borgo Sansepolcro and Grosseto. Most, though, were from or about

Florence, and so I began to methodically put these onto the smaller pile. It was still barely light outside, and the room was in near-darkness. I had found an iron candlestick with three good wax candles to light my work. My eyes are sharp, but not as sharp as a youth's, and some of the writing was so bad that I could only make out one word in ten, if that. As sergeant of a fighting company I had done my share of ledger work; in fact, I had had a reputation for efficiency and had enjoyed the simple pleasure of bringing order to jumbles of figures, facts and names. But I had never intended to make a career of it, and now I was wondering if that was precisely what I had just done.

In the interests of speed – I hoped this was some sort of test that Scarfa was inflicting on me that I needed to pass as quickly as possible, so that I could be released for something more active – I merely glanced at the letters at first, enough to see on which pile they belonged (I had added a second pile, for places beyond the city), but as I worked, my eyes naturally drifted across the lines of text. Names began to snag my attention, then, without my intending it, I began to notice patterns in the words, which when I followed them, became voices whispering in my head. The handwriting, the way the words came into being from the scarring of paper with ink, the strange sensation of being talked to by a man – they were all men, these writers – whom I had never met, and who might be ten, twenty, a hundred miles away. It was enthralling.

Because I had never received a letter, except for the one from Don Orazio, calling me to Rome. I had, in fact, taken great care to avoid getting involved with anyone to the extent that they might, perhaps, choose to write to me with . . . with whatever it was that people, ordinary people, wrote to each other about. Things like dowries, and being chased for unpaid bills, and horses for sale. And love. I had heard men read aloud their letters from home countless times, around campfires, or sitting in dirty, stinking revetments in France or Flanders. I had myself read aloud to men who had no schooling and could not read the pages they had been sent. I had listened, and thought about how complicated it all was, and whether I should be envious. I was, a little. But I'd always found it stifling as well, all the connections, all the bindings. I had enough of those already.

Most of the correspondence dealt with laughably petty stuff: suspicions, proof of minute wrongdoings, hearsay about other men's wives and daughters, or fathers, or uncles. It seemed extraordinary to me that the state of Tuscany should bother itself with any of it, let alone that someone like me should be getting paid, albeit poorly, to deal with such nonsense. But, petty or not, it was fascinating, like eavesdropping on a great crowd of gossips in full cry. I finished an accusation against a friar-priest accused of swindling one of his parishioners out of a hog and picked up the next document. It was written in a strong, ugly hand, and something about it made me guess that the author was a soldier. Something had happened in the Maremma, that marshy, fever-ridden land between the sea and Monte Amiata. A group of bandits under the command of a nobleman had captured the mule train of a salt trader. I gathered from the report that this had happened before. It was the name of the nobleman, though, that caught my attention: Vico Aldobrandeschi. I put the letter aside and kept reading.

The next day, Scarfa assigned me the same task. And the next.

The other men – a big sergeant called Andrea, two more sergeants who spent most of their time out on the streets, a pair of corporals and a number of clerks who seemed to drift between our offices and those of the magistrates next door – made no attempt to be friendly, and watched me with slightly hostile indifference, a gang of shabby owls. On the sixth day, I waited until the captain had come back from his lunch and went over to his desk with the letter concerning the Maremma bandits.

'What happens with things like this?' I asked. Scarfa put on his eyeglasses and glanced at the letter. His eyebrows went up, and he chuckled.

'Looking for some action already, Celavini? Good luck. The state doesn't have the money to fight bandits in the middle of nowhere.'

'It's just that I came across something like this when I was coming north with Don Orazio's body. I gather that there are noble families around Amiata and in the Val d'Orcia who run their own little kingdoms. I was surprised, as Duke Cosimo is renowned for enforcing the rule of law.'

Scarfa tutted. 'The further you get from Florence . . . Amiata is under the jurisdiction of the Bargello of Siena, which in turn is under us – in theory. In practice they turn a blind eye until the situation gets too bad, then do something half arsed, claim they've solved the problem, and the whole thing starts all over again. I think – and I'm not alone – that old Sienese families like the Aldobrandeschi and the Piccolomini, who used to run things when Siena was a republic, have a lot of support down there.'

'The ones I heard about, down near Radicofani, were the Ellebori,' I said, innocently. 'Lodovigo Ellebori. Has his own village.'

'Ellebori? Oh, yes. Plenty of stuff about the Ellebori in our files,' said Scarfa.

'Surely it would be a good thing to guard the pilgrims on the Francigena,' I said. Scarfa rolled his eyes and was about to reply when a man in the red and white livery of a *sbirro* burst into the room, sweating and out of breath.

'Capo!' He saluted reasonably smartly.

'Renzi?' Scarfa said, eyebrows raised.

'You need to send some men to Chiasso di Malacucina,' Renzi panted. 'There's a mob gathering.'

Scarfa folded his arms and looked at me. 'What happened?' I asked.

'A whore stabbed a customer,' the man said, and twisted his face to show just how monstrous this was. 'Now the mob wants to lynch her.' He looked from Scarfa to me and back again, as if waiting for our approval.

'Will you deal with this, Comandante?' Scarfa asked. 'I sense that you are bored with all that correspondence.'

'Gladly,' I said.

'Take some men with you.'

'If I need reinforcements, I'll come back for some,' I said. My sword belt was hanging from my chair. I buckled it on and told Renzi that I'd follow him.

Chiasso di Malacucina is one of those narrow, smelly streets just to the north of the Mercato Vecchio and inside the brothel quarter administered by the *Onestà*, the Magistrates of Decency. As soon as we had crossed Via Calimala, we were swallowed up in a welter of noise. Women were leaning out of windows overhead, some dressed in the sheerest muslin that hid almost nothing, some simply naked from the waist up, yelling and cackling at the men down in the street, who were prowling, alone or in groups, furtive or unabashed, drunk and sober, singing and yelling back at the women. I watched the men: most of them were young, hardly any older than twenty-five, but there were older men too, and several red-faced, round-eyed specimens who were plainly visitors from foreign parts. Renzi's uniform attracted a barrage of hoots and cat-calls, and some choice and inventive insults. Towards the middle of the street a crowd had blocked the thoroughfare, and more people, all of them men, were joining it. Renzi was carrying a halberd and he had to use it to force a way for us through the press of bodies. The smell of wine-spiked sweat, unwashed clothes and male excitement was almost too much to bear in the airless street. We finally reached an open doorway, which another uniformed policeman was desperately trying to block with his halberd.

'Thank fuck you're here, Renzi!' he said, then scowled at me. 'Who's this?'

'The new *comandante*, Nencio.'

'Shit.' Nencio saluted hurriedly.

'So . . .' I had no idea what I was supposed to do here. 'What happened?' I asked, because I had to start somewhere.

'A whore knifed her customer, sir,' said Nencio. 'Upstairs.'

'Right, then. You'd better show me.'

'Bring her out here!' someone yelled from the street.

'Yes! Bring us the slut! We're the magistrates now!'

'Shut that door, and keep it shut,' I told Nencio, and started up the stairs, looking around me as I climbed. The house was quite old and cheaply built, judging by the creaking stairs and smell of damp. There was a large room on the ground floor – I had glimpsed it through a stone arch – decorated with garish frescoes. There were more frescoes in the stairwell: writhing women with strange proportions and blancmange-like flesh, men endowed with both muscles and paunches, brandishing gargantuan members. The painter seemed to have had limited experience of the human body, which struck me as strange, given that he had been working in a bawdy house. His work reminded me quite strongly of Maestro Vasari's frescoes inside the dome of Santa Maria del Fiore, but with copulation involved. I had seen worse, both in the pamphlets and chapbooks that circulate in soldiers' camps, and in life. This wasn't the first bawdy house I had been in, though before this I had always been there to retrieve deserters and stragglers from my company. There were real women at the top of the stairs, herded against the flimsy-looking bannister by more policemen. There must be a full patrol here. The whores stared at me as I came up the stairs. I suppose I looked like a client: my sword marked me out as a nobleman, or at least as someone who could pay the hefty licence to carry one. But they didn't flirt, they glared. The youngest was no more than fifteen; the oldest probably older than fifty. Her breasts, barely hidden by a silk shift, were hanging flat against her chest. The youngest had elaborately braided hair pinned against her scalp. She was strongly built but pale, like the girls from the Pietà. Every one of them carried some mark of the French pox: a sore on a lip, a blistered nipple. They watched me in silence, and I realised that they were not cowed, they were angry.

'In here, Comandante,' said Renzi. He opened a door, one of a row along one long, lavishly frescoed wall. I stepped into a narrow room which looked startlingly like a convent cell but for the crudely coloured Venetian prints framed on the back wall: scenes cut from the infamous book *I Modi*, dog-eared pages of which could be found in most cavalrymen's saddlebags.

A man was sitting on the rucked-up sheets of the bed in nothing but his shirt. He had a hand clamped around his arm above the elbow, and there was some blood on his forearm. Sprawled at his feet was a naked woman. She was lying face down, her arms flung out. The floor was dark wood planking, and it took me a moment to realise that she was surrounded by a thickening pool of blood. I bent down and touched her shoulder. She didn't move, and her skin was only just warm.

'This woman is dead,' I said, and looked up to see Renzi and the man on the bed regarding me as if I had just said something incredibly stupid. 'I . . . Constable Renzi, you reported that a man had been knifed here.'

'So I have been,' said the half-naked man petulantly. 'Look what she did to me!' He took his hand away to reveal a gash about an inch long on his arm. It was only skin deep; it wasn't even bleeding any more. Then I noticed a bloodstained knife on the bed next to him, a wooden-handled country blade like a fishmonger might use. 'There, you see?' the man said, following my eyes. 'She cut me with that, the little bitch!' Renzi rolled his eyes and nodded with obvious sympathy.

'And you killed her,' I said. He stared at me as if I was an idiot. I could smell wine coming off him, and that sour stink of men in rut as I bent down and gently turned the body over. She was young, and her eyes were open and round with the final shock of violent death. She might have looked surprised, but it would hardly have been a surprise to her, would it, to come to this end. She had been stabbed at least five times in the chest, a ragged scatter of wounds from her left shoulder to her left breast.

'Why?' I asked the man.

'She went mad.' He shrugged.

'And again, why?'

'I wanted to do it in the other place. You know. She wouldn't let me. I even told her I'd pay a little more. For God's sake! I began to take my pleasure anyway, and she took a knife from under the mattress and did this.' He squeezed his arm and pouted in self-pity.

'So you took the knife from her . . .'

'I was defending myself, signore,' he said, as though it was the most reasonable thing in the world.

I had been here before, of course. Not this exact room, with this exact corpse. But in other places: Brussels, Trieste, a village near Orléans, a garrison town on the Hungarian border. I would have found some man from the company spattered in blood, either slack-faced with drink or ready with his defence, his excuse. Those men would be hanging in the town square or from a prominent tree by morning. I had made sure of that – mercenary justice is expedient and swift. Other companies allowed their men to rape and murder, but mine did not. Here, though, I wasn't the judge. Here, there was an angry mob waiting to lynch a woman who had already been executed for the crime of refusing to be sodomised.

'Your name?' I demanded.

247

The man blinked. 'Rienzo di Giovanni da Empoli,' he said.

'Take him to the Stinche,' I told Renzi. The constable extended a friendly hand to the man on the bed.

'Better get dressed, mate,' he said.

'No!' I barked. 'Take him like this. And tie his hands.' Renzi looked at me in amazement.

'But the crowd outside—' Renzi began.

'You've got a full patrol here,' I told him. 'If you can't deal with a few drunks, you can hand in your resignations in the morning. Or you can suggest that they lynch this piece of dung instead. Your choice, Constable.'

I left Renzi and the killer muttering to each other and went to find the madam, who Renzi told me was called Mother Chiara. She was downstairs, standing in the corner of what passed for a kitchen, a dark little room with bare brick walls stained black with smoke, smelling of boiled kale and old onions. A fleshy woman in third-hand clothes that had, perhaps ten years ago, been the height of fashion in Venice. When she turned around I saw that she was in early middle-age, wide-faced, wide-bodied, the white lead with which she had painted her cheeks streaked with tears and spattering her exposed neck and chest with chalky blotches. One of her hands was gripping the sleeve of her dress so hard that her nails had gone through the cloth.

'My name is Onorio Celavini. I'm *comandante* of the *sbirri* of the *Otto di Guardia*,' I said. The woman glared at me. 'I'm sorry that this trouble has come under your roof,' I went on. 'The man is under arrest and will be taken to the Stinche. Can you tell me the name of the poor girl upstairs?'

The woman still glared, though her expression was less hostile now and more surprised. 'Her name?' There was a long pause. 'It was Sofia.'

'And was the man who . . .' I saw the woman flinch in anticipation of my words. 'Was he a regular customer of hers?' I asked.

'No. He's never come in here before now,' she said. Her voice was hoarse and heavily tinged with the accent of San Frediano across the river.

'He tried to make her do something she didn't want,' I told her. 'She refused and pulled a knife on him.'

'What is *his* name?' the woman said, raising her head and staring at me with so much anger that I almost stepped backwards.

'Rienzo di Giovanni da Empoli,' I said.

The woman hissed. 'May his guts be eaten by snakes!' She spat on the floor in front of her. 'I know that name. He is a rapist and a sodomite. He's caused trouble in other houses. He should never have been allowed through our door. I wasn't here. I . . . Oh, Holy Mother! I went out to fetch a bottle of wine from Falco down the street. One of the girls must have let him in . . .' She let go of her sleeve and began to tear at her elaborately plaited and pinned hair. It came loose and fell around her like sleek brown snakes, which she gathered up and pressed against her face, her shoulders heaving with sobs.

'It was this Rienzo who killed the girl, signora,' I said gently. 'No one is to blame except him. He will face justice.'

'What justice?' she burst out. 'He will pretend remorse and be fined a month's wages! Damn his soul!'

'I will do everything I can to see that he is given what he deserves,' I said. 'I give you my word.'

'Your word?' She let go of her hair and it fell loose, wet and plastered with white lead. She was smiling, an awful, joyless curl of her mouth. 'I've not seen you before, Signor Comandante. You don't seem to be new to brothels, but you are plainly very new to Florence. So don't talk to me about justice. You are a man, and he is a man. Your loyalty is to that thing between your legs, which you share with Rienzo di Giovanni, and with the magistrates of the *Otto*, and every man who comes in here quivering like a dog who's smelt a bitch. Justice doesn't apply to a man's cock if its owner has money. That pig has enough money to spend in brothels, so he has enough to pay a little fine. So to hell with your justice.'

'I'm sorry, signora. I swear I'll do my best,' I said. I was trembling, full of my own rage and my own sadness. She was right, though she didn't know why. I shared nothing at all with Rienzo, least of all my anatomy, but I wasn't the *capo* of a mercenary company now, I was a paid functionary. A servant of the Grand Duke, on thirty-five *scudi* a year. I had some power, but I didn't yet know how much. In the brothel kitchen that night, I felt almost as helpless as I had ever felt in my life.

'I will make sure that the Misericordia are informed, so they can collect your girl.'

'The Misericordia? Why, signore, would the Misericordia come for her, as though she were a nameless corpse pulled from the river? Sofia will stay here tonight. This is her home.'

'I only meant . . .' I searched for something else to tell her, some fragment of consolation. 'I would be glad to pay for a decent funeral,' I said.

'You think I can't pay?' she whispered. 'You think I . . . I *would* not pay? For my own girl to be properly buried?' She groaned and bit her lip, her whole body quivering as she strained to keep control, to stay on her feet. Her lip split, and a bead of blood ran down and collected in the white lead crease of her chin. 'Sofia was my daughter. There, signore. Now please, get out and leave us in peace.'

I stayed a little longer, talking to the women who were willing to answer my questions. By the time I left, the crowd had wandered away. A dead whore promised no entertainment for them when there were live ones all around. I visited each brothel on the street and questioned the women about the murderer. Then I went back to the Bargello and wrote a report for the magistrates, making sure that every detail of Rienzo di Giovanni's life, his character and his habits were there to help with his interrogation, which I recommended should be as thorough as his evil reputation deserved. There were wounded girls, violated women, even a missing girl whose disappearance trailed Rienzo's name. It was getting dark by the time I left the Bargello. Borgo Ognissanti was still bustling. Girls were returning to the Pietà like shabby bees to a hive. Bells started ringing all over Florence. The door to the Pietà's chapel was ajar, and something made me stop in the middle of the street, hesitate, and go inside. It was a plain, whitewashed space with a beamed ceiling. A dreadful painting of the dead Christ in his mother's arms, done in cheap colours and unskilled lines, hung behind the altar, which was just a table, though covered with a gorgeous silk cloth of intricate detail. A few girls were sitting in the plain black pews. I took a seat at the very back and bowed my head. I prayed, as I always did, to the Virgin and Santa Celava, holding her medal in my hand as I listened to the comings and goings in the home next door. Looms were still clacking, and the air was full of the smells of smoke, steam, wet silk, boiling cabbage. Yesterday I had passed a little funeral, a coffin of rough pine boards leaving this chapel, trailing a short procession of girls. An older woman in black robes led the coffin. They headed up the *borgo* towards the city walls and were soon enveloped by the morning throng. Here in the chapel, one of the girls was coughing, a deep, wet cough that she was trying to stifle but could not. Another, sitting almost opposite me, had clear signs of the French pox. They were all thin, and pale from their lives spent working in dark rooms. Yet they came into the chapel arm in arm, some of them; I could hear merry voices and laughter in the house, and somewhere above me, I could faintly hear singing: a bawdy tune that was doing the rounds of the Mercato Vecchio. Then the older woman I had seen leading the funeral came in. Some of the girls got up and curtsied. There was a chorus of soft voices: 'Good evening, Sister Brigida!' I couldn't help noticing that there were smiles, that Sister Brigida touched the girl with the cough gently on the shoulder as she walked past. She saw me, and her serene expression didn't change, but she came over and sat down next to me.

'Welcome to our church, signore,' she said. She was older than I had thought. Her face was deeply lined, and age had thinned her lips and revealed the sinews of her neck, but she gave off a sort of calm vitality. Her voice was surprisingly rough, and she spoke in the accent of this eastern quarter. 'We welcome guests, although perhaps a man might find himself out of place, or indeed in the wrong place.'

'I hope I'm not out of place,' I said. 'I have not been in Florence long. My name is Onorio Celavini. I'm one of the *comandantes* of the Bargello *sbirri*.'

'Oh dear,' she said, frowning. 'None of my girls is in trouble, I hope.'

'No. Not at all. I'm simply your neighbour, and . . .' I took a deep breath. 'Another girl was murdered today. A prostitute,' I went on, not entirely sure why, but feeling oddly secure next to this woman. 'She was murdered. By a man, a client, and no one . . .' I shrugged and looked down at my knees. 'I wanted to see a place where women seemed safe, I suppose.'

Sister Brigida looked at me in surprise. 'Girls aren't safe anywhere, Signor Comandante. Here we simply do the best we can. We rely on charity and most of all on God's kindness. The one is hardly sufficient and the other I accept with a glad heart, though He seems to want to take my girls to Himself when I should like to keep them here with me. But you are welcome here. It will be good to have a gentleman of the *sbirri* who looks at my girls with kindness and not with suspicion. Or greed,' she added. 'Who is that?' She nodded at the medal that was hanging against my doublet.

'Her name is Santa Celava,' I said.

'Santa Clara?'

'No, signora. She's just a local saint from where I was born. People there call her the patron of lost and hidden things.'

'Would that not be Saint Anthony?'

'People used to say that Saint Anthony had enough work to do. Celava listened to us because she had been one of us. They also used to say that women are better at finding things.'

We both smiled. 'Well, you may pray to her here as often as you wish,' said Sister Brigida. 'I think the Pietà has great need of a patron for the lost.'

She nodded to me, rose and went down to the front of the chapel. Soon afterwards, a priest came in, a Dominican. As he began to celebrate Mass, I retreated into my thoughts. What did I want for the dead girl in Chiasso di Malacucina? Justice? Or simple revenge? It was both, I supposed. Justice for Sofia, and for Mother Chiara, though scant, very scant. Revenge for me. Or was I just feeding my ghosts, giving them the blood they craved? I couldn't stop myself imagining Sofia's last moments, because I had lived them myself. Except that I was here, still breathing, though strangely transformed, so much so that I had not recognised a grieving mother, nor she a bereaved daughter. And yet it was my signature on the report that damned her killer. There was power there after all. Hidden, yes – it would take me a while to find out how to wear it. But it was there.

BOOK III

CHAPTER NINETEEN

For a while I lay curled up on the bed, cradling the tiny rind of gold to me as if it were a child. The ring that Zanobia Linucci's murderer had given her, that her cook had stolen, which I had taken from a fence in a dirty Florence warehouse. I had carried it all day without knowing what it was. But when I had recognised it in the chapel of the Pietà the past had come crashing in on me like the roofbeam of a burning house.

It was my mother's betrothal ring. I slipped it onto my finger and put it to my lips. Two hounds: Maria Capacci and Amerigo Ormani. I could hear their voices telling me: 'See here. That is Mamma, that is Papà.' I had teethed on that ring, mumbled my sore gums against the stone and the hounds. Two hounds for fidelity. I could barely remember my mother's face. The last time I had seen her, she had looked as Zanobia Linucci had looked this morning. Or perhaps that had been another murdered woman. I had seen so many. I sometimes wonder if I'm the only one who sees each poor dead woman as a person, not as a chattel, an inconvenience, a stain on someone else's honour. Then again, I suppose they are always Maria Ormani.

I didn't sleep that night, the night after Zanobia Linucci's murder. It was stiflingly hot, and the miasma of the dyeworks and the river mud had finally managed to creep into the house. The stench curled itself around me, ripe with rot and sharp with minerals, as clinging and insistent as the memories that wandered through the empty rooms, whispering in my ears. My nightshirt felt like a lead sheet and itched. When I sat down, the wood of the chair seemed to suck at my skin. I went out into the courtyard, but the air was thicker there, and a rat was fidgeting around in the dry fronds of the date palm. At last I lay down on the flagstones in the kitchen and floated in a twilight where the cold stone brought relief but was painful as well; however, I couldn't have one without the other. At some point in the early hours I felt something unfamiliar on my hand and found that I was wearing my mother's ring. When had I put it on? I couldn't remember. I twisted it around my finger, the contours of the faithful hounds rolling like a familiar, distant landscape. Golden hills seen from above, beautiful and safe. And then I saw my mother, sprawled on a floor like I was sprawled now, like Zanobia had lain, like a broken doll. Augusto Ellebori killed my father in his sleep, and when my mother had woken, had killed her too as she fought to understand if she was still dreaming. Then he had come for me.

A crooked back: that's what Simone the steward had told me. He'd imitated a man twisted unnaturally, a man with a wound, who was still angry about his condition, though he must have come about it a long time ago. I turned over and pressed my forehead against the stone, and saw myself picking up a heavy sword, saw the man writhing on bloodied sheets, felt the weight of the sword as I lifted it above my head and brought it down across his back. I'd felt the edge bite. I'd felt his body break beneath it. I'd seen him die. *He's dead*: I'd heard the men say it, before the flames rose, before . . .

The rat was still scuffling outside, and bats were piping as they hunted midges through the dense air. I got up and sat cross-legged on the floor. I was trying to think but my mind felt numb. I had waited patiently in the Bargello for six years. Everyone comes to Florence sooner or later, Scarfa had said, so I had waited, like a spider in the funnel of its web. Had I really believed that Augusto Ellebori would come to me, though? I decided that it didn't matter. I would have waited. I would have waited for ever. Two hounds for fidelity. I had been faithful. Had I been rewarded?

I went upstairs and got dressed, binding the linen tight around my breasts, slipping on my lightest black doublet, buttoning the high collar up under my chin so that the black ruff hid most of my scar. I didn't need to look in the mirror: I always knew when Onoria became Onorio. From one skin and into another. This morning the metamorphosis seemed incomplete, even though I studied myself again and again in the mirror. I understood: my mother's ring around my finger. It was a gift from the dead, sent to me out of the darkness. Wearing it, I would always be a daughter. I tried to drown out these thoughts as I clattered down the stairs and unlocked the door, all manly bustle and noise.

I wandered down to Ponte Santa Trìnita. Footsteps and horse piss had more or less erased Pietro Vennini and his attackers from the pavement, but there was still a rotten taint in the air where he had died. The sun was an hour away from rising but the sky was already a dirty orange above Vallombrosa, fine layers of cloud hanging in the air, as though a vast rubbish heap was on fire beyond the horizon. Church bells clanged sullenly. I walked over to the Pietà and let myself into the chapel. The girls were already awake: I could hear looms clattering inside the main building, and the hoarse chatter of women who should, in a just world, be lying between cool sheets, dreaming until well after sunrise. I sat on the hard, narrow pew, and after a while, the girls began to drift in and out. Some of them simply walked to the altar, dropped a quick curtsey and left. Others lit candles and knelt in prayer. One older woman prostrated herself full-length on the floor. They barely noticed me: I was a familiar face in the Pietà, a friend, a protector. I drifted in and out of prayer, holding my medal of Santa Clara of Assisi, talking to Santa Celava of Pietrodoro, asking her for help with whatever lost thing had just been found. Every now and again one of the girls caught my eye, some painfully thin child, cheekbones showing through, perhaps stifling a racking cough or scratching at a scaly rash or sore. It wasn't an unkind place, the Pietà. Prioress Brigida was kind-hearted but overworked; there was never enough money. Girls came. Girls died. I could hardly bear to think what it must be like, spinning or weaving silk in an airless room on days like this one. I knew the girl with the bad cough wouldn't see the first day of September. The chapel was beginning to fill up; soon the old friar who celebrated Mass would arrive. I slipped out. It was still early, but my office was always open.

Lieutenant Poverini was the only one there when I arrived at the Bargello.

'Quiet night?' I asked.

'Incredible. Not one death,' he said wryly. 'Four stabbings, and some unlucky chap had his ears cut off by persons unknown. But no deaths. Is that a first for this month?'

'I think it must be,' I said. Although the summer was always a time when tempers became dangerous and worse, the city had been getting more lawless recently. No one wanted to say it aloud, but since Duke Cosimo had retired and left Don Francesco in charge, violence had started to creep back onto the streets in a way that people hadn't seen since the reign of Duke Alessandro, nearly forty years ago. 'Listen: is anyone saying anything about the Vennini affair?'

'Is anyone *not* talking about Vennini, you mean. It's all just gossip and poisoned tongues. But we arrested that surgeon. He's locked up.'

'Excellent! I want to talk to him.'

'No need. They already put him to the torture. Three lifts. He didn't know the man he treated, and he was told to go for payment to the Banco Miniati.'

'That's the bank of Donna Zanobia's man. Three lifts, though? Seems a bit zealous.'

Poverini shrugged. 'Don Francesco's taken an interest. He told Scarfa and the magistrates that he wants a result.'

I went to see if any of the magistrates were in, but their offices were empty. I peered through the door of the torture chamber, just in case, but it was empty too. The rack stood in one corner, and the rope for the *strappado* hung down from its pulley in the middle of the room, one end terminating in a leather strap, the other attached to a windlass. The surgeon, Spinelli, would have had his hands tied behind his back, that strap wrapped around his wrists, and a man, usually Pandolfo the regular torturer, would have cranked the windlass until Spinelli was dangling a few feet from the ground. It only took a minute or two before the muscle and sinew of the shoulders began to part, and arm bones started to dislocate. For a recalcitrant suspect, or an unpopular one, the man on the windlass might be ordered to let the wheel slip through his hands so that the hanging man plunged, weightless for an instant, before he was brought up short. A drop would finish what a lift had started. After a couple of drops, some men would never be able to use their arms again. Three lifts just to question a surgeon who had treated a wounded man was grotesque. It wouldn't have been done to punish him, though, just to make sure that he wasn't lying. It had been the hardest part of my job, the torture. Depending on the case, even witnesses friendly to the prosecution might be given a short lift, just to make them more credible. Just last week, a serving woman who had happened to witness a fight between two gentlemen had been given the *strappado*, just the merest of lifts but still agonising, and the poor woman had even been grateful to the magistrates as now her honesty was proved for all to see. I didn't like to have my suspects tortured but the magistrates decided, and there was nothing I could do about it. Spinelli hadn't deserved to suffer like that. And why was Don Francesco concerning himself with two honour killings? I decided that I couldn't wait for the magistrates. I left a vague note for Scarfa and went out again.

* * *

The Banco Miniati occupied the ground floor of a small palazzo between the Duomo and the Innocents' Hospital. They weren't open yet, but I banged on the door, and when a well-dressed clerk opened it, already scolding me for the disturbance, I held out the duke's seal and he became a little more polite.

'How can I help a *comandante* of the *sbirri*?' he asked. Bankers can't seem to help being unctuous, and this one was no exception.

'You have a client called Bartolomeo Ormani, I believe? And perhaps another: Donna Zanobia Linucci?' I said.

'Ah. All client information is of course confidential,' said the clerk. I just smiled and pushed past him into a neatly furnished room lined with shelves and drawers. Ledgers and stacks of documents tied with ribbons and sealed with wax or lead lined the walls behind a horseshoe-shaped counter, which was draped with new-looking Turkey carpets. A French tapestry filled one of the empty wall spaces, and a portrait of a bulbous-nosed man in last century's headwear kept an eye on things from an ornate gilded frame. A bench and several chairs upholstered in satin with the blue-on-white crest of the Miniati. The bank had been in the family for at least two centuries. It was one of the smaller banks in Florence, and its public reputation was spotless, although I happened to know that it had narrowly avoided the scandal that, indirectly, had destroyed my predecessor, Comandante Milanesi. I leant on the counter and began to fiddle absently with a set of silver-inlaid scales.

'Those are rather finally calibrated, signore,' the clerk said tactfully.

'I would hope so,' I said, treating him to my emptiest grin.

'Don't worry. Balance is my trade.' I picked up one of the little gilded weights and dropped it into one of the pans of the scale, which tilted, shuddering. 'Balance. Harmony in the affairs of men.'

'Justice,' said the clerk, still smiling encouragingly, although he was eyeing the weight I was currently bouncing in the palm of my hand. 'Justice, with her scales.'

'Ah. Well, you see, Messer . . . Messer . . .'

'Giardini,' he supplied. 'I am the head clerk here.'

'You see, Messer Giardini, you say justice. Blind justice, impartial and fair.'

'Of course.'

'I'm not talking about that at all.'

'Ah ' Giardini blinked.

'Harmony. My job is to restore harmony here in the city. From the greatest to the smallest. A dispute between neighbourhoods, guilds. A feud between two families. A petty dispute between petty street traders. All these things upset the balance of life. Robbery. Murder.' I dropped the weight into the already tilting pan and the arm dropped with a loud clunk. Giardini blinked again, more rapidly. His smile had grown more artificial.

'You look like a man of integrity,' I told him. 'A man who isn't interested in gossip. So perhaps you haven't heard that Donna Zanobia was murdered the night before last, around the same time that one Pietro Vennini was cut to ribbons on the Ponte Santa Trìnita. Vennini, a brave swordsman to the last, managed to kill two of his assailants and gave at least one more of them a nasty wound, right here.' I smacked my arse, and the clerk winced involuntarily. 'Nasty enough that he had to be treated by a surgeon here in Florence before making his escape. A surgeon called Spinelli, who was told to collect payment for his services from the Banco Miniati, on the account of one Bartolomeo Ormani. Who was also the lover and benefactor of Donna Zanobia. The *Otto di Guardia* believe that the men who committed the murders were paid by Messer Ormani, and seeing that he appears to put all his expenses through this bank, it would be interesting to see, in the interests of harmony, whether the Banco Miniati has been complicit – unwittingly, no doubt – in a double and extremely sensational murder, and the incidental deaths of at least two other men.'

Giardini had gone milk-white. 'You would need a warrant from the *Otto*. And besides, Messer Orlando Miniati, my employer, is travelling at the moment. Without his—'

'That surgeon I just mentioned? The *Otto* arrested him last night. They gave him three lifts of the *strappado*; and he'd already told them all he knew. Three lifts!' I held up my hands in disbelief – not entirely feigned, but Giardini wasn't to know that. 'On the other hand, the magistrates like cooperation. They value it very highly.'

'And . . . umm . . . are the *Otto* going to request this information officially?'

'Yes. But the level of *officially* depends quite a bit on how cooperative you are with me now.'

Giardini took off his silk cap and ran his hands through his hair. 'Is there anything you particularly need to know?' he asked after a heavy silence.

'The Ormanis.' Only when I said the words did I realise how much I had been keeping myself in check, how much emotion had built up inside me. 'I want everything you know about the Ormani family. Who this Don Bartolomeo is. Where he is from. What business he's involved in. The same for Donna Zanobia. I – we – want to know every last detail.'

'I can't give you figures or . . .'

'I don't care about figures. Just tell me about the people.'

Giardini took a deep breath. 'Please,' he said, indicating one of the upholstered chairs. 'Take a seat, Comandante. I will bring you what you need.'

The next few minutes passed as slowly as any in my entire life. I fidgeted. I ran my fingernail up and down the wire wrapping of my sword hilt until the little ratcheting noise put my teeth on edge. The linen binding around my breasts was digging into my skin below my armpits, which in turn made me aware of my nipples, aching and sore. I would begin to bleed tomorrow or the next day. I shifted in the chair, trying to ease the discomfort. It was as if Onoria was trying to get out. When Giardini came back, I jumped to my feet as if an invisible string had jerked me upright. The clerk didn't appear to notice. He held a book and a sheet of paper with some hastily scribbled lines on it. I had to bite the inside of my mouth to resist the urge to snatch it from him.

'You promise to keep this in the strictest confidence?' he said.

'I'll share it with the magistrates only.'

Giardini seemed as satisfied as he was going to be. He locked the main door and sat down beside me. 'The Ormanis have banked with us for ten years. First, they were clients of our Siena branch. Then . . .' He opened the book and held it at an angle, so that I couldn't quite see the figures. 'About ten years ago, the account was transferred here. The principle client is Bartolomeo Ormani, though we handle transactions for one Smeralda, wife of Messer Ditto Salvucci, who lives here in Florence. Ormani has made it known that Donna Smeralda is his sister.'

Smeralda. Smeralda . . . 'Where?' My throat had suddenly tightened, and my voice was hardly more than a hiss. Giardini handed me the sheet of paper.

'All the relevant details are here.'

I barely glanced at the paper. 'The Ormanis.' I tried to swallow, but it was as if my throat was full of molten lead. 'They aren't from Florence.'

'No indeed. From the south. Signor Ormani is the lord of Pietrodoro. A place I have never heard of.'

The picture that had been forming inside my head since before dawn, a painting of lost things found, of reunions, redemption, painted in the bright colours of hope, dissolved like a sheet of burnt paper which, though it looks almost perfect, falls to dust the moment it is touched. I thanked Giardini for his willingness to help the Eight and left, walking out into the street feeling strangely disembodied, as though there was nothing inside my clothes but aching and a growing sense of dread.

CHAPTER TWENTY

The clerk had written an address for Smeralda Salvucci. I had to blink a few times before his elegant but studiedly illegible handwriting made sense to me. Borgo San Lorenzo: a fashionable street behind the old Palazzo de' Medici. Not far. I walked fast, sword bumping against my thigh, wrappings chafing beneath my doublet, the first nagging pain in my ovaries.

The Palazzo Salvucci was an old patrician mansion from before the time of the Medici, the front decorated with worn stone shields blazoned with cockerels and crescent moons. I knocked on the door, and a smartly dressed slave girl opened it. Her master was travelling, she regretted to inform me. Her mistress was at church and would return around eleven of the clock. Would I leave my name? I said I would come back later and left before she could see that my hands were trembling.

Secretary Boschi was perched on a high stool behind his desk at the tax office. He scowled when he saw me, and I probably did the same in return. I was still in a sort of daze, almost drugged by the riot of thoughts in my head. My skull felt like the inside of the Duomo after a busy service, filled with the chatter of thousands. I had to force myself back into the shell of Onorio Celavini.

'Do you have anything for me, Segretario?' I asked.

Boschi sucked in his cheeks and narrowed his eyes. 'This Zanobia Linucci, who was murdered,' he said. 'Do you know who she was?'

'Obviously not, Segretario,' I said, forcing my mouth into a rigid smile. 'I'm presuming you remember our conversation yesterday.'

'She was Zanobia Orsini, daughter – illegitimate – of Niccolò Orsini, Duke of Pitigliano. Widow of Giovanni de Giorgio Linucci of Pitigliano, knight, who died eleven years ago in the service of the King of Spain.'

'And what about Ormani?'

Boschi frowned, plainly annoyed that I wasn't more impressed by his information. 'You sent me on a wild goose chase, Comandante. Your Bartolomeo Ormani owns no property in Florence or anywhere else in the Duchy. Admittedly some records were lost in the recent flooding, but to find nothing . . .'

'Nothing at all?'

'No. But I admit that the search threw up a few interesting bits and pieces. I'd assumed the Ormani name to have been extinct for centuries, but it seems that a line, rather an obscure one, had survived in a place called Pietrodoro. One Amerigo Ormani, hereditary knight, three dependants, paid taxes until 1557, and then payments cease. No mentions after that. Fascinating, though. Some offshoot of the family must have taken root down there after the White Guelphs were expelled. I don't suppose that interests you, though, Comandante.'

'I assure you that it does, Segretario,' I said, barely able to form the words. 'You have . . . you have answered all my questions.'

I found myself back at the Bargello. One of the magistrates, Messer Alessandro del Caccia, was waiting for me.

'What in Christ's name is going on, Celavini?' he demanded.

'Good morning, Cavaliere,' I rasped. 'What can I do for you?'

'This damned Vennini business. The city is full of it. I don't want that bloody fornicator to become some sort of hero. They're already printing pamphlets about him.'

I took a deep breath. Vennini. Always Vennini. 'I'll have some new information later today,' I said.

'Good. The sooner the better.' He dismissed me with a distracted wave. I left by the magistrates' entrance so that I wouldn't have to talk to Scarfa. He'd want his report, and I didn't want to stand in front of him without it and pretend to be contrite. The clock on the Palazzo Vecchio told me that it was after the eleventh hour. As I walked across the piazza, one of my men came out of the crowd, saluted me, and reported that his patrol had caught a pair of cutpurses. I feigned interest, clapped him on the back and slipped away. Elbowing my way through the Mercato Vecchio, I caught sight of Sergeant Gherardi arguing with a well-known pimp. Florence was going about its business all around me, teeming with life like a midden, or some dead thing that is forever rotting, but never rotted away, and I was one of the creatures battened onto it, one of those misshapen things that shun the light and turn from it to burrow deeper into the warm foulness. *Amerigo Ormani. Three dependants. Payments cease. Fascinating.* A sudden desire came over me, like the first surge of a tertian fever, to unbutton my doublet, unlace my shirt, loosen the bindings and show this world of strangers what kind of monster walked among them.

I was still in this state when I came once again to the door of the Palazzo Salvucci. The sensation that I had already stripped myself naked was so strong that I had to run my hands down my clothing to make sure I was still Comandante Onorio Celavini. The slave girl opened the door and led me into a wood-panelled room hung with smoke-darkened portraits and a large allegorical scene of Daphne pursued through a forest by Apollo. It must have come from an old wedding chest. I found myself staring at the little figures in their antique clothes: at Apollo, in high boots, holding a bow, running through orange trees heavy with fruit; at Daphne, slender girl, reaching up towards the blue sky, stretching, her thin mantle falling away from her white breasts, her clasped hands bursting into branches, twigs, a crown of glossy green. Between the trees, gentle hills of gold and grey fading into light.

'It's very old,' came a voice from behind me. I felt myself jump out of my skin, though in reality, years of training had kept my flesh steady. 'From the days of Cosimo il Vecchio. My husband's grandmother's wedding chest.'

'A lovely thing,' I said with difficulty. My scar was stinging as if the whip of a jellyfish had just been drawn across my face. I forced myself to turn around. In front of me was a woman of about my age, dressed in a gown of dove grey damask patterned with golden lilies, over an embroidered petticoat of pale blue. She had freckled skin, a delicately curved nose and eyes that were slightly too small for her face, offset by the heavy curve of dark eyebrows. Her black hair was pulled back and fixed with a silver tiara. Even though when I had last seen her she had been a girl of fourteen, sitting across from me in the village square on the Feast of Santa Clara, I knew her at once. She was smiling, a polite, neutral smile, but as our eyes met it froze in place across her lips. She gasped and took a step backwards.

'Smeralda Ellebori,' I said.

'Oh! Holy Mother . . .' She gasped, and her hand jumped to the cameo locket around her neck. 'Bartolomeo . . .' She squeezed her eyes shut, breathed, and recomposed her smile. She opened her eyes again. 'Your deepest pardon, Comandante. It is this awful heat. It gives one fancies.' But her expression changed again, her body began to tremble, and she staggered backwards, feeling behind her, and sank into the nearest chair.

'Are you not well, signora?' I asked. 'Or did you take me for someone else?'

'Someone . . . ? Yes. How foolish.' She fanned herself with a stiff hand. Her lips had gone white. 'Perhaps . . .'

'Perhaps I look like someone from Pietrodoro,' I said. My voice was nothing more than a hiss of air, the scrape of a whetstone along a steel edge.

'Who are you?' she shrieked. Bolt upright in the chair, one hand at her neck, the other gripping the armrest. It was carved in the form of a long, supple dog. 'Who—?' The word ended abruptly, as though a hand had been clamped across her mouth.

I almost told her. It took everything in my power, all that I had taught myself over the years, all that I had learnt. But at the last moment, as it seemed as though the body beneath my clothes was going to burn through them of its own accord, I remembered the old Mother Superior, sitting beside my bed, years ago. 'It must be hard to have saved your life at the cost of your nature,' she had said, and she had sounded so sad, because yes, it was true. It was hard. But I had saved myself. Survival over nature. I rubbed the scar on my neck, my gesture mirroring that of the woman sitting before me.

'I am Onorio Celavini,' I said. 'Bartolomeo Ormani was my cousin. Do you not remember me?'

'You look so very much like him,' she whispered.

'Do I?'

She nodded faintly.

'Which Bartolomeo do I resemble? The one who was murdered in Pietrodoro, or the one who kept a mistress here in Florence, before he had her head almost hacked from her body two nights ago?'

'I don't know what you mean,' she said.

'In the name of God!' I barked, and she winced at the violence in my voice, the ugliness of it. 'Why would you take the trouble to lie? You cannot comprehend the offence you cause me!' She stared at me, her eyes showing white, seeing a ghost, but seeing the commander of the Grand Duke's police as well.

'I'm s-sorry,' she stammered. 'I knew the magistrates would come, after . . . after . . .'

'Zanobia Linucci was killed like peasants kill their autumn sow, and left for the world to stare at, to slander,' I said. I was standing over her now, legs apart, balled-up hands on my hips, and I saw myself as she saw me, a man with power, with weapons, who could reach out and take her life with no more consequence than if she beat one of her slaves. 'They left her with no honour or dignity. And a man who stole my . . . my cousin's name caused it to be done.'

'I hate him!' Suddenly she was out of her chair and facing me. We were less than an arm's length apart. I could see the fine down of dark hair on her upper lip, the sweat beading on her freckled forehead. 'Do you hear me? I hate him! Arrest him! Make him pay!'

'But who is he?' I said quietly.

She blinked. 'Augusto,' she said. 'Don't you remember Augusto, my older brother? If you are who you say you are. I'm confused!' She turned away and paced stiffly towards the window. 'I shouldn't be talking to a policeman!'

'Look at me, Smeralda! We used to play in the terraces below the walls,' I said. 'You, me, Bartolomeo's sister. Your brother Federigo. We would hunt rats with your father's dog in the priest's barn. Once you thought a snake had bitten you when you put your hand inside a hollow tree, but it was a hornet. Your hand swelled up like a melon.'

'I don't remember you at all,' she said, her voice soft with confusion. 'But there's so much I don't remember. I don't want to. I've never wanted to. And now this has come to me.' Her hands were fists around the rich fabric of her skirt. I felt a wave of cold fury. This woman, who had drifted unchanged, from then to now, into this soft existence, was inconvenienced by the past.

'Your family killed them all,' I said. 'You gave them the lie of friendship, of love, and then you destroyed them!'

'Not me! I tried to stop them! I tried to prevent it, but what was I? Nothing! They brushed me aside like a moth! I thought they would kill me like a moth, a beetle – like this!' She clapped her hands. I flinched in surprise. 'Because once they knew, once Father and Augusto found out, there was nothing, not in the whole of Creation, that could have stopped them.' She was facing me now, her back pressed against one of the Flemish tapestries on the wall.

'What did they find out?' I asked. 'What could they possibly have cared about? We . . . They were going to leave Pietrodoro. Bartolomeo told me. Don Amerigo was buying land in Montalcino. There was nothing. Your families were at peace.'

'At peace? Dear God!' She pulled viciously at a lock of her hair. 'Yes, yes, we thought so. We believed that everything had healed. But we were so young, and so blind.'

'Who are you talking about?' It was all I could do to stop myself grabbing her shoulders. I didn't understand this at all. My world, my memories seemed to be lurching in an unknown direction.

'Bartolomeo and me,' she said, and she seemed to have let all of her vitality out with those three words. Her legs buckled, and then I had to catch her under the arms and help her down onto the bench beneath the window.

'I don't understand,' I said. I was kneeling too, because I wasn't sure what my body would do if it wasn't anchored to the ground.

'We were betrothed,' she said, so quietly that her voice was almost drowned out by a pair of friars bantering out in the street.

'Betrothed.' I fumbled with the buttons on my collar. The ruff was too tight against my scar; I felt as if I were choking.

'We were in love. So in love. And that was perfect – don't you see? We would unite our two families. We would heal the whole of Pietrodoro. Don't you remember it, how the piazza between our house and the Ormanis' felt like a wound? All the blood they'd spilt there, for centuries. Since the mountains were

275

made – that's what they used to say. We believed that my father and Amerigo were ready. There would be a great, beautiful wedding and we would be . . . we would be happy.'

'But he was going into the Church. Bartolomeo was going to be a cardinal,' I said in disbelief.

'He'd changed his mind. That was another thing that was going to be wonderful. Don Amerigo always wanted a son who would share his passions: a soldier son. Instead he had little Onoria, who turned herself into a boy just to please her father. Don't you remember her? It was so sad.'

'She could fight,' I managed to say.

'Yes, she could fight! But girls ought not to fight. Bartolomeo was going to give up his books and become his father's pupil, and poor Onoria would have gone back to being a girl. Everything would have been put right. Put into order. And then I . . . Oh, God. Stupid, stupid.'

'Tell me.'

'I told my brother Federigo. I didn't know that he was angry with Augusto about something. But he was. He was raging. He told Augusto about us. I don't know why – perhaps to show that he knew things, that he had secrets. He wanted to be like Augusto, like Onoria wanted to be like Don Amerigo. But Augusto became like a madman. He told my father, and then I found out that my family was a flask of poison. Father had inherited a hatred of the Ormanis from his father, and after Florence attacked Siena and the republic fell, he loathed them even more. Augusto fought at Scannagallo, on the Sienese side. He's never forgiven the Medicis, and neither did Father. I didn't understand that the warmth that seemed to have grown between us and the Ormanis was all a pretence. When Father found out about Bartolomeo and me, he and Augusto decided to act. Did you ever come to our village feast, for Santa Clara's day? They waited, smiled, plotted until that night. I didn't know. I watched them pouring wine, more and more wine, heard them laughing, sang the old songs. God help me, but I thought: *One day, my love and I will be at the head of a great, happy, united family.'* Smeralda buried her face in her hands. Her tiara slipped out of the thick braid and fell to the floor. 'Then I woke up in the night, and there were screams, and fire . . . They killed them all. Don Amerigo, Donna Maria, Onoria and . . . and Bartolomeo. The servants. Everyone.' She looked up defiantly. 'But my love died with honour, the only honour in my village that night. He fought Augusto hand to hand and made him a cripple before he died. And I was glad. The last pleasure I have ever felt in this world was when I saw Augusto carried back to our house and knew he would suffer for ever.'

She stopped, and sat there, gasping as though she had just run a race. The expression on her face was half disbelief, half terror.

'And then?' *What happened while I was wandering alone?* I wanted to ask. *What happened while your poor Onoria was dying, and had to save herself by hiding inside her own skin? What happened after your foolishness brought ruin to us all?* But then I discovered that there was no hatred in me for this woman. We had both been destroyed by the same men. We both walked through the world hiding our open wounds.

'Then?' She laughed bitterly and turned her face away from me. 'Then I heard my mother pleading with my father not to kill me too and throw me into the blaze across the piazza, for the dishonour I had brought to the Ellebori. Augusto was screaming as they carried him upstairs, and Father was screaming outside my bedroom. Both of them, howling for my death. I heard him order his groom to strangle me. I was getting ready to throw myself out of the window rather than being slaughtered like that, but then my mother put her body across the doorway, and Federigo was begging . . . God knows what happened. Their blood cooled. A few days later I was sent off to the priory in Radicofani, and the year after that I was married off to my husband in San Giminiano, where the Salvuccis have most of their lands. We moved here soon afterwards, to the fury of my father and Augusto. Their hatred of the Medicis and of this city never dimmed. Meanwhile, they had declared themselves lords of Pietrodoro and stole everything that the Ormanis had once owned, because there was no one left to challenge them. I have heard that you cannot even speak the name Ormani in the village now, and if you do, no one remembers, or pretends not to.

'Then my father and Augusto allied themselves with the Aldobrandeschis and made a sort of rebellion against the power of Florence. They aren't rebels, though: they're bandits, outlaws. Girolamo is with them. He became a brute as well.' She twisted her face into a mask of loathing. 'Antonio died of tertian fever along with my mother within a few years of the Ormanis. My father died two years ago, in his bed.'

'May his soul be in hell,' I muttered. Smeralda gave no sign of having heard.

'I thought I was free of them here in Florence,' she said. 'But around the time of my father's death – I didn't go back to Pietrodoro to see him buried, or to say a prayer for him, I can assure you – Augusto appeared. He came here, to my house, grinning like the Devil himself. "I have a new name," he said. "Can you guess it? Bartolomeo Ormani!" He had come back into my life just to torment me. I mean, what other explanation could there have been? He made my husband introduce him to his bank, the Miniati, and forced a loan out of him. Then I heard that Augusto had installed a mistress here, under my nose. Under my family's nose. I am a Salvucci now, I washed Pietrodoro and Ellebori from me like the dust from that stinking charnel house of a village. My brother delighted in his masquerade, Comandante. Satisfying his lust here in the city of his enemies, passing himself off as the man he'd killed, the man I loved.'

'Did you know that Donna Zanobia was an Orsini?' I asked, bringing up the dead because I couldn't bear to hear any more of this living woman's suffering.

Smeralda's shoulders stiffened. 'I made friends with her, you know,' she said. 'Out of pity, at first, because what woman deserves to be tied to a man like Augusto? But I discovered that I liked her. She was so different to me. Her family had used her as a gaming piece, which was something we shared. But she was outgoing and worldly, and I am . . . as you see me. We kept our friendship from Augusto, but I tell you, Comandante, the last two years were the most carefree of my life.'

'Your brother's mistress. It sounds like a strange friendship.'

'Mistress? Oh, no, Comandante. Zanobia was Augusto's wife.'

I stared at her. 'I don't believe you!'

'But it's true. They married in secret. Augusto dreams about an alliance with the barons of Pitigliano against Duke Francesco. The present baron is in debt to the Medicis, but his brother is more independent: he knew about the marriage. Augusto wooed Zanobia and she saw some advantage for herself, though I never understood it. She soon realised what a monster he is.' Smeralda gave me an almost defiant half-smile. 'Pietro wasn't the first, Comandante. But he wasn't worth dying for. Or perhaps he was. How would I know?'

'Where is Augusto now?'

'On his way back to Pietrodoro, I suppose. I don't care. Can I tell you something that is horribly selfish, Comandante? Although my friend is dead, I rejoice that my brother will have no cause to visit Florence ever again.'

I reached out and took her hands. 'He never will, signora. On behalf of the *Otto di Guardia*, I can make that promise.'

'Bartolomeo's cousin.' She smiled for the first time. 'You look so much like him. But he would be . . . older.' Tears were streaming down her face, but she let them fall unchecked.

'He would be. A little,' I said. 'Donna Smeralda, would you bear witness in front of the *Otto*? I'll see to it that you are treated graciously.'

She hesitated and bit the inside of her mouth. She had used to do that. How strange, to remember such a thing. 'Yes. Gladly,' she said at last.

I laid her hands in her lap and stood up. 'Perhaps it won't be necessary.'

'I am ready, Comandante. And then perhaps you will come back and talk with me about . . . about the old days, and Bartolomeo, and Onoria?' she said, almost tripping over the words.

'I'd like that,' I said. I was at the door when my thoughts cleared enough to ask one last question. 'What happened to Federigo?'

Smeralda was dabbing at her face with a handkerchief. When she turned to me, half in light, half in shadow, her face streaked red, she seemed to have become a child again. 'He joined the Church,' she said. 'He went to Spain and became a bishop. Now he's a cardinal in Rome. One of the youngest.' The pride in her voice was heartbreaking.

'That was Bartolomeo's destiny.'

'Yes. Federigo hated fighting. He hated cruelty. I don't know what it was that made him so angry with Augusto.' She smiled again and shook her head. 'I don't know whether Federigo would ever have married. But after . . . after it happened, it was little Onoria that he cried over. There was nothing left of them. Just ash. Just . . .' She hugged herself and didn't say anything more. I left silently, and when I stepped out into the street, for a moment I didn't know where I was.

CHAPTER TWENTY-ONE

I went back to the Bargello. That forbidding, impersonal place felt almost comforting as its grim smells and sounds wrapped themselves around me. Scarfa beckoned me over as soon as I walked in, but I pretended not to see him. The file I had been compiling on the Ellebori was locked in one of the drawers of my desk. I took it out. The weight of it in my hand, which still remembered the feel of Smeralda Ellebori's own hands, took me by surprise; the papers shifted inside the binder like bones inside a dead limb. Scarfa was scowling at me. He waved at me again, but I shook my head. 'Come with me, please, Capo,' I called, and headed for the magistrates' chambers.

Cavaliere del Caccia was conferring with another magistrate when I walked in, Scarfa grumbling behind me. I dropped the file on his desk and clasped my hands behind my back.

'What's this?' del Caccia snapped, annoyed at the interruption.

'The activities of the bandit Lodovigo Ellebori and his son Augusto Ellebori, of Pietrodoro,' I said.

Del Caccia made an exasperated grunt. 'This is hardly apposite, Celavini. I clearly told you that I wanted answers regarding the murders on Ponte Santa Trìnita.'

'Here is your answer,' I said, fighting to keep my voice under control.

'Do we really have time for this?' asked the other magistrate, whose name was Bondoni.

'This isn't a good idea, Onorio,' hissed Scarfa, touching my arm.

'If you'll just give me a moment, sirs,' I said. 'This is your answer. I can name both victim and culprits.'

'The victim was Pietro Vennini,' said del Caccia shortly.

'The true victim was Donna Zanobia Linucci,' I said. 'Widow of Giovanni Linucci of Pitigliano.' Bondoni opened his mouth to say something but I cut him off. 'Prior to her marriage she was Zanobia Orsini, daughter – illegitimate – of the Count of Pitigliano.'

'Orsini?' del Caccia repeated.

'Segretario Boschi will confirm it. And, Capo Scarfa, you have the pendant that belonged to Donna Zanobia?' I asked.

He nodded. 'It certainly bears the arms of Pitigliano,' he said.

'Orsini . . .' Del Caccia seemed to have the word attached to his tongue. 'Dear God. There'll be such a scandal. We'll have to tell His Highness at once. Go on, Celavini.'

'She was killed on the orders of one Bartolomeo Ormani, her lover and patron. The motive is as obvious as it seems: she betrayed him with Pietro Vennini. An affair of honour. Vennini has had something like this coming to him for years, but God knows, his end was spectacular. Which cannot be said for Donna Zanobia.'

'Have you arrested this Ormani?'

'He left the city with his gang of assassins, if indeed he was ever here. I think it likely that he wasn't.'

'Damn him!' Bondoni exclaimed. 'A band of assassins in our city! Where is he?'

'With respect, Cavaliere, the question is, who is he?' I said. 'Ormani is a false name. The Ormanis were thrown out of Florence with the rest of the White Guelphs nearly three hundred years ago, and . . .' I paused and licked my dry lips. 'And they never came back. But they hadn't vanished from the earth. A branch of the family had thrived in the south of Tuscany.'

'Then we know where to find him!'

'Ah. Except that Bartolomeo Ormani died twenty years ago.' My audience all threw up their hands in frustration. I'd caught them, all right. Crimes so rarely make for good stories. They are simply the muddy distillate of humanity's worst impulses. And anyway, this was no different from any other crime, any other report, after all: lust, jealousy, rage, revenge, arrogance and, finally, stupidity. But I wasn't drawing my story out for effect. It felt like each link of it was part of a chain wrapped around my heart, and the telling was a painful disgorging, as though I was purging some long-held poison. 'The Ormanis are all dead,' I managed, because that was the poison: the tincture of truth and falsehood which for twenty years had corrupted my true nature. For a moment I felt as I had earlier, as if I had discarded my clothes, my shell, and revealed myself. I was dead. Yet I was standing here.

'Go on,' said Capo Scarfa. I realised that I'd fallen silent.

'I'm sorry,' I said, and forced myself back into the present.

'The Ormani family was destroyed in a feud by the Ellebori family, with whom they shared the lands belonging to a village called Pietrodoro. We know – the Grand Duchy knows – the Ellebori very well.' I laid my hand on the file of documents. 'I can prove that the man calling himself Bartolomeo Ormani is really Augusto Ellebori, lord of Pietrodoro, bandit and outlaw. And more: that Zanobia Linucci was not his mistress but his secret wife, and that it was Ellebori's plan to form an alliance with the County of Pitigliano against His Highness Don Francesco.'

They all bombarded me with questions. How did I know? What proof did I have? Were there witnesses?

'What is this file?' asked Bondoni after he had banged on the desk for quiet.

'Every report on the Ellebori, Cavaliere. Every mention. Every trace, going back almost twenty years.'

'And why . . . ? What was your interest in them before this sorry affair?' asked del Caccio, puzzled.

I kept my face impassive, though at last I wanted to smile. 'When I was escorting the body of Don Orazio del Forese here from Rome, our company passed through the Val d'Orcia. I heard that there was an army of bandits operating beyond the laws of the Grand Duke, keeping the land in fear, harassing pilgrims on the Via Francigena, plundering mule trains and holding merchants and their goods to ransom. I'm a soldier, sirs, and I suppose I always will be. You might say it was out of habit, but whatever the reason, I began to wonder how bandits like the Ellebori – and the Piccolomini and Aldobrandeschi, who claim to be rebels but are just common thieves – could take hold of a country like Tuscany, and how they could be fought.

It's been a . . . a personal interest of mine. A bit of a nail in the head.' I tapped my temple. 'I thought that one day I might suggest a military solution.'

'That would be far outside the jurisdiction of the *sbirri*,' said Bondoni sternly, but Scarfa was stifling a grin.

'Of course, of course,' I said. 'This is something I've done on my own time, sirs. We old soldiers' – I glanced at Scarfa – 'can't help dreaming of action.'

'Comandante Celavini is still young and ambitious,' Scarfa said. 'And he's right, the bandits are a growing problem to the south and west. Even around Arezzo. At some point something will have to be done.'

'It is not a priority for His Highness,' Bondoni said, with a shrug that said: *Nothing that we do is a priority for the Grand Duke.*

'No, indeed it isn't. But this is good work, Comandante. Very good. Holy Virgin, what a mess,' said del Caccio. 'Now leave us, please. We need to work out how we will proceed. That bastard Vennini – even dead he's making us all step in shit.'

'That was impressive,' Scarfa told me when we were back in the *sbirri* offices.

'Thank you, Capo,' I said. I felt exhausted, and the griping pain in my belly had returned, along with the first tendrils of a headache.

'I mean it. You know, of course, that nothing else will happen?' he went on. I stopped on the way to my desk and stared at him.

'What do you mean?'

'I mean that the criminals are no longer in Florence. They're probably at the far end of the country by now, if they're even still in Tuscany. The magistrates are perfectly happy that Vennini got himself killed – they're delighted, in fact. And that poor woman . . .' He shrugged his shoulders. 'An adulteress. Who cares?'

'Capo!' I said, appalled.

'No, really. You are a truly honourable man and the way you stand up for women is commendable, though a lot of people don't understand exactly why you bother. We're the police, is the general feeling, not the Umiltà. I don't agree with them, but I think you've got more than one nail in your head, Onorio. Let it go. Remember that we're servants of the law, and, in the end, of the Grand Duke. Do you think for one minute . . . ?' He lowered his voice and came over to where I was standing. He leant and almost whispered into my ear. 'Do you think that the *Otto* will want any of this to be public? The death of an Orsini in our city is a great embarrassment. The quicker this is all put to bed the better.' He must have seen that I was dumb with shock, because he took my shoulder and shook it gently, one man talking sense to another. 'You've done fine work, Onorio. My advice is this: go out, get drunk, wake up tomorrow and stretch out in bed knowing you don't have to come back to this shithole for a month. Let Carnesecchi deal with the Vennini business.'

'But, Capo . . .'

'Go home. You're my best officer, Onorio. After this, you'll have everyone's eye. I'll wager that you could be *capo* one day, if you want to be. But for God's sake, man, it *is* just a job.'

I was still a soldier – God help me, would I always be a soldier? – so I obeyed my superior's order and went home. But first I stopped at the Pietà and knelt in the chapel. I prayed for the soul of Zanobia

Linucci, and for Smeralda Ellebori, asking the Virgin to bring them peace. The house was empty, though my housekeeper, Gherarda, had left the place swept and smelling faintly of lemon and rosemary. I tied a cloth between my legs, went to the kitchen, lit a small fire in the stove and boiled some water. I steeped dried motherwort leaves and caraway seeds, and drank the hot tisane from a bowl, sitting on the lichen-crusted stone bench in the courtyard. Sparrows piped busily in the bushes, and martens swooped down and around the walls on scissored wings, shrilling with what seemed like delight but was perhaps something else entirely. Perhaps, for the martens, this was just a job.

I didn't go out and get drunk. Instead I went to Zanobia Linucci's funeral. Wearing my best black doublet and hose, black sleeves damasked with silver and a simple black velvet cap, and carrying only a dagger, I waited in the shadows near the church of San Biagio until I heard the clang of a muffled bell coming down Via Pellicceria. First came the usual gaggle of street children, out when they should have been long asleep, skipping in front of Father Iacopo and behind him, the figures draped in long black cloaks, hoods drawn down over their faces, each carrying a long white candle. It was a still, close night and the flames barely wavered as the marchers came on, treading slowly to the pulse of the bell. I watched as the coffin, draped in silver-spangled black velvet and carried by six hooded brothers of the Misericordia, swayed into the little piazza in front of the church. There weren't many mourners. As the coffin bearers climbed the steps into the church, I recognised the usual professionals, men and women who made their living by following the coffins of the unpopular or the lonely. But mingled with these familiar faces were others:

Simone, Donna Zanobia's steward; Lisabetta, her maid; and some of the other servants, although Riccio the cook had absented himself. Smeralda was not there, but that wasn't a surprise. The Salvuccis wouldn't want any association with scandal.

Another man, in inconspicuous clothes, slipped into the church behind Father Iacopo. I recognised his hollow eyes and neatly clipped beard: a secretary from the Signoria who acted as one of Don Francesco's intelligencers, a gatherer of information whose gleanings were sometimes shared with the magistrates of the Eight but never with us humble policemen. As I came up the steps behind him I nodded familiarly, and he nodded back with blank politeness, as though I was a stranger, though he knew my face very well.

It was a short funeral. Father Iacopo did little to hide his disdain for the proceedings, and very soon Zanobia Linucci was being lowered down into oblivion through a hole in the floor, a dark rectangle lit from below by the dirty red glow of the sextons' torches as they waited for the coffin. I could hear them scraping and shunting it unceremoniously into some less cluttered part of the crypt as I left the church, a corner of a room crowded with the bones and dust of countless strangers. It was a long way from Pitigliano, but then again, as the illegitimate sister of a count, it had always been her destiny to be forgotten, no matter how brightly she had tried to burn. The thought lowered my spirits even further, and I paused on the threshold and said a prayer to Santa Celava, asking her to watch over the lost woman. When I came out onto the small landing in front of the church door, I found the piazza still crowded with people, most of them professional mourners waiting for Simone the steward to pay them. Two

Misericordia brothers were chatting with Father Iacopo, and the usual curious drunks and beggars of the neighbourhood were drifting around the edges of the crowd. I didn't want to linger: my stomach was cramping, and my breasts were aching and swelling uncomfortably inside their binding. I was thinking of another tisane and my bed as I jogged down the steps, and so I wasn't paying attention when a figure slipped out of the dark alley that led down to Via del Terme. Most people coming from there at night looked furtive, and usually for good reason, so I gave him no more thought. I was making my way through the mourners, hoping that no one would notice me leaving, when there was a shrill scream. I spun around and saw, outlined against the torchlit wall of the building opposite, a raised hand and the flash of metal. The crowd was flinching in one collective movement, like a shoal of minnows when a pebble is dropped into their midst, and I was suddenly leaning against moving bodies, but I still heard a voice, pitched loud enough to carry above the confusion.

'My brother sends you this payment, with his regards!'

I drew my knife and pushed Father Iacopo to one side. One of the long white candles fell across me, spattering my clothes with wax. I grabbed it with my free hand as I almost tripped over a man on the ground. I glimpsed the tangled eyebrows of Simone. His eyes were screwed shut and his tongue was sticking straight out between his teeth. Above him stood a man holding a dagger blade downwards in his fist, poised to strike again.

'Ho!' I yelled, and swung the candle backhanded at his head. It struck him on the ear and snapped in two. The man, unhurt but surprised, lurched backwards. I saw his eyes register the knife in my hand, saw him hesitate. And recognised . . . something. I took the guard of the unicorn, blade above my head, and took a step across Simone's body. But instead of coming on, the man turned and, shoving aside a couple of professional mourners who were still waiting with their purses in their hands, took off at a sprint up Via Pellicceria. 'Call out the *sbirri*!' I shouted to the nearest person, a Misericordia brother who was hurrying towards Simone. Then I set off after him.

Via Pellicceria runs straight north into the Mercato Vecchio. The man was dashing along it, the few passers-by jumping out of his way when they saw the knife in his hand. Soon he was crossing the Mercato itself, still crowded with empty stalls and strewn with rubbish. He was taller than me, and younger. Two years younger. I knew I wasn't going to catch him. Then I saw him slow down to pass a throng of people outside a tavern. Something about his movements told me that he thought he'd lost me. I ducked behind a row of stalls and ran as quietly as I could to the tavern. There he was, half a street ahead of me. He had sheathed his dagger and was moving at a fast walk, a young man late for an assignation. I followed, keeping to the shadows.

He stopped at the corner of Via dei Pecori, looked up and down the street, and then turned left. He had slowed down, and I realised that he hadn't quite got his bearings. Pausing at the next corner, he looked around again, and started up Via de' Vecchietti. At the end he paused again, crossed the street and turned right towards the baptistery. When he hesitated at the corner of Borgo San Lorenzo, I realised where he was going. By the time I had reached the corner myself, he was already at the door of the Palazzo Salvucci. I heard him knock, and as I began to run, saw the glint as he drew his dagger.

'Girolamo Ellebori!' I yelled. He turned, and I drew my blade. The palazzo door was opening. 'Stop!' I yelled again. He looked from me to the door, turned, and sprinted off up the street. I flew past Smeralda Salvucci's door, seeing only the puzzled face of a servant peering into the street, and followed him into the square in front of San Lorenzo.

'Family, to me!' I shouted, because there was often a police patrol around here, but there was no answer. Girolamo Ellebori was gaining on me again.

And then he made a mistake, one that a Florentine perhaps would not have made. Instead of carrying on up Via de' Ginori, which was straight and empty, he crossed the square at an angle and darted into Borgo la Noce. Perhaps he had shied away from the empty streets and, hearing the sound of a crowd up ahead, thought that he would more easily lose me there. He must not have known that Borgo la Noce was one of the officially licensed brothel streets in the city. It was crowded, all right, but at this time of night it was full, not with people going about their peaceable business who would be frightened by an armed man but with young men inflamed by drink and by the entreaties of the women leaning out of windows, wearing nothing but gauzy tunics that hid nothing of their bodies, or calling to them from the doorways of taverns from which even more noise – laughter, singing and often fights and despair – spilt out.

I followed him. He was still a good twenty paces ahead of me and drawing away all the time. But almost at once his path was blocked by a knot of young fellows who were all looking up at three women leaning far out of a window, shaking their breasts and flicking their long plaits of hair like fishing lines. The man barged into them like a football player, sending them flying. I had to jump over one of them, and when another stepped in front of me I yelled '*Sbirri!*' in his face and short-armed him out of my way. A little further on a group of young aristocrats was standing in front of a tavern. They were all wearing swords and had certainly paid for that privilege. I might perhaps have written out their licenses myself. My quarry was forced to dodge around them in the narrow street, and as he passed he must have caught one of them with his elbow because all at once there was an explosion of oaths and threats. Someone put out his foot and the running man went down, landing heavily on his face. Two or three of the gentlemen had drawn their swords. I was still running towards them. The man rolled and sprang to his feet. His dagger was lying a few feet away from him. He picked it up and turned to run again, but I pushed past the gentlemen, who were standing over their friend in drunken confusion, and faced him.

'Girolamo Ellebori!' I said. He frowned. I pointed my dagger at him. 'I am Comandante Onorio Celavini, and I am arresting you in the name of the *Otto di Guardia*.'

He spat. 'Go to hell,' he said, and grinned. Taking a couple of paces back, he dropped into a low guard. The young men were all jabbering and shaking their swords. I needed to get away from them. 'Put down your blades, or I'll lock all of you up,' I said, stepping beyond the wavering points, knowing that they were as likely to go for me as for the man who was facing me, his dagger point down and his arm flexed to strike.

Girolamo Ellebori. He had been a rather thin, pale boy with a long and freckled face, given to throwing stones at cats and bullying the village children, but also to crying when he lost even the most trivial games. Two years younger than me, he was always telling tales on his brother Federigo and getting us into trouble. It was hard to believe that this man, sinewy and sunburnt, with a beard and a curled moustache, was the same person. But his face was still long, and his eyes . . . His eyes looked like the eyes of his brother, Augusto. I could almost feel the tension, the power in his body. It seemed to be reaching across the space between us, pressing against me, forcing me backwards. The air, already thick, tightened around me, plastering itself against my face like wet linen. Like bedsheets soaked with my own blood. The leash tightened around my neck. I couldn't breathe. *He's found me,* a voice inside my head was whining. Onoria's voice. *He's come back for me.* Then one of the drunken gentlemen cursed and lunged past me with his sword, his arm jogging my shoulder.

'You bastard,' he yelled, and aimed a thrust at Girolamo. It was weak and badly timed, and Girolamo turned it aside with a deft twist of his blade and lashed out, catching the man across the forehead. The man dropped his sword and staggered back, his face a veil of red. Girolamo dropped his dagger, bent down and scooped up the sword. He was laughing. Suddenly, though, my body, if not my mind, was awake. It knew what this was. It understood battle.

I have always disliked fighting with only a dagger. It usually means that something has gone badly wrong, that you've miscalculated or wandered into the wrong tavern. As I watched Girolamo, I wondered why he hadn't kept hold of his own dagger in his left hand. Then I saw that he was holding it wrong: his wrist was bent, and the fingers crabbed. He must have fallen on it and damaged it somehow. That was good. I stepped to the side and watched him track me with his eyes. The sword was long and new-looking, something for a young lord to wave around, but Girolamo knew what he was doing with it. I moved again, trying to get away from the drunkards. Perhaps there was a police patrol nearby, I thought. They usually came up and down this street a few times a night. I needed to arrest Girolamo and hand him over to the Eight alive. But a crowd was gathering. A half-naked girl hanging onto the neck of a fat merchant was yelping at us as though she was at a cockfight. *I should have let him run*, I was thinking. *He couldn't have left the city. We'd have hunted him down tomorrow.*

'Put down the sword,' I said, in my most reasonable policeman's voice, but it came out as a twisted rasp. I could still feel the leash against my throat. Girolamo grinned.

'Get fucked, you Florentine queer,' he said, and lunged. I was holding the blade of my dagger along my forearm and I parried easily, knocking his sword wide and jumping back out of range. He came at me again, probing. I still wasn't sure what I was going to do. A woman was screaming somewhere above us, calling for the police and God to help her. Girolamo swished his blade, took a decorative guard and leered at me, posing like a drawing in a fencing manual. He stepped forward, and I stepped back. I could sense the shadows growing behind me and realised that he was backing me into a doorway, a tight space where I wouldn't be able to use my arms. He lunged again, and this time I trapped him, trying to stab his arm but instead catching it between my blade and my own forearm, at the same time as I tried to get a leg across his body and throw him. But he was strong, and angry, and twisted himself free, wrenching his arm back so that the hilts of our weapons tangled, and the dagger was nearly pulled from my hand. I grabbed his blade with my free hand, turned my back to him and kicked backwards with all my strength. My heel struck his shin, and he grunted and punched my head with his injured hand, making my ears ring. I was twisting the quillons of my dagger and they suddenly came free. Still holding his blade, I jabbed my elbow back into his face and pulled the edge of my dagger up across the inside of his arm. He shouted, and the sword clattered out of his limp fingers. Turning, I grabbed his neck and put my dagger against his face.

'Girolamo Ellebori, I'm arresting you for the murders of Zanobia Linucci, Pietro Vennini and Simone da Fiesole, and for plotting the murder of your own sister, Donna Smeralda Salvucci. We're going to the Bargello, and the *Otto* are going to ask you a lot of questions. You know how the *Otto* asks questions, don't you? And when they're done with you, you'll hang.'

Girolamo bared his teeth at me. 'My arm, you cunt. You've ruined my arm! May your balls shrivel up and be eaten by pigs!'

'That should be interesting,' I said. 'Save your stinking breath for the magistrates.' He opened his mouth to say something else, and I twisted my hand around his ruff in warning when suddenly he went limp and the flimsy lace was tearing in my fist as he dropped to his knees. I looked up to see one of the young aristocrats trying to pull his sword out of Girolamo's side. It had gone in under one right armpit and come out near the other.

'What . . . what have you done?' I said to the young fool, who was grinning with bloodlust and wine-kindled pride. 'In Jesus's name . . .' Girolamo's mouth was making a noise like air escaping from a bloated horse's punctured belly, and his eyes were rolling back in his head. I knelt in front of him, took hold of his hair and leant in so that my lips were almost touching his ear.

'Do you remember the Ormanis?' I whispered. 'I can tell you that they have never forgotten you. I can tell you . . .' But his head was lolling in my grasp. I let go of him, and his body folded sideways onto the paving stones.

A patrol, with Lieutenant Poverini at its head, had only been two streets away. When they finally arrived, I had put the idiot who had killed Girolamo Ellebori under arrest, and a whore was bandaging the head of his friend, who had bled all over several hundred *scudi* worth of silk doublet. The Misericordia were summoned to take the body away. The rest of the patrol was detailed to guard Smeralda's house, in case there were more assassins in the city. I walked back to the Bargello with Poverini and the young nobleman, who had passed through rage and threats, and was now gibbering with terror. I doubted anything would happen to him beyond a small fine, perhaps, and the inconvenience of being summoned by the Eight. I would see to it that he spent a few uncomfortable hours in a cell, though. I made my report to the magistrates' clerk on duty. He told me that Simone da Fiesole was still alive, though not expected to live.

By the time I got back to the house, the sky was already beginning to glow faintly, and Venus was shining high in the east. As I undressed in my curtained room, I found that my beautiful silver-spangled sleeves were covered in blood. It was on my hands as well. It was almost blissful to unbind the cloth around my chest, and there was blood on the cloth between my legs too. I stood in front of the mirror and studied myself. A pale woman, lean and muscled, with a scarred neck and small, reddened, cloth-marked breasts. Delicate face too tired to be anything but a blank. I cocked my hip, rested one stained hand on the curve of it and saw the statue of David in the courtyard of the Palazzo Vecchio: the sexless boy, deed done; the monster's head lolling, pointless now, nothing but meat, underfoot. David had girls' hair and a boy's prick, and I had neither, so I was his reverse. If Donatello had cast me in bronze I would have been just as baffling, just as unnatural. There was no giant's head at my feet, but I had a monster's blood on my hands, and I felt just as forlorn as David looked, his work done, and the world still the same.

I went outside and washed in cold water from the well, tipping the bucket over my head and listening to the rats scuttle away at the sound of the water. Then I put on some shapeless clothes, slipped out into the streets and let myself into the church of San Biaggio. I was gone long before anyone else was awake, and as I stretched myself out between sheets that were fleetingly cool, I repeated to myself the promise I'd whispered to Zanobia Linucci through the cracks in the stone floor, above the place where they'd lowered her into the dark.

CHAPTER TWENTY-TWO

I rose late, which felt strange, because it has never been my habit, or one which life has allowed me. I heard Gherarda let herself in, and the sounds of the fire being lit, pans being moved around: ordinary, domestic sounds, which I still found as exotic, in their way, as the skirl of a Turkish military band. When I got up, I found that I had bled a little on the sheets. Muttering, I stripped them from the bed, made it up again with clean linen from the press, and hid the soiled sheets beneath the neatly folded ones. I would take them out again tonight and use them until my bleeding stopped. Then I would have to boil them at night, or if they were too bad, leave them outside the Pietà when no one was looking, for the girls to clean and use. Gherarda was forbidden to come into my bedroom, but though I felt almost content to give her the run of the rest of my house, in the end I didn't trust her. I didn't trust anyone.

I was getting dressed when I heard Gherarda calling out, 'Coming, sirs! Coming!' and unlatch the front door. I knew she was irritated by my insistence on keeping the street door locked, and as I buttoned my doublet – green velvet the colour of bottle glass, which I sometimes wore in the summer when I was off duty – I pictured her limping across the courtyard. Her feet were bad: she had bunions that made her big toes lie across their neighbours, but she was inclined to exaggerate her aches and pains when it suited her. It was something I envied, in a way, this ability to be oneself, to display one's infirmities as badges of selfhood, as virtues. I would never be able to complain about the burdens of my own flesh. The cramps in my belly, the headaches, the swelling of my breasts: I had never told a soul about them. My mother had never known me as a woman. I had never sat down in a comfortable room with others of my sex, and talked of . . . what? I couldn't even imagine it. I sighed as I did up my hose and stepped into my shoes. Drawing back the curtains, I looked down into the street. Some girls from the Pietà were walking by, chatting together, happy and apparently carefree, but the greyish-white of their skin gave that the lie. They were orphans or abandoned by their parents for lack of money or kindness, or thrown out of home for being raped, or sick, or deformed. The women who ran the house were kind in their way, but pragmatic above all, and the girls below me spent most of their waking hours unravelling silk cocoons in one of the ill-lit rooms above the chapel. Some of them escaped into service and a few into marriage – the lucky ones. Many others left on a stretcher wrapped in a stained bedsheet, on their way to a perfunctory burial. I supposed their names must be written down somewhere, because if not, they might never have lived at all.

'Don Onorio!' Gherarda was calling up the stairs. 'A gentleman has visited you!'

'I'm coming.' I ran my hands down my front, wincing at the pressure against my breasts but satisfied that the bulge of the peascod doublet and the fashionably baggy folds of my hose had satisfactorily transformed me.

I never had visitors unless they were colleagues from the *sbirri*, so I assumed that one of them was waiting for me downstairs. Instead, standing elegantly in the hallway and pretending to admire the rather shabby Brussels tapestry that hung near the door, was the hollow-eyed man who had been at the funeral last night. The courtier. The Grand Duke's spy.

'Comandante Celavini,' he said. 'Let me congratulate you on your actions last night.'

'Thank you,' I said. 'It was no more than my duty as a servant of His Highness. How may I be of service to you, Don . . . ?'

'Angelo Ruspi.' He bowed in the elaborate manner of the court, and I replied in kind, not without noticing Gherarda's raised eyebrows as she watched the ritual.

'Gherarda, could you fetch some of that good Malvasia wine and something to eat?' I asked, but Ruspi held up his hand.

'I would adore a glass of your wine, but actually I'm here to bring you to the Signoria. The Grand Duke desires to speak with you.'

'The Grand Duke?' I repeated. I felt a lurch of unease, which Ruspi must have noticed. He was probably used to it.

'About last night and the unfortunate circumstances surrounding it,' he said. 'The Grand Duke feels that you are the man who understands them best.'

301

'Of course, signore.' I buckled on my sword and dagger, gave Gherarda some vague instructions on what she might leave me for my supper, and followed Ruspi out into the courtyard. 'I need to put this place to rights,' I said apologetically, but the courtier just smiled.

'Nonsense! Doesn't do to be too ostentatious,' he said, and led me out into Borgo Ognissanti.

'The man who was attacked, Donna Zanobia's steward, is likely to live after all, his doctor says,' he told me as we walked. 'If he does, he has you to thank.'

'I'm glad,' I said. 'He seems like a good fellow. Loyal.'

'Ah, loyalty. An excellent quality, but only if offered to the right party. Otherwise it becomes the source of boundless difficulty, wouldn't you say? He arranged the funeral. Do you think he let anyone know about her death – outside Florence?'

'If you mean her family in Pitigliano, I don't think he knew that Donna Zanobia was an Orsini by birth. She seems to have been a secretive person.'

'Ah. And the other servants?'

'I don't think any of them are bright enough, or curious enough, to have looked into it.'

'Good. Very good.' We walked in what might have been companionable silence for a while. 'You were a soldier, weren't you, Comandante? With Don Orazio del Forese.'

'That's right.'

'You don't seem like the usual run of soldier, if you don't mind me saying.'

'Oh? Why so?'

'You aren't a drunkard, or a braggart. You're a famous

swordsman – don't deny it. Witnesses say you could easily have killed that fellow last night.'

'Instead I let some wine-soaked boy do it for me,' I said ruefully.

'Young Pitti? Yes, that was unfortunate. He's an idiot in a family of idiots. But there, you see? You are a modest man. Modest home, modest dress. Soft-spoken.'

'I don't have much choice in the matter,' I told him, pointing to my scarred throat.

'Oh, it isn't a criticism, Celavini. It's a compliment. In any case, Girolamo Ellebori is better off dead.'

'I'd like to have brought him to justice.'

'I'm inclined to think that justice was served. Here we are,' he added, as we started across the Piazza della Signoria. 'Have you met His Highness before?'

'Once, after I joined the *sbirri*. I bowed, and he nodded.'

'Then you know what to expect,' Ruspi said, and I was pondering the ambiguity of this as we passed through the doorway on the piazza and into the courtyard beyond. There was the bronze boy leaning on his huge sword, and opposite him Judith about to behead Holofernes. I had seen them a hundred times before, but this morning they seemed more alive, somehow, the naked, sexless boy and the hooded, merciless girl. I followed Ruspi up to the first floor and waited while he spoke to the guard outside an unassuming door. The guard knocked, there was an indistinct noise from within, and Ruspi opened the door. 'I'll wait for you downstairs,' he said.

I had never been inside the Studiolo of Don Francesco,

though I had heard a great deal about it. Nothing that I had heard prepared me for the reality, though. I had expected something grand and strange. The room I entered was certainly strange, but there was no grandeur. Instead, as the guard discreetly closed the door behind me, I found myself inside an alarmingly small room, a narrow rectangle with a high, barrel-vaulted ceiling. Virtually the whole of the floor, from where I stood to the back wall, was crammed with a promiscuous jumble of lecterns, telescopes, a printing press, various stoves of different sizes, tripods and braziers, pestles and mortars, one of them so tall that I could have climbed inside it. There were glass alembics, spirals of copper tubing, sacks of charcoal spilling out onto the grimy floor, bellows and tongs. One of the braziers was alight, and a huge pear-shaped glass vessel full of greenish yellow liquid was bubbling above it. A layer of smoke hung just above my head. The walls themselves were lined with paintings, which added a further layer of hysteria to the room's atmosphere.

'What is it?' An impatient voice came from somewhere within the thicket of implements. I blinked – my eyes were already smarting from the acrid fumes that were almost stifling me – and saw a dark shape crouching behind the lit brazier. A man stood up, batting at the smoke rising from the handful of fresh charcoal that he had just dropped onto the fire. He had close-cropped black hair and a beard to match, a thin mouth and large eyes, red and running with tears, that seemed to hint at some great disappointment with the world. His black doublet was buttoned up to his neck and the white ruff that spread above his collar was no longer white, but grey with ash and sweat.

'Comandante Onorio Celavini of the *sbirri*, Your Highness,' I said, standing to attention. 'You sent for me, sir,' I added, when the man showed no sign of recognition. The large eyes kept straying to the bubbling liquid, and to the sheaf of dog-eared papers in his hand.

'Oh. Yes.' Grand Duke Francesco de' Medici frowned. 'Do you know anything about feldspar? I'm having difficulty with temperature and flux.'

'I'm afraid not, Your Highness,' I said. 'I believe you wanted to talk to me about last night's business in Borgo la Noce.'

'You have the tax figures from the brothels, do you?' Duke Francesco said wearily. 'Please don't bother me with those again. Just leave them.' He started to kneel again.

'No, Your Highness,' I said hurriedly. 'I tried to arrest a man called Girolamo Ellebori. Unfortunately, he was killed.'

'Ellebori . . .' The duke stood up again. 'Ellebori. Yes. Yes indeed.' His whole demeanour seemed to change. His back stiffened, and the look in his eyes changed from disappointment to a sullen hardness. 'You're the one who investigated the murders. Who discovered that the woman was the Count of Pitigliano's bastard sister.'

'Yes, Your Highness.'

'Sit down.'

I looked around for a chair but found nothing but a rope-bound barrel. I perched on the rim and watched as the duke fished out an empty packing case from beneath an easel covered by sheets of paper which were almost black with scrawled figures and obscure geometric symbols. He upended the case and sat down opposite me.

'Tell me everything you know,' he said, gripping his knees. He was almost rigid with attention. So I told him.

'Niccolò Orsini is an old monster, but he still has teeth,' the duke muttered when I was finished. Suddenly his attention had shifted elsewhere. I wasn't sure whether he was even talking to me. 'My father spent a fortune in gold and men to try and take Pitigliano. He should have taken it when Duke Niccolò sided with the Sienese and lost in 1555, but he let the old devil get stronger again.'

I knew men who had fought on both sides of the little wars between Pitigliano and Sovana, but I said nothing.

'My father played Niccolò and his brother Orso off against each other,' the duke went on. 'Orso took Pitigliano and we supported him. But Niccolò had Orso killed two years ago and has taken back the county. So I have decided to support the old swine, who is afraid his son is planning to depose him. In return he's let us put garrisons in the county. But now I hear that somehow, he has contrived to marry this bastard, who must be the sport of one of his Jewish concubines, to a notorious bandit. He sees an alliance of the old feudal lords, no doubt about it: Aldobrandeschi, Piccolomini, Orsini, Ellebori.' His fingers were claws digging into the stained black serge of his hose. 'Doomed. Yes, doomed: his son Alessandro will get rid of him, and Alessandro is deep in my pocket. But to give a villain like Ellebori permission to act against us, to set Augusto Ellebori up, to puff him up so that he feels sufficiently bold to come and go in our city, to cause scandal and disgrace, bloodshed . . .' The duke trailed off. His eyes were fixed on the far wall, burning with cold rage. Despite the suffocating heat in the room, I could almost feel a chill radiating from him.

'Your Highness, surely the matter is solved. Ellebori . . .' I paused. It felt dangerous to be uttering his name in this little underworld of a room. 'He has killed Orsini's daughter, so surely the alliance is at an end.'

Duke Francesco cracked his knuckles. He was still staring at the wall. 'Oh, I doubt that! I doubt that very much! Niccolò Orsini can spare a bastard daughter! She hardly matters. She's in her box and forgotten.' He waved his white hand and it passed through the air like a claw. His eyes narrowed, as if he was exploring some vivid idea that had come to life inside his skull. I imagined his mind must be like the easel: a mass of dark scrawls and speculations that only he could decipher. Then he grunted and seemed to relax.

'Comandante,' he said. 'Do you enjoy serving us?'

'Of course, Your Highness!' I said quickly. Sweat was starting to pool in the hollows at the base of my spine.

'You have a soldier's loyalty, a soldier's fixity of purpose. Your Capo . . .' He frowned, and I realised that he didn't know Scarfa's name. 'He recommends you highly. All well and good. I require something from you.'

'Of course, Your Highness.'

'I would be pleased if you would forget everything about this business.'

'My lord, I'm not sure what you are asking me,' I said, aware that my voice was little more than a whisper.

'I want the Vennini affair forgotten about. The dead are buried. Let their memories and all that you have found out be buried too.'

'We have enough to bring Augusto Ellebori to justice,' I said, thinking that perhaps he wasn't aware what had happened yesterday.

'Would two hundred *scudi* be enough?'

'I'm afraid I don't understand.'

'For your silence, man. For your promise to leave things exactly as they are.'

I stood up. The smoke had thickened, and was hanging like a heavy, gently rippling blanket. Some of the taller objects in the room were poking through it like mountains rising through mist in some dreary, hellish dawn. 'With the head of the family removed, the rest of his band will run away,' I said, struggling to hold on to what I was, a soldier, and officer of the *sbirri*. 'The bandits could be eradicated.'

'This matter will not be settled by destroying a few bandits. It will not be settled by a . . . by a . . .' He looked me up and down with a sort of revulsion. 'By a *policeman*.'

'But justice, Your Highness!'

'Three hundred, then. Would three hundred *scudi* satisfy you?' He sighed in exasperation. 'I wish to reward you, man. I am offering you a choice. This reward, or its reverse. You talk of justice, but every law, every judgement ultimately rests with me. And I am not a kindly judge. Do as I say and rise like the sun in the service of Tuscany. Refuse me, and you will be meddling in affairs of state. Which I would judge to be the action of a traitor.' He stood and turned his gaze absently towards the curved ceiling. His eyes were bored again. Eternally disappointed. 'Three hundred and fifty *scudi*, Comandante,' he said. I could tell by his voice that his mind had already drifted away from these worldly matters. 'You were a mercenary. We believe that is an excellent rate of pay.'

'Your Highness . . .' My collar was limp with sweat, which was trickling down my neck and into the binding around my breasts. I tugged the stiff linen away from my scar, and swallowed, wincing. And at that moment I understood that the emotion I was feeling was not revulsion or shame, but a strange sort of peace.

'I am at your service, Your Highness,' I said.

'Very good. Ruspi will see to the details.' Duke Francesco turned his back on me and squatted down in front of the brazier. As he leant over the glass vessel, the light from the burning charcoal cast a dull orange halo around his head. I watched him feeling around with one of his white hands for a pair of tongs, his dirty fingernails scrabbling through drifts of cinders and ash. I opened the door, and he didn't look back.

CHAPTER TWENTY-THREE

'Tell no one about this,' Ruspi said. We were strolling like a pair of old friends through the Mercato Nuovo.

'My God, sir! Who would I tell?' I snapped. The stink of the Grand Duke's alchemical smoke was all over me. Whatever sense of peace I had felt in the *studiolo* had dissolved in the heat of noon. 'Signor Ruspi, is this the way the Grand Duchy of Tuscany usually conducts its affairs?'

'You are the police, Comandante Celavini. What do you think?'

'I think that His Highness has a great deal on his mind, though little of it relates to the running of this city. And that is his right. Who am I to question the dealings of princes? But as the police, as you call me, what I see is . . .' I paused. I didn't know this man. But he plainly lived and worked in a wholly different world from mine, and I had now stepped across into it as well. 'The *sbirri* have been wading through blood these past four years, since Duke Cosimo's death,' I said. 'Florence, and Tuscany beyond it, has become lawless and bloodthirsty. In

310

the other pan of the scale, His Highness has found the secret of making porcelain. As I said, it is far beyond my remit to look into the mind of a prince.'

'And my remit also,' said Ruspi. 'We'll go to His Highness's bank and get your money – you drive a hard bargain, Comandante,' he added approvingly. 'You think like a magistrate and act like a soldier. There will be certain advantages if you please His Highness. You'll find you won't have to worry about advancement. If indeed you worry about that at all.'

'I don't,' I said, shortly.

'I believe you. But you aren't beyond wants and desires, Comandante.'

'I keep my desires simple. Work and solitude.'

'You'd have made an excellent monk. Though that would have been our loss. But you aren't being entirely truthful. I think you desire justice.'

'I want it. Otherwise, why would I have joined the *sbirri*?'

'Want and desire are different things, Comandante.' He stopped for a moment and regarded me with those hollow eyes. 'You care a great deal about women,' he said. 'I've noticed how you work. The Linucci woman, for instance: you seem to have been more touched by her death than by Vennini and the others. When you speak of justice, I think you mean it in a particular way. Unfortunate women, girls in trouble, wives killed by husbands . . . And yet you live alone.'

'As I told you, I like solitude,' I said.

'Every sort of opportunity – you have a good position, some money. And access to less . . . genteel pleasures. The city has its legs open for you, Comandante. But unless you are a far more secretive man than you appear, you ignore it all.'

'Yes, I do,' I said, taking great care not to show anything. 'My work is to seek redress for misery, not add to it.'

'You take the side of women, but you haven't sought out one of your own?'

'Of my own?' I let the fissures in my voice hide the outrage I felt. 'No, signore. I don't have one *of my own.*' I rubbed my throat, trying to ease the words. 'My life would not be a good one to share. I have been alone for a long time, and I have seen and done dreadful things. I don't wish to share the battlefields of Flanders or the corpse pits on Malta, because those would be my gifts to a wife, together with melancholy and bad dreams. Who would deserve that?'

Ruspi touched my shoulder reassuringly. 'You are right. How could that be a good thing, indeed? How I prattle on! We're almost at the bank, and then we should say our goodbyes. We understand each other, I think.'

Gherarda had already left when I got back to Borgo Ognissanti. It felt strange to wash myself in daylight, and I had the unpleasant feeling that Signor Ruspi was watching me with those dark-ringed eyes of his, so I put on a long shift before I went outside and washed myself through the clinging linen. It took me only a few minutes to pack my old valise and to change into the clothes I had been wearing when I first came to Florence: slashed pumpkin hose in black serge, a black leather doublet of defence with sleeves in the darkest maroon, a soft, faded black cap that I could pull down to shade my face. The shiver of pleasure I felt as I pulled on my riding boots surprised me. There was a journey ahead. Solitude, and a road on which to enjoy it. I hadn't been dissembling when I'd confessed to that desire of mine. I decided to take my old German sword, as it had always brought me good luck; and I wrapped my good Brescia pistol in oilcloth and stuffed it down the side of the valise, along with a powder flask and bullets. When I was packed, I took out the bloody sheet from last night and my soiled cloths, and tied them up into a neat parcel. I counted out fifty *scudi* and put the rest into a leather purse. Making sure the bedroom door was securely locked, I wrote a brief note for Gherarda and left it on the kitchen table along with two weeks' worth of wages.

Sister Brigida was in the entrance hall of the Pietà, arguing with a man I assumed was a silk jobber, no doubt trying to underpay the girls who made his cloth. I waited until they had come to an agreement and asked her to step into the chapel with me.

'Here,' I said, handing her the leather purse that held Duke Francesco's gold. 'This is for your girls.'

She hefted the purse and her eyes widened. Then she looked at my valise, my riding boots.

'Surely you aren't leaving Florence, my son?' she asked. 'Will you come back?'

'I don't know, sister,' I said. 'I have to do something.'

'But there is enough here for . . .' I could almost see her thoughts: a new roof, a bigger infirmary, new beds, a laundry.

'Probably,' I said. 'I give it with all my heart. Thank you for helping me.'

I left before she could say anything else. Out in Borgo Ognissanti the vapours from the dye vats were so strong that people's eyes were running, so no one noticed that I was crying, though I wasn't sad.

I was thinking of the abandoned girls, of Sister Vittoria and the Mother Superior of Izvor, and the tears were tears of gratitude.

I kept my horse at a livery stables next to the convent of Santa Anna, near the Porta al Prato. On the way, I threw the bundle of stained linen onto a rubbish fire that was smouldering on one of the patches of waste ground beyond the dyers' yards. The horse, a young roan I called Sultan, seemed pleased to see me, though I was surprised that he remembered my face: I hadn't ridden him for weeks. We went back through the city, across the Porta Santa Trìnita and through the Porta Romana. The guards at the gate knew me well, and I had to stop and gossip with them for a while. They asked where I was going, and I said I was planning to visit some relatives near Orvieto. One of them decided that I must be going to meet a prospective bride, and I didn't try too hard to deny it, so that when I finally rode off, I was followed by shouts of good-natured ribaldry. I waved and put my heels to the horse. Sultan was glad to stretch his legs, and we raised a cloud of dust until I could see the walls of the monastery at Galluzzo. I reined him in then, because I needed to think. Now I was outside the city, I was aware of two things: the first was that it had been so easy to leave; the second was that I was going back to Pietrodoro, and I had no idea what was waiting there for me.

I joined the Via Francigena a few miles south of San Gimignano and reached Siena the next day. I left my horse at a modest tavern I had used before and went straight to the Palazzo Pubblico. I knew the commander there from a few public functions in

Florence. Another old soldier, blunt and cynical, we had both fought at Jemmingen, though on opposite sides, though that meant nothing to mercenaries. Paolo di Monterrigione was his name, and he was on duty in the prison at the side of the building. We embraced warmly, and he immediately brought out a jug of wine and began to cut up a salami with his dagger. We ate, drank and talked shop for a while: I told him the same vague story about being on my way to Orvieto, we swapped a few bits of gossip about our offices and we brought each other up to date on the most notable crimes in our respective cities.

'Which reminds me, I don't know how fast our news reaches Siena, but did you hear about the murder of Pietro Vennini?'

'Vennini . . . Vennini.' Paolo scratched his grey stubbled chin. 'We haven't got wind of that one yet. So many killings in Florence, though, Onorio. It's as bad as it was before Duke Cosimo came along.'

I told him about the bloodbath on Ponte Santa Trìnita and he shook his head. 'A man's greatest fight, and no audience for it,' he said. 'Where's the fairness in that?'

'Knowing Vennini, he's bragging about it in purgatory as we speak,' I said. 'Meanwhile, the woman he'd been sleeping with was murdered in her own bedroom.'

'Ah. Jealous husband.'

'She was the mistress of a certain Bartolomeo Ormani.' I paused and washed down a mouthful of salami with some wine.

'I know an Ormani,' Paolo said at once. 'Bartolomeo, yes. Fellow from Pitigliano. He's rich: he's been buying property here in Siena and Montalcino. So he's got himself in trouble, has he? I can't say I'm surprised.'

'Oh, no?'

'No. He puts himself about as one of those country noblemen with a pedigree going back to Julius Caesar's third cousin, but he's very rough around the edges. Mind you, a lot of them are, down that way. Old republicans, the lot of them.' Paolo thumped his cup down. The authorities in Siena were all Medici loyalists; even now, twenty-five years after the fall of the Sienese Republic, there were many who hated Florence, and it was worse the further south you went. *Nothing ever really changes*, I thought to myself. 'Yes, he has a brother and a couple of sons, all ruffians,' Paolo went on. 'No word of any wife, though. As far as I knew, he was a widower. And he has a twisted back. I believe he tells people he was wounded at Scannagallo.'

'Does he, indeed,' I muttered. 'Have you seen him recently?'

'I thought you said you were on your way to Orvieto,' Paolo said, raising his eyebrows knowingly.

'I am. But that whole business has really got under my skin,' I said.

'I know what that's like. Don't worry, I'll put my ear to the ground,' Paolo said. 'Talking of Pitigliano, did you hear about the count? Old Niccolò finally got kicked out by his son. Happened yesterday, by all accounts. A messenger came charging through here this morning, on his way to the Signoria. Well, it's Count Alessandro now. I'd say it's over for the county. Alessandro's reckless, and a spendthrift, and he doesn't have the sense of his ogre of a father.'

'Really? That's interesting news.' *Don Francesco can move quickly if he wants to*, I thought. Or perhaps it was just coincidence, though I doubted it.

I told Paolo where I was lodging, and he told me to come back in the morning. I spent the evening wandering around the city, looking for a bookseller, because I'd forgotten to bring anything to read. When I found a little shop belonging to a man called Sigismondi, my eye was caught by a translation of Ovid's *Metamorphoses*. I paid Sigismondi more than it was worth, but it seemed like an omen, or perhaps a talisman. I was going back to where I had first read these stories, although my mother would never have allowed me to read a translation. At the tavern I had my dinner sent to my room, which was expensive because it had a door that locked. When the noise of the tavern had faded, late in the night, I took out the book-sized leather case I had packed, carefully wrapped in a Turkish silk shawl, in my valise. Opening my mirror, I set it on the table and stood in front of the glass. In the light of the cheap tallow candle I looked tired, with wan skin and soft, sexless limbs. Onoria, who had stood before a grand duke and somehow been given the thing she had desired above all other things but could never had asked for.

Paolo was waiting for me at dawn. Police hours. He was eating a bowl of porridge and offered me some. I accepted for politeness' sake though I never ate in the morning. It felt as though it was choking me, and I had to force it down with some watered wine.

'So, I made some enquiries,' said Paolo at last. 'More porridge? My wife makes it with trout roes.'

'Thank you. It was delicious. But I like to ride with an empty belly.'

'Habit from the days when we didn't have a choice, eh,

Onorio? Do you remember the sky the morning of Jemmingen? My belly was empty that morning . . .'

'Mine too. Any word of the Ormanis?' I prompted.

'Curiously enough, one of my informants at the Monte di Paschi told me that Don Bartolomeo withdrew a lot of money from his account there. Nearly a thousand *scudi*. That sort of thing doesn't go unnoticed, as you well know.'

The Monte di Paschi was the biggest bank in Siena and one of the biggest in Tuscany. Respectable to a fault. 'When was this?'

'Two days ago. He was with a man who looked as if he'd been riding with the devil behind him, my informant said. The bank clerk remembered that very distinctly. I got the feeling that they don't fully approve of your Signor Ormani.'

'Perceptive of them. Tell me, Paolo, do you have much trouble with bandits around here?'

'Not between Siena and Pienza. Or Montepulciano, in the direction you're heading. Why do you ask? Don't tell me you've become a nervous traveller!'

'A nervous man is a sensible man. No, it's an interest of mine. I suppose I still dream of action.'

'I dream of bums, mostly,' said Paolo. 'But yes, if I were the Grand Duke I would put a small army together and clear out all those warlords. The Aldobrandeschi are making life impossible in the Maremma.'

'And the Ellebori, so I hear.'

'Oh, the Ellebori. They keep to the Val d'Orcia. A repulsive clan. I'd love to hang them all here in the piazza, but they live in some impregnable village – not that I've gone anywhere near them. Fortunately for me, they're someone else's problem.'

'So they are. Perhaps I'll see you on my way back to Florence. And give my compliments to your wife: the porridge was delicious.'

I left Siena and took to the Francigena. Because it was high summer, the road was crowded with pilgrims and it was hard to make any headway. As soon as we got to the gentle hills of the Crete Senesi I left the road and gave Sultan his head. Augusto Ellebori was two days ahead of me, but I had no way of knowing how much haste he was making. He had gone to the Monte di Paschi with a messenger or a retainer two days ago. Siena was a hard day's ride from Florence. Assuming that the rider had brought news of Girolamo's death, he must have left a few hours ahead of me. So Augusto knew that his plans had only half succeeded. His sister was still alive, and under the city's protection: a dangerous witness. An enemy. But Augusto would have had no way of knowing that Smeralda had told me everything. As I sped southward, I knew he had ordered his own sister's death simply because he suspected that she had played some part in the affair between Donna Zanobia and Vennini. What had been in Augusto's heart when he had sent Girolamo into Florence? Spite? Vanity? Weakness? Had the idea that two women could be friends damaged the family honour so terribly, enough that a brother would go to his sister's house to kill her with a dagger, face-to-face, with no proof of betrayal?

Proof . . . I was starting to think like the rest of Florence, like every other man to whom it was fine, if not in truth required, to put a woman to death for daring to seek some morsel of pleasure. Or to help a friend find happiness. Or even, God forbid, be caught harbouring thoughts of her own. I had worked on a case

319

this very year where a man had battered his wife to death with a hammer just for looking at a handsome apprentice. The Eight had merely sent the husband to work in Livorno for half a year and fined him fifty lire.

I reached Buonconvento in the early afternoon and stopped by the Ombrone river that lies across the road there. I dismounted and let Sultan drink while I rested underneath the poplar trees that grew close to the bank. The water was sluggish and turtle-dove grey. Rivers are borders, and though this one was meaningless, I felt that I had crossed over some invisible but powerful dividing line. Behind me was Florence and the lands civilised by the Medici. In front of me were bandits and warlords. The wild lands. My home.

It was half a day's ride to Pietrodoro from here. I could be there by nightfall. I hid in a ditch and changed my cloth. Then I mounted Sultan and took us back to the road, going south.

CHAPTER TWENTY-FOUR

Sultan lost a shoe outside San Quirico d'Orcia. Our gallop must have loosened the nails. I led him the last three miles into the town, found a blacksmith, and decided that it was too late to press on south. All the inns were full of pilgrims, and there were no single rooms to be had. I paid the blacksmith a few coins to let me sleep in his barn and made a bed for myself in the straw. Strangely for me, I slept well, but woke early. Pilgrims were already gathering in the streets. I heard English being spoken, and Flemish. They had come a long way. For them, the journey was almost over. More than one of them looked ill, and I wondered whether they were going to Rome to die, or whether they had fallen sick on the road. Still, in another two weeks or less, most of them would be walking into Saint Peter's. For these pilgrims, arrival would be an end in itself. Fulfilment, blessings, vows discharged, absolution – all by the act of arriving. It would be easy to become one of them: slip into the noisy crowd, let them carry me along to where my soul might find some healing.

But no, the Rome I knew wouldn't bring me absolution. That would have to come later, if it ever came at all.

The blacksmith had reshod Sultan, though he told me that he was a little lame, and that I should be gentle with him for a few days. So I joined the pilgrims after all as they walked down the hill towards the golden swell of the valley, leading Sultan, who was indeed limping slightly. They were a friendly lot, laughing and chattering away in their tongues. The last time I had passed along this road I had been in very different company, following Don Orazio's hearse as it lumbered north through December rain. I had learnt a pinch of many languages in my years as a mercenary, and I understood a few of my companions' jokes and some of their songs.

'Are you on pilgrimage?' a friendly, sunburnt Englishman asked me in English, almost bellowing in that habit they have, as if all the peoples of the world beyond their island are hard of hearing.

'Yes,' I said, because it seemed easier than denying it, and he clapped me on the back and began to tell me something about his journey, most of which I couldn't understand but might have had something to do with bad food. I nodded politely, but I was thinking about the last time I had been in Rome. Don Orazio had died, and I had gone to witness the embalming of his body. Lying on the bed where he'd died in his brother the cardinal's palazzo, he hadn't looked like one of the great soldiers of Italy. His cheeks were stretched tight over the bones of his face, and his eyes had sunk into their sockets. He was naked, lying on a white sheet laid over a rough palliasse of straw. Death had already given his skin a tallow-yellow translucency. In the room with me were the surgeon, assisted by the cardinal's cook and a couple of servants who might have been grooms, together with Don Orazio's priest-confessor, and my own second in command, Lorenzo.

I had looked on, my unease growing, as the men did their work. Though I'd seen every aspect of death countless times, I had still winced as the knife went into his flesh just above his manhood. It wasn't the corpse or the controlled violence now being committed against it that had troubled me. It was that a man who had seemed like a giant to me was now lying here in front of a dozen eyes, reduced to stiff, ungainly limbs, ugly hair, blemishes and wrinkles, a manhood of surprising modesty. What had once been a man was no more, really, than a thing. And yet that thing had once been the man who had saved my life. Orazio del Forese could not keep his secrets any longer. He had left himself defenceless, and I hadn't wanted to be complicit.

'He wanted this,' I had whispered to Lorenzo, aware that I was trying to convince myself.

Lorenzo had nodded. He was watching the proceedings with frank interest. 'We're taking Don Orazio more than two hundred miles,' he had whispered back. 'He'll travel better this way.'

'True.' I had sighed and winced as the surgeon began to snip through the commander's ribs with a pair of heavy shears. There it all was, all the hidden complexity. Soon it would all be scooped into jars, the body rinsed in wine and strong spirits, stuffed with rosemary, sage, flax and scented grass, then sewn up again. The cardinal's plumber was waiting to seal the body into a sheath of lead. Then, only then, would it be secret again. But not from anyone in this room.

'Lorenzo, I want you to swear that you'd never let anyone do this to me. Just bury me where I fall.'

'Sure, Condottiere.' Lorenzo had been frowning at Don Orazio's heart, which the surgeon was handing to the cook. 'Look at that. I thought it would be bigger, you know?'

'That's what a man's heart looks like. If you're looking for his courage . . .' I breathed out slowly. *Where's your bravery now, old friend?* I had been thinking. *Where's your skill?* 'Listen, Lorenzo, I'm serious. Don't let anyone get their bloody hands on me. Just put me in a box and bury me.'

Lorenzo had given me a curious look. 'I didn't think you were scared of anything, Condottiere.'

'It isn't fear,' I'd hissed, 'it's . . .' But what was it? 'Dignity,' I'd whispered finally. But that hadn't been it at all. I had been afraid, then – not of death, but of what would happen to me afterwards. I'd be stripped, and then everything would be revealed. The confusion, the mockery, the revulsion . . . I would be dead, but I still feared it. Perhaps it was the thought of all my guile, all my discipline, my artfulness, reduced in a moment to pointing fingers and bawdy laughter. Or maybe it was pride. But I believe what I had feared the most was that those who discovered the secret of my life would think that I had been ashamed of my true sex. That they would assume I had rejected womanhood, that I had made some sort of choice. And I wouldn't be able to tell them the truth.

Soon the distant bulk of Monte Amiata appeared in the south-west. It hadn't been very far from here that Don Orazio had found me, though I didn't know where the little valley was, because I had been lost then. Lost, alone, hiding. I had had nothing left but prayer. And then I had been found. The surgeon's wagon had carried me along this very road, feverish, half alive, with a new name and a new sex. My prayers had been heard – and then I realised that I was on a pilgrimage after all.

I left the pilgrims before they arrived at the next station on their itinerary, which was Bagno Vignoni, where I had talked to the fat landlord about the Ellebori, almost seven years ago. I had no idea whether he was still there, but I didn't want to be recognised in these lands. The towers of Rocca d'Orcia were a handy way marker: I got up on Sultan and let him amble along past the castle up on its hill, and paused in the village of Castiglione to buy a slab of bacon, a bag of chestnut flour, some cord and a dented copper pot in the market. Beyond the village, I found a track that led towards the straggling clumps of woodland spreading out from the feet of Amiata. People were working in the fields and groves: it was harvest time. They turned away when I rode by – plainly, an armed man in these parts did not signify anything good for them. After a while the trees began to close in around me: holm oaks and maples at first, then, as the track began to climb, beech and chestnut. I skirted a gully of exposed limestone and climbed a low, round hill. Another ravine led into a grove of young chestnut trees. Beyond, the track bit into the slope of the mountain itself. It was littered with dead leaves which crunched under Sultan's hooves. As we climbed higher, they grew thicker and dryer. No one seemed to have come this way for a long time.

Finally, I was surrounded by trees. It was very quiet. Every now and then a bird would cross my path, and once a deer bounded away, its gruff bark echoing. I saw the smoke from charcoal burning rising through the trees here and there across the slopes, but I never saw the burners. After a while the track I was following began to narrow, and then it petered out altogether. I dismounted and led my puzzled horse through the trees, climbing higher and higher. I was getting lost, but that was good. Memories were coming back to me, swelling like a choir. The abandoned garden where I'd sheltered must be nearby, but I didn't find it. Rabbits watched me from clearings. I skirted a cliff and came across an old charcoal burners' path that pointed southwards and up. Several times I had to get up on Sultan and have him trample through tangles of brambles and dying bracken. The sun had long ago dropped behind the summit of the mountain, but below me, the great valley was still bright, stretching away towards the low mountains I remembered so well, that were beginning to turn orange as the day ebbed. When the path turned a sharp corner around a bastion of rock, I found myself looking down on Pietrodoro.

It was two miles away, balanced on the end of another fold in the mountain, already in shadow, a grey silhouette against the grasslands below. My heart jolted, and I had to gasp for breath. Even though I couldn't see anything more than a shape, I knew my home with every drop of my blood, every splinter of bone.

The path turned, and Pietrodoro dropped out of sight. But I had my bearings now. I followed it a little further, until a much smaller path dropped away downhill, a way etched through the undergrowth by generations of boar and deer. Leading an ever-more-reluctant Sultan, I followed it, sometimes scrambling, briars plucking at my clothes. It was getting dark. Sultan was beginning to stumble.

'I know, I know: you aren't a pack horse,' I told him. I was looking for a piece of level ground where we might make camp when, in the gloom, I saw what looked like the tentacles of a sea creature waving above the ground. A little further, and I came to a place on the steep hillside where some landslip had felled a patch of huge trees many years ago. With another clench of my heart, I recognised the place where I had been terrified by the howling of wolves and had spent my second night alone.

I decided to make camp there, in a grassy pit where a great plug of roots, soil and rock had been torn up. There was grass for Sultan, and plenty of dead wood to make a fire. I cooked myself a porridge of chestnut flour and bacon, and it seemed marvellous to me that I had salt to season it with, and pepper from a silver box, because what man leaves on a journey without those things? A man . . . As I sprinkled my salt, my pepper all the way from India, I wondered at the creature I had become, many years ago, among these very trees. Like Daphne fleeing from Apollo, I had passed through the forest and been changed beyond all recognition. I was coming home, but I was not the same person who had left, so was this a return, or something else?

There were no wolves tonight. A waning moon drawing to the end of its last quarter was rising in the east. The bright scrape of crickets came from every thicket, and somewhere nearby, a nightjar whirred monotonously. On an impulse I took off my doublet and my shirt, unbound my breasts and stepped out into the dark wood. Strange creature. If anyone had seen me in the light of the waning moon, they might have believed they were looking at a forest spirit, a satyress, human above, beast below, stalking among the rocks and the twisted roots. And they would have feared me, because such a creature would be free: from humanity and its constraints, from God, from Mother Church – and freedom fills men with terror. But I wasn't free. I felt alive, more alive than I had ever felt in my entire life. Not free, though. Not yet.

I wrapped myself in my blanket and watched the stars flicker through the leaves. It was hardly light when I got up, stretched my stiff limbs, buttoned up my shirt over my unbound flesh and made my way quietly, carefully downhill, my sword belt across my shoulder. What had taken me a whole day all those years ago took me almost no time at all now. After less than an hour, judging by the gathering dawn, I heard the sound of water. Another few minutes brought me to a clearing beneath a rocky outcrop, from which a trickle of clear water was falling into an ancient stone basin. I scrambled down to it and, kneeling on the damp stone, looked down at my reflection in Santa Celava's spring.

Time had finished what had just been started when I had last seen myself in this water. What had been an open wound was now an old scar. The girl was gone: she had vanished a long time ago. But she'd be gone anyway, I told myself. Onoria would be a woman now. It seemed to me, suddenly, that I had never stopped staring at that first reflection, the bloodied, frightened girl with butchered hair and eyes that had already seen the worst they would ever see. She was who I saw whenever I thought about myself, whenever I looked in my mirror or glanced down at a puddle in the street. And yet looking back at me now was a woman in a man's shirt, a sword hanging from her shoulder, a scar that didn't shape her face but made it fragile and at the same time defiant. Not a monster or a freak or an abomination, but a woman. Onoria had survived. She was here, where the saint who found lost things had come to drink, before Pietrodoro had existed, before Amiata had given birth to Ormanis and Ellebori.

I had been found. Celava's medal was hanging between my breasts. I took it off and hung it from a jut of rock beside the trickle of water. The saint had heard my prayers. She had found me; I was here.

Above me and a little way around the curve of the mountain there was another outcropping of rock that stuck out beyond the trees. I climbed up to it and looked out across the deep, wooded valley below me to where my village basked on its sunny crag. It had been the topography of my dreams for so long that for a moment it seemed less real than the place I visited almost every night. But then I saw the *campanile* of the church; the tall, narrow tower of the Palazzo Ellebori; and there, the bigger, square tower of the Rocca. I reached out into the air and held the tip of a finger so that it seemed to rest on the tiny keep, rippling in the warm air.

After that, there seemed to be no need to hurry any more. I made myself a rough hut out of branches, a soldier's bivouac. My supplies would last me at least a week. There were springs all around and enough grass for Sultan, whose ankle was a little swollen and who seemed perfectly happy to do nothing. Every morning I went down to Celava's spring to pray and bathe in the icy water. Sometimes I found other footprints in the soft earth beside the stone basin: others came here, but they didn't stay long. I never saw any other sign of them. It had been a more important place, surely, when I was young. I couldn't really remember, though. Perhaps it had only been the old folk who had come up here. I guessed, with a pang of sadness, that most of them would be dead now.

After I had bathed, I would climb up to my overlook and sit, staring across at Pietrodoro. I should have been planning, but somehow, I was content just to rest there, watching the kites, the morning mists roll down the mountains on the far side of the valley and the shadow of Amiata move across the hills and fields far below, as if the world was a vast sundial and the mountain its gnomon. There would be plenty of time to do what needed to be done. One day I saw a golden eagle being mobbed by ravens, which it barely seemed to notice as it wheeled above me on its great fingered wings. Ormani ravens, three of them. *They should be flying above a field of blood*, I thought. One day soon, they would be. Then the eagle tilted its wings and rose effortlessly through the air, a hundred, a thousand feet, and the ravens dived away, tumbling and croaking with joy, towards the shining carpet of leaves.

In the afternoons I would patrol the forest, scouting paths and trails, picking early mushrooms, keeping watch for other people. There were none. One morning, when I rose, I went further into the forest and set some rabbit snares made from the cord I'd bought down in the valley. By the time I climbed up to my overlook it was mid-morning. The three ravens were black dots in the sky over the crag, circling a pillar of black smoke that was rising, thick, greasy and as straight as a bowstring, from the walls of Pietrodoro.

CHAPTER TWENTY-FIVE

I ran back to my camp, threw on my doublet, buttoned it tight across my breasts and loaded my pistol. I heaved the saddle up onto Sultan's back, fumbling with the girth and harness while he whinnied nervously. Buckling on my sword belt, I stuck the pistol through it crossways, grabbed Sultan's reins and all but dragged him up the through the trees until we reached the charcoal burners' path. Mounting, I urged him into a canter. He was bored and needed no encouragement. His hooves seemed terrifyingly loud to me after my days of silence. Once a family of snipe burst from cover and clattered past us, making Sultan shy and almost throw me.

A mile down the path I came to a place where another track appeared through the trees below us. I had found it on one of my patrols. I had to lead Sultan down a dangerous slope, but once we were on the track, which had been used not too long ago and was free from dead wood and brambles, I gave the horse his head. Only then, when we were hurtling along the uneven track, kicking up stones and dust, and sending flocks of birds screeching out of the bushes, did I ask myself what I was doing.

I had come back to Amiata to kill Augusto Ellebori. That was the whole of my plan, and all of my intention. I hadn't thought how I was going to do it, but I had doubted that it would be very difficult. At some point, when the time seemed right, I would go down the mountain, find a place from where I could keep an eye on the comings and goings from the village, and when Augusto came out – which he would do, sooner or later – I would kill him. What would happen after that concerned me even less. Perhaps I would die with him. If I survived, I supposed I would ride away from Pietrodoro and keep riding until I found a war in which I could lose myself. I wouldn't be able to go back to the *sbirri*, and fighting was the only other life I knew. Then again, I had never forgotten the Convent of Izvor. If the Turks hadn't overrun it; if the sisters were still leading their gentle, timeless life there . . .

But everything had gone wrong. The smoke, which was now rising from much closer to hand, was the smoke of battle. I knew it as well as I knew anything. I had waited too long in the forest. That was no accidental fire: war had come to Pietrodoro, and someone else had brought it. I cursed as I ducked under a branch and saw the proper road just below me, the road which connected the village to the outside world. Someone had come for the Ellebori. What if it was Duke Francesco's soldiers? The thought that Augusto might be arrested, that he might escape me that way, was maddening. It could just as well be another bandit company, I reasoned. Yes, that seemed most likely. Don Francesco wouldn't bother with Pietrodoro. He had his porcelain and his alchemy to keep him amused. This was likely some local dispute, I decided. Maybe I could drive them off. And then what? Save Augusto Ellebori so that I could kill him myself? It was absurd. And yet I kept riding.

In what seemed like no time at all, I was clattering around the last bend in the road that twisted back and forth across the steep slope of Pietrodoro's mountain spur. I came out of the chestnut forest, and there in front of me was a long saddle of land sloping gently away to left and right in stone-walled terraces. The road ran along the ridge line between old holm oaks and cypress trees towards a fortified gateway set into an ancient wall the colour of burnt sugar. Caper plants grew in thick festoons from cracks in the masonry and cascaded down from the battlements. Beyond the walls, narrow towers rose, closely packed together. It was all achingly familiar. The contorted olive trees that stood in lines across the terraces: some of them had had names, like people. Surely the oaks had been smaller. And then I saw what was happening.

A company of cavalry was lined up where the road left the body of the mountain. I counted twenty men. A smaller group of men on foot were rushing to and fro in front of the gateway. It was the gate that was burning, and the two watchtowers on either side of it. I guessed that the attackers had doused the gate with pitch, piled brushwood against it and set it alight. They had cut down one of the old trees and were lashing ropes to the trunk, getting ready to use it as a battering ram. Every so often a rattle of arquebus fire sounded from the walls, but the attackers didn't seem very worried. As I got closer I saw that one of the cavalrymen was carrying a flag. It was white, divided horizontally by a yellow band. Below, oblique red lines. Above, a single red rose. Orsini of Pitigliano.

I could have reined Sultan in. I could have wrenched his head around and fled back down the road, or lost myself again in the silence of Amiata. Instead I kept on, at full gallop, until the nearest horseman saw me. They were mercenaries, of course. I could tell by their gear, and by their discipline. For one queasy moment I thought I recognised one of them, but they were all strangers. I raised my hand as I brought Sultan to a prancing, twirling halt.

'I'm in time, then!' I said.

'And who might you be?' said one of the men. He was wearing half-armour. His morion helmet was extravagantly plumed, and his face, in the shadow of its peak, was tanned and bearded. A southerner, I guessed. Second son of a Neapolitan noble family, like half the mercenary officers I'd ever known. His troop were dressed for a fight, not a parade: doublets of defence, cuirasses, mail shirts, morion helmets or steel caps.

'Amerigo di . . . Capacci,' I said, my parents' names landing on my tongue from nowhere, or perhaps from the smoke, which was so familiar, rising above the ancient walls. I could just see the tower of the Rocca through the roiling black cloud. It seemed to have been rebuilt, but streaks of black still stained the walls.

'Don't know you,' said the man curtly. His hand was on the hilt of his sword.

'I've come on behalf of Signor Ruspi of Florence,' I said. 'To make sure that this endeavour is accomplished to the satisfaction of all parties.'

'Ruspi?'

'From the Signoria. Perhaps one isn't supposed to say that but . . .' I grinned and shrugged, reached into the purse on my belt and pulled out the Grand Duke's seal, my badge of office, and held it out to him. He took it, squinted and handed it back. He'd plainly never had dealings with the *sbirri*.

'You're in time,' he said, far more warmly. 'But only just.'

'What do you intend?' I was doing my best to keep my voice level. I knew the harshness kept most of the emotion out of it at the best of times, but the strangeness of the moment was overwhelming.

The man shrugged. 'We'll be through that gate any moment now. Then, I'd say it's all up for anyone inside who keeps hold of a weapon. I'm not interested in the village. My orders are to rid these lands of the Ellebori.'

'So he's in there, then? Augusto Ellebori?'

'So we believe. The filthy beast who murdered Count Alessandro's sister.' He grinned, revealing gapped teeth and mottled gums. 'I'm to bring back his head.'

I swallowed and rubbed my neck. 'I should like to be in at the kill,' I said, my voice sounding like fingers dragged through broken glass. 'To assure them' – I patted the seal in its pouch – 'that all is well done.'

The man eyed my sword, and the pistol in my belt. 'You look as if you can handle yourself, Messer Capacci. But try not to get in the way. My name is de Tranzano.' He held out a gauntlet-sheathed hand, and I shook it. 'This gentleman has come all the way from Florence to keep an eye on things,' he called to his men. 'Try not to kill him by accident.' He winked at me, and I nodded. Another shot cracked and echoed, and some of the men jeered.

'Are there many men inside?' I asked.

'You aren't from these parts,' said another man. 'Or else you'd know that the plague went through here a few years ago and killed almost everyone. Pietrodoro's hardly a village any more: hardly even a fortress. We couldn't have done this in the old days. Old Lodovigo Ellebori wouldn't have let us get halfway up this mountain.'

'And Augusto?'

'Everyone fears him, and everyone hates him. He's nothing but a petty tyrant. Even his own people want to see the back of him. This little carnival is just for show. Why do you think they've barely wounded any of us?'

'So you're from Pietrodoro?'

'From this very place.' He spat.

'I suppose the Ellebori live in the Rocca now,' I said.

'The Rocca? Christ, no! After they butchered the Ormanis – our other noble family, signore – Lodovigo rebuilt it, but people said it was haunted. It's a priory now. I suppose monks don't care about ghosts.'

'Do you remember the Ormanis, then?'

'No. I was too young. I remember the fire though. And the screaming.' He shook his head. 'Left as soon as I could. I wanted to see the world.'

'You can see the world from up here,' I said, and he gave me an odd look, but just then someone whistled. A cloud of sparks was rising up from the gateway. There was a quick rattle of arquebus fire, and then the walls went silent.

'Here we go, boys!' de Tranzano called. He trotted to the head of the company and turned to face them. 'Kill anyone who resists, but if they surrender, leave them be. Don't touch the women or the children. If anyone comes out of the Ellebori house, kill them. Kill everyone inside – everyone, do you understand?'

De Tranzano wheeled around again and drew his sword. His horse plunged forward into a slow canter. As the troop moved off behind him I managed to work Sultan around them until I was riding just behind him. We clattered down the old, worn pavement, along which I'd once raced my friends. I was strangely numb. The gateway was just ahead, smoke pouring from the towers, the opening itself a blackened mouth with a tongue of burning embers, with sunlight in its throat.

In my memory, the gate had opened straight onto the piazza, but instead there was a narrow street between houses, a slot with a gutter running down the middle, old arched doorways. A place I only remembered from dreams. A woman was screaming from an upper window. As we rode past, a man ran out of one of the doorways, struggling to cock his arquebus. The trooper next to me leant down casually, put his pistol to the man's head and fired. The body fell and rolled under the hooves of the company behind us. We burst out into the piazza. Too soon, too soon. I wasn't ready. How long had I been waiting? Could it be twenty years? I wasn't prepared for the smallness of this place, the way the buildings rose around the worn flagstones that sunk gently towards the well in the centre, everything whitish-yellow, the colour of bone. It was an upturned skull cup, the bowl of a cranium. There was the church. There was the palace of the Ellebori. And there was the gate of the Rocca, with two white-

robed monks peering around the pillars. The two buildings –
tall tower and square, burnt tower . . . How could they be so
close together? How could this begging bowl be the vast, bright
arena of my childhood?

Sultan's hooves clacked and skidded on the smooth
flagstones. The company was pressing through the entrance to
the street, momentum carrying them pell-mell into the piazza.
The noise was deafeningly sharp. I didn't even notice the gunfire
until one of the troopers, whose horse had just swerved to avoid
the well head, doubled over in his saddle and fell sideways.
Then I saw puffs of smoke coming from the windows of the
Palazzo Ellebori. Another horse shrieked and went down. I
looked around for de Tranzano, saw his absurd yellow and green
plumes bobbing in front of the church. He was pointing to the
doorway of the palazzo. Four men were swinging the cypress
battering ram against the iron-strapped double doors and
another had just fired his arquebus through one of the ground
floor windows. I jumped down off Sultan and sent him running
through the gate of the Rocca. An arquebus ball cracked against
the lip of the well, showering me with shards of stone. Ducking,
I ran between panicked horses, stopped and looked up. The
barrel of an arquebus was poking out of an upper window;
most of the other windows were shuttered. There weren't many
defenders after all. We'd just ridden into a crude, weak trap. De
Tranzano was off his horse as well. His men were disciplined:
they were already pulling their mounts behind the wall of the
Rocca, returning fire with their pistols. There were two dead
horses in the piazza and another was rolling in agony. The
wounded man had crawled behind the well and seemed to be

cursing rather than dying. I walked across to the palazzo. De Tranzano loped over to join me. The men with the tree trunk had already splintered the boards of the doors and the iron straps were bending.

'You're a cool fellow,' de Tranzano said, with a certain amount of admiration. 'But you're very keen to get inside, aren't you?'

I shrugged and tugged the pistol from my belt, drew my dagger with my left hand. The men swung the tree again, and the two halves of the door split and buckled inwards, still held by a stout wooden bar. The muzzle of a gun jabbed through the gap. There was a flash and a bang, and one of the men lurched backwards, clutching his neck. Another man grabbed the rope handle and they swung again, and again. There was a screech of twisting metal, and the bar tore loose. The doors slammed inwards. I stepped into the opening, pistol levelled. A man was walking backwards, in the act of priming the lock of his arquebus. I sighted on his face and shot him under the left eye. There was a cheer from outside and the sound of running feet. I was still walking through the smoke from my pistol, trying to remember how the house was laid out, when I was shouldered aside by first one trooper, then another, fanning out into the rooms off the hall. There was a shot, and another. An unarmed man in a bloodied shirt ran out from the corridor which, now I remembered, led to the kitchens. One of the troopers ran him through, and he crumpled. The stairs were in front of me. I'd hated to go up there, because Lodovigo would be lurking, or worse, Donna Benedetta, whose misery filled the air like the smell of dead flowers. I was sure Augusto was up there, though. I had my foot on the bottom step when someone grabbed my arm. It was de Tranzano.

'No, you don't, Signor Florence,' he said coldly. 'We'll see to business. You're just here to observe – isn't that what you told me?'

'Do you think I'll want a slice of your prize money? Don't worry, Capo. I assure you that's the very last thing I care about.'

'You care about something. I'm warning you: keep out of it.'

De Tranzano shouted an order and started up the stairs, six or seven of his men stamping and clattering behind him. I followed, reloading my pistol as I went. I could hear boots stamping on the boards above me, swords clashing. An old man's voice raised in prayer, suddenly cut off in the middle of a word. I wound the lock of the pistol and took the last stairs two at a time.

'He's here! He's here!'

Shouting from the back of the house. I saw de Tranzano's plumes vanishing around a corner and ran after him. The body of a grey-haired man in the black robes of a priest lay across the narrow corridor, his cap askew over staring eyes. I jumped over him. Around the corner, a door led into a large, open room with a painted ceiling, the walls completely covered with Flemish tapestries. With a shock I recognised the one straight in front of me: Hercules wrestling with the Nemean Lion, which had once hung in the entrance hall of the Rocca – one of the things I had loved most, which I had pressed my face against countless times, imagining myself swallowed up by the dazzling forest of threads, sinking into that vivid, magical landscape. Tumbling in the embrace of the lion, the great beast as soft as the warp and weft of the cloth. For a brief moment, the figures were more real than what was happening in the room. There was noise, and motion, and a man's sharp cry. I stepped back over whatever invisible line divides the past from the present, and saw a tall man with a sallow face and bristling mustachios standing behind an upturned table, a sword and a dagger in his hand. He was grinning, showing a row of big, stained teeth, and his eyes were thumbprints of black in the middle of wide white circles. A man, the soldier from Pietrodoro, was staggering away from him, his hand clamped around his right forearm, which was leaking blood. The room moved around me, or was I moving through it? The light from the window caught the shiny stump of a missing finger on the hand that gripped the sword.

I think he saw me. His head turned, at least. I looked into his eyes, but there was nothing there.

No, I must tell the truth. There was something: pain, and terror. The grin was a rictus. If Augusto was thinking anything at all, it would have been about the hand's breadth of space between him and the wall behind him, that contained the rest of his life.

'Augusto Ellebori!' I shouted, forcing his name out through the scars in my throat, through all the scars and unhealed wounds I still carried, that he had put in me. My voice cracked, and the end of his name came out as empty air, as nothing. De Tranzano raised his pistol and shot him through the chest.

Augusto toppled forward over the table. Another man leant over and fired his pistol into the back of his head. The man from Pietrodoro cursed and thrust his sword into Augusto's side. Men were pushing past one another to stab the corpse. I stood, my own pistol hanging limp in my hand, my breath coming in short, painful gasps.

I could have shot him as he stood there. I'd had his face in my sights. But I'd seen his fear and I'd known it for what it was. What he had seen in my eyes that night, when I'd still been someone who could feel joy, who loved, whose body had been made for so many things other than concealment: that was what I'd seen in his. For the last moments of his life, Augusto had become my mirror.

'His son.' I looked up. 'I think that's the lot.' De Tranzano was prodding something with his foot. The corpse of a young man, very young, was lying on his face half under a writing desk. 'In at the kill. Wasn't that what you said?' I nodded blankly. 'So you can report to your masters on an endeavour well executed.'

'That's so,' I said. I gently uncocked the pistol and put it back in my belt. I thought I might be sick: the smell of blood and gunpowder in the airless room was overwhelming. Strange that it should bother me now. I needed to leave. There was nothing more important than getting away from this place. Then the crash and thud of a door being kicked open came from upstairs, and a long, piercing shriek.

'Oh, *dio stronzo*,' de Tranzano spat. 'What now?'

One of the cavalrymen, bandy-legged, in landsknecht hose and a mail shirt, came cursing into the room. He was dragging two young girls by the collars of their dresses, pulling them along heedless of the way they twisted in his grasp, or of the fact that his spurs had slashed one of them, the smaller one, across her stockinged shin. 'Two little pigeons, hiding in the tower,' he said.

'Daughters?' De Tranzano shook his head in exasperation. 'Menno! Did Ellebori have daughters?'

343

The wounded man, whose arm was being bandaged by one of his comrades, glanced over. 'Aye. Two of them.'

'Fuck.' The officer shrugged. 'Oh, well.' He drew his sword and tapped the nearest girl on the arm with the flat of the blade, like a schoolmaster with his stick. 'Over there, please.' He gestured with the point towards the open space in front of the fireplace. The older girl screamed again. She had seen her brother's body.

'Sir!' I said. 'What are you going to do?'

'I was ordered not to leave a single one of this cursed family alive, signore.'

'You're going to kill them? Here?'

'Where else, signore? Do you think your Secretary Ruspi will care where we do it? Did he give you instructions, like a playwright?'

The man in the mail shirt was already twisting his fists around the delicate grey organza of the children's matching dresses. One was nine, perhaps, and the other ten, both very alike, with Smeralda's curved nose, huge grey eyes, delicate ears that stuck out below their tightly coiffed hair. They were both as white as though their throats had already been cut. The younger girl was whimpering slightly, her upper lip quivering; her older sister was staring at the ceiling, mouth open, breathing in tiny gasps. I could see the vein in her neck pulsing. If I put my hand there, I thought suddenly, it would feel like a kitten's heart beating.

'You cannot,' I said to de Tranzano.

'Ach. You didn't strike me as being delicate, signore. But then you are a Florentine.' He gestured again, and the man started to drag the girls out into the room.

'Delicate . . .' I said. 'Yes, I am delicate, sir.' I stepped between de Tranzano and the girls. 'You!' I said. 'Let them go!' The man in the mail shirt gave a start at the tone of command and opened his hands. The girls stumbled forward.

'For God's sake!' De Tranzano put his left hand on his hip. 'You are wasting time.'

'You will not kill them,' I said, and put my hand on the hilt of my sword.

'I will, sir!' he said. 'If you get in the way, I'll give them to the men first, and you may watch the fruits of your meddling.'

'My orders, sir, *my* orders . . .' My voice was drying up. It couldn't fail me now, though. 'My orders are as specific as yours. They are to take, to whit: two girls, the female offspring of said Augusto Ellebori, and convey them to a convent in Rome. This is at the command of my Grand Duke, who has considered the pleas of the girls' uncle, Cardinal Federigo Ellebori.'

'A cardinal? I don't believe you. Get out of my way, little fellow.' He put his fist on his hip and lifted the tip of his sword. I stepped back and drew my own, darting my eyes around the room. There were eight men here, and at least another twelve downstairs. I had no chance at all. But I'd make them suffer. But then . . . I pictured my corpse, and one of these brutes backing the girls into a corner at the point of a sword, or a knife. Behind us was an open window. I remembered that the palazzo was built right at the very edge of the cliff, and that there was nothing but air below these windows for three hundred feet.

I slid my sword back into its sheath. 'Take my hands, girls,' I said. 'You're safe now.' Not taking my eyes off de Tranzano, I put down my arms and gently wiggled my fingers. A cold, damp hand crept into one of mine, and then into the other. I squeezed, and felt the warmth of my flesh pass into theirs. I began to back towards the window. 'You haven't been abandoned, little ones,' I said. 'I won't leave you. I'll never leave you.'

'Enough of this!' De Tranzano took a high guard, the guard of the unicorn, and came forward. I stepped back, and back, the girls walking too, backwards into something better, into safety. I could already feel my arms slipping around their waists, holding them as tight as I could, as tightly as a mother holds her frightened children. I could imagine taking one more step backwards until my back touched the window ledge and I took them out and into the air. Three ravens, above a field of blood.

'Wait, Capo. There is a cardinal.' It was Menno, who was born in Pietrodoro. *In a minute you'll have seen an Ormani die twice,* I thought, and almost laughed. 'No, there is,' Menno went on. He wasn't even looking at us. 'The story is that he was in love with one of the Ormani children. This bastard' – he prodded Augusto's corpse with his boot – 'found out and went mad. Slaughtered the Ormanis. The brother was so heartbroken that he joined the Church. Now he's supposed to be good friends with Duke Francesco's brother – you know: Cardinal Ferdinando.'

'Cardinal Ferdinando. Damn it.' De Tranzano stepped back and sheathed his sword. 'You have no papers, signore? Nothing to prove this?'

It took me a moment to understand that he was talking to me. There was nothing in my mind beyond the touch of the little hands in mine. 'Papers?' I said. 'No papers.'

'Then how do I know—'

'You do not know!' My voice seemed to knit itself together. 'This is none of your business, Signor de Tranzano. It is between His Highness and Cardinal Ellebori. These children will disappear. You never saw them. Neither did I. But they will disappear into a convent, not into a grave. Now let us go. Take your trophy and do not speak of this to anyone. Duke Francesco is a man full of strange humours, and he cares very little for the world, but I can tell you that he finds a special relish in revenge.'

'The devil take you all,' said de Tranzano, and turned his back on us. I walked, slowly at first, then faster, towards the door.

'We'll go now,' I whispered to the girls. 'Shall we say a prayer? Do you ever pray to Santa Celava?'

'My name is Clara,' whispered the older girl, glancing in terror at the soldiers in the corridor. 'I'm named for the saint in our church.'

'That's wonderful,' I said. 'Don't look.' I led us around the body of the priest. We were at the stairs now. 'And you, little heart?' I squeezed the younger girl's hand. 'What's your name?'

'Ismeralda,' she whispered, and began to weep silently. We went carefully, slowly down the stairs, one step at a time. At the bottom, the girls began to sob again at the sight of the dead bodies in the hallway.

'Can you ride, girls? Do you have your own horses?'

'We . . . we're not allowed to,' said Clara.

'It doesn't matter. You can get up on my horse. Would you like that? His name's Sultan. He's very gentle.'

'But I'll be scared,' said little Ismeralda. We were outside now, in the piazza, which was full of men holding horses, and women drawing water from the well as if nothing was any different. The keep of the Rocca loomed over everything, the tongues of soot that lapped up from every window making it seem as though it was still ablaze with invisible fire.

'Yes, you will,' I said. 'For a while. And then you'll find that nothing will ever frighten you again.'

'I don't believe you,' said Clara, but she held on tightly to my hand.

'You don't have to,' I said. 'But it's true.'

We went out through the charred gateway, passing through the smoke and out onto the old paved track between the trees. Ismeralda in front, Clara behind, both held snugly in the saddle. I led Sultan across the ridge and along the road that led down to the valley. None of us looked back. When Pietrodoro was out of sight I found a trail that led up onto the mountain. We climbed up through the chestnuts until the dappled shade and the sharp green scent of Amiata had calmed the girls' breathing, and they began to look about them. I could sense that their fear was leaving them, but not their horror, nor their grief. That would take longer. It might take the rest of their lives.

Amiata was in shadow by the time we reached Celava's spring. I lifted them down and tied Sultan to a tree nearby. I unbuckled my sword belt and hung it from the saddle. The pistol I took by its barrel and threw out over the trees, and the girls watched it tumble end over end until it crashed into the branches far below us. Then I unbuttoned my doublet and took it off. If the girls saw me change from a man into a woman, they showed no sign of it. I sat down on one of the flat rocks next to

PHILIP KAZAN was born in London and grew up in Devon. His first novel for Allison & Busby, *The Black Earth*, was a commercial and critical success and he is also the author of two previous novels set in fifteenth-century Florence. He lives on the edge of Dartmoor with his family.

philipkazan.wordpress.com
@pipkazan